TED BELL
STEVE BERRY
GRANT BLACKWOOD
LEE CHILD
LINCOLN CHILD
DAVID DUN
HEATHER GRAHAM
JAMES GRIPPANDO
DENISE HAMILTON
RAELYNN HILLHOUSE
GREGG HURWITZ
ALEX KAVA
J. A. KONRATH
JOHN LESCROART
ROBERT LIPARULO
DAVID LISS
ERIC VAN LUSTBADER
DENNIS LYNDS
GAYLE LYNDS
CHRIS MOONEY
DAVID MORRELL
KATHERINE NEVILLE
MICHAEL PALMER
DOUGLAS PRESTON
CHRISTOPHER REICH
CHRISTOPHER RICE
JAMES ROLLINS
M. J. ROSE
JAMES SIEGEL
BRAD THOR
M. DIANE VOGT
F. PAUL WILSON

TED BELL
STEVE BERRY
GRANT BLACKWOOD
LEE CHILD
LINCOLN CHILD
DAVID DUN
HEATHER GRAHAM
JAMES GRIPPANDO
DENISE HAMILTON
RAELYNN HILLHOUSE
GREGG HURWITZ

THRILLER

ALEX KAVA
J.A. KONRATH
JOHN LESCROART
ROBERT LIPARULO
DAVID LISS
ERIC VAN LUSTBADER
DENNIS LYNDS
GAYLE LYNDS
CHRIS MOONEY
DAVID MORRELL
KATHERINE NEVILLE
MICHAEL PALMER
DOUGLAS PRESTON
CHRISTOPHER REICH
CHRISTOPHER RICE
JAMES ROLLINS
M. J. ROSE
JAMES SIEGEL
BRAD THOR
M. DIANE VOGT
F. PAUL WILSON

EDITED BY
JAMES PATTERSON

MIRA

MIRA®

ISBN-13: 978-0-7783-2456-0
ISBN-10:   0-7783-2456-7

THRILLER

Copyright © 2006 by International Thriller Writers, Inc.

Printed in U.S.A.

The publisher acknowledges the copyright holders of the original works as follows:

THE POWDER MONKEY
Copyright © 2006 by Ted Bell

THE DEVILS' DUE
Copyright © 2006 by Steve Berry

SACRIFICIAL LION
Copyright © 2006 by Grant Blackwood

JAMES PENNEY'S NEW IDENTITY
Copyright © 2006 by Lee Child

SPIRIT WALKER
Copyright © 2006 by David Dun

OPERATION NORTHWOODS
Copyright © 2006 by James Grippando

To Dennis Lynds and all thriller writers,
past and present.
May their stories live forever.

TABLE OF CONTENTS

Introduction

This book is a trailblazer on two counts. It's the first short-story anthology of thrillers ever done, and it's the first publication of a new professional organization: International Thriller Writers, Inc.

By nature writers tend to be loners, happy with their work, their families and a few close friends. But we also yearn occasionally for collegiality. For years we've all said to one another, "Why don't we organize?" Then in June 2004, Barbara Peters, of the legendary Poisoned Pen bookstore in Scottsdale, Arizona, held the first-ever thriller conference in the United States. She invited six writers—Lee Child, Vince Flynn, Steve Hamilton, Gayle Lynds, David Morrell and Kathy Reichs—and one editor, Keith Kahla, of St. Martin's Press, to give presentations about the various aspects of writing and publishing thrillers. Clive Cussler spoke at the luncheon.

With only two weeks to publicize the event, Barbara thought she'd be lucky if a hundred people registered. In the end some 125 attended and, to everyone's surprise, not all were there to learn about writing. Many were readers who wanted to meet some of their favorite thriller authors. Here for the first time was concrete evidence of what most of us had long suspected: there was a demand among fans for a thriller writers' organization, too. If we held conventions, readers would likely attend, as well as us. And if we awarded prizes—there have never been awards specifically for thriller books, stories and films in the English language—that interest would only grow.

On the last day of the conference, in the sunny restaurant at the Biltmore Hotel in Scottsdale, several of the attendees stood around talking. Gayle Lynds, a highly accomplished thriller writer, mentioned that she thought the conference indicated the time had come to create an association for thriller writers. Adrian Muller, a journalist and freelance conference organizer, pointed out that the association should not be limited to the United States. Barbara Peters said she'd be willing to hold another, larger convention. Realizing that she'd almost committed herself, Gayle quickly announced, "I can't organize this alone, though." Her husband, the incomparable Dennis Lynds, added, "She's right. She can't." Barbara merely smiled and said, "Pull in David Morrell. He's perfect."

And that's what happened.

Adrian Muller volunteered to send out e-mails to every thriller author he could find to see if there was enough interest among writers to form a group. A few days later, Gayle and David had a long telephone call, discussing their workloads and a potential thriller organization that would be international in scope. They agreed to jointly head the effort, and over the summer of 2004 Adrian, David and Gayle talked and exchanged e-mails. Adrian arranged with Al Navis, who was orchestrating Bouchercon 2004, the great congregation of mystery readers and writers, to assign a room in which the thriller authors could meet.

The response to Adrian's e-mail was impressive. Author after author said that an association was a great idea. A meeting was held on October 9 in the Metro Toronto Convention Centre and, after many discussions, International Thriller Writers, Inc. was born. In November 2004, members were solicited. That response was likewise incredible. Currently there are over four hundred members, with combined sales exceeding 1,600,000,000 books.

This is all quite astonishing, and fitting because thrillers provide such a rich literary feast. There are all kinds. The legal thriller, spy thriller, action-adventure thriller, medical thriller, police thriller, romantic thriller, historical thriller, political thriller, religious thriller, high-tech thriller, military thriller. The list goes go on and on, with new variations constantly being invented. In fact, this openness to expansion is one of the genre's most enduring characteristics. But what gives the variety of thrillers a common ground is the intensity of emotions they create, particularly those of apprehension and exhilaration, of excitement and breathlessness, all designed to generate that all-important thrill. By definition, if a thriller doesn't thrill, it's not doing its job.

Thrillers, though, are also known for their pace, and the force with which they hurtle the reader along. They're an obstacle race in which an objective is achieved at some heroic cost. The goal can be personal (trying to save a spouse or a long-lost relative) or global (trying to avert a world war) but often it's both. Perhaps there's a time limit imposed, perhaps not. Sometimes they build rhythmically to rousing climaxes that peak with a cathartic, explosive ending. Other times they start at top speed and never ease off. At their best, thrillers use scrupulous research and accurate details to create environments in which meaningful characters teach us about our world. When readers finish a thriller, they should feel not only emotionally satisfied but also better informed—and hungry for the next riveting tale.

Henry James once wrote, "The house of fiction has many windows." That observation certainly applies to thrillers, and this anthology is an excellent example. When Gayle Lynds suggested producing it, International Thriller Writers, Inc. sent out a call to its members for stories. Many replied, and thirty were ultimately selected for inclusion. I was contacted about acting as editor and readily agreed, while Steve Berry, another ITW member and thriller author, took on the responsibility of managing director. When the book proposal was finally shopped by agent Richard Pine, himself an ITW member, several publishers expressed interest and, after a bidding war, MIRA Books acquired the rights.

Generously, each of the contributors to this book donated his or her story. Only ITW will share in the royalties, the proceeds earned going into the corporate treasury to fund the expansion of this worthwhile organization. The theme of this anthology is simple. Each writer has used a familiar character or plotline from their body of work and crafted an original story. So you have something known, along with something new. As you'll see, the variations are captivating, as the writers' imaginations soared. Each story is prefaced by an introduction from me that sets up the writer, his or her work and the story. At the book's end, there are short biographies of each contributor. What a pleasure it was to read the stories as they came in, and it's my hope that you'll likewise relish the tales.

So prepare to be thrilled.

And enjoy the experience.

—James Patterson

June 2006

P.S. More can be learned about ITW through its Web site at www.internationalthrillerwriters.com. Check it out.

LEE CHILD

Lee Child's debut novel was *Killing Floor*, a first-person narrative introducing his series character Jack Reacher, and although clearly a fast-paced thriller it shared characteristics with the classic limited-universe Western. At the time Child was also an experienced media professional, aware that his second book had to be written before significant reaction to his first had even been received. To avoid stereotyping—which can affect a writer as much as any performer—Child determined to make his second book, *Die Trying*, as different as possible, albeit part of the same series. His plan was to stake out a wide "left field, right field" territorial span between books one and two, one in which the rest of the series could happily roam. Therefore *Die Trying* featured third-person narration and a classic high-stakes, multistrand thriller structure. But, in its first draft, that structure went one strand too far. There was a character—James Penney—who had an appealing introduction and backstory, but who clearly didn't have any valid place to go. So Penney wasn't featured in the completed novel. Instead, he languished on Child's hard drive until a request came from an obscure British anthology for a short story. Child repackaged Penney's narrative and added a prequel-style ending, featuring a brief glimpse of Jack Reacher's early career. The story was published, but with limited distribution. Now it comes to life again, revised and renewed, in hopes of reaching a wider audience.

JAMES PENNEY'S NEW IDENTITY

The process that turned James Penney into a completely different person began thirteen years ago, at one in the afternoon on a Monday in the middle of June, in Laney, California. A hot time of day, at a hot time of year, in a hot part of the country. The town squats on the shoulder of the road from Mojave to L.A. Due west, the southern rump of the Coastal Range Mountains is visible. Due east, the Mojave Desert disappears into the haze. Very little happens in Laney. After that Monday in the middle of June thirteen years ago, even less ever did.

There was one industry in Laney. One factory. A big spread of a place. Weathered metal siding, built in the sixties. Office accommodations at the north end, in the shade. The first floor was low grade. Clerical functions took place there. Billing and accounting and telephone calling. The second story was high grade. Managers. The corner office on the right used to be the personnel manager's place. Now it was the human resources manager's place. Same guy, new title on his door.

Outside that door in the long second-floor corridor was a line of chairs. The human resources manager's secretary had rustled them up and placed them there that Monday morning. The line of chairs was occupied by a line of men and women. They were silent. Every five minutes the person at the head of the line would be called into the office. The rest of them would shuffle up one place. They didn't speak. They didn't need to. They knew what was happening.

Just before one o'clock, James Penney shuffled up one space to the head of the line. He waited five long minutes and stood up when he was called. Stepped into the office. Closed the door behind him. The human resources manager was a guy called Odell. Odell hadn't been long out of diapers when James Penney started work at the Laney plant.

"Mr. Penney," Odell said.

Penney said nothing, but sat down and nodded in a guarded way.

"We need to share some information with you," Odell said.

Penney shrugged at him. He knew what was coming. He heard things, same as anybody else.

"Just give me the short version, okay?" he said.

Odell nodded. "We're laying you off."

"For the summer?" Penney asked him.

Odell shook his head.

"For good," he said.

Penney took a second to get over the sound of the words. He'd known they were coming, but they hit him like they were the last words he ever expected Odell to say.

"Why?" he asked.

Odell shrugged. He didn't look as if he was enjoying this. But on the other hand, he didn't look as if it was upsetting him much, either.

"Downsizing," he said. "No option. Only way we can go."

"Why?" Penney said again.

Odell leaned back in his chair and folded his hands behind his head. Started the speech he'd already made many times that day.

"We need to cut costs," he said. "This is an expensive operation. Small margin. Shrinking market. You know that."

Penney stared into space and listened to the silence breaking through from the factory floor. "So you're closing the plant?"

Odell shook his head again. "We're downsizing, is all. The plant will stay open. There'll be some maintenance. Some repairs, overhauls. But not like it used to be."

"The plant will stay open?" Penney said. "So how come you're letting me go?"

Odell shifted in his chair. Pulled his hands from behind his head and folded his arms across his chest defensively. He had reached the tricky part of the interview.

"It's a question of the skills mix," he said. "We had to pick a team with the correct blend. We put a lot of work into the decision. And I'm afraid you didn't make the cut."

"What's wrong with my skills?" Penney asked. "I got skills. I've worked here seventeen years. What's wrong with my damn skills?"

"Nothing at all," Odell said. "But other people are better. We have to look at the big picture. It's going to be a skeleton crew, so we need the best skills, the fastest learners, good attendance records, you know how it is."

"Attendance records?" Penney said. "What's wrong

with my attendance record? I've worked here seventeen years. You saying I'm not a reliable worker?"

Odell touched the brown file folder in front of him.

"You've had a lot of time out sick," he said. "Absentee rate just above eight percent."

Penney looked at him incredulously.

"Sick?" he said. "I wasn't sick. I was post-traumatic. From Vietnam."

Odell shook his head again. He was too young.

"Whatever," he said. "That's still a big absentee rate."

James Penney just sat there, stunned. He felt like he'd been hit by a train.

"We looked for the correct blend," Odell said again. "We put a lot of management time into the process. We're confident we made the right decisions. You're not being singled out. We're losing eighty percent of our people."

Penney stared across at him. "You staying?"

Odell nodded and tried to hide a smile but couldn't.

"There's still a business to run," he said. "We still need management."

There was silence in the corner office. Outside, the hot breeze stirred off the desert and blew a listless eddy over the metal building. Odell opened the brown folder and pulled out a blue envelope. Handed it across the desk.

"You're paid up to the end of July," he said. "Money went in the bank this morning. Good luck, Mr. Penney."

The five-minute interview was over. Odell's secretary appeared and opened the door to the corridor. Penney walked out. The secretary called the next man in. Penney walked past the long quiet row of people and made it to the parking lot. Slid into his car. It was a red Firebird, a year and a half old, and it wasn't paid for yet. He started it up and drove the mile to his house. Eased to a stop in his driveway and sat there, thinking, in a daze, with the engine running.

He was imagining the repo men coming for his car. The only damn thing in his whole life he'd ever really wanted. He remembered the exquisite joy of buying it. After his divorce. Waking up and realizing he could just go to the dealer, sign the papers and have it. No discussions. No arguing. He'd gone down to the dealer and chopped in his old clunker and signed up for that Firebird and driven it home in a state of total joy. He'd washed it every week. He'd watched the infomercials and tried every miracle polish on the market. The car had sat every day outside the Laney factory like a bright red badge of achievement. Like a shiny consolation for the shit and the drudgery. Whatever else he didn't have, he had a Firebird.

He felt a desperate fury building inside him. He got out of the car and ran to the garage and grabbed his spare can of gasoline. Ran back to the house. Opened the door. Emptied the can over the sofa. He couldn't find a match, so he lit the gas stove in the kitchen and unwound a roll of paper towels. Put one end on the stove top and ran the rest through to the living room. When his makeshift fuse was well alight, he skipped out to his car and started it up. Turned north toward Mojave.

His neighbor noticed the fire when the flames started coming through the roof. She called the Laney fire department. The firefighters didn't respond. It was a volunteer department, and all the volunteers were in line inside the factory, upstairs in the narrow corridor. Then the warm air moving off the Mojave Desert freshened up into a hot breeze, and by the time James Penney was thirty miles away the flames from his house had set fire to the dried scrub that had been his lawn. By the time he was in the town of Mojave itself, cashing his last paycheck at the bank, the flames had spread across his lawn and his neighbor's and were licking at the base of her back porch.

Like any California boomtown, Laney had grown in a hurry. The factory had been thrown up around the start of Nixon's first term. A hundred acres of orange groves had been bulldozed and five hundred frame houses had quadrupled the population in a year. There was nothing really wrong with the houses, but they'd seen rain less than a dozen times in the thirty-one years they'd been standing, and they were about as dry as houses can get. Their timbers had sat and baked in the sun and been scoured by the dry desert winds. There were no hydrants built into the streets. The houses were close together, and there were no windbreaks. But there had never been a serious fire in Laney. Not until that Monday in June.

James Penney's neighbor called the fire department for the second time after her back porch disappeared in flames. The fire department was in disarray. The dispatcher advised her to get out of her house and just wait for their arrival. By the time the fire truck got there, her house was destroyed. And the next house in line was destroyed, too. The desert breeze had blown the fire on across the second narrow gap and sent the old couple living there scuttling into the street for safety. Then Laney called in the fire departments from Lancaster and Glendale and Bakersfield, and they arrived with proper equipment and saved the day. They hosed the scrub between the houses and the blaze went no farther. Just three houses destroyed, Penney's and his two downwind neighbors. Within two hours the panic was over, and by the time Penney himself was fifty miles north of Mojave, Laney's sheriff was working with the fire investigators to piece together what had happened.

They started with Penney's place, which was the up-wind house, and the first to burn, and therefore the coolest. It had just about burned down to the floor slab, but the layout was still clear. And the evidence was there to see. There was tremendous scorching on one side of where the living room had been. The Glendale investigator recognized it as something he'd seen many times before. It was what is left when a foam-filled sofa or armchair is doused with gasoline and set afire. As clear a case of arson as he had ever seen. The unfortunate wild cards had been the stiffening desert breeze and the proximity of the other houses.

Then the sheriff had gone looking for James Penney, to tell him somebody had burned his house down, and his neighbors'. He drove his black-and-white to the factory and walked upstairs, past the long line of people and into Odell's corner office. Odell told him what had happened in the five-minute interview just after one o'clock. Then the sheriff had driven back to the Laney station house, steering with one hand and rubbing his chin with the other.

And by the time James Penney was driving along the towering eastern flank of Mount Whitney, a hundred and fifty miles from home, there was an all-points-bulletin out on him, suspicion of deliberate arson, which in the dry desert heat of southern California was a big, big deal.

The next morning's sun woke James Penney by coming in through a hole in his motel-room blind and playing a bright beam across his face. He stirred and lay in the warmth of the rented bed, watching the dust motes dancing.

He was still in California, up near Yosemite, in a place just far enough from the park to be cheap. He had six weeks' pay in his billfold, which was hidden under the center of his mattress. Six weeks' pay, less a tank and a half of gas, a cheeseburger and twenty-seven-fifty for the room. Hidden under the mattress, because twenty-seven-fifty doesn't get you a space in a top-notch place. His door was locked, but the desk guy would have a passkey, and he wouldn't be the first desk guy in the world to rent out his passkey by the hour to somebody looking to make a little extra money during the night.

But nothing bad had happened. The mattress was so thin he could feel the billfold right there, under his kidney. Still there, still bulging. A good feeling. He lay watching the sunbeam, struggling with mental arithmetic, spreading six weeks' pay out over the foreseeable future. With nothing to worry about except cheap food, cheap motels and the Firebird's gas, he figured he had no problems at all. The Firebird had a modern engine, twenty-four valves, tuned for a blend of power and economy. He could get far away and have enough money left to take his time looking around.

After that, he wasn't so sure. But there would be a call for something. He was sure of that. Even if it was menial. He was a worker. Maybe he'd find something outdoors, might be a refreshing thing. Might have some kind of dignity to it. Some kind of simple work, for simple honest folks, a lot different than slaving for that grinning weasel Odell.

He watched the sunbeam travel across the counterpane for a while. Then he flung the cover aside and swung himself out of bed. Used the john, rinsed his face and mouth at the sink and untangled his clothes from the pile he'd dropped them in. He'd need more clothes. He only had the things he stood up in. Everything else he'd burned along with his house. He shrugged and reran his calculations to allow for some new pants and work shirts. Maybe some heavy boots, if he was going to be laboring outside. The six weeks' pay was going to have to stretch a little thinner. He decided to drive slow, to save gas and maybe eat less. Or maybe not less, just cheaper. He'd use truck stops, not tourist diners. More calories, less money.

He figured today he'd put in some serious miles before stopping for breakfast. He jingled the car keys in his pocket and opened his cabin door. Then he stopped. His heart thumped. The blacktop rectangle outside his cabin was empty. Just old oil stains staring up at him. He glanced desperately left and right along the row. No red Firebird. He staggered back into the room and sat down heavily on the bed. Just sat there in a daze, thinking about what to do.

He decided he wouldn't bother with the desk guy. He was pretty certain the desk guy was responsible. He could just about see it. The guy had waited an hour and then called some buddies who had come over and hot-wired his car. Eased it out of the motel lot and away down the road. A conspiracy, feeding off unsuspecting motel traffic. Feeding off suckers dumb enough to pay twenty-seven-fifty for the privilege of getting their prize possession stolen. He was numb. Suspended somewhere between sick and raging. His red Firebird. Gone. Stolen. No repo men involved. Just thieves.

The nearest police station was two miles south. He had seen it the previous night, heading north past it. It was small but crowded. He stood in line behind five other people. There was an officer behind the counter, taking details, taking complaints, writing slow. Penney felt like every minute was vital. He felt like his Firebird was racing down to the border. Maybe this guy could radio ahead and get it stopped. He hopped from foot to foot in frustration. Gazed wildly around him. There were notices stuck on a board behind the officer's head. Blurred Xeroxes of telexes and faxes. U.S. Marshal notices. A mass of stuff. His eyes flicked absently across it all.

Then they snapped back. His photograph was staring out at him. The photograph from his own driver's license, Xeroxed in black and white, enlarged, grainy. His name underneath, in big printed letters. JAMES PENNEY. From Laney, California. A description of his car. Red Firebird. The plate number. James Penney. Wanted for arson and criminal damage. He stared at the bulletin. It grew larger and larger. It grew life-size. His face stared back at him like he was looking in a mirror. James Penney. Arson. Criminal damage. All-points-bulletin. The woman in front of him finished her business and he stepped forward to the head of the line. The desk sergeant looked up at him.

"Can I help you, sir?" he said.

Penney shook his head. Peeled off left and walked away. Stepped calmly outside into the bright morning sun and ran back north like a madman. He made about a hundred yards before the heat slowed him to a gasping walk. Then he did the instinctive thing, which was to duck off the blacktop and take cover in a wild-birch grove. He pushed through the brush until he was out of sight and collapsed into a sitting position, back against a thin rough trunk, legs splayed out straight, chest heaving, hands clamped against his head like he was trying to stop it from exploding.

Arson and criminal damage. He knew what the words meant. But he couldn't square them with what he had actually done. It was his own damn house to burn. Like he was burning his trash. He was entitled. How could that be arson? And he could explain, anyway. He'd been upset. He sat slumped against the birch trunk and breathed easier. But only for a moment. Because then he started thinking about lawyers. He'd had personal experience. His divorce had cost him plenty in lawyer bills. He knew what lawyers were like. Lawyers were the problem. Even if it wasn't arson, it was going to cost plenty in lawyer bills to start proving it. It was going to cost a steady torrent of dollars, pouring out for years. Dollars he didn't have, and never would have again. He sat there on the hard, dry ground and realized that absolutely everything he had in the whole world was right then in direct contact with his body. One pair of shoes, one pair of socks, one pair of boxers, Levi's, cotton shirt, leather jacket. And his billfold. He put his hand down and touched its bulk in his pocket. Six weeks' pay, less yesterday's spending.

He got to his feet in the clearing. His legs were weak from the unaccustomed running. His heart was thumping. He leaned up against a birch trunk and took a deep breath. Swallowed. He pushed back through the brush to the road. Turned north and started walking. He walked for a half hour, hands in his pockets, maybe a mile and three-quarters, and then his muscles eased off and his breathing calmed down. He began to see things clearly. He began to appreciate the power of labels. He was a realistic guy, and he always told himself the truth. He was an arsonist because they said he was. The angry phase was over. Now it was about making sensible decisions, one after the other. Clearing up the confusion was beyond his resources. So he had to stay out of their reach. That was his first decision. That was the starting point. That was the strategy. The other decisions would flow out of that. They were tactical.

He could be traced three ways. By his name, by his face, by his car. He ducked sideways off the road again into the trees. Pushed twenty yards into the woods. Kicked a shallow hole in the leaf mold and stripped out of his billfold everything with his name on. He buried it all in the hole and stamped the earth flat. Then he took his beloved Firebird keys from his pocket and hurled them far into the trees. He didn't see where they fell.

The car itself was gone. Under the circumstances, that was good. But it had left a trail. It might have been seen in Mojave, outside the bank. It might have been seen at the gas stations where he filled it. And its plate number was on the motel form from last night. With his name. A trail, arrowing north through California in neat little increments.

He remembered his training from Vietnam. He remembered the tricks. If you wanted to move east from your foxhole, first you moved west. You moved west for a couple hundred yards, stepping on the occasional twig, brushing the occasional bush, until you had convinced Charlie you were moving west, as quietly as you could, but not quietly enough. Then you turned around and came back east, really quietly, doing it right, past your original starting point and away. He'd done it a dozen times. His original plan had been to head north for a spell, maybe into Oregon. He'd gotten a few hours into that plan. Therefore, the red Firebird had laid a modest trail north. So now he was going to turn south for a while and disappear. He walked back out of the woods, into the dust on the near side of the road, and started walking back the way he had come.

His face he couldn't change. It was right there on all the posters. He remembered it staring out at him from the bulletin board in the police building. The neat side-parting, the sunken gray cheeks. He ran his hands through his hair, vigorously, backward and forward, until it stuck out every which way. No more neat side-parting. He ran his palms over twenty-four hours of stubble. Decided to grow a big beard. No option, really. He didn't have a razor, and he wasn't about to spend any money on one. He walked on through the dust, heading south, with Excelsior Mountain towering on his right. Then he came to the turn dodging west toward San Francisco, through Tioga Pass, before Mount Dana reared up even higher. He stopped in the dust on the side of the road and pondered. Keeping on south would take him nearly all the way back to Mojave. Too close to home. Way too close. He wasn't comfortable about that. Not comfortable at all. So he figured a new move. He'd hitch a ride west, and then decide.

Late in the afternoon he got out of some old hippie's open Jeep on the southern edge of Sacramento. He stood by the side of the road and waved and watched the guy go. Then he looked around in the sudden silence and got his bearings. All the way up and down the drag he could see a forest of signs, bright colors, neon, advertising motels, air and pool and cable, burger places, eateries of every description, supermarkets, auto parts. Looked like the kind of place a guy could get lost in, no trouble at all. Big choice of motels, all side by side, all competing, all offering the lowest prices in town. He figured he'd hole up in one of them and plan ahead. After eating. He was hungry. He chose a burger chain he'd never used before and sat in the window, idly watching the traffic. The waitress came over and he ordered a cheeseburger and two Cokes. He was dry from the dust on the road.

The Laney sheriff opened a map. Thought hard. Penney wouldn't be aiming to stay in California. He'd be moving on. Probably up to the wilds of Oregon or Washington State. Or Idaho or Montana. But not due north. Penney was a veteran. He knew how to feint. He would head west first. He would aim to get out through Sacramento. But Sacramento was a city with an ocean not too far away to the left, and high mountains to the right. Fundamentally six roads out, was all. So six roadblocks would do it, maybe on a ten-mile radius so the local commuters wouldn't get snarled up. The sheriff nodded to himself and picked up the phone.

Penney walked north for an hour. It started raining at dusk. Steady, wetting rain. Northern California, near the mountains, very different from what Penney was used to. He was hunched in his jacket, head down, tired and demoralized and alone. And wet. And conspicuous. Nobody walked anywhere in California. He glanced over his shoulder at the traffic stream and saw a dull olive Chevrolet sedan slowing behind him. It came to a stop and a long arm stretched across and opened the passenger door. The dome light clicked on and shone out on the soaked roadway.

"Want a ride?" the driver called.

Penney ducked down and glanced inside. The driver was a very tall man, about thirty, muscular, built like a regular weight lifter. Short fair hair, rugged open face. Dressed in uniform. Army uniform. Penney read the insignia and registered: military police captain. He glanced at the dull olive paint on the car and saw a white serial number stenciled on the flank.

"I don't know," he said.

"Get in out of the rain," the driver said. "A vet like you knows better than to be walking in the rain."

Penney slid inside. Closed the door.

"How do you know I'm a vet?" he asked.

"The way you walk," the driver said. "And your age, and the way you look. Guy your age looking like you look and walking in the rain didn't beat the draft for college, that's for damn sure."

Penney nodded.

"No, I didn't," he said. "I did a jungle tour."

"So let me give you a ride," the driver said. "A favor, one soldier to another. Consider it a veteran's benefit."

"Okay," Penney said.

"Where you headed?" the driver asked.

"I don't know," Penney said. "North, I guess."

"Okay, north it is," the driver said. "I'm Jack Reacher. Pleased to make your acquaintance."

Penney said nothing.

"You got a name?" the guy called Reacher asked.

Penney hesitated.

"I don't know," he said.

Reacher put the car in drive and glanced over his

shoulder. Eased back into the traffic stream. Clicked the switch and locked the doors.

"What did you do?" he asked.

"Do?" Penney repeated.

"You're running," Reacher said. "Heading out of town, walking in the rain, head down, no bag, don't know what your name is. I've seen a lot of people running, and you're one of them."

"You going to turn me in?"

"I'm a military cop," Reacher said. "You done anything to hurt the army?"

"The army?" Penney said. "No, I was a good soldier."

"So why would I turn you in?"

Penney looked blank.

"What did you do to the civilians?" Reacher asked.

"You're going to turn me in," Penney said helplessly.

Reacher shrugged at the wheel. "That depends. What did you do?"

Penney said nothing. Reacher turned his head and looked straight at him. A powerful, silent stare, hypnotic intensity in his eyes, held for a hundred yards of road. Penney couldn't look away. He took a breath.

"I burned my house," he said. "Near Mojave. I worked seventeen years and got canned yesterday and I got all upset because they were going to take my car away so I burned my house. They're calling it arson."

"Near Mojave?" Reacher said. "They would. They don't like fires down there."

Penney nodded. "I was real mad. Seventeen years, and suddenly I'm shit on their shoe. And my car got stolen anyway, first night I'm away."

"There are roadblocks all around here," Reacher said. "I came through one south of the city."

"For me?" Penney asked.

"Could be," Reacher said. "They don't like fires down there."

"You going to turn me in?"

Reacher looked at him again, hard and silent. "Is that all you did?"

Penney nodded. "Yes, sir, that's all I did."

There was silence for a beat. Just the sound of the wet pavement under the tires.

"I don't have a problem with it," Reacher said. "A guy does a jungle tour, works seventeen years and gets canned, I guess he's entitled to get a little mad."

"So what should I do?"

"Start over, someplace else."

"They'll find me," Penney said.

"You're already thinking about changing your name," Reacher said.

Penney nodded. "I junked all my ID. Buried it in the woods."

"So get new paper. That's all anybody cares about. Pieces of paper."

"How?"

Reacher was quiet another beat, thinking hard. "Classic way is find some cemetery, find a kid who died as a child, get a copy of the birth certificate, start from there. Get a social security number, a passport, credit cards, and you're a new person."

Penney shrugged. "I can't do all that. Too difficult. And I don't have time. According to you, there's a roadblock up ahead. How am I going to do all of that stuff before we get there?"

"There are other ways," Reacher said.

"Like what?"

"Find some guy who's already created false ID for himself, and take it away from him."

Penney shook his head. "You're crazy. How am I going to do that?"

"Maybe you don't need to do that. Maybe I already did it for you."

"You got false ID?"

"Not me," Reacher said. "Guy I was looking for."

"What guy?"

Reacher drove one-handed and pulled a sheaf of official paper from his inside jacket pocket.

"Arrest warrant," he said. "Army liaison officer at a weapons plant outside of Fresno, peddling blueprints. Turns out to have three separate sets of ID, all perfect, all completely backed up with everything from elementary school onward. Which makes it likely they're Soviet, which means they can't be beat. I'm on my way back from talking to him right now. He was running, too, already on his second set of papers. I took them. They're clean. They're in the trunk of this car, in a wallet."

Traffic was slowing ahead. There was red glare visible through the streaming windshield. Flashing blue lights. Yellow flashlight beams waving, side to side.

"Roadblock," Reacher said.

"So can I use this guy's ID?" Penney asked urgently.

"Sure you can," Reacher said. "Hop out and get it. Bring the wallet from the jacket in the trunk."

He slowed and stopped on the shoulder. Penney got out. Ducked away to the back of the car and lifted the trunk lid. Came back a long moment later, white in the face. Held up the wallet.

"It's all in there," Reacher said. "Everything anybody needs."

Penney nodded.

"So put it in your pocket," Reacher said.

Penney slipped the wallet into his inside jacket pocket. Reacher's right hand came up. There was a gun in it. And a pair of handcuffs in his left.

"Now sit still," he said quietly.

He leaned over and snapped the cuffs on Penney's wrists, one-handed. Put the car back into drive and crawled forward.

"What's this for?" Penney asked.

"Be quiet," Reacher said.

They were two cars away from the checkpoint. Three highway patrolmen in rain capes were directing traffic into a corral formed by parked cruisers. Their light bars were flashing bright in the shiny dark.

"What?" Penney said again.

Reacher said nothing. Just stopped where the cop told him and wound his window down. The night air blew in, cold and wet. The cop bent down. Reacher handed him his military ID. The cop played his flashlight over it and handed it back.

"Who's your passenger?" he asked.

"My prisoner," Reacher said. He handed over the arrest warrant.

"He got ID?" the cop asked.

Reacher leaned over and slipped the wallet out from inside Penney's jacket, two-fingered like a pickpocket. Flipped it open and passed it through the window. A second cop stood in Reacher's headlight beams and copied the plate number onto a clipboard. Stepped around the hood and joined the first guy.

"Captain Reacher of the military police," the first cop said.

The second cop wrote it down.

"With a prisoner name of Edward Hendricks," the first cop said.

The second cop wrote it down.

"Thank you, sir," the first cop said. "You drive safe, now."

Reacher eased out from between the cruisers. Accelerated away into the rain. A mile later, he stopped again on the shoulder. Leaned over and unlocked Penney's handcuffs. Put them back in his pocket. Penney rubbed his wrists.

"I thought you were going to turn me in," he said.

Reacher shook his head. "Looked better for me that way. I wanted a prisoner in the car for everybody to see."

Reacher handed the wallet back.

"Keep it," he said.

"Really?"

"Edward Hendricks," Reacher said. "That's who you are now. It's clean ID, and it'll work. Think of it like a veteran's benefit. One soldier to another."

Edward Hendricks looked at him and nodded and opened his door. Got out into the rain and turned up the collar of his leather jacket and started walking north. Reacher watched him until he was out of sight and then pulled away and took the next turn west. Turned north and stopped again where the road was lonely and ran close to the ocean. There was a wide gravel shoulder and a low barrier and a steep cliff with the Pacific tide boiling and foaming fifty feet below it.

He got out of the car and opened the trunk and grasped the lapels of the jacket he had told Penney about. Took a deep breath and heaved. The corpse was heavy. Reacher wrestled it up out of the trunk and jacked it onto his shoulder and staggered with it to the barrier. Bent his knees and dropped it over the edge. The rocky cliff caught it and it spun and the arms and legs flailed limply. Then it hit the surf with a faint splash and was gone.

JAMES GRIPPANDO

It's no accident that five of James Grippando's ten thrillers are legal thrillers featuring Jack Swyteck, an explosive criminal defense lawyer. Grippando is a lawyer himself, though fortunately with far fewer demons than Jack. What's it like to be Jack? Simply imagine that your father is Florida's governor, your best friend was once on death row and your love life could fill an entire chapter in *Cupid's Rules of Love and War (Idiot's Edition)*. Throw in an indictment for murder and a litany of lesser charges, and you'll begin to get the picture.

Readers of the Swyteck series know that Jack is a self-described half-Cuban boy trapped in the body of a gringo. That's a glib way of saying that Jack's Cuban-born mother died in childbirth, and Jack was raised by his father and stepmother, with no link whatsoever to his Cuban heritage. Grippando is not Cuban, but he considers himself an "honorary Cuban" of sorts. His best friend since college was Cuban born and that family dubbed him their *otro hijo*, other son. Quite remarkable, considering that Grippando grew up in rural Illinois and spoke only "classroom" Spanish. When he first arrived in Florida, he had no idea that Cubans made better rice than the Chinese, or that a jolt of Cuban coffee was as much a part of mid-afternoon in Miami as thunderclouds over the Everglades. He'd yet to learn that if you ask a nice Cuban girl on a date, the entire family would be waiting at the front door to meet you when you picked her up. In short, Grippando—like Jack Swyteck—was the gringo who found himself immersed in Cuban culture.

In *Hear No Evil*, the fourth book in the Swyteck series, Jack Swyteck travels back to Cuba to discover his roots. Naturally, he runs into a mess of trouble, all stemming from a murder on the U.S. naval base at Guantanamo Bay. Grippando prides himself on his research, and threw himself into all things Cuban when researching the thriller. At the time it was impossible to speak to anyone about the U.S. naval base at Guantanamo Bay without the problem of the detainees dominating the conversation. It was then that Grippando came across a forty-year-old plan—Operation Northwoods—which, in the hands of someone with an extremely devious mind, could cause a mountain of trouble.

So was born this story.

In *Operation Northwoods*, Jack and his colorful sidekick, Theo Knight, find themselves in the heat of a controversy after an explosion at the U.S. naval base at Guantanamo Bay, Cuba—an explosion that rocks the world.

OPERATION NORTHWOODS

6:20 a.m., Miami, Florida

Jack Swyteck swatted the alarm clock, but even the subtle green glow of liquid-crystal digits was an assault on his eyes. The ringing continued. He raked his hand across the nightstand, grabbed the telephone and answered in a voice that dripped with a hangover. It was Theo.

"Theo who?" said Jack.

"Theo Knight, moron."

Jack's brain was obviously still asleep. Theo was Jack's best friend and "investigator," for lack of a better term. Whatever Jack needed, Theo found, whether it was the last prop plane out of Africa or an explanation for a naked corpse in Jack's bathtub. Jack never stopped wondering how Theo came up with these things. Sometimes he asked; more often, he simply didn't want to know. Theirs was not exactly a textbook friendship, the Ivy League son of a governor meets the black high-school dropout from Liberty City. But they got on just fine for two guys who'd met on death row, Jack the lawyer and Theo the inmate. Jack's persistence had delayed Theo's date with the electric chair long enough for DNA evidence to come into vogue and prove him innocent. It wasn't the original plan, but Jack ended up a part of Theo's new life, sometimes going along for the ride, other times just watching with amazement as Theo made up for lost time.

"Dude, turn on your TV," said Theo. "CNN."

There was an urgency in Theo's voice, and Jack was too disoriented to mount an argument. He found the remote and switched on the set, watching from the foot of his bed.

A grainy image filled the screen, like bad footage from one of those media helicopters covering a police car chase. It was an aerial shot of a compound of some sort. Scores of small dwellings and other, larger buildings dotted the windswept landscape. There were patches of green, but overall the terrain had an arid quality, perfect for iguanas and banana rats—except for all the fences. Jack noticed miles of them. One- and two-lane roads cut across the topography like tiny scars, and a slew of vehicles seemed to be moving at high speed, though they looked like matchbox cars from this vantage point. In the background, a huge, black plume of smoke was rising like a menacing funnel cloud.

"What's going on?" he said into the phone.

"They're at the naval base in Guantanamo Bay. It's about your client."

"My client? Which one?"

"The crazy one."

"That doesn't exactly narrow things down," said Jack.

"You know, the Haitian saint," said Theo.

Jack didn't bother to tell him that he wasn't actually a saint. "You mean Jean Saint Preux? What did he do?"

"What did he *do?*" said Theo, scoffing. "He set the fucking naval base on fire."

6:35 a.m., Guantanamo Bay, Cuba

Camp Delta was a huge, glowing ember on the horizon, like the second rising of the sun. The towering plume of black smoke rose ever higher, fed feverishly by the raging furnace below. A gentle breeze from the Windward Passage only seemed to worsen matters—too weak to clear the smoke, just strong enough to spread a gloomy haze across the entire southeastern corner of the U.S. Naval Station at Guantanamo Bay, Cuba.

Major Frost Jorgenson was speeding due south in the passenger seat of a U.S. marine Humvee. Even with the windows shut tight, the seeping smoke was making his eyes water.

"Unbelievable," he said as they drew closer to the camp.

"Yes, sir," said his driver. "Biggest fire I've ever seen."

Major Jorgenson was relatively new to "Gitmo," part of the stepped-up presence of U.S. Marines that had come with the creation of a permanent detention facility at Camp Delta for "enemy combatants"—suspected terrorists who had never been charged formally with a crime. Jorgenson was a bruiser even by marine standards. Four years of college football at Grambling University had prepared him well for a life of discipline, and old habits die hard. Before sunrise, he'd already run two miles and peeled off two hundred sit-ups. He was stepping out of the shower, dripping wet, when the telephone call had come from Fire Station No. 1. An explosion at Camp Delta. Possible casualties. Fire/Rescue dispatched. No details as yet. Almost immediately, he was fielding calls from his senior officers, including the brigadier general in charge of the entire detainee program, all of whom were demanding a situation report, *pronto*.

A guard waved them through the Camp Delta checkpoint.

"Unbelievable." The major was slightly embarrassed for having repeated himself, but it was involuntary, the only word that seemed to fit.

The Humvee stopped, and the soldiers rushed to strap on their gas masks as they jumped out of the vehicle. A wave of heat assaulted the major immediately, a stifling blow, as if he'd carelessly tossed a match onto a pile of oversoaked charcoal briquettes. Instinctively he brought a hand to his face, even though he was protected by the mask. After a few moments, the burning sensation subsided, but the visibility was only getting worse. Depending on the wind, it was like stepping into a foggy twilight, the low morning sun unable to penetrate the smoke. He grabbed a flashlight from the glove compartment.

Major Jorgenson walked briskly, stepping over rock-hard fire hoses and fallen debris, eventually finding himself in the staging area for the firefighting team from Fire Station No. 2. Thick, noxious smoke made it impossible to see beyond the three nearest fire trucks, though he was sure there were more, somewhere in the darkness. At least he hoped there were more. Once again, the heat was on him like a blanket, but even more stifling was the noise all around him—radios crackling, sirens blaring, men shouting. Loudest of all was the inferno itself, an endless surge of flames emitting a noise that was peculiar to fires this overwhelming, a strange cross between a roaring tidal wave and a gigantic wet bedsheet flapping in the breeze.

"Watch it!"

Directly overhead, a stream of water arched from the turret of a massive, yellow truck. It was one of several three-thousand-gallon airport rescue and firefighting machines on the base, capable of dousing flames with 165 gallons of water per minute. It wasn't even close to being enough.

"Coming through!" A team of stretcher bearers streaked past. Major Jorgenson caught a glimpse of the blackened shell of a man on the gurney, his arms and legs twisted and shriveled like melted plastic. On impulse, he ran alongside and then took up the rear position, relieving one of the stretcher bearers who seemed to be on the verge of collapse.

"Dear God," he said. But his heart sank even further as the lead man guided the stretcher right past the ambulance to a line of human remains behind the emergency vehicles. The line was already too long to bear. They rolled the charred body onto the pavement.

"Major, in here!"

He turned and saw the fire chief waving him toward the side of the fire truck. An enlisted man stepped in to relieve his commanding officer of stretcher duty. The major commended him and then hurried over to join the chief inside the cab, pulling off his mask as the door closed behind him.

The fire chief was covered with soot, his expression incredulous. "With all due respect, sir, what are you doing out here?"

"Same as you," said the major. "Is it as bad as it looks?"

"Maybe worse, sir."

"How many casualties?"

"Six marines unaccounted for so far. Eleven injured."

"What about detainees?"

"Easier to count survivors at this point."

"How many?"

"So far, none."

The major felt his gut tighten. None. No survivors. A horrible result—even worse when you had to explain it to the rest of the world.

The fire chief picked a flake of ash from his eye and said, "Sir, we're doing our best to fight this monster. But any insight you can give me as to how this started could be a big help."

"Plane crash," the major reported. "That's all we know now. Civilian craft. Cessna."

Just then, a team of F-16s roared across the skies overhead. Navy fighter jets had been circling the base since the invasion of airspace.

"Civilian plane, huh? It may not be my place to ask, but how did that happen?"

"You're right. It's not your place to ask."

"Yes, sir. But for the safety of my own men, I guess what I'm getting at is this: if there's something inside this facility that we should know about...I mean something of an explosive or incendiary nature—"

"This is a detention facility. Nothing more."

"One heck of a blaze for a small civilian aircraft that crashed into nothing more than a detention facility."

The major took another look through the windshield. He couldn't argue.

The chief said, "I may look like an old geezer, but I know a thing or two about fires. A little private plane crashing into a building doesn't carry near enough fuel to start a fire like this. These bodies we're pulling out of here, we're not talking third-degree burns. Upward of eighty-five, ninety percent of them, it's fourth- and even fifth-degree, some of them cooked right down to the bone. And that smell in the air, benzene all the way."

"What is it you're trying to tell me?"

"I know napalm when I see it."

The major turned his gaze back toward the fire, then pulled his encrypted cellular phone from his pocket and dialed the naval station command suite.

7:02 a.m., Miami, Florida

Jack increased the volume to hear the rapid-fire cadence of an anchorwoman struggling to make sense of the image on the TV screen.

"You are looking at a live scene at the U.S. naval base in Guantanamo Bay," said the newswoman. "We have no official confirmation, but CNN has obtained unofficial reports that, just after sunrise, there was an explosion on the base. A large and intense fire is still burning, but because both the United States and the Cuban military enforce a buffer zone around the base, we cannot send in our own camera crew for a closer look.

"Joining me now live by telephone is CNN military analyst David Polk, a retired naval officer who once served as base commander at Guantanamo. Mr. Polk, as you watch the television screen along with us, can you tell us anything that might help us better understand what we're viewing?"

"As you can see, Deborah, the base is quite large, covering about forty-five square miles on the far southeastern tip of Cuba, about four hundred air miles from Miami. To give you a little history, the U.S.

has controlled this territory since the Spanish American War, and the very existence of a military base there has been a source of friction in U.S./Cuba relations since Fidel Castro took power. There is no denying that this is Cuban soil. However, for strategic reasons, the U.S. has clung to this very valuable turf, relying on a seventy-year-old treaty that essentially allows the United States to stay as long as it wishes."

"We've heard reports of an explosion. Has anything of this nature ever happened before at Guantanamo?"

"No. Tensions have certainly run high over the years, spiking in the early sixties with the Bay of Pigs and Cuban Missile Crisis, and spiking again in 1994 when sixty-thousand Cuban and Haitian refugees were detained at Guantanamo. But never anything like this."

"What might cause an explosion and fire like this at the base?"

"That would be pure speculation at this juncture. We'll have to wait and see."

"Can you pinpoint the location of the fire for me? What part of the base appears to be affected?"

"It's the main base. What I mean by that is that Guantanamo is a bifurcated base. The airstrip is on the western or leeward side. The main base is to the east, across the two-and-a-half-mile stretch of water that is Guantanamo Bay. You can see part of the bay in the upper left-hand corner of your television screen."

"What part of the main base is burning?"

"It's the southern tip, which is known as Radio Range because of the towering radio antennae that you can see in your picture. Interestingly enough, the fire is concentrated in what appears to be Camp Delta, which is the new high-security detention facility."

"Camp Delta was built to house suspected terrorists, am I right?"

"The official terminology is 'enemy combatant.' Originally, the only detainees there were the alleged members of the al-Qaeda terrorist network. In recent months, however, the United States has broadened the definition of 'enemy combatant.' As a result, Camp Delta now houses drug lords and rebels from South America, suspected war criminals from Chechnya, kidnappers and thugs from Cambodia and a host of others who meet the Defense Department's definition of 'enemy combatant' in the ever-widening war on terrorism."

"This whole issue of detainees—this has become quite an international sore spot for President Howe, has it not?"

"That's an understatement. You have to remember that none of the detainees at this facility has ever been charged with a crime. This all goes back to what I said earlier—the base is on Cuban soil. The Department of Defense has successfully argued in the U.S. federal courts that the base is not 'sovereign' territory and that inmates therefore have no due-process rights under the U.S. Constitution. The White House has taken the position that the military can hold the prisoners indefinitely. But pressure has steadily risen in the international community to force the U.S. either to charge the detainees with specific crimes or release them."

"Some of these detainees are quite dangerous, I'm sure."

"Even the president's toughest antiterrorism experts are beginning to worry about the growing clamor over holding prisoners indefinitely without formal charges. On the other hand, you could probably make a pretty strong case that some of these guys are among the most dangerous men in the world. So Camp Delta is a bit of a steaming political hot potato."

"Which has just burst into flames—literally."

"I think this is on the verge of becoming one of the toughest issues President Howe will face in his second term—What should be done with all these enemy combatants that we've rounded up and put into detention without formal charges?"

"From the looks of things, someone may have come up with a solution."

"I wasn't suggesting that at all, but—"

"Mr. Polk, thank you for joining us. CNN will return with more live coverage of the fire at the U.S. naval base in Guantanamo Bay, Cuba, after these commercial messages."

Jack hit the mute button on the remote. "You still there?" he asked over the phone.

"Yeah," said Theo. "Can you believe he did it?"

"Did what?"

"They said it was a Cessna. Wake up, dude. It's Operation Northwoods."

There was a pounding on the door. It had that certain thud of authority—law enforcement. "Open up. FBI!"

Jack gripped the phone. "Theo, I think this lawyer may need a lawyer."

There was a crash at the front door, and it took Jack only a moment to realize that a SWAT team had breached his house. Jack could hear them coming down the hall, see them burst through the bedroom door. "Down, down, on the floor!" someone shouted, and Jack instinctively obeyed. He had never claimed to be the world's smartest lawyer, but he was sharp enough to realize that when six guys come running into your bedroom in full SWAT regalia before dawn, generally they mean business. He decided to save the soapbox speech on civil liberties for another day, perhaps when his face wasn't buried in the carpet and the automatic rifles weren't aimed at the back of his skull.

"Where's Jack Swyteck?" one of the men barked at him.

"*I'm* Jack Swyteck."

There was silence, and it appeared that the team leader was checking a photograph to confirm Jack's claim. The man said, "Let him up, boys."

Jack rose and sat on the edge of the bed. He was wearing gym shorts and a Miami Dolphins jersey, his version of pajamas. The SWAT team backed away. The team leader pointed his gun at the floor and introduced himself as Agent Matta, FBI.

"Sorry about the entrance," Matta said. "We got a tip that you were in danger."

"A tip? From who?"

"Anonymous."

Jack was somewhat skeptical. He was, after all, a criminal defense lawyer.

"We need to talk to you about your client, Jean Saint Preux. Did he act alone?"

"I don't even know if he's done anything yet."

"Save it for the courtroom," Matta said. "I need to know if there are more planes on the way."

Jack suddenly understood the guns-drawn entrance. "What are you talking about?"

"Your client has been flying in the Windward Passage for some time now, hasn't he?"

"Yeah. He's Haitian. People are dying on the seas trying to flee the island. He's been flying humanitarian missions to spot rafters lost at sea."

"How well do you know him?"

"He's just a client. Met him on a pro bono immigration case I did ten years ago. Look, you probably know more than I do. Are you sure it was him?"

"I think you can confirm that much for us with the air traffic control recordings." He pulled a CD from inside his pocket, then said, "It's been edited down to compress the time frame of the engagement, but it's still highly informative."

Jack was as curious as anyone to know if his client was involved—if he was alive or dead. "Let's hear it," he said.

Matta inserted the CD into the player on Jack's credenza. There were several seconds of dead air. Finally a voice crackled over the speakers: *"This is approach control, U.S. Naval Air Station, Guantanamo Bay, Cuba. Unidentified aircraft heading one-eight-five at one-five knots, identify yourself."*

Another stretch of silence followed. The control tower repeated its transmission. Finally, a man replied, his voice barely audible, but his Creole accent was still detectable. *"Copy that."*

Jack said, "That's Jean."

The recorded voice of the controller continued, *"You are entering unauthorized airspace. Please identify."*

No response.

"Fighter planes have been dispatched. Please identify."

Jack moved closer to hear. It sounded as though his client was having trouble breathing.

The controller's voice took on a certain urgency. *"Unidentified aircraft, your transponder is emitting code seven-seven-hundred. Do you have an emergency?"*

Again there was silence, and then a new voice emerged. *"Yeah, Guantanamo, this is Mustang."*

Matta leaned across the desk and paused the CD just long enough to explain, "That's the navy fighter pilot."

The recording continued: *"We have a visual. White Cessna one-eighty-two with blue stripes. N-number—November two six Golf Mike. One pilot aboard. No passengers."*

The controller said, *"November two six Golf Mike, please confirm the code seven-seven-hundred. Are you in distress?"*

"Affirmative."

"Identify yourself."

"Jean Saint Preux."

"What is the nature of your distress?"

"I…I think I'm having a heart attack."

The controller said, *"Mustang, do you still have a visual?"*

"Affirmative. The pilot appears to be slumped over the yoke. He's flying on automatic."

"November two six Golf Mike, you have entered unauthorized airspace. Do you read?"

He did not reply.

"This is Mustang. MiGs on the way. Got a pair of them approaching at two-hundred-forty degrees, west-northwest."

Matta looked at Jack and said, "Those are the Cuban jets. They don't take kindly to private craft in Cuban airspace."

The recorded voice of the controller said, *"November two six Golf Mike, do you request permission to land?"*

"Yes," he said, his voice straining. *"Can't go back."*

The next voice was in Spanish, and the words gave Jack chills. *"Attention. You have breached the sovereign airspace of the Republic of Cuba. This will be your only warning. Reverse course immediately, or you will be fired upon as hostile aircraft."*

The controller said, *"November two six Golf Mike, you*

must alter course to two-twenty, south-southwest. Exit Cuban airspace and enter the U.S. corridor. Do you read?"

Matta paused the recording and said, "There's a narrow corridor that U.S. planes can use to come and go from the base. He's trying to get Saint Preux into the safety zone."

The recording continued, *"November two six Golf Mike, do you read?"*

Before Saint Preux could reply, the Cubans issued another warning in Spanish. *"Reverse course immediately, or you will be fired upon as hostile aircraft."*

"November two six Golf Mike, do you read?"

"He's hand signaling," said Mustang. *"I think he's unable to talk."*

The controller said, *"November two six Golf Mike, steer two-twenty, south-southwest. Align yourself with the lead navy F-16 and you will be escorted to landing. Permission to land at Guantanamo Bay has been granted."*

Jack's gaze drifted off toward the window, the drama in the Cuban skies playing out in his mind.

"Mustang, what's your status?" asked the controller.

"We're in the corridor. Target is back on automatic pilot."

"Do you have the craft in sight?"

"Yes. I'm on his wing now. That maneuver away from the MiGs really took it out of him. Pilot looks to be barely conscious. Dangerous situation here."

"November two six Golf Mike, please hand signal our pilot if you are conscious and able to hear this transmission."

After a long stretch of silence, Mustang said, *"Got it. He just signaled."*

The controller said, *"Permission has been granted to land on runway one. You are surrounded by four F-16s, and they are authorized to fire immediately upon any deviation from the proper course. Do you read?"*

There was silence, then a response from Mustang. *"He's got it."*

"Roger. Mustang, lead the way."

After thirty seconds of dead air, the controller returned. *"Mustang, what's your unaided visibility?"*

"Our friend should be seeing fine. Approaching the south end of the main base."

Matta used another stretch of silence to explain, saying, "The main base is to the east of the landing strip. They have to pass over the main base, and then fly across the bay in order to land."

"Whoa!" shouted Mustang. *"Target is in a nosedive!"*

"November two six Golf Mike, pull up!"

"Still in a nosedive," shouted Mustang, his voice racing.

"Pull up immediately!"

"No change," said Mustang.

"November two six Golf Mike, final warning. Regain control of your craft or you will be fired upon."

"He's headed straight for Camp Delta."

"Fire at will!"

A shrill, screeching noise came over the speakers. Then silence.

Matta hit the STOP button. "That's it," he said in a matter-of-fact tone. Slowly, he walked around the desk and returned to his seat in the wing chair.

Jack was stone silent. He wasn't particularly close to Saint Preux, but it was still unnerving to think of what had just happened to him.

Matta said, "Did Mr. Saint Preux have heart trouble?"

"Not to my knowledge. But he had pancreatic cancer. The doctors gave him only a few months to live."

"Did he ever talk of suicide?"

"Not to me."

"Was he depressed, angry?"

"Who wouldn't be? The guy was only sixty-three years old. But that doesn't mean he deliberately crashed his plane into Camp Delta."

Matta said, "Do you know of any reason he might have to hate the U.S. government?"

Jack hesitated.

Matta said, "Look, I understand that you're his lawyer and you have confidentiality issues. But your client's dead, and so are six U.S. Marines, not to mention scores of detainees. We need to understand what happened."

"All I can tell you is that he wasn't happy about the way the government treats refugees from Haiti. Thinks we have a double standard for people of color. I'm not trying to slap a Jesse Jackson rhyme on you, but as the saying goes—If you're black, you go back."

"Was he unhappy enough to blow up a naval base?"

"I don't know."

"I think you do know," said Matta, his voice taking on an edge. He was suddenly invading Jack's space, getting right in his face. "I believe that the heart attack was a ruse. I think this was a planned and deliberate suicide attack by a man who had less than six months to live. And I suspect the logistical support and financial backing for an organization that only you can help us identify."

"That's ridiculous," said Jack.

"Are you going to sit there and pretend that he didn't mention any plans to you, any organizations?"

Jack was about to tell him that he couldn't answer that even if he'd wanted to, that conversations with his client—even a dead client—were privileged and confidential. But one thing did come to mind, and it wasn't privileged. Jean had said it in front of Jack, in front of Theo and in front of about a half-dozen other drunks at Theo's tavern. Jack could share it freely.

"He mentioned something called Operation Northwoods."

Matta went ash-white. He turned, walked into the next room, and was immediately talking on his encrypted cell phone.

7:40 p.m., Two Weeks Later

Sparky's Tavern was on U.S. 1 south of Homestead, one of the last watering holes before a landscape that still bore the scars of a direct hit from Hurricane Andrew in 1992 gave way to the splendor of the Florida Keys. It was a converted old gas station with floors so stained from tipped drinks that not even the Environmental Protection Agency could have determined if more flammable liquids had spilled before or after the conversion. The grease pit was gone but the garage doors were still in place. There was a long, wooden bar, a TV permanently tuned to ESPN, and a never-ending stack of quarters on the pool table. Beer was served in cans, and the empties were crushed in true Sparky's style at the old tire vise that still sat on the workbench. It was the kind of dive that Jack would have visited if it were in his own neighborhood, but he made the forty-minute trip for one reason only: the bartender was Theo Knight.

"Another one, buddy?"

He was serving Jack shots of tequila. "No thanks," said Jack.

"Come on. Try just one *without* training wheels,"

he said as he cleared the lemons and saltshaker from the bar top.

Jack's thoughts were elsewhere. "I met with a former military guy today," said Jack. "Says he knows all about Operation Northwoods."

"Does he also know all about the tooth fairy and the Easter Bunny?"

"He worked in the Pentagon under the Kennedy administration."

Theo poured another shot, but Jack didn't touch it. "Talk to me," said Theo.

"He showed me a memo that was top secret for years. It was declassified a few years ago, but somehow it never got much press, even though it was titled 'Justification for U.S. Military Intervention in Cuba.' The Joint Chiefs of Staff submitted it to the Defense Department a few months after the Bay of Pigs invasion. No one denies that the memo existed, though former Secretary of Defense McNamara has gone on record saying he never saw it. Anyway, it outlines a plan called Operation Northwoods."

"So there really was an Operation Northwoods? Pope Paul wasn't just high on painkillers?"

"His name was Saint Preux, moron. And it was just a memo, not an actual operation. The idea was for the U.S. military to stage terrorist activities at Guantanamo and blame them on Cuba, which would draw the United States into war with Cuba."

"Get out."

"Seriously. The first wave was to have friendly Cubans dressed in Cuban military uniforms start riots at the base, blow up ammunition at the base, start fires, burn aircraft, sabotage a ship in the harbor and sink a ship near the harbor entrance."

"Sounds like a plot for a bad movie."

"It gets better—or worse, depending on your perspective. They talked about having a 'Remember the *Maine*' incident where the U.S. would blow up one of its own ships in Guantanamo Bay and blame Cuba."

"But how could they do that without hurting their own men?"

"They couldn't. And this was actually in the memo—I couldn't believe what I was reading. It said, 'Casualty lists in U.S. newspapers would cause a healthy wave of national indignation.'"

Theo winced, but it might have been the tequila. "They didn't actually do any of this shit, did they?"

"Nah. Somebody in the Pentagon came to their senses. But still, it makes you wonder if Jean was trying to tell us something about a twenty-first-century Operation Northwoods."

Theo nodded, seeming to follow his logic. "A plane crash on the base, a few U.S. casualties, and *voilà!* The burning question of what to do with six hundred terrorists is finally resolved. Could never happen, right?"

"Nah. Could never—" Jack stopped himself. President Lincoln Howe was on television. "Turn that up, buddy."

Theo climbed atop a bar stool and adjusted the volume. On screen, President Lincoln Howe was delivering a prime-time message with his broad shoulders squared to the microphone, his forceful tone conveying the full weight of his office. The world could only admire the presidential resolve of a former general in the United States Army.

"The FBI and Justice Department have worked tirelessly and swiftly on this investigation," said the president. "It is our very firm conclusion that Mr. Saint

Preux acted alone. He filled a civilian aircraft with highly explosive materials to create the equivalent of a flying eight-hundred-pound napalm bomb. Through means of deception, which included a fake medical emergency, he gained permission to land at the U.S. Naval Air Station in Guantanamo. In accordance with his premeditated scheme, the plane exploded and created a rain of fire over Camp Delta, killing six U.S. Marines and over six hundred detainees, and injuring many others.

"Naturally, our prayers and sympathies go out to the victims and their families. But I wish to emphasize that the speed with which we addressed this incident demonstrates that we will pursue terrorists and terrorist groups in whatever criminal guise they take, irrespective of whether they target American soldiers, innocent civilians or even foreign enemy combatants whom the United States has lawfully detained and taken into custody."

The president paused, as if giving his sound bite time to gel, then narrowed his eyes for a final comment. "Make no mistake about it. Although most of the victims were detained enemy combatants, this attack at Guantanamo was an attack on democracy and the United States of America. With Mr. Saint Preux's death, however, justice has been done. Good night, thank you, and may God bless America."

Jack remained glued to the television as the president stepped away from the podium. Reporters sprang from their seats and started firing questions, but the president simply waved and turned away. The network commentators jumped in with their recap and analysis, but Jack's mind was awhirl with his own thoughts. Was Operation Northwoods for real? Did

Jack's client do this as a favor to the U.S. government? Or did he do it to embarrass the Howe administration, as a way to make the world think that the president had put him up to this? None of those questions had been answered.

Or maybe they had.

Theo switched off the television. "Guess that settles it," he said, laying on a little more than his usual sarcasm. "Just another pissed-off Haitian crashing his airplane into a naval base to protest U.S. immigration policy."

Jack lifted his shot glass of tequila. "I'm ready."

"For what?"

He glanced at the lemon and saltshaker, then stiffened his resolve. "I'm losing the training wheels."

J. A. KONRATH

J. A. Konrath is relatively new to the thriller scene. The Lieutenant Jacqueline "Jack" Daniels series features a forty-something Chicago cop who chases serial killers. Konrath's debut, *Whiskey Sour*, was a unique combination of creepy chills and laugh-out-loud moments. *Bloody Mary* and *Rusty Nail* used the same giggle-then-cringe formula—likable heroes in scary situations. Konrath believes that a lot of the fun in writing a thriller series comes from the supporting characters. People are defined by the company they keep. Jack has a handful of sidekicks who both help and hinder her murder investigations.

Phineas Troutt is one of the helpful ones.

Introduced in *Whiskey Sour*, Phin operates outside the law as a problem solver—someone who takes illegal jobs for big paydays. Jack is never quite sure what Phin does to earn a living. Konrath himself didn't know, but thought it would be fun to find out.

Forsaking the cannibals, necrophiles, snuff filmers and serial killers of his Jack Daniels books, *Epitaph* revolves around a more familiar and accessible evil—street gangs. The result is something grittier, darker and more intimately violent than the series that spawned Phin. No tongue in cheek here. No goofy one-liners. Konrath has always enjoyed exploring where shadows hide when the sun goes down, but this time there's no humorous safety net. What motivates a man to drop out of society and kill for money? Is there a tie between morality and dignity? And most important of all, what is Phin loading into the shells of that modified Mossberg shotgun?

Let the body count begin.

There's an art to getting your ass kicked.

Guys on either side held my arms, stretching me out crucifixion style. The joker who worked me over swung wildly, without planting his feet or putting his body into it. He spent most of his energy swearing and screaming when he should have been focusing on inflicting maximum damage.

Amateur.

Not that I was complaining. What he lacked in professionalism, he made up for in mean.

He moved in and rabbit-punched me in the side. I flexed my abs and tried to shift to take the blow in the center of my stomach, rather than the more vulnerable kidneys.

I exhaled hard when his fist landed. Saw stars.

He stepped away to pop me in the face. Rather than tense up, I relaxed, trying to absorb the contact by letting my neck snap back.

It still hurt like hell.

I tasted blood, wasn't sure if it came from my nose or my mouth. Probably both. My left eye had already swollen shut.

"Hijo calvo de una perra!"

You bald son of a bitch. Real original. His breath was ragged now, shoulders slumping, face glowing with sweat.

Gangbangers these days aren't in very good shape. I blame TV and junk food.

One final punch—a halfhearted smack to my broken nose—and then I was released.

I collapsed face-first in a puddle that smelled like urine. The three Latin Kings each took the time to spit on me. Then they strolled out of the alley, laughing and giving each other high fives.

When they got a good distance away, I crawled over to a Dumpster and pulled myself to my feet. The alley was dark, quiet. I felt something scurry over my foot.

Rats, licking up my dripping blood.

Nice neighborhood.

I hurt a lot, but pain and I were old acquaintances. I took a deep breath, let it out slow, did some poking and prodding. Nothing seemed seriously damaged.

I'd been lucky.

I spat. The bloody saliva clung to my swollen lower lip and dribbled onto my T-shirt. I tried a few steps forward, managed to keep my balance, and continued to walk out of the alley, onto the sidewalk, and to the corner bus stop.

I sat.

The Kings took my wallet, which had no ID or credit cards, but did have a few hundred in cash. I kept an emergency fiver in my shoe. The bus arrived, and the portly driver raised an eyebrow at my appearance.

"Do you need a doctor, buddy?"

"I've got plenty of doctors."

He shrugged and took my money.

On the ride back, my fellow passengers made heroic efforts to avoid looking at me. I leaned forward, so the blood pooled between my feet rather than stained my clothing any further. These were my good jeans.

When my stop came up, I gave everyone a cheery wave goodbye and stumbled out of the bus.

The corner of State and Cermak was all lit up, twinkling in both English and Chinese. Unlike NYC and L.A., each of which had sprawling Chinatowns, Chicago has more of a *Chinablock*. Blink while you're driving west on Twenty-second and you'll miss it.

Though Caucasian, I found a kind of peace in Chinatown that I didn't find among the Anglos. Since my diagnosis, I've pretty much disowned society. Living here was like living in a foreign country—or a least a square block of a foreign country.

I kept a room at the Lucky Lucky Hotel, tucked between a crumbling apartment building and a Chinese butcher shop, on State and Twenty-fifth. The hotel did most of its business at an hourly rate, though I couldn't think of a more repulsive place to take a woman, even if you were renting her as well as the room. The halls stank like mildew and worse, the plaster snowed on you when you climbed the stairs, obscene graffiti lined the halls and the whole building leaned slightly to the right.

I got a decent rent: free—as long as I kept out the drug dealers. Which I did, except for the ones who dealt to me.

I nodded at the proprietor, Kenny-Jen-Bang-Ko, and asked for my key. Kenny was three times my age, clean-shaven save for several black moles on his cheeks that sprouted long, white hairs. He tugged at these hairs while contemplating me.

"How is other guy?" Kenny asked.

"Drinking a forty of malt liquor that he bought with my money."

He nodded, as if that was the answer he'd been expecting. "You want pizza?"

Kenny gestured to a box on the counter. The slices were so old and shrunken they looked like Doritos.

"I thought the Chinese hated fast food."

"Pizza not fast. Took thirty minutes. Anchovy and red pepper."

I declined.

My room was one squeaky stair flight up. I unlocked the door and lumbered over to the bathroom, looking into the cracked mirror above the sink.

Ouch.

My left eye had completely closed, and the surrounding tissue bulged out like a peach. Purple bruising competed with angry red swelling along my cheeks and forehead. My nose was a glob of strawberry jelly, and blood had crusted black along my lips and down my neck.

It looked like Jackson Pollock had kicked my ass.

I stripped off the T-shirt, peeled off my shoes and jeans, and turned the shower up to *scald*.

It hurt but got most of the crap off.

After the shower I popped five Tylenol, chased them with a shot of tequila and spent ten minutes in front of the mirror, tears streaming down my face, forcing my nose back into place.

I had some coke, but wouldn't be able to sniff anything with my sniffer all clotted up, and I was too exhausted to shoot any. I made do with the tequila, thinking that tomorrow I'd have that codeine prescription refilled.

Since the pain wouldn't let me sleep, I decided to do a little work.

Using a dirty fork, I pried up the floorboards near the radiator and took out a plastic bag full of what appeared to be little gray stones. The granules were the size and consistency of aquarium gravel.

I placed the bag on the floor, then removed the Lee Load-All, the scale, a container of gunpowder, some wads and a box of empty 12-gauge shells.

Everything went over to my kitchen table. I snapped on a fresh pair of latex gloves, clamped the loader onto my countertop and spent an hour carefully filling ten shells. When I finished, I loaded five of them into my Mossberg 935, the barrel and stock of which had been cut down for easier concealment.

I liked shotguns—you had more leeway when aiming, the cops couldn't trace them like they could trace bullets, and nothing put the fear of God into a guy like the sound of racking a shell into the chamber.

For this job, I didn't have a choice.

By the time I was done, my nose had taken the gold medal in throbbing, with my eye coming close with the silver. I swallowed five more Tylenol and four shots of tequila, then lay down on my cot and fell asleep.

With sleep came the dream.

It happened every night, so vivid I could smell Donna's perfume. We were still together, living in the suburbs. She was smiling at me, running her fingers through my hair.

"Phin, the caterer wants to know if we're going with the split-pea or the wedding-ball soup."

"Explain the wedding-ball soup to me again."

"It's a chicken stock with tiny veal meatballs in it."

"That sounds good to you?"

"It's very good. I've had it before."

"Then let's go with that."

She kissed me; playful, loving.

I woke up drenched in sweat.

If someone had told me that happy memories would one day be a source of incredible pain, I wouldn't have believed it.

Things change.

Sun peeked in through my dirty window, making me squint. I stretched, wincing because my whole body hurt—my whole body except for my left side, where a team of doctors had severed the nerves during an operation called a chordotomy. The surgery had been purely palliative. The area felt dead, even though the cancer still thrived inside my pancreas. And elsewhere, by now.

The chordotomy offered enough pain relief to allow me to function, and tequila, cocaine and codeine made up for the remainder.

I dressed in some baggy sweatpants, my bloody gym shoes (with a new five-dollar bill in the sole) and a clean white T-shirt. I strapped my leather shotgun sling under my armpits and placed the Mossberg in the holster. It hung directly between my shoulder blades, barrel up, and could be freed by reaching my right hand behind me at waist level.

A baggy black trench coat went on over the rig, concealing the shotgun and the leather straps that held it in place.

I pocketed the five extra shells, the bag of gray granules, a Glock 21 with two extra clips of

.45 rounds and a six-inch butterfly knife. Then I hung an iron crowbar on an extra strap sewn into the lining of my coat, and headed out to greet the morning.

Chinatown smelled like a combination of soy sauce and garbage. It was worse in the summer, when stenches seemed to settle in and stick to your clothes. Though not yet seven in the morning, the temperature already hovered in the low nineties. The sun made my face hurt.

I walked up State, past Cermak, and headed east. The Sing Lung Bakery had opened for business an hour earlier. The manager, a squat Mandarin Chinese named Ti, did a double take when I entered.

"Phin! Your face is horrible!" He rushed around the counter to meet me, hands and shirt dusty with flour.

"My mom liked it okay."

Ti's features twisted in concern. "Was it them? The ones who butchered my daughter?"

I gave him a brief nod.

Ti hung his head. "I am sorry to bring this suffering upon you. They are very bad men."

I shrugged, which hurt. "It was my fault. I got careless."

That was an understatement. After combing Chicago for almost a week, I'd discovered the bangers had gone underground. I got one guy to talk, and after a bit of friendly persuasion he gladly offered some vital info; Sunny's killers were due to appear in court on an unrelated charge.

I'd gone to the Daly Center, where the prelim hearing was being held, and watched from the sidelines. After matching their names to faces, I followed them back to their hidey-hole.

My mistake had been to stick around. A white guy in a Hispanic neighborhood tends to stand out. Having just been to court, which required walking through a metal detector, I had no weapons on me.

Stupid. Ti and Sunny deserved someone smarter.

Ti had found me through the grapevine, where I got most of my business. Phineas Troutt, Problem Solver. No job too dirty, no fee too high.

I'd met him in a parking lot across the street, and he laid out the whole sad, sick story of what these animals had done to his little girl.

"Cops do nothing. Sunny's friend too scared to press charges."

Sunny's friend had managed to escape with only ten missing teeth, six stab wounds and a torn rectum. Sunny hadn't been as lucky.

Ti agreed to my price without question. Not too many people haggled with paid killers.

"You finish job today?" Ti asked, reaching into his glass display counter for a pastry.

"Yeah."

"In the way we talk about?"

"In the way we talked about."

Ti bowed and thanked me. Then he stuffed two pastries into a bag and held them out.

"Duck egg moon cake, and red bean ball with sesame. Please take."

I took.

"Tell me when you find them."

"I'll be back later today. Keep an eye on the news. You might see something you'll like."

I left the bakery and headed for the bus. Ti had paid me enough to afford a cab, or even a limo, but cabs and limos kept records. Besides, I preferred to save my money for more important things, like drugs and hookers. I try to live every day as if it's my last.

After all, it very well might be.

The bus arrived, and again everyone took great pains not to stare. The trip was short, only about two miles, taking me to a neighborhood known as Pilsen, on Racine and Eighteenth.

I left my duck egg moon cake and my red bean ball on the bus for some other lucky passenger to enjoy, then stepped out into Little Mexico.

It smelled like a combination of salsa and garbage.

There weren't many people out—too early for shoppers and commuters. The stores had Spanish signs, not bothering with English translations: *zapatos, ropa, restaurante, tiendas de comestibles, bancos, teléfonos de la célula.* I passed the alley where I'd gotten the shit kicked out of me, kept heading north, and located the apartment building where my three amigos were staying. I tried the front door.

They hadn't left it open for me.

Though the gray paint was faded and peeling, the door was heavy aluminum and the lock solid. But the jamb, as I'd remembered from yesterday's visit, was old wood. I removed the crowbar from my jacket lining, gave a discreet look in either direction and pried open the door in less time than it took to open it with a key, the frame splintering and cracking.

The Kings occupied the basement apartment to the left of the entrance, facing the street. Last night I'd counted seven—five men and two women—including my three targets. Of course, there may be other people inside that I'd missed.

This was going to be interesting.

Unlike the front door, their apartment door was a joke. They apparently thought being gang members meant they didn't need decent security.

They thought wrong.

I took out my Glock and tried to stop hyperventilating. Breaking into someone's place is scary as hell. It always is.

One hard kick and the door burst inward.

A guy on the couch, sleeping in front of the TV. Not one of my marks. He woke up and stared at me. It took a millisecond to register the gang tattoo, a five-pointed crown, on the back of his hand.

I shot him in his forehead.

If the busted door didn't wake everyone up, the .45 did, sounding like thunder in the small room.

Movement to my right. A woman in the kitchen, in panties and a Dago-T, too much makeup and baby fat.

"*Te vayas!*" I hissed at her.

She took the message and ran out the door.

A man stumbled into the hall, tripping and falling to the thin carpet. One of mine, the guy who'd pinned my right arm while I'd been worked over. He clutched a stiletto. I was on him in two quick steps, putting one in his elbow and one through the back of his knee when he fell.

He screamed falsetto.

I walked down the hall in a crouch, and a bullet zinged over my head and buried itself in the ceiling. I kissed the floor, looked left, and saw the shooter in the bathroom; the guy who had held my other arm and laughed every time I got smacked.

I stuck the Glock in my jeans and reached behind me, unslinging the Mossberg.

He fired again, missed, and I aimed the shotgun and peppered his face.

Unlike lead shot, the gray granules didn't have deep penetrating power. Instead of blowing his head off, they peeled off his lips, cheeks and eyes.

He ate linoleum, blind and choking on blood.

Movement behind me. I fell sideways and rolled onto my back. A kid, about thirteen, stood in the hall a few feet away. He wore Latin Kings colors; black to represent death, gold to represent life.

His hand ended in a pistol.

I racked the shotgun, aimed low.

If the kid was old enough to be sexually active, he wasn't anymore.

He dropped to his knees, still holding the gun.

I was on him in two steps, driving a knee into his nose. He went down and out.

Three more guys burst out of the bedroom.

Apparently I'd counted wrong.

Two were young, muscular, brandishing knives. The third was the guy who'd worked me over the night before. The one who'd called me a bald son of a bitch.

They were on me before I could rack the shotgun again.

The first one slashed at me with his pig-sticker, and I parried with the barrel of the Mossberg. He jabbed again, slicing me across the knuckles of my right hand.

I threw the shotgun at his face and went for my Glock.

He was fast.

I was faster.

Bang bang and he was a paycheck for the coroner. I spun left, aimed at the second guy. He was already in midjump, launching himself at me with a battle cry and switchblades in both hands.

One gun beats two knives.

He took three in the chest and two in the neck before he dropped.

The last guy, the guy who'd broken my nose, grabbed my shotgun and dived behind the couch.

Chck chck. He ejected the shell and racked another into the chamber. I pulled the Glock's magazine and slammed a fresh one home.

"Hijo calvo de una perra!"

Again with the *bald son of a bitch* taunt. I worked through my hurt feelings and crawled to an end table, tipping it over and getting behind it.

The shotgun boomed. Had it been loaded with shot, it would have torn through the cheap particleboard and turned me into ground beef. Or ground *hijo calvo de una perra*. But at that distance, the granules didn't do much more than make a loud noise.

The banger apparently didn't learn from experience, because he tried twice more with similar results, and then the shotgun was empty.

I stood up from behind the table, my heart a lump in my throat and my hands shaking with adrenaline.

The King turned and ran.

His back was an easy target.

I took a quick look around, making sure everyone was down or out, and then went to retrieve my shotgun. I loaded five more shells and approached the downed leader, who was sucking carpet and whimpering. The wounds in his back were ugly, but he still made a feeble effort to crawl away.

I bent down, turned him over and shoved the barrel of the Mossberg between his bloody lips.

"You remember Sunny Lung," I said, and fired.

It wasn't pretty. It also wasn't fatal. The granules blew out his cheeks and tore into his throat, but somehow the guy managed to keep breathing.

I gave him one more, jamming the gun farther down the wreck of his face.

That did the trick.

The second perp, the one I'd blinded, had passed out on the bathroom floor. His face didn't look like a face anymore, and blood bubbles were coming out of the hole where his mouth would have been.

"Sunny Lung sends her regards," I said.

This time I pushed the gun in deep, and the first shot did the trick, blowing through his throat.

The last guy, the one who made like Pavarotti when I took out his knee, left a blood smear from the hall into the kitchen. He cowered in the corner, a dishrag pressed to his leg.

"Don't kill me, man! Don't kill me!"

"I bet Sunny Lung said the same thing."

The Mossberg thundered twice; once to the chest, and once to the head.

It wasn't enough. What was left alive gasped for air.

I removed the bag of granules from my pocket, took out a handful and shoved them down his throat until he stopped breathing.

Then I went to the bathroom and threw up in the sink.

Sirens wailed in the distance. Time to go. I washed my hands, and then rinsed off the barrel of the Mossberg, holstering it in my rig.

In the hallway, the kid I emasculated was clutching himself between the legs, sobbing.

"There's always the priesthood," I told him, and got out of there.

My nose was still clogged, but I managed to get enough coke up there to damper the pain. Before closing time I stopped by the bakery, and Ti greeted me with a somber nod.

"Saw the news. They said it was a massacre."

"Wasn't pretty."

"You did as we said?"

"I did, Ti. Your daughter got her revenge. She's the one that killed them. All three."

I fished out the bag of granules and handed it to her father. Sunny's cremated remains.

"*Xie xie*," Ti said, thanking me in Mandarin. He held out an envelope filled with cash.

He looked uncomfortable, and I had drugs to buy, so I took the money and left without another word.

An hour later I'd filled my codeine prescription, picked up two bottles of tequila and a skinny hooker with track marks on her arms, and had a party back at my place. I popped and drank and screwed and snorted, trying to blot out the memory of the last two days. And of the last six months.

That's when I'd been diagnosed. A week before my wedding day. My gift to my bride-to-be was running away so she wouldn't have to watch me die of cancer.

Those Latin Kings this morning, they got off easy. They didn't see it coming.

Seeing it coming is so much worse.

HEATHER GRAHAM

Heather Graham has spent her life in the Miami
area and frequently uses her home arena as the setting in her novels. She sometimes considers that
it's quite a bit like living in a theater of the absurd.
Where else can you mix such a cosmopolitan, big-
city venue with traces of a distant past? The place
has it all. Snowbirds blending with the Old South.
The Everglades, where proud tribes of Native
Americans still live. And the sultry "river of
grass," which affords deadly opportunities for the
drug trade and convenient hiding spots for bodies
that may never surface again.

Graham loves her hometown, the water, boat-
ing, and one of her main passions, scuba diving.
She says that loving Miami is like loving a child.
You have to accept it for the good and bad. Graham is known for creating locations that live and
breathe—becoming as much a character in her
books as the people who propel them. A multi-
award-winning author, continually reaching *New*

York Times and USA TODAY lists, she's glad to work in several venues, including vampire, historical, ghost and suspense. Whatever time or place she's dealing in, Graham loves to keep her readers on edge. With *The Face in the Window* she takes characters from her thriller, *The Island*, and sets them in the midst of an unexpected storm with unexpected consequences.

THE FACE IN THE WINDOW

Lightning flashed.

Thunder cracked.

It might have been the end of the world.

And there, cast eerily in the window, pressed against it, was a face. The eyes were red; they seemed to glow, like demon eyes. There was a split second when it seemed the storm had cast up the very devil to come for her.

Startled, Beth Henson let out a scream, backing away from the image, almost tripping over the coffee table behind her. The brilliant illumination created by the lightning faded to black, and along with it, the image of the face.

Beyond the window, darkness reigned again.

A lantern burned on the table, a muted glow against the shadowed darkness of night. The storm had long since blown out the electricity as it should have removed other inhabitants from the area. The wind railed with the sharpness of a banshee's shriek, even though the hurricane had wound down to tropical-storm strength before descending upon the lower Florida Keys.

Instinctive terror reigned in Beth's heart for several long seconds, then compassion overrode it. Someone was out there, drenched and frightened in the storm. She had gone to the window to see if she could find any sign of Keith. He had left her when their last phone communication with the sheriff had warned them that Mrs. Peterson—one of the few full-time residents of the tiny key—had failed to evacuate. She wouldn't leave for a shelter, not when the shelters wouldn't allow her to bring Cocoa, her tiny Yorkie. Okay, so Cocoa could be a pain, but she and Keith could understand the elderly woman's love for her pup and companion, and Beth had convinced Keith they could listen to a bit of barking.

The appearance of the face in the window was followed by a banging on the door. Beth jumped again, startled. For a moment, she froze. *What if it was a serial killer?* Normally, she would never just open a door to anyone.

But the pounding continued, along with a cry for help. She sprang into action, chiding herself. Someone was out there who needed shelter from the storm. Some idiot tourist without the sense to evacuate when told to. And if that someone *died* because she was too frightened to give aid in an emergency…

And how ridiculous. Sure, the world had proven to be a rough place, with heinous and conniving criminals. But to assume a serial killer was running around in the midst of what might have been a killer storm was just ludicrous.

She hurried forward, hand firmly on the door as she

opened it against the power of the wind. Again, compassion surged through her as the soaked and bedraggled man came staggering in, desperately gasping for breath. He was a thin man with dark, wet hair that clung to his face and the back of his neck. When he looked at Beth, his eyes were wide and terrified. He offered her a faltering smile. "God bless you! You really must be an angel!" he cried.

Beth drew the quilted throw from the sofa and wrapped it around the man's shoulders, demanding, "What were you doing out there? How could you *not* have heard the evacuation orders issued for all tourists?"

He looked at her sheepishly. "Please, don't throw me back out," he told her. "I admit, I was on a bender in Key West." He staggered to his feet. "When I realized we were told to go, I started out, but my car was literally blown off the road. Then I saw light. Faint light—your place. God must look after fools. I mean…if you don't throw me out." He was tall and wiry, perhaps about thirty. She realized, when not totally bedraggled, he was surely a striking young fellow, with his brilliant blue eyes and dark hair.

"I'm not going to throw you out," she told him.

He offered her a hand suddenly. "I'm Mark Egan. A musician. Maybe you've heard of my group? We're called Ultra C. Our first CD just hit the stores, and we were playing the bars down in Key West. You haven't heard of me—or us?" he said, disappointed.

"No, I'm afraid I haven't."

"That's okay, I guess most of the world hasn't," he said.

"Maybe my husband will have heard of you. He's in Key West often and he really loves to listen to local groups."

He offered her his engaging grin once again. "It

doesn't matter—you're still wonderful. You're an angel—wow, gorgeous, too."

"Thanks. I can give you something dry to put on. My husband is somewhat larger than you are, but I'm sure you can make do."

"Your husband? Is he here?"

She felt a moment's unease. "Yes, of course. He's just…battening down a few things. He's around, close," she said.

"I hope he doesn't stay out too long. It's brutal. Hey, you guys don't keep a car here?" he asked.

An innocent question? she wondered.

"Yes, we have a car," she said, determined not to explain further. "I'm Beth Henson," she said, and offered him a hand. They shook. His grip was more powerful than what she had expected. "Hang on, I'll get you those clothes," she said.

She picked up one of the flashlights and headed for the bedroom. She couldn't help looking over her shoulder, afraid that he had followed her. He hadn't. She went to the closet and decided on an old pair of Keith's jeans and a T-shirt. Best she could do. She brought them back out and handed them to the dripping man. "Bathroom is the first door on the left, and here's a flashlight."

"Thanks. Truly, you are an angel!" he said, and walked down the hall.

Keith's friends liked to make fun of him for the Hummer. Hell, Beth liked to rib him about it, shaking her head with bemused tolerance as she did so. It was a gas guzzler. Not at all eco-friendly. It was a testosterone thing, a macho thing he felt he had to have. He mused he could now knock it all back in their faces—

the Hummer was heavy enough to make it through the wind, tough enough to crawl through the flooding.

So there, guys. Testosterone? Maybe. But Beth had been the one who had been worried sick about Mrs. Peterson. She had been worried sick again when he had left to retrieve Mrs. Peterson and the dog. She'd wanted to come; he'd convinced her that if she was home, he wouldn't be worried about her in the storm as well.

He fiddled with the knob on the radio again, trying to get something to come in. At last, he did. He expected the news stations in the south of the state to be carrying nothing but storm coverage—even if the storm had lost momentum.

"…serial killer on the loose. Authorities suspect that he headed south just before evacuation notices went into effect…" Static, damn! Then, "Parker managed to disappear, 'as if into thin air,' according to Lieutenant Abner Gretsky, prison guard. Downed poles and electrical failures have made pursuit and apprehension difficult. John Parker was found guilty in the slaying of Patricia Reeves of Miramar last year. He is suspected of the murders of at least seven other women in the southeastern states. He is a man of approximately—"

Keith couldn't believe it when another earful of static slammed him instead of statistics on the man. Headed south?

Not this far south. Only a suicidal maniac would have attempted to drive down into the dark and treacherous keys when a storm of any magnitude was in gear. Still, it felt as if icy fingers slid down his throat to his heart.

Beth was alone at the house.

He was tempted to turn back instantly. But Mrs. Peterson's trailer was just ahead now. All he had to do was grab the old woman, hop back in the Hummer and turn around.

The first thing he noted was that her old Plymouth wasn't in the drive.

He hesitated, then reached in the glove compartment for the .38 Smith & Wesson he was licensed to carry. He exited the car, swearing against the savage pelting of the rain.

"Mrs. Peterson!" he roared, approaching the trailer. Damn, the woman was lucky the thing hadn't blown over yet. He could hear the dog barking. Yappy little creature, but hell, it was everything in the world to the elderly widow.

"Mrs. Peterson!" He pounded on the door. There was no response. He hesitated, then tried the knob. The door was open.

He walked in. Mrs. Peterson's purse was on the coffee table. Cocoa could be heard but not seen. "Mrs. Peterson?"

The trailer was small. There was nowhere to hide in the living room or kitchen. He tried her sewing room, and then, not sure why, he hesitated at the door to her bedroom. He slipped the Smith & Wesson from his waistband, took a stance and threw open the door.

Nothing. No one. He breathed a sigh of relief, then spun around at a flurry of sound. Cocoa came flying out from beneath the bed.

The small dog managed to jump into his arms, terrified. As Keith clutched the animal, he heard a noise from the front, and headed back out.

A drenched man in what was surely supposed to be a waterproof jacket stood just inside the doorway. "Aunt Dot?" he called.

The fellow was about thirty years old. Dark hair was

plastered to his head. He stood about six feet even. He saw Keith standing with the gun and cried out, stunned and frightened.

"Who are you?" Keith demanded.

"Joe. I'm Joe Peterson. Dot Peterson's nephew," he explained.

"How did you get here?"

"Walked." The fellow swallowed. "My car broke down. Um…where's my aunt?" he inquired.

"You tell me," Keith demanded warily.

"I…I don't know. I was on my way down here…the car gave out. Man, I went through some deep flooding…walked the rest of the way here. Um, who are you and why are you aiming a gun at me?" There was definite fear in his voice. "Wait, no, never mind. I don't want to know your name. Hey, if you're taking anything, go ahead. I'll just walk back out into the storm. I'll look for my aunt."

"We'll look for her together," Keith said.

He indicated that Joe should walk back out. The fellow hesitated uneasily and then voiced an anxious question. "Aunt Dottie…she's really not here?"

Keith shook his head. "Move."

Joe moved toward the door. "Back out into the storm?" he demanded.

Keith nodded grimly. Outside, he put the dog in the car, stuck the gun in his waistband and opened the driver's side. "Get in," he shouted to Joe Peterson.

"Maybe I should wait here," Peterson shouted back.

"Maybe we should look for your aunt!"

They both got into the car. Cocoa scampered to the back seat, whimpering. Keith eased the Hummer out of the drive. "Search the sides of the road, see if she drove off somehow!" Keith commanded.

"Search the side of the road?" Peterson repeated. He looked at Keith so abruptly that water droplets flew from his face and hood. "I can't see a damn road! It's all gray."

"Look for a darker gray blob in the middle of the gray then," Keith said.

The windshield wipers were working hard, doing little.

But then he saw it. Something just barely visible. Peering forward more closely, he saw the Plymouth. It had gone off the road heading south.

Keith stared at Peterson, drew out the gun and warned the man, "Sit still."

"Right, yeah, right!" Peterson said nervously, staring at the gun.

Keith stepped from the car. He sloshed through the flooded road to the mucky embankment. He looked in the front and saw nothing. *Why would the old lady, who always held tight to her handbag, have left the purse on the table when she was taking off in her own car?*

Fighting against the wind, he opened the front doors and the back. No sign of a struggle, of a person, of…anything.

Then he noted the trunk. It was ajar. He lifted the lid.

And found Mrs. Peterson.

"So…you live out here, year-round?"

"No. This is just a vacation home."

"Lonely place," he said.

Beth shrugged. "We live in Coconut Grove, but actually spend a lot of time down here. My husband is a diver."

"A professional diver?"

Beth could have explained that Keith's work went

much further than simple diving, that his contracts often had to do with the government or law enforcement, but she didn't want to explain—she wasn't sure why. Her uninvited guest had changed his clothing. He was warm and dry. She had given him a brandy, and he had been nothing but polite and entirely circumspect. The unease of having let someone into her house hadn't abated, although she didn't know why. This guy seemed to be as benign as a hibiscus bush.

"Um, yes. He's a professional diver," she agreed.

"Great," he said, grinning. He pointed a finger at her. "Didn't you get that original evacuation notice?"

"We got it, but this place was built in the mid-1800s. It's weathered many a storm. The evacuation wasn't mandatory for residents—only visitors." She was pleased to hear a sudden burst of static and she leaped to her feet. "The radio! I don't know why, my batteries are new, but I wasn't getting anything on it. And the cell phones right now are a total joke." She offered him a rueful smile and went running through the hall for the kitchen, at the back of the house.

" …be on the lookout…extremely dangerous…"

She nearly skidded to a stop as she heard the words come from the radio on the dining table.

"…serial killer…"

Like a stick figure, she moved over to the table, staring at the radio. It had gone to static again. She picked it up and shook it, feeling dizzy, ill.

"…suspected to be running south, into the keys…"

"Turn it off!"

Beth looked up. Her guest had followed her from the living room to the kitchen. He stood in the doorway, hands tightly gripping the wood frame as he stared at her. His eyes were wild, red-rimmed…

Like they had appeared when she'd first seen his face in the window.

And there *was* a serial killer loose in the keys....

Mrs. Peterson was trussed up like a fresh kill, wrists and ankles bound, a gag around her mouth. There was no blood, and though her linen pants and shirt were muddied and soaked, there were no signs of violence on her. Keith checked for any sign of life. Her body was so cold.

But she was alive. He felt a faint pulse and snapped open the blade on the Swiss Army knife attached to his key chain. He cut the tight gag from her mouth and then the ropes binding her.

He didn't know if she had broken bones or internal injuries. She could wind up with pneumonia or worse, but this wasn't the kind of situation that left him much choice. He hoisted her fragile body from the trunk and returned to the car, staggering against the wind. He shouted for Joe Peterson to help, but there was no response. He managed to wrench open the rear door of the vehicle on his own.

Cocoa yapped.

Keith swore.

"Dammit! Why didn't you *help?*" he demanded of his passenger, depositing his human burden as best he could.

There was no answer, other than Cocoa's excited woofs.

His passenger had disappeared.

"You're right!" Beth managed to say, forcing her frozen mind into action. "The storm is rough enough. Let's not listen to bad news!"

She turned the radio off.

"Hey, I have a Sterno pot, if you're hungry. I can whip up something."

He shook his head, not moving, staring at her with his red-rimmed eyes. *You've been through worse than this! she reminded herself.*

Worse?

Yes! When she had met Keith, when there had been a skull in the sand, when she had become far too curious…

Toughen up! she chastised herself. You've come through before!

"I think I'll make myself something." *Stay calm. Appear confident.* How did one deal with a serial killer? She tried to remember all the sage things that had been said, recommendations from the psychiatrists who had spent endless hours talking with killers that had been incarcerated. *Talk. Yes. Just keep talking….*

Then she remembered her husband's own words of caution. *If you ever pull out a gun, intend to use it. If you find that you have to shoot, shoot to kill.*

She didn't have a gun.

But then again, there was another question.

What if he wasn't the serial killer? Just because she had found herself alone with this man and heard that there was a killer on the loose, did that mean this man was the one?

Weapon! She needed some kind of weapon.

And would it be the same? *If you ever pull out a gun, intend to use it.* Would that work with, if you ever pull out a frying pan, intend to use it?

She reached into one of the shelves for a can of Sterno and matches, trying to pretend the man who now looked like a psycho and stood in the door frame—still just staring at her—wasn't doing so. She forced herself to hum as she lit the Sterno, and then reached for the frying pan. She held it as she rummaged through the cabinet.

Then she felt him coming nearer…

Her back was to him, he was making no sound. The air around her seemed to be the only hint of his stealth.

She pretended to keep staring at the objects in the cabinet.

She turned.

God!

He was next to her, before her, staring at her, starting to smile…

She swung the frying pan around with all of her might. She caught him on the side of his skull, and the pan seemed to reverberate in her hands. He was still there, still standing, just staring at her.

And then…

He reached out.

She screamed as his hands fell upon her shoulders.

The flooding had grown worse. Still, Keith had no choice but to trust in his knowledge of the area and his instincts. He took the turn-off, then said a silent prayer of relief as the tires found the gravel and rock of his driveway.

The man calling himself Joe Peterson was missing. He had run from the car. Leaving his aunt. There was only one house in the area—his. And Beth was in it.

Something streaked out of the windblown brush and pines that lined the drive.

Someone ahead of him, making his way to the house.

Mark Egan's hands fell upon Beth's shoulders. His eyes met hers.

They held a dazed and questioning look.

He sank slowly to the floor in front of her, trying to catch hold of her to prevent his fall. She stepped back, then turned to flee.

His hand, his grip still incredibly strong, wound around her ankle. She fell, stunned. She still had her frying pan.

Never pull out a frying pan unless you intend to use it!

She raised it to strike again. She didn't need to. The vise of his fingers around her ankle eased. She scurried to the far side of the kitchen floor, staring at him. Was he dead? She inched ever so slightly closer on her knees, frying pan raised to strike.

He didn't move.

She remained still, desperately thinking. She loathed a movie wherein the victim had the attacker down—then just ran, eschewing the idea that a killer might rise again. She lifted the pan to strike again, then gritted her teeth in agony.

What if she was wrong? What if he was just a drugged-out musician?

She looked around the kitchen, desperate to find something. She saw what she needed. A bottom cabinet was just slightly ajar. She saw an extension cord. The good thing about spending her life around the water and boats was that she could tie one sturdy knot.

She scrambled for the extension cord and turned back to tie up her victim. To her astonishment, he had risen.

He was staring at her again.

His eyes were no longer dazed.

They were deadly.

The elements were still raging. The area in front of the house looked like a lake. Keith knew if he left the old lady in the car, he might well be signing her death certificate. He fought the temptation to leave her, to rush out in a panic, thinking only of his wife.

The dog was yapping.

"Cocoa, if you don't shut up...!" Keith warned.

To his astonishment, the Yorkie sat still, staring at him gravely. Keith opened the door, reached into the back, picked up his human burden. Cocoa barked once—just reminding Keith he was there. "Come on, then!" he said, and Cocoa jumped up, landing on the old woman's stomach. Keith hurried toward the house. *Was the man in the trailer really just the old woman's nephew—who had run because of him? Or was he a killer? What if he were in the house, if he had come upon Beth...?*

Keith made his way to the front door.

Run. There was no other option.

The rear door was at the back of the kitchen. She ran; he was right behind her.

When she opened the door, the wind rushed in with a rage. She had been ready. He hadn't. The door slammed shut in his face.

Beth ran out into the storm.

Keith burst into the house, Mrs. Peterson in his arms, Cocoa on top of her.

"Beth?"

To his astonishment, a man staggered out of the kitchen. Wearing his clothes. The fellow stared at him like an escapee from the nearest mental institute.

He was unarmed.

Keith quickly strode to the sofa to deposit Mrs. Peterson. Cocoa stayed on her stomach—growling.

Keith pulled his gun from his waistband.

"Whoa!" the man said.

"Where's my wife?" Keith barked.

"She hit me with a frying pan and ran out!" the man said. "Oh my God, I've been rescued by loonies!" he wailed. "She hits me—now you're going to *shoot* me?"

"Who the hell are you?" Keith barked.

"Mark Egan." He sighed, rubbing his hand. "I'm a musician. What is the matter with you people?"

Holding his gun on the intruder, loath to take his eyes from him, Keith draped a throw, tossed on the back of the rocker, over Mrs. Peterson. "Get in there," he ordered, indicating the guest room. "Now!"

"I'm going!" the man said, lifting a hand. He sidled against the wall, heading for the room. The lantern caused ominous shadows to invade the house.

"You know, you're crazy," he said softly. "You're both crazy!"

"If you've hurt her, I'm going to take you apart piece by piece."

"She attacked me!" the fellow protested.

"Get in there!"

It was then they both heard the scream, long and sharp, rising above the lashing sound of wind and rain.

The shed had seemed to offer the only escape from the violent elements, and she could arm herself there. Their shed held scuba equipment; she could grab a diving knife.

She couldn't get the door to open at first because of the wind. At last, it gave.

An ebony darkness greeted her.

She slipped inside, reaching in her pocket for the matches with which she had lit the Sterno. Her hands were shaking, wet and cold.

Her first attempt was futile. She was wet; she had to stop dripping on the matches.

At last, she got a match lit.

There, in the brief illumination of flame, was a face.

Eyes red-rimmed.

Flesh pasty white.

Hand gripping a diver's knife.

"Don't scream!" she heard.

Too late.

She screamed.

Keith sped out of the house.

He was forced to pause, slightly disoriented. The wind and rain were loud, skewing sounds around him. Then he realized that the scream had to have come from the shed, and he raced in that direction, his gun drawn. He wrenched the door open.

There was darkness within.

"Beth!"

"Put the gun down!" came a throaty, masculine reply.

Beth appeared. Soaked, hair plastered around her beautiful face. There was a man behind her. The fellow who had claimed to be Joe Peterson. He had a knife, and it was against Beth's throat as he emerged.

"Put the gun down!" Peterson raged again.

"Let go of my wife," Keith commanded, forcing himself to be calm.

"You'll kill me. He's not sane at all, did you know that?" the man demanded of Beth.

She stared hard at Keith, eyes wide on his. He frowned. She seemed to be trying to tell him she was all right. Insane, yes, it was all insane, there was a knife against her throat.

"We're all getting soaked out here. Let's go back to

the house. Keith, did you know we had another visitor?" she asked, as if there wasn't honed steel pressing her flesh.

"I've seen him."

"Where's Mrs. Peterson?" she asked.

"He tried to kill her—stuffed her into the trunk of her car," Keith said. "She's on our sofa now. And, uh, your guest is in the house. I imagine."

"I did not try to kill Aunt Dot! You had to be the one!" Peterson protested, the knife twitching in his hand.

"Let's get to the house," Beth said again. "Mr. Peterson, I'll walk ahead of you, and Keith will walk ahead of us."

Keith frowned fiercely at her.

"Yeah, all right, go!" Peterson said.

Keith started forward uneasily. There was one man in the house, and another behind him with a knife to Beth's throat. There was no doubt one of them was a murderer.

He entered the house. The door had been left open. Rain had blown in.

He was followed by Beth.

And the man with the knife.

Mrs. Peterson remained as a lump on the sofa; nothing more than a dark blob in the shadows. Cocoa, however, was no longer with her. He had run to the far side of the room, and wasn't even yapping. He hugged the wall, near the guest-room door, whining pathetically as they entered.

"There was another fellow with us, too, a musician. Plays for a group called Ultra C," Beth said to Peterson. She swallowed carefully before looking at Keith again. "What happened to him? He was, uh, in the house when I left."

"Gone—I hope!"

They heard a sound of distress. It was Joe Peterson. He was staring at the lump on the sofa.

"Mr. Peterson," Keith said softly. "I'm not going to shoot you. But you are going to get that knife away from my wife's throat this instant."

Beth pushed Peterson's arm, stepping away from him. Peterson barely reacted. He stared at the sofa. "God! Is she dead?" he asked.

Cocoa whined. Beth stared at Keith, shaking but relieved. "Cocoa," she said softly. "Well, I could have been wrong, but if this man had attacked Mrs. Peterson, the dog would be barking right now."

"Aunt Dot!" Peterson said numbly.

"She isn't dead—wasn't dead," Keith said. He looked at Beth. "So it's your musician."

"You realized it, too… But—"

"He's out there somewhere. And we'll have that to deal with. But for the moment…we've got to try to keep Mrs. Peterson alive."

"Keith, would you get me some brandy and the ammonia from the kitchen?" Beth asked. "We'll see if we can rouse her. Then we can try to make it to the hospital." She grimaced. "With the Hummer."

Keith walked to the kitchen, then stopped, pausing to pick up the frying pan that lay on the floor. He froze in his tracks as he heard a startled scream rise above the pounding of the rain. He turned to race back to the living room, then came to a dead stop.

Their living room had been pitched into absolute darkness.

Terror struck deep into Beth's heart. She had pulled back the blanket, anxious to be there first, to assure herself that the woman hadn't died.

A hand snaked out for her from beneath the cover, dragging her down with a ferocity that was astounding. Fingers wound around her throat and she was tossed about as if she weighed nothing.

Egan. Mark Egan. Drugged-out musician. No. Psychotic killer.

She saw his deranged grin right before he doused the lantern, holding her in the vise of his one hand like a rag doll.

"What ya gonna do, big man?" a throaty voice called out in the darkness, next to her ear. "Shoot me—you might kill her. Don't come after me, or she's dead."

Beth tensed every muscle. She didn't know if the man had a weapon or not, anything more than the hideous strength of his hands.

She could hear nothing other than the wind and rain. Stars began to burst into the darkness as his grip choked her. There was no sound of voice. No sound of movement.

Not even Cocoa let out a whine.

Then there was a muffled groan. *Not Keith, the sound had not come from Keith! It was Peterson who had groaned. So…where was Keith?*

"That's right," Egan—or whoever he was—said. "You stay right where you are. The missus and I are going to take the car. Your car. We'll go for a little ride. Will she be all right? Who knows? But try to stop me now, and you'll probably kill her yourself."

He began to drag her toward the door. He chuckled softly. "I don't see too badly in the dark. I like the dark."

They were nearly there; she could sense it. He threw open the door. Her heart was thundering so that she didn't hear the *whoosh* of motion at first.

She gasped, the air knocked from her as the *whoosh* became an impetus of muscle and movement. Keith. He flew into them from the porch side, taking both her and Egan by storm and surprise. She twisted. Egan's grip had been loosened by the fall. She bit into his wrist. The man howled, then went rolling away as he and Keith became engaged in a fierce physical battle.

Cocoa began to bark excitedly. She felt the little dog run over her hand and begin to growl. Egan cried out in pain again. She could hear Cocoa wrenching and tearing at something—Egan. In pain or not, Egan was still wrestling on the floor with vehemence. Rain washed in from the open doorway. The faintest light showed through, glittering on something...

The frying pan.

She picked it up, and in the darkness, desperately tried to ascertain her husband's form from that of the killer. She saw a head rise—

She nearly struck.

Keith!

The other head was on the ground. There was a hand around Keith's throat, fingers tightening...

Blindly, she slammed the frying pan down toward the floor. A scream was emitted....

She struck again. And again.

And then arms reached out for her.

"It's all right now. It's all right."

The lantern was lit. Good old Cocoa was in the bedroom, standing guard over Mrs. Peterson who—despite having been dumped unceremoniously on the floor—was still alive and breathing. Her nephew, Joe Peterson, was tending to her.

Keith hadn't moved the form on the floor yet. Beth

didn't know if he was dead or alive, but he wouldn't be blithely getting up this time.

She'd seen his face. Before Keith had covered it with the throw.

"Is it…him? The serial killer?" she said.

"I think so," Keith murmured, slipping an arm tightly around her shoulders.

"But you knew it wasn't Peterson when I did."

He turned to her, a pained and rueful smile just curving his lips. "Because anyone who spends any time in Key West knows that Ultra C is an all-girl band," he said softly.

"I told him you knew music," she said.

They both jumped, hearing the sudden loud blare of a horn. A second later there was a pounding on the door.

Keith, still gripping his gun, strode to it, pulling it open. Andy Fairmont, from the Monroe County Sheriff's Office, was there.

"Jesus!" Andy shouted. "There's a serial killer on the loose! Have you heard?"

Keith looked at Beth. She shrugged, and turned to Andy. "Never pull out a frying pan unless you intend to use it," she said gravely.

"What?"

"You'd better come in, Andy," Keith said, and he set his arm around his wife's shoulders again, pulling her close.

JAMES SIEGEL

James Siegel says the most common question he's asked by readers is, *Where do you get your ideas?* His standard answer is, *I don't know—do you have any?* The real answer, of course, is, *Everywhere*. Siegel tends to write about ordinary people caught up in extraordinary events. Being a self-described "ordinary person," Siegel doesn't find it hard to place himself in the protagonist's shoes. Riding the Long Island railroad for instance—where attractive women would sometimes occupy the seat beside him—sent Siegel into reveries of *what if?* That ended up as *Derailed*—the story of an ordinary ad guy whose life goes awry when he meets a woman on the train. Adopting kids in Colombia gave him the notion for *Detour*, where an adoption goes terribly, murderously wrong. And then there was the day he was lying in a massage room at the Four Seasons Hotel in Beverly Hills. The masseuse touched his neck and said, *What's bothering you?* Siegel's response: *How do you know something's bothering me?* And she said, *Because I'm an empath.*

Siegel was puzzled.

An empath? What's that?

EMPATHY

I sit in a dark motel room.

It's pitch-black outside, but I've pulled the shades down tight anyway, so she won't see me when she walks in. So she'll be sure to turn away from me to switch on the light.

I don't like the dark.

I live on Scotch and Ambien so I never have to stare at it, because sooner or later it becomes the dark of the confessional and I'm eight years old again. I can smell the garlic on his breath and hear the rustle of his clothing. For a moment, I'm a shy, sweet-natured, baseball-crazy boy again, and I physically shrink away from what's coming.

Then everything turns red and the world's on fire.

I look back in anger, because anger is what I've become—a fist of a man.

Anger is what cost me my home, and anger is what put me into court-ordered therapy, and anger is what finally kicked me off the LAPD and into hotel security, where I can be angry without killing anyone.

Not yet.

You've heard of the hotel I work in. It's considered top-shelf and is patronized by various Hollywood wannabes and occasional bona fide celebrities. As downward spirals go, mine hasn't sucked me to the bottom yet, only to Beverly and Doheny.

I get to wear a suit and earpiece, something like a Secret Service man. I get to stand around and look semi-important and even give orders to the hotel employees who don't get to wear suits.

She was a masseuse in the hotel spa.

Kelly.

She was known for her deep-tissue and hot stone. I first talked to her in the basement alcove where I went to be alone—but I'd noticed her before that. I'd heard the music seeping out of her room on my way to the back elevators, and when she entered the basement to grab a smoke, I complimented her on her taste. Most of the hotel masseuses were partial to Enya, to Eastern sitar or the monotonous sound of waves lapping sand. Not her. She played the Joneses—Rickie Lee and Nora and Quincy, too, on occasion.

"Do your customers like it?" I asked her.

She shrugged. "I don't know. Most of them are just trying to not get a hard-on."

"Occupational hazard, I guess?"

"Oh, yeah."

She was pretty, certainly. But there was something else, a palpable aura that made it feel humid even in full-blast air-conditioning.

I believe she noticed the ugly swelling on the

knuckles of my right hand, and the place in the wall where I'd dented it.

"Bad day?"

"No. Pretty ordinary."

She reached out and touched my face, fanning her fingers across my right cheek. Which is more or less when she told me she was an empath.

I won't lie and tell you that I knew what an empath was.

A look had come over her when she touched my face—as if she'd felt that part of me which I rarely touch myself, and then only in the dark before the Johnny Walker has worked its magic.

"I'm sorry," she said.

"For what?"

"For whatever did this to you."

This is what an empath can do—their special gift. Or curse, depending on the day.

I learned all about empaths from her over the next few weeks. As we talked in the basement, or bumped into each other on the way into the hotel, or grabbed smokes outside on the corner.

Empaths touch and know. They feel skin and bone but they touch soul. They see through their hands. Everything—the good, the bad and the truly ugly.

She saw more ugly than she wanted to.

The ugliness had begun to get to her, to send her into a very dark place.

It was one of her customers, she explained.

"Mostly I just see emotions," she confided, "you know, happiness, sadness, fear—longing—all that. But sometimes…sometimes I see more…I know who they *are,* understand?"

"No. Not really."

"This guy—he's a regular. The first time I touched him, I had to pull my hands away. It was that strong."

"*What?*"

"The sense of evil. Like touching—I don't know…a black hole."

"What kind of evil are we talking about?"

"The worst."

Later, she told me more. We were sitting in a bar on Sunset having drinks. Our first date, I guess.

"He hurts kids," she said.

I felt that special nausea. The kind that used to subsume me back in the confessional, when he would come for me, that dark wraith of hurt. The nausea that came when my little brother dutifully followed me into altar-boyhood and I kept my mouth zipped tight like a secret pocket. *Don't tell…don't tell.* There's a price for not telling. It was paid years later, on the afternoon I found my sweet, sad brother hanging from a belt in our childhood bedroom. Over his teenage years, he'd furiously sought solace in various narcotics, but they could only do so much.

"How do you know?" I asked Kelly.

"I know. He's going to do something. He's done it before."

When I told her she might want to report him to the police, she shot me the look you give to intellectually challenged children.

"Tell them I'm an empath? That I *feel* one of my clients is a pedophile? That'll go over well."

She was right, of course. They'd laugh her out of the station.

It was maybe a week later, after this customer had come and gone from his regular appointment and

Kelly was looking particularly miserable, that I volunteered to keep an eye on him.

"How?"

We were lying in my bed, having taken our relationship to the next level as they say, both of us using sex as a kind of opiate, I think—a way to forget things.

"His next appointment?" I asked her. "When is it?"

"Tuesday at two."

"Okay, then."

I waited outside the pool area where the clients saunter out looking sleepy and satiated. He looked frazzled and anxious. She'd slipped out of the room while he undressed to tell me what he was wearing that day. She needn't have bothered—I would've known him anyway.

He carried his burden like a heavy bag.

When he got into the Volvo brought out from the hotel-parking garage, I was already waiting in my car.

I followed him onto the 101, then into the valley. We exited onto a wide boulevard and stayed on it for about five miles, finally making a turn at the School Crossing sign.

He parked by the playground and sat there in his car.

It came back.

The paralytic sickness that made me want to crawl into a ball.

I stayed in the front seat and watched as he exited the car and sidled up to the fence. As he took his glasses off and wiped them on the pocket of his pants. As he scoped out the crowd of elementary-school kids flowing out the front gate. As his attention seemed to fixate on one particular boy—a fourth-grader maybe, a sweet-looking kid who reminded me of someone. As he began to follow this boy down the street, edging closer and closer the way lions separate calves from the herd. I watched and felt every bit as powerless and inert as I did back when my brother bounded down the steps of our house on the way to his first communion.

I couldn't move.

He stepped up behind the boy and began conversing with him. I didn't have to see the boy's face to know what it looked like. The man reached out and grabbed the boy by the arm and I still sat there in the front seat of my car.

It was only when the boy broke away, when he turned and ran, when the man took a few halting steps toward him and then slumped, gave up—that I actually moved.

Anger was my enemy. Anger was my long-lost friend. It came in one red-hot surge, sending the sickness scurrying away in terror, propelling me out of the car, ready to finally protect him.

Joseph, I whispered.

My brother's name.

The man slipped back into his car and drove away. I stood there with my heart colliding against my ribs.

That night, I told Kelly what I was going to do.

We lay in bed covered in sweat, and I told her that I *needed* to do this. The anger had come back and claimed me, wrapped me in its comforting bosom and said, *You're home*.

I waited at the school the next afternoon, and the one after that. I waited all week.

He came the next Monday—parking his Volvo directly across from the playground.

When he got out, I was standing there to ask him if he could point me toward Fourth Street. When he turned and motioned over *there,* I placed the gun up against his back.

"If you make a sound, you're dead."

He promptly wilted. He mumbled something about just taking his money, and I told him to shut up.

He entered my car as docile as a lamb.

A mother stared at us as we drove away.

I went to a place in the valley that I'd used before, when the redness came and made me do certain things to suspects with big mouths and awful résumés. Things that got me tossed off the force and into mandated anger management where the class applauded when I said I'd learned to count to ten and avoid my triggers. Triggers were the things that set me off—there was an entire canon of them.

Men in collar and vestment. That was trigger number one.

We had to walk over a quarter of a mile to the sandpit. They'd turned it into a dumping ground filled with water the color of mud.

"Why?" he said to me when I made him stand there at the lip of the pit.

Because when I was eight years old, I was turned inside out. Because I killed my brother as surely as if I'd tied that belt around his neck and kicked away the chair. That's why.

His body flew into the subterranean tangle of junk and disappeared.

Because you deserve it.

When I showed up at work the next day, she wasn't there.

I wanted to let her know; I wanted to ease her burden.

When I called her cell—she didn't answer.

I asked hotel personnel for her address—we'd always slept at my place because she had a roommate. Two days later I went to her second-floor flat in Ventura and knocked on the door.

No answer.

I found the landlord puttering around the backyard, mostly crabgrass, dandelions and dirt.

"Have you seen Kelly?" I asked him.

"She's gone," he said without really looking up.

"*Gone?* Gone where? Gone to the store?"

"No. *Gone.* Not here anymore."

"What are you talking about? Where'd she go?"

He shrugged. "She didn't leave an address. Her and the kid just left."

"What kid?"

He finally looked up.

"Her *kid*. Her son. Who are *you*, exactly?"

"A friend."

"Okay, Kelly's friend. She took the kid and left. That lowlife of a boyfriend picked them up. End of story."

I will tell you that I still did not understand what happened.

I will tell you that I went back to the hotel and calmly contemplated the situation. That when another masseuse walked out of her room—Trudy, one of the girls Kelly used to talk to—I said tell me about Kelly. She's an empath, I said.

"A *what?*"

"An empath. She touches people and knows things about them."

"Yeah. That they're horny and out of shape."

"She knows what they're feeling—what kind of people they are."

"Ha. Who told you that? *Kelly?*"

I still didn't understand.

Even with Trudy staring at me as if I'd arrived from a distant galaxy. Even then, I refused to grasp what was right there.

"Kelly has a son," I said.

"Uh-huh. Nice kid, too. No thanks to her. Okay, that's not fair. She just needs to develop better taste in men."

"You mean the father?"

"No. I mean the boyfriend. She's got a dope problem—she's always doing it, and she's always doing *them.* Dopes."

"What about the father?"

"Nah, he's kind of nice actually. A real job and everything. She dumped him naturally. He's fighting her for custody."

"Why?"

"Maybe he doesn't think junkies are the best company for an eight-year-old. And she's always trying to poison the kid against him. It's a fucking shame. You should've heard them going at it in the Tranquillity Room last week."

"Last week…when? What day?"

"I don't know. He comes by to drop off money for the kid. Tuesday, I think."

Now it was coming. And it wouldn't stop coming.

"What time Tuesday?"

"I don't know. After lunch. Why?"

Look at it. It wants you to look at it.

Tuesday, I think. After lunch.

"What does he look like, Trudy?"

"Geez…I don't know. About your height, I guess. Glasses. He didn't look too fucking terrific after seeing her. She told him she was going to take the kid and disappear if he didn't drop the whole custody thing. You know what I think? Her boyfriend wants that child support."

About your height. Glasses.

Don't look. Do not look.

Tuesday. After lunch.

When he argued with her in the meditation room, and then walked out looking anxious and upset.

Tuesday.

When he drove to his son's school.

Tuesday.

When he tried to tell him that he was fighting for him and to please not believe the things his mother said about him. When he reached out to make the boy listen, but his son pulled away because all that poison had done its work.

"The boy," I said. "He has brown hair. Cut real short—like a crew. He's sweet looking."

"Yeah. That's him."

I'm an empath, she said. I'm touching this bad man, this sexual predator, and what can I do about it—nothing, because the police won't believe an empath like me. He's coming Tuesday at two, but what can I do? Nothing.

How?

How did she pick *me*?

How?

Because.

Because she'd made me open that secret pocket.

Because one day they'd pointed me out to her—one of the masseuses—oh *him*, stay away, an ex-cop who used to beat people half to death.

But she didn't stay away—she came down to the basement room where I punched holes in the wall. She talked to me. And then I ripped that pocket wide open for her and spilled my dreadful secrets all across the bed.

My brother. My guilt. My anger.

My trinity.

A kind of religion with one acolyte, and one commandment.

Vengeance is yours.

He's a bad man, she said. He's coming Tuesday at two. Tuesday.

At two.

This man who loved his son. Who was simply trying to protect him.

From her.

Why, he said, standing at the top of that sandpit. *Why?*

Because anger is as blind as love, and she gave me both.

I will tell you that a drought took hold of L.A. and turned the brush in the Malibu hills to kindling. That twenty-million-dollar homes went up in smoke. That the drought dried up half the Salton Sea and sucked the water right out of that dump, and that a man disposing of his GE washing machine saw the body wrapped around an old engine casing.

I will tell you that he was ID'd and the bullet in his heart identified as a Walther .45—the kind security guards are partial to, and that a mother came forward and said she'd seen him being coerced into a car near her son's school by another man.

I will tell you that the wheels of justice were grinding and turning and rolling inexorably toward me.

I will tell you that I am not liked much by the police officers I once worked with, but there is a code that is sometimes thick as blood. That makes an ex-partner whom you almost took down with you get hold of bank records so you might know where a Kelly Marcel has been using her VISA card.

I will tell you that there's a motel somewhat south of La Jolla where the down-and-out pay by the week.

I will tell you that I drove there.

That I saw her drop the boy at his grandmother's, who lived in a trailer park by the sea.

That the boyfriend took off for parts unknown.

That it's down to her.

I will tell you that I sit in a dark motel room.

That I've pulled the shades down tight so she won't see me when she walks in. So she'll be sure to turn away from me to switch on the light.

I will tell you that I hear her now, the slam of her car door, the crunch of gravel leading up to her door.

I will tell you that my Walther .45 has two bullets in it. Two.

I will tell you the door is opening.

I will tell you that finally and at last the dark no longer scares me, that there is a peace more comforting than anger.

"I'm sorry," I say.

Who do I say this to?

This I *won't* tell you.

I won't.

JAMES ROLLINS

James Rollins's *Sandstorm* (2003) and *Map of Bones* (2004), were departures from his usual work. His prior thrillers were all stand-alones, with a separate cast of characters. But in these two, Rollins introduced his first series with recurring characters. He pursued that course based on input from his readers and from personal desire. For years, fans had contacted him and asked questions about various cast members from his earlier thrillers. What became of Ashley and Ben's baby after *Subterranean* (1999)? What is the next port of call for the crew of the *Deep Fathom* (2001)?

Eventually, Rollins came to realize that *he* wanted to know those answers, too. So he challenged himself to construct a series—something unique and distinct. He wanted to build a landscape of three-dimensional characters and create his own mythology of these people, to watch them grow over the course of the series, balancing personal lives and professional, some succeeding, some failing. Yet at the same time, Rollins refused to let go of his roots. Trained as a biologist with a degree in veterinary medicine, his new series, like his previous thrillers, folded scientific intrigue into stories of historical mystery. His new characters belong to *Sigma Force*, an elite team of ex-Special Forces soldiers retrained in scientific disciplines (what Rollins jokingly describes as "killer scientists who operate outside the rule of law"). Finally, from his background as a veterinarian, the occasional strange or exotic animal often plays a significant role in the plot.

And this short story is no exception.

Here, Rollins links his past to the present. He brings forward a minor character, one of his personal favorites, from his earlier stand-alone thriller *Ice Hunt* (2003). Joe Kowalski, a naval seaman, is best described as someone with the heart of a hero but lacking the brainpower to go with it. So how does Seaman Joe Kowalski end up being recruited by such an illustrious team as Sigma Force?

As they say…dumb luck is better than no luck at all.

KOWALSKI'S IN LOVE

He wasn't much to look at...even swinging upside down from a hog snare. Pug-nosed, razor-clipped muddy hair, a six-foot slab of beef hooked and hanging naked except for a pair of wet gray boxer shorts. His chest was crisscrossed with old scars, along with one jagged bloody scratch from collarbone to groin. His eyes shone wide and wild.

And with good reason.

Two minutes before, as Dr. Shay Rosauro unhitched her glide-chute on the nearby beach, she had heard his cries in the jungle and come to investigate. She had approached in secret, moving silently, spying from a short distance away, cloaked in shadow and foliage.

"Back off, you furry bastard...!"

The man's curses never stopped, a continual flow tinged with a growled Bronx accent. Plainly he was American. Like herself.

She checked her watch.

8:33 a.m.

The island would explode in twenty-seven minutes.

The man would die sooner.

The more immediate threat came from the island's other inhabitants, drawn by the man's shouts. The average adult mandrill baboon weighed over a hundred pounds, most of that muscle and teeth. They were usually found in Africa. Never on a jungle island off the coast of Brazil. The yellow radio collars suggested the pack were once the research subjects belonging to Professor Salazar, shipped to this remote island for his experimental trials. *Mandrillus sphinx* were also considered *frugivorous,* meaning their diet consisted of fruits and nuts.

But not always.

They were also known to be opportunistic carnivores.

One of the baboons stalked around the trapped man: a charcoal-furred male of the species with a broad red snout bordered on both sides by ridges of blue. Such coloration indicated the fellow was the dominant male of the group. Females and subordinate males, all a duller brown, had settled to rumps or hung from neighboring branches. One bystander yawned, exposing a set of three-inch-long eyeteeth and a muzzle full of ripping incisors.

The male sniffed at the prisoner. A meaty fist swung at the inquisitive baboon, missed, and whished through empty air.

The male baboon reared on its hind legs and howled, lips peeling back from its muzzle to expose the full length of its yellow fangs. An impressive and horrifying display. The other baboons edged closer.

Shay stepped into the clearing, drawing all eyes. She lifted her hand and pressed the button on her sonic device, nicknamed a *shrieker*. The siren blast from the device had the desired effect.

Baboons fled into the forest. The male leader bounded up, caught a low branch and swung into the cloaking darkness of the jungle.

The man, still spinning on the line, spotted her. "Hey…how about…?"

Shay already had a machete in her other hand. She jumped atop a boulder and severed the hemp rope with one swipe of her weapon.

The man fell hard, striking the soft loam and rolling to the side. Amid a new string of curses, he struggled with the snare around his ankle. He finally freed the knotted rope.

"Goddamn apes!"

"Baboons," Shay corrected.

"What?"

"They're baboons, not apes. They have stubby tails."

"Whatever. All I saw were their big, goddamn teeth."

As the man stood and brushed off his knees, Shay spotted a U.S. Navy anchor tattooed on his right bicep. Ex-military? Maybe he could prove handy. Shay checked the time.

8:35 a.m.

"What are you doing here?" she asked.

"My boat broke down." His gaze traveled up and down her lithe form.

She was not unaccustomed to such attention from the male of her own species…even now, when she was unflatteringly dressed in green camouflage fatigues and sturdy boots. Her shoulder-length black hair had been efficiently bound behind her ears with a black bandanna, and in the tropical swelter, her skin glowed a dark mocha.

Caught staring, he glanced back toward the beach. "I swam here after my boat sank."

"Your boat sank?"

"Okay, it blew up."

She stared at him for further explanation.

"There was a gas leak. I dropped my cigar—"

She waved away the rest of his words with her machete. Her pickup was scheduled at the northern peninsula in under a half hour. On that timetable, she had to reach the compound, break into the safe and obtain the vials of antidote. She set off into the jungle, noting a trail. The man followed, dragged along in her wake.

"Whoa…where are we going?"

She freed a rolled-up poncho from her daypack and passed it to him.

He struggled into it as he followed. "Name's Kowalski," he said. He got the poncho on backward and fought to work it around. "Do you have a boat? A way off this friggin' island?"

She didn't have time for subtlety. "In twenty-three minutes, the Brazilian navy is going to firebomb this atoll."

"What?" He checked his own wrist. He had no watch.

She continued, "An evac is scheduled for wheels up at 8:55 a.m. on the northern peninsula. But first I have to retrieve something from the island."

"Wait. Back up. Who's going to firebomb this shithole?"

"The Brazilian navy. In twenty-three minutes."

"Of course they are." He shook his head. "Of all the goddamn islands, I had to shag my ass onto one that's going to blow up."

Shay tuned out his diatribe. At least he kept moving. She had to give him that. He was either very brave or very dumb.

"Oh, look…a mango." He reached for the yellow fruit.

"Don't touch that."

"But I haven't eaten in—?"

"All the vegetation on this island has been aerial sprayed with a transgenic rhabdovirus."

He lowered his hand.

"Once ingested, it stimulates the sensory centers of the brain, heightening a victim's senses. Sight, sound, smell, taste and touch."

"And what's wrong with that?"

"The process also corrupts the reticular apparatus of the cerebral cortex. Triggering manic rages."

A growling yowl echoed through the jungle behind them. It was answered by coughing grunts and howls from either flank.

"The apes…?"

"Baboons. Yes, they're surely infected. Experimental subjects."

"Great. The Island of Rabid Baboons."

Ignoring him, she pointed toward a whitewashed hacienda sprawled atop the next hill, seen through a break in the foliage. "We need to reach that compound."

The terra-cotta-tiled structure had been leased by Professor Salazar for his research, funded by a shadowy organization of terrorist cells. Here on the isolated island, he had conducted the final stages of perfecting his bioweapon. Then two days ago, Sigma Force—a covert U.S. science team specializing in global threats—had captured the doctor in the heart of the Brazilian rain forest, but not before he had infected an entire Indian village outside of Manaus, including an international children's relief hospital.

The disease was already in its early stages, requiring the prompt quarantine of the village by the Brazilian army. The only hope was to obtain Professor Salazar's antidote, locked in the doctor's safe.

Or at least the vials *might* be there.

Salazar claimed to have destroyed his supply.

Upon this assertion, the Brazilian government had decided to take no chances. A storm was due to strike at dusk with hurricane-force winds. They feared the storm surge might carry the virus from the island to the mainland's coastal rain forest. It would take only a single infected leaf to risk the entire equatorial rain forest. So the plan was to firebomb the small island, to burn its vegetation to the bedrock. The assault was set for zero nine hundred. The government could not be convinced that the remote possibility of a cure was worth the risk of a delay. Total annihilation was their plan. That included the Brazilian village. Acceptable losses.

Anger surged through her as she pictured Manuel Garrison, her partner. He had tried to evacuate the children's hospital, but he'd become trapped and subsequently infected. Along with all the children.

Acceptable losses were not in her vocabulary.

Not today.

So Shay had proceeded with her solo op. Parachuting from a high-altitude drop, she had radioed her plans while plummeting in free fall. Sigma command had agreed to send an emergency evac helicopter to the northern end of the island. It would touch down for one minute. Either she was on the chopper at that time…or she was dead.

The odds were fine with her.

But now she wasn't alone.

The side of beef tromped loudly behind her. Whistling. He was *whistling*. She turned to him. "Mr. Kowalski, do you remember my description of how the virus heightens a victim's sense of hearing?" Her quiet words crackled with irritation.

"Sorry." He glanced at the trail behind him.

"Careful of that tiger trap," she said, stepping around the crudely camouflaged hole.

"What—?" His left foot fell squarely on the trap-door of woven reeds. His weight shattered through it.

Shay shoulder-blocked the man to the side and landed atop him. It felt like falling on a pile of bricks. Only, bricks were smarter.

She pushed up. "After being snared, you'd think you'd watch where you were stepping! The whole place is one big booby trap."

She stood, straightened her pack and edged around the spike-lined pit. "Stay behind me. Step where I step."

In her anger, she missed the trip cord.

The only warning was a small *thwang*.

She jumped to the side but was too late. A tethered log swung from the forest and struck her knee. She heard the snap of her tibia, then went flying through the air—right toward the open maw of the tiger trap.

She twisted to avoid the pit's iron spikes. There was no hope.

Then she hit…bricks again.

Kowalski had lunged and blocked the hole with his own bulk. She rolled off him. Agony flared up her leg, through her hip, and exploded along her spine. Her vision narrowed to a pinprick, but not enough to miss the angled twist below her knee.

Kowalski gained her side. "Oh, man…oh, man…"

"Leg's broken," she said, biting back the pain.

"We can splint it."

She checked her watch.

8:39 a.m.

Twenty-one minutes left.

He noted her attention. "I can carry you. We can still make it to the evac site."

She recalculated in her head. She pictured Manuel's shit-eating grin…and the many faces of the children. Pain worse than any broken bone coursed through her. She could not fail.

The man read her intent. "You'll never make it to that house," he said.

"I don't have any other choice."

"Then let me do it," he blurted out. His words seemed to surprise him as much as it did her, but he didn't retract them. "You make for the beach. I'll get whatever you want out of the goddamn hacienda."

She turned and stared the stranger full in the face. She searched for something to give her hope. Some hidden strength, some underlying fortitude. She found nothing. But she had no other choice.

"There'll be other traps."

"I'll keep my eyes peeled this time."

"And the office safe…I can't teach you to crack it in time."

"Do you have an extra radio?"

She nodded.

"So talk me through it once I get there."

She hesitated—but there was no time for even that. She swung her pack around. "Lean down."

She reached to a side pocket of her pack and stripped out two self-adhesive patches. She attached one behind the man's ear and the other over his Adam's apple. "Microreceiver and a subvocal transmitter."

She quickly tested the radio while explaining the stakes involved.

"So much for my relaxing vacation under the sun," he mumbled.

"One more thing," she said. She pulled out three sections of a weapon from her pack. "A VK rifle. Variable Kinetic." She quickly snapped the pieces together and shoved a fat cylindrical cartridge into place on its underside. It looked like a stubby assault rifle, except the barrel was wider and flattened horizontally.

"Safety release is here." She pointed the weapon at a nearby bush and squeezed the trigger. There was only a tiny whirring cough. A projectile flashed out the barrel and buzzed through the bush, severing leaves and branches. "One-inch razor-disks. You can set the weapon for single shot or automatic strafe." She demonstrated. "Two hundred shots per magazine."

He whistled again and accepted the weapon. "Maybe you should keep this weed whacker. With your bum leg, you're going to drag ass at a snail's pace." He nodded to the jungle. "And the damn apes are still out there."

"They're baboons...and I still have my handheld shrieker. Now get going." She checked her watch. She had given Kowalski a second timepiece, calibrated to match. "Nineteen minutes."

He nodded. "I'll see you soon." He moved off the trail, vanishing almost instantly into the dense foliage.

"Where are you going?" she called after him. "The trail—"

"Screw the trail," he responded through the radio. "I'll take my chances in the raw jungle. Fewer traps. Plus, I've got this baby to carve a straight path to the mad doctor's house."

Shay hoped he was right. There would be no time for backtracking or second chances. She quickly dosed herself with a morphine injector and used a broken tree branch for a crutch. As she set off for the beach, she heard the ravenous hunting calls of the baboons.

She hoped Kowalski could outsmart them.

The thought drew a groan that had nothing to do with her broken leg.

Luckily Kowalski had a knife now.

He hung upside down…for the second time that day. He bent at the waist, grabbed his trapped ankle and sawed through the snare's rope. It snapped with a *pop*. He fell, clenched in a ball, and crashed to the jungle floor with a loud *oof*.

"What was that?" Dr. Rosauro asked over the radio.

He straightened his limbs and lay on his back for a breath. "Nothing," he growled. "Just tripped on a rock." He scowled at the swinging rope overhead. He was not about to tell the beautiful woman doctor that he had been strung up again. He did have some pride left.

"Goddamn snare," he mumbled under his breath.

"What?"

"Nothing." He had forgotten about the sensitivity of the subvocal transmitter.

"Snare? You snared yourself again, didn't you?"

He kept silent. His momma once said, *It is better to keep your mouth shut and let people think you're a fool than to open it and remove all doubt.*

"You need to watch where you're going," the woman scolded.

Kowalski bit back a retort. He heard the pain in her voice…and her fear. So instead, he hauled back to his feet and retrieved his gun.

"Seventeen minutes," Dr. Rosauro reminded him.

"I'm just reaching the compound now."

The sun-bleached hacienda appeared like a calm oasis of civilization in a sea of nature's raw exuberance. It was straight lines and sterile order versus wild overgrowth and tangled fecundity. Three buildings sat on manicured acres, separated by breezeways, and nestled around a small garden courtyard. A three-tiered Spanish fountain stood in the center, ornate with blue and red glass tiles. No water splashed through its basins.

Kowalski studied the compound, stretching a kink out of his back. The only movement across the cultivated grounds was the swaying fronds of some coconut palms. The winds were already rising with the approaching storm. Clouds stacked on the southern horizon.

"The office is on the main floor, near the back," Rosauro said in his ear. "Careful of the electric perimeter fence. The power may still be on."

He studied the chain-link fencing, almost eight feet tall, topped by a spiral of concertina wire and separated from the jungle by a burned swath about ten yards wide. No-man's-land.

Or rather no-*ape's*-land.

He picked up a broken branch and approached the fence. Wincing, he stretched one end toward the chain links. He was mindful of his bare feet. *Shouldn't I be grounded for this?* He had no idea.

As the tip of his club struck the fence, a strident wail erupted. He jumped back, then realized the noise was not coming from the fence. It wailed off to his left, toward the water.

Dr. Rosauro's shrieker.

"Are you all right?" Kowalski called into his transmitter.

A long stretch of silence had him holding his breath—then whispered words reached him. "The baboons must sense my injury. They're converging on my location. Just get going."

Kowalski poked his stick at the fence a few more times, like a child with a dead rat, making sure it was truly dead. Once satisfied, he snapped the concertina wire with clippers supplied by Dr. Rosauro and scurried over the fence, certain the power was just waiting to surge back with electric-blue death.

He dropped with a relieved sigh onto the mowed lawn, as bright and perfect as any golf course.

"You don't have much time," the doctor stressed needlessly. "If you're successful, the rear gardens lead all the way to the beach. The northern headlands stretch out from there."

Kowalski set out, aiming for the main building. A shift in wind brought the damp waft of rain… along with the stench of death, the ripeness of meat left out in the sun. He spotted the body on the far side of the fountain.

He circled the man's form. The guy's face had been gnawed to the bone, clothes shredded, belly slashed open, bloated intestines strung across the ground like festive streamers. It seemed the apes had been having their own party since the good doctor took off.

As he circled, he noted the black pistol clutched in the corpse's hand. The slide had popped open. No more bullets. Not enough firepower to hold off a whole pack of the furry carnivores. Kowalski raised his own weapon to his shoulder. He searched the shadowed corners for any hidden apes. There were not even any bodies. The shooter must either be a poor marksman, or the ruby-assed monkeys had hauled off their brethren's bodies, perhaps to eat later, like so much baboon takeout.

Kowalski made one complete circle. Nothing.

He crossed toward the main building. Something nagged at the edge of his awareness. He scratched his skull in an attempt to dislodge it—but failed.

He climbed atop the full-length wooden porch and tried the door handle. Latched but unlocked. He shoved the door open with one foot, weapon raised, ready for a full-frontal ape assault.

The door swung wide, rebounded, and bounced back closed in his face.

Snorting in irritation, he grabbed the handle again. It wouldn't budge. He tugged harder.

Locked.

"You've got to be kidding."

The collision must have jiggled some bolt into place.

"Are you inside yet?" Rosauro asked.

"Just about," he grumbled.

"What's the holdup?"

"Well…what happened was…" He tried sheepishness, but it fit him as well as fleece on a rhino. "I guess someone locked it."

"Try a window."

Kowalski glanced to the large windows that framed either side of the barred doorway. He stepped to the right and peered through. Inside was a rustic kitchen with oak tables, a farmer's sink and old enamel appliances. Good enough. Maybe they even had a bottle of beer in the fridge. A man could dream. But first there was work to do.

He stepped back, pointed his weapon and fired a single round. The silver razor-disk shattered through the pane as easily as any bullet. Fractures spattered out from the hole.

He grinned. Happy again.

He retreated another step, careful of the porch edge. He thumbed the switch to automatic fire and strafed out the remaining panes.

He poked his head through the hole. "Anyone home?"

That's when he saw the exposed wire snapping and spitting around a silver disk imbedded in the wall plaster. It had nicked through the electric cord. More disks were impaled across the far wall…including one that had punctured the gas line to the stove.

He didn't bother cursing.

He twisted and leaped as the explosion blasted behind him. A wall of superheated air shoved him out of the way, blowing his poncho over his head. He hit the ground rolling as a fireball swirled overhead, across the courtyard. Tangled in his poncho, he tumbled—right into the eviscerated corpse. Limbs fought, heat burned, and scrambling fingers found only a gelid belly wound and things that squished.

Gagging, Kowalski fought his way free and shoved the poncho off his body. He stood, shaking like a wet dog, swiping gore from his arms in disgust. He stared toward the main building.

Flames danced behind the kitchen window. Smoke choked out the shattered pane.

"What happened?" the doctor gasped in his ear.

He only shook his head. Flames spread, flowing out the broken window and lapping at the porch.

"Kowalski?"

"Booby trap. I'm fine."

He collected his weapon from his discarded poncho. Resting it on his shoulder, he intended to circle to the back. According to Dr. Rosauro, the main office was in the rear.

If he worked quickly—

He checked his watch.

8:45 a.m.

It was hero time.

He stepped toward the north side of the hacienda. His bare heel slipped on a loop of intestine, slick as any banana peel. His leg twisted out from under him. He tumbled face-first, striking hard, the weapon slamming to the packed dirt, his finger jamming the trigger.

Silver disks flashed out and struck the figure lumbering into the courtyard, one arm on fire. It howled—not in agony, but in feral rage. The figure wore the tatters of a butler's attire. His eyes were fever bright but mucked with pasty matter. Froth speckled and drooled from lips rippled in a snarl. Blood stained the lower half of his face and drenched the front of his once-starched white shirt.

In a flash of insight—a rarity—Kowalski realized what had been nagging him before. The lack of monkey corpses here. He'd assumed the monkeys had been cannibalized—if so, then why leave a perfectly good chunk of meat out here?

The answer: no apes had attacked here.

It seemed the beasts were not the only ones infected on the island.

Nor the only cannibals.

The butler, still on fire, lunged toward Kowalski. The first impacts of the silver disks had struck shoulder and neck. Blood sprayed. Not enough to stop the determined maniac.

Kowalski squeezed the trigger, aiming low.

An arc of razored death sliced across the space at knee height.

Tendons snapped, bones shattered. The butler collapsed and fell toward Kowalski, landing almost nose to nose with him. A clawed hand grabbed his throat, nails digging into his flesh. Kowalski raised the muzzle of his VK rifle.

"Sorry, buddy."

Kowalski aimed for the open mouth and pulled the trigger, closing his eyes at the last second.

A gargling yowl erupted—then went immediately silent. His throat was released.

Kowalski opened his eyes to see the butler collapse face-first.

Dead.

Kowalski rolled to the side and gained his legs. He searched around for any other attackers, then ran toward the back of the hacienda. He glanced in each window as he passed: a locker room, a lab with steel animal cages, a billiard room.

Fire roared on the structure's far side, fanned by the growing winds. Smoke churned up into the darkening skies.

Through the next window, Kowalski spotted a room with a massive wooden desk and floor-to-ceiling bookshelves.

It had to be the professor's study.

"Dr. Rosauro," Kowalski whispered.

No answer.

"Dr. Rosauro..." he tried a little louder.

He grabbed his throat. His transmitter was gone, ripped away in his scuffle with the butler. He glanced back toward the courtyard. Flames lapped the sky.

He was on his own.

He turned back to the study. A rear door opened into the room. It stood ajar.

Why did that not sit well with him?

With time strangling, Kowalski edged cautiously forward, gun raised. He used the tip of his weapon to nudge the door wider.

He was ready for anything.

Rabid baboons, raving butlers.

But not for the young woman in a skintight charcoal wet suit.

She was crouched before an open floor safe and rose smoothly with the creak of the door, a pack slung over one shoulder. Her hair, loose and damp, flowed as dark as a raven's wing, her skin burnt honey. Eyes, the smoky hue of dark caramel, met his.

Over a silver 9mm Sig-Sauer held in one fist.

Kowalski ducked to the side of the doorway, keeping his weapon pointed inside. "Who the hell are you?"

"My name, *señor*, is Condeza Gabriella Salazar. You are trespassing on my husband's property."

Kowalski scowled. The professor's wife. Why did all the pretty ones go for the smart guys?

"What are you doing here?" he called out.

"You are American, *sí*? Sigma Force, no doubt." This last was said with a sneer. "I've come to collect my husband's cure. I will use it to barter for my *marido's* freedom. You will not stop me."

A blast of her gun chewed a hole through the door. Splinters chased him back.

Something about the easy way she had handled her pistol suggested more than competence. Plus, if she'd married a professor, she probably had a few IQ points on him.

Brains and a body like that…

Life was not fair.

Kowalski backed away, covering the side door.

A window shattered by his ear. A bullet seared past

the back of his neck. He dropped and pressed against the adobe wall.

The bitch had moved out of the office and was stalking him from inside the house.

Body, brains, *and* she knew the lay of the land.

No wonder she'd been able to avoid the monsters here.

Distantly a noise intruded. The *whump-whump* of an approaching helicopter. It was their evac chopper. He glanced to his watch. Of course their ride was early.

"You should run for your friends," the woman called from inside. "While you still have time!"

Kowalski stared at the manicured lawn that spread all the way to the beach. There was no cover. The bitch would surely drop him within a few steps.

It came down to do or die.

He bunched his legs under him, took a deep breath, then sprang up. He crashed back-first through the bullet-weakened window. He kept his rifle tucked to his belly. He landed hard and shoulder-rolled, ignoring the shards of glass cutting him.

He gained a crouched position, rifle up, swiveling.

The room was empty.

Gone again.

So it was to be a cat-and-mouse hunt through the house.

He moved to the doorway that led deeper into the structure. Smoke flowed in rivers across the ceiling. The temperature inside was furnace hot. He pictured the pack over the woman's shoulder. She had already emptied the safe. She would make for one of the exits.

He edged to the next room.

A sunroom. A wall of windows overlooked the expanse of gardens and lawn. Rattan furniture and floor screens offered a handful of hiding places. He would have to lure her out somehow. Outthink her.

Yeah, right.

He edged into the room, keeping close to the back wall.

He crossed the room. There was no attack.

He reached the far archway. It led to a back foyer.

And an open door.

He cursed inwardly. As he made his entrance, she must have made her exit. She was probably halfway to Honduras by now. He rushed the door and out to the back porch. He searched the grounds.

Gone.

So much for outthinking her.

The press of the hot barrel against the back of his skull punctuated how thick that skull actually was. As he had concluded earlier, she must have realized a sprint across open ground was too risky. So she had waited to ambush him.

She didn't even hesitate for any witty repartee…not that he'd be a good sparring partner anyway. Only a single word of consolation was offered. *"Adiós."*

The blast of the gun was drowned by a sudden siren's wail.

Both of them jumped at the shrieking burst.

Luckily, he jumped to the left, she to the right.

The round tore through Kowalski's right ear with a lance of fire.

He spun, pulling the trigger on his weapon. He didn't aim, just clenched the trigger and strafed at waist level. He lost his balance at the edge of the porch, tumbling back.

Another bullet ripped through the air past the tip of his nose.

He hit the cobbled path, and his skull struck with a distinct ring. The rifle was knocked from his fingers.

He searched up and saw the woman step to the edge of the porch.

She pointed her Sig-Sauer at him.

Her other arm clutched her stomach. It failed to act as a dam. Abdominal contents spilled from her split belly, pouring out in a flow of dark blood. She lifted her gun, arm trembling—her eyes met his, oddly surprised. Then the gun slipped from her fingers, and she toppled toward him.

Kowalski rolled out of the way in time.

She landed with a wet slap on the stone path.

The bell-beat of the helicopter wafted louder as the winds changed direction. The storm was rolling in fast. He saw the chopper circle the beach once, like a dog settling for a place to sleep, then lower toward the flat rocky expanse.

Kowalski returned to Gabriella Salazar's body and hauled off her pack. He began to sprint for the beach. Then stopped, went back, and retrieved his VK rifle. He wasn't leaving it behind.

As he ran, he realized two things.

One. The siren blast from the neighboring jungle had gone silent. And two. He had heard not a single word from Dr. Rosauro. He checked the taped receiver behind his ear. Still in place.

Why had she gone silent?

The helicopter—a Sikorsky S-76—touched down ahead of him. Sand swirled in the rotorwash. A gunman in military fatigues pointed a rifle at him and bellowed over the roar of the blades.

"Stand down! Now!"

Kowalski stopped. He lowered his rifle but lifted the pack. "I have the goddamn antidote."

He searched the surrounding beach for Dr. Rosauro, but she was nowhere in sight.

"I'm Seaman Joe Kowalski! U.S. Navy! I'm helping Dr. Rosauro!"

After a moment of consultation with someone inside the chopper, the gunman waved him forward. Ducking under the rotors, Kowalski held out the satchel. A shadowy figure accepted the pack and searched inside. Something was exchanged by radio.

"Where's Dr. Rosauro?" the stranger asked, clearly the one in charge here. Hard blue eyes studied him.

Kowalski shook his head.

"Commander Crowe," the pilot called back. "We must leave now. The Brazilian navy had just ordered the bombardment."

"Get inside," the man ordered Kowalski, the tone unequivocal.

Kowalski stepped toward the open door.

A shrieking wail stopped him. A single short burst. It came from beyond the beach.

In the jungle.

Dr. Shay Rosauro clung to the tangle of branches halfway up the broad-leafed cocoa tree. Baboons gibbered below. She had sustained a deep bite to her calf, lost her radio and her pack.

Minutes ago, after being chased into the tree, she had found that her perch offered a bird's-eye view of the hacienda, good enough to observe Kowalski being led out at gunpoint. Unable to help, she had used the only weapon still at hand—her sonic shrieker.

Unfortunately, the blast had panicked the baboons

below her, their sudden flight jostling her branch. She'd lost her balance…and the shrieker. As she'd regained her balance, she'd heard two gunshots.

Hope died inside her.

Below, one of the baboons, the dominant male of the pack, had recovered her sonic device and discovered the siren button. The blast momentarily scattered the pack. But only momentarily. The deterrent was becoming progressively less effective—only making them angrier.

Shay hugged the tree trunk.

She checked her watch, then closed her eyes.

She pictured the children's faces…her partner's…

A noise drew her attention upward. The double *whump* of a passing helicopter. The leaves whipped around her. She lifted an arm—then lowered it.

Too late.

The chopper lifted away. The Brazilian assault would commence in a matter of seconds. Shay let her club, her only remaining weapon, drop from her fingers. What was the use? It tumbled below, doing nothing but drawing the attention of the baboons. The pack renewed its assault, climbing the lowest branches.

She could only watch.

Then a familiar voice intruded.

"Die, you dirty, rabid, motherfucking apes!"

A large figure appeared below, blazing out with a VK rifle.

Baboons screamed. Fur flew. Blood splattered.

Kowalski strode into the fray, back to nothing but his boxers.

And his weapon.

He strafed and fired, spinning, turning, twisting, dropping.

Baboons fled now.

Except for their leader. The male rose up and howled as loudly as Kowalski, baring long fangs. Kowalski matched his expression, showing as many teeth.

"Shut the hell up!"

Kowalski punctuated his declaration with a continuous burst of firepower, turning monkey into mulch. Once finished, he shouldered his rifle and strode forward. Leaning on the trunk, he stared up.

"Ready to come down, Doctor?"

Relieved, Shay half fell out of the tree. Kowalski caught her.

"The antidote…?" she asked.

"In safe hands," he assured her. "On its way to the coast with Commander Crowe. He wanted me to come along, but well…I…I guess I owed you."

He supported her under one shoulder. They hobbled quickly out of the jungle to the open beach.

"How are we going to get off—?"

"I've got that covered. Seems a nice lady left us a going-away present." He pointed down the strand to a beached Jet Ski. "Lucky for us, Gabriella Salazar loved her husband enough to come out here."

As they hurried to the watercraft's side, he gently helped her on board, then climbed in front.

She circled her arms around his waist. She noted his bloody ear and weeping lacerations across his back. More scars to add to his collection. She closed her eyes and leaned her cheek against his bare back. Grateful and exhausted.

"And speaking of the love of one's life," he said, igniting the watercraft's engine and throttling it up. He glanced back. "I may be falling in love, too…"

She lifted her head, startled, then leaned back down. Relieved.

Kowalski was just staring at his shouldered rifle.

"Oh, yeah," he said. "This baby's a real keeper."

GAYLE LYNDS

Gayle Lynds did not intend to start a series. When she wrote her first book, *Masquerade*, in the mid-1990s, she was simply creating a modern espionage thriller. But in those early post-Iron Curtain days, not only was there serious discussion in Congress about dissolving the CIA, the *New York Times* eliminated its regular review column titled, "Spies & Thrillers." Within book publishing, the spy novel was declared as dead as the cold war.

Still, *Masquerade* became a *New York Times* bestseller. A great adventure story, it was infused with fascinating doses of history and psychology. In an odd way, Sarah Walker, the heroine, was Lynds. Both were magazine journalists, but Sarah had the misfortune to have an uncle who was a notorious assassin called the Carnivore, although she did not know this. In the novel, Asher Flores, the hero, is a CIA man of the fascinating ilk—charming, terribly smart, with the soul of a rogue. Together, Sarah and Asher must unearth the Carnivore.

Lynds went on to publish two more stand-alone thrillers, *Mesmerized* and *Mosaic*, and collaborated with Robert Ludlum to create the Covert-One series. Through it all, she continued to receive mail from fans who wanted her to bring back Sarah, Asher and the Carnivore. So *The Coil*, a novel about the Carnivore's only child, Liz Sansborough, was born. A former CIA operative, Liz had played a pivotal role in *Masquerade*, just as Sarah and Asher would play pivotal roles in *The Coil*.

Liz and Sarah are two matched flames, not only in appearance but in spirit, with quick wit and the sort of personal courage that is both admirable and sometimes daunting. Costarring with Liz in *The Coil* is Simon Childs of MI6. For him, the "M" means maverick. Hotheaded and coolly charming, Simon reflects Lynds's endless fascination with politics—he's a penetration agent in the antiglobalization movement.

Lynds's latest espionage thriller is *The Last Spymaster*, and will be followed by another book in the Carnivore series. *The Hunt for Dmitri* is part of that continuum.

It's a Liz Sansborough story.

Which means the Carnivore must appear, too.

THE HUNT FOR DMITRI

The French never got enough credit. The Germans never got enough control. The Romanians had a guilt complex. And the Americans hadn't a clue. As the good-natured slanders continued, Liz Sansborough, Ph.D., peered around the Faculty Club for her close friend and colleague Arkady Albam. He was late.

The dimly lit bar was packed, every table filled. The rich aromas of wine and liquor were intense. As glasses clinked, a world atlas of languages electrified the air. Academics all, they were celebrating the conclusion of a highly successful international conference on cold war political fallout, post-9/11, which she had helped to organize. Still, there was no sign of Arkady.

The economist from the University of London grinned pointedly at Liz—the only American in their group. "I hear Russia's economy is so rotten that the Kremlin has had to sack dozens of its American moles."

"Only because we don't sell ourselves cheap." She

grinned back at him. "Moscow can afford to keep your MI6 turncoats on the payroll forever."

As laughter erupted, the sociologist from the Sorbonne nodded at the empty bar stool beside Liz and asked in French, "Where's Arkady? He isn't here to defend his country!"

"I've been wondering, too." Liz's gaze swept the lounge once more.

Arkady was a visiting scholar in Russian history, on campus here at the University of California at Santa Barbara since January. They had met soon after he arrived, when he sat beside her at a mass faculty meeting, peered at the empty seat on his other side, then introduced himself to her. "I'm the new kid," he said simply. They discovered a shared European sensibility, a love of movies, and that each had pasts neither would discuss. In her mind, she could see his kindly wrinkled face, feel the touch of his fingertips on her forearm as he leaned toward her with an impish smile to impart some piece of wisdom or gossip.

The problem was, he was elderly—almost seventy years old—and so unwell the past week that he had missed all of Monday's events, including his own seminar. He had phoned to tell her, but stubbornly refused to see a doctor.

As the lighthearted banter continued, and more people arrived, there was still no Arkady. He was never late. Liz speed-dialed his number on her cell phone. No answer again. Instead of leaving another message, she toasted her colleagues farewell and wound through the throngs to the door. His apartment was only minutes away. She might as well look in on him.

The night sky was dull black, the stars pinpricks, remote. Liz hurried to her car, threw her shoulder bag across the front seat, turned on the ignition and peeled out, speeding along streets fringed with towering palms until at last she parked in front of Arkady's building. He lived in 2C. In a rare admission, he had joked once that he preferred this "C" to the one that referred to the Cellar, Soviet intelligence's name for the basement in the Lubyanka complex where the KGB executed dissidents and spies and those who crossed them. He barely escaped, he had told her, then refused to say more, his profile pinched with bad memories.

Liz ran upstairs and knocked. There was no answer. His drapes were closed, but a line of light showed in a center gap. She knocked again then tried the knob. It turned, and she cracked open the door. Just inside, magazines were strewn in piles. A lamp lay on its side, its ceramic base shattered. Her chest tightened.

"Arkady? Are you here?"

The only sound was the ticking of the wall clock. Liz opened the door wider. Books lay where they had been yanked from shelves, spines twisted. She peered around the door—and saw Arkady. His brown eyes were wide and frightened, and he seemed small, shriveled, although he was muscular and broad-chested for his age. He was sitting in his usual armchair, drenched in the light of his tall, cast-iron floor lamp.

She drank in the sight of him. "Are you all right?"

Arkady sighed. "This is what greeted me after the last seminar." He spoke English with an American accent. "It's a mess, isn't it?" He still wore his battered tweed jacket, his gray tie firmly knotted against his throat. His left hand held a blue envelope, while the other was tucked inside his jacket as if clutching at his heart. He was a man of expressive Rus disposition and ascetic Mongol habits and was usually vibrant and talkative.

She frowned. "Yes, but you didn't answer my question. Are you hurt?"

When he shook his head, experience sent her outside to the balcony again. A gust of wind rustled the leaves of a pepper tree, cooling her hot face. As she inspected the street and parked cars, then the other apartment buildings, uneasy memories surged through her, transporting her back to the days she had been a CIA NOC—nonofficial cover operative—on roving assignment from Paris to Moscow. No one at the university knew she had been CIA.

Seeing nothing unusual, she slipped back inside and locked the door. Arkady had not moved. In the lamplight, his thick hair and heavy eyebrows were the muted color of iron shavings.

"What happened, Arkady? Who did this? Is anything missing?"

He shrugged, his expression miserable.

Liz walked through the kitchen, bedroom and office. Nothing else seemed out of place. She returned to the living room.

Arkady rallied. "Sit with me, dear Liz. You're such a comfort. If I'd been blessed with a daughter, I'd want her to be you."

His words touched her. As a psychologist, she was aware of her desire for this older man's attention, that he had become a surrogate father, a deep bond. Her real father was her most closely guarded secret: He was an international assassin with a code name to match his reputation—the Carnivore. She hated what he had done, what he was. That his blood flowed through her veins haunted her—except when she was with Arkady.

She sank into her usual armchair, where only the

low reading table separated them. "Have you phoned the sheriff's department?"

He shrugged. "There's no point."

"I'll call for you."

Arkady gave his head a rough shake. "Too dangerous. He'll be back."

She stared. "Too dangerous? *Who'll* be back?"

Arkady handed her the blue envelope he had been holding. She turned it over. The postmark was Los Angeles.

"Ignore that," he told her. "The letter was sent originally from Moscow to New York in a larger envelope. A friend there opened it and put the letter into another big envelope and mailed it to Los Angeles. That's where my address was added."

Liz pulled out folded stationery. Inside were three tiny dried sunflowers. In Russia, an odd number of blooms was considered good luck. The writing was not only different, it was in the Cyrillic alphabet—Russian.

"Dearest," it began. She peered up at him.

"It's from my wife, Nina." He looked past her to another time, another life. "She wouldn't escape with me. We'd never had children, and she knew I could take care of myself. She said she'd rather have me alive far away than dead in some Moscow grave." He paused. "I suspect she knew I'd have a better chance alone."

Liz took a long breath. With the stationery in one hand, and the sunflowers on the palm of the other, she bent her head and read. The letter recounted the ordinary life of an ordinary woman living on a small pension in a tiny Moscow flat. "I've enclosed three pressed sunflowers, my love," the letter finished, "to remind you of our happy times together. You are in my arms forever."

Liz gazed a moment longer at the dried blossoms,

now the color of desert sand. She folded the letter and slid the flowers back inside.

Arkady looked at her alertly, as if hoping she would say something that would rectify whatever had happened, what he feared might happen.

"It's obvious Nina loves you a lot," she told him. "Surely she can join you now."

"It's impossible."

She frowned. "I don't understand what's going on."

"Nina and I decided before I left that if either of us ever suspected our mail was being read, we'd write that we were enclosing three sunflowers. Some snooper must've thought they'd fallen out, so he covered himself by adding them. The mistake confirms what Nina surmised, and it fits with this." He gestured at the damage around them. "I thought I was being followed yesterday and today. The vandalism proves he's here. And it's a message that he can have someone in Moscow scrub Nina to punish me if I try to escape now. He knows I know that."

Liz remembered an official statement during the Communist show trial of Boris Arsov, a Bulgarian defector: *The hand of justice is longer than the legs of the traitor.* A few months later, Arsov was found dead in his prison cell. The Kremlin had been relentless about liquidating anyone who escaped. Even today, some former operatives prowled the globe for those they felt had betrayed the old Soviet Union.

"You expect him to kill you," she said woodenly.

"You must go, Liz. I accept my fate."

"Who is this man?"

"A KGB assassin called Oleg Olenkov. He's a master of impersonation and recruiting the unsuspecting. Even after the Soviet Union dissolved, he hunted me.

So I decided to become Arkady Albam—I thought he'd never look for me in academia. But for him, eliminating me is personal." He peered at her. "My name is actually Dmitri Garnitsky. I was a dissident. Those were desperate times. Do you really want to hear?"

"Tell me." Liz's eyes traveled from window to door and back again. "Quickly." As her gaze returned to Arkady, a small, strange smile vanished from his face. A smile she had never seen. For an uncomfortable instant, she was suspicious.

Day after day in the bitter winter of 1983, Moscow's gray sky bled snow through the few hours of light into the black well of night. From their flat, Dmitri and Nina Garnitsky could hear the caged wolves in the zoo howl. Across the city, vodka poured until bottles were empty. Meanwhile in Europe, Washington was deploying Pershing missiles aimed at the Soviet Union. A sense of helpless desolation shrouded Moscow, escalating the usual paranoia. The Kremlin became so convinced of a surprise nuclear attack that it not only secretly ordered the KGB to plan a campaign of letter bombs against Western leaders but also to immediately erase Moscow's dissident movement.

Dmitri was the city's ringleader. Still, he managed to evade surveillance and disappear for a week to print anti-Soviet pamphlets on an old press hidden in a tunnel beneath the sprawling metropolis. Nina was with him in the early hours before sunrise of that last day, making fresh cups of strong black tea to keep them awake.

Suddenly Sasha Penofsky hurtled in, snow flying off his muskrat *shapka* hat and short wool coat. "The KGB has surrounded our building!"

"Tell us." Dmitri pulled Nina close. She trembled in his arms.

"That KGB animal, Oleg Olenkov, is under specific orders to get you, Dmitri. When he couldn't find you, he decided to go ahead and arrest our people. They took everyone to Lubyanka." He swallowed hard. "And there's more. The KGB wants you so much that they brought in a specialist to wipe you. He's an assassin with a reputation for never failing. They call him the Carnivore."

Nina stared at Dmitri, her face white. "You can't wait. You have to leave *now*."

"She's right, Dmitri!" Sasha turned on his heel and ran. He had his own escape plans. No one knew them, just as no one knew Dmitri's. It was safer that way.

"I'll tell them where your cell met, darling." Nina's voice broke. "I'll be fine." They would interrogate and release her in hopes they could find him through her. But if they believed she was also a subversive, her life would be at risk, too.

His heart breaking, they rushed down the tunnel. He shoved up a manhole cover, and she climbed out. His last sight of her was her worn galoshes hurrying away through the alley's fresh snow.

Dmitri paced the tunnel five minutes. Then he accelerated off through the bleak dawn, too, carrying a lunch pail like any good worker. The cold pierced to his marrow. Little Zhigulis and Moskvich cars roared past, a stream of bloodred taillights. He watched nervously. He knew Olenkov by sight but had never heard of the Carnivore.

On the other side of Kalininsky Bridge, he was running down steps toward a pedestrian underpass when the skin on the back of his neck suddenly puckered.

He glanced back. Walking behind were a young couple, an older man with a briefcase and two more men alone, each carrying lunch pails like his. One had a mustache; the other was clean-shaven. All were strangers.

When an evergreen hedge appeared on his right, he yanked open a wooden gate and slipped into a small park beside an apartment building for the privileged *nomenklatura*. The skeletal branches of a giant linden tree spread overhead like anemic veins. He grabbed a snow-covered lawn chair, carried it to the trunk and jumped onto the chair. Reaching up to a hole in the trunk, he pawed through icy layers of leaves until he found his waterproof bundle. In it were rubles, rare U.S. greenbacks and a good fake passport.

But as he pulled it out, Dmitri heard the quiet *click* of the gate. He stiffened. Turned awkwardly—and looked at a pistol with a sound suppressor aimed steadily at him. Pulse hammering, he raised his gaze, saw the mustache. The gunman was one of the workers behind him in the underpass.

"You are Dmitri Garnitsky." The man spoke Russian with a slight accent and stood with feet planted apart for balance, knees slightly bent. About six feet tall, he was muscular but not heavy, with a bland, expressionless face and nearly colorless eyes. There was something predatory about him that had nothing to do with his weapon.

Dmitri tried to think. *"Nyet.* I don't know—"

Abruptly, the gate swung open again. The gunman tensed, and his head moved fractionally, watching as the notorious Olenkov marched in, impressive in his mink *shapka* hat and black cashmere overcoat. He was taller and broader—and smiling. He unbuttoned his coat and removed a pistol, which he, too, pointed at Dmitri.

"Very good," he told the first man. "You've found him." Then to Dmitri: "Come along, Comrade Garnitsky." He held up handcuffs. "We'll make a good show of it. A lesson for others who would harm our Soviet."

Dmitri climbed off the chair and tucked the packet under his arm. "Why bother with handcuffs? You want me dead to scare the others into recanting publicly before you send them to the gulags. You'll kill me here anyway."

"That's almost true," Olenkov said easily. "But I see no reason to make myself sweat carrying you. And my specialist was not hired to lug corpses. No, it makes much more sense to shoot you at the van where there'll be witnesses that you resisted."

The other man's head whipped around. Expressionless, he studied Olenkov.

Dmitri's rib cage clenched. Olenkov's words thundered in his mind "—my *specialist* was not *hired*." The other man must be the Carnivore.

"What about my wife?" Dmitri demanded.

"I'll deal with her later." Olenkov gestured with his weapon and ordered the other man, "Bring him!"

The Carnivore did not move. "A man in my business must be careful." His tones were quiet, commanding. "You're the only one who was to know who I am, yet you had me followed."

"So?" Olenkov asked impatiently.

"I never do wet work in public." His eyelids blinked slowly as he considered the KGB officer. "Never on the street. Never where there are witnesses who can identify me. My security rules are absolute. You knew what they were." It seemed almost as if he was giving Olenkov a chance to come to his senses. "I work alone."

But the muscles in Olenkov's jaw bunched. His face

tightened. "Not this time!" he snapped. "The chief's in a hurry for Garnitsky's corpse. *Get him!*"

Disgust flashed across the Carnivore's face. His silenced pistol lashed around in a single smooth motion. He fired. *Pop.* The bullet slammed into Olenkov's overcoat, burning a hole blacker than the black cashmere. Blood and tissue exploded, spraying the gray air pink.

Rage twisted Olenkov's features. As he staggered sideways, he swung his pistol around to aim at the assassin. The Carnivore took two nimble steps and slammed a foot into Olenkov's knee.

The KGB man grunted and toppled onto his back, a black Rorschach blot against the white snow. His pistol fell. He stretched for it. The Carnivore smashed a foot down onto the arm, scooped up the gun, and pocketed it, watching as Olenkov struggled to free himself, to sit up, to fight back. But his face drained of color. His eyes closed. Finally, he lay motionless. Air gusted from his lungs.

Dmitri fought nausea and terror. He waited to be shot, too.

The Carnivore glanced at him, showing no emotion. "The contract on you is canceled." He opened the gate and was gone.

For a long moment, Liz said nothing, suffocated by the past. During the cold war, government officials and private individuals on both sides of the Iron Curtain had alternately used the Carnivore and tried to eliminate him. He was ruthless, a legend. Allegedly, he had only one loyalty—to money. He always worked in disguise, so no one knew what he really looked like, much less his true identity. All of the protocols in the story were accurate.

Still, his appearance in it was too much of a coincidence. Ignoring Arkady's gaze, she lifted the blue envelope, examining it closely against the bright light of the floor lamp. There was no hint of a covert French opening—slitting one end of the envelope then gluing it back together. No sign of a roll-out—Soviet tradecraft using two knitting needles on the flap. And no indication of steam or one of the new chemical compounds.

Breathing shallowly, she lowered the letter. She remembered Arkady's strange smile before he told her the story. "You know the Carnivore is my father, don't you?" she asked.

"How did you figure that out?"

Liz did not respond. Instead, she peered pointedly across the low table to the bulge in his jacket where his right hand remained near his heart. She had to know.

Acknowledging her unspoken question, he used the other hand to push aside the lapel.

Shocked, she stared. As she feared, he held a pistol trained on her. What she had not guessed was that it was hers—her Glock, which had been locked in her bedroom safe. She looked up into the face of the kindly man who was a close friend. A better father. His sweetness had vanished, a mask. Raw hatred burned from his dark eyes.

A fundamental of survival was to adapt. Liz erased emotion from her face. She had to find a way to take him or escape.

"It was the envelope," she told him. "No one opened it before you received it."

He inclined his head once. "Where is the Carnivore?"

"If you know he's my father, then you know he's dead." That was a lie. It was possible he was still alive. When she was CIA, she had discovered his real work when she spotted him in the middle of a wet job in Lisbon. She stopped it, and he promised to let her take him in. But before that could happen, he was apparently killed—yet his body was never found. "Was there any truth in your story?"

"There was a Dmitri and Nina Garnitsky, an Oleg Olenkov and a Carnivore. Olenkov was shot, and Dmitri Garnitsky escaped."

She thought swiftly, trying to understand. Then she remembered his words—*Oleg Olenkov...a master of impersonation and recruiting the unsuspecting*—and everything made a crazed kind of sense: last January, it had been no accident that "Arkady Albam" sat beside her at the faculty meeting. That was the beginning of his campaign to cultivate her, make her vulnerable to him. At some point, he wrote the "Nina" letter, and on Monday, when he claimed to be sick, he drove down to Los Angeles to mail it to himself. Tonight he set her up so she would worry and come to check on him. That was why he had been waiting, with her Glock hidden under his jacket, pointed at the chair where she always sat.

"You're Olenkov!"

His thin lips curved in a smile, pleased with his ruse. Chilled, Liz listened as footsteps sounded faintly, climbing the outside staircase. He had created the envelope and story to distract her, keep her from causing trouble as long as possible because someone else really was coming—but not to terminate him.

She kept her voice calm. "Dmitri Garnitsky, I assume."

Olenkov pulled a 9mm Smith & Wesson from between his back and the chair. Neither it nor her Glock was equipped with a sound suppressor, which told her he had no intention of trying to hide what he planned.

"You think you'll walk away from this," she realized. "I'll bet the sheriff's department will find my place was tossed, too, so you can tell them that I was carrying my Glock for protection. That I'd found out somehow that Oleg Olenkov was hunting me because he couldn't get revenge on my father." She was beginning to have a sense the envelope and story were a test of her, too.

He chuckled, pleased with the results of his operation. "You have given me my answer—the daughter is confirmed as a worthy substitute for the father. Naturally you must defend yourself. In the end, sadly, you and Dmitri will have wiped each other. I'll be very convincing when I talk to the authorities."

A trickle of sweat slid down her spine. "But what you're angry about happened long ago. No one cares anymore!"

"*I* care! I nearly *died*. I spent two years in hospital! Then when I was finally able to go back to work, they demoted me because of Garnitsky's escape. My career was over. My life was ruined. They *laughed* at me!"

The most powerful psychological cause of violent behavior was the feeling of being slighted, rejected, insulted, humiliated—any of which could convey the ultimate provocation: the person was inferior, insignificant, a nobody. Olenkov was a venomous and volatile man, probably with an inferiority complex, who could easily act irrationally and against his own interests—including relating tonight's tale, in which he appeared to be both arrogant and incompetent.

"You have no reason to feel ashamed," Liz tried.

"*I did nothing wrong*. It was all your goddamn father's—"

There was a knock on the door. It sounded like a jackhammer in the small apartment.

Olenkov rose lithely and walked sideways away, never moving the aim of the Glock from her. He lowered the S&W and unlocked the door, then retraced his steps. He sat again, pointing the S&W at her now, while he trained the Glock on the doorway.

"Come in!" he called.

The door opened, and fresh salt-tinged air gusted inside. A man stood on the threshold, the drab night sky and distant stars framing him.

"Liz Sansborough?" He had a Russian accent. "I got a note to come—" He saw the pistols. His soft blue eyes darkened with fear. His boxy shoulders twitched as if he was preparing to bolt.

Liz recognized him. He was a historian from the University of Iowa, not using the name Dmitri Garnitsky. He had a flat, tired face and large hands. Dressed in chinos and a tan corduroy sports jacket, he was probably in his late forties.

"Don't try it," Olenkov warned. "I'll shoot before you finish your first step away. Come in and close the door."

Dmitri hesitated, then moved warily inside. Gazing at Olenkov, he shoved the door shut with the heel of a tennis shoe. For a moment, puzzlement replaced his fear.

"Who are you? What do you want?" Dmitri peered quickly at Liz.

"You don't recognize me?" Olenkov asked.

"Your voice maybe."

Olenkov laughed loudly. "I didn't recognize you either until I saw you walk. It's a rule—never forget how a person moves." He looked him over carefully. "The CIA has taken good care of you. I had plastic surgery, too."

Olenkov's reaction was a classic example of the compelling nature of deep shame. It not only inflamed, it consumed. He was engrossed in Dmitri, hanging on every word, milking pleasure from every shock, every surprise—which was the distraction she needed. She gazed swiftly around, searching for a weapon, a way to disarm him. She checked the cast-iron floor lamp just behind the little table between Olenkov and her.

Dmitri seemed to shrink. "Oleg Olenkov." His voice rose. "You bastard. Where's Nina? You've done nothing to Nina!"

Olenkov laughed again. "I have something more important for you—this is the Carnivore's daughter, Liz Sansborough. You remember the Carnivore—your savior?"

Liz leaned toward the tall lamp, hoping Dmitri would recognize what she had in mind. She rested her right elbow on the arm of her chair. From here, she would be able to reach up and back with both hands and pull the lamp's heavy pole down onto Olenkov's skull.

But Dmitri gave no indication he understood. He returned his focus to Olenkov and announced, "The Carnivore didn't save me. Your *stupidness* did!"

Everything happened in seconds. Olenkov jerked erect as if someone had just stretched his spine. Without a word, he glanced at each of them and leveled the guns.

As Liz's hands shot up and yanked down the lamp, Olenkov saw her. He ducked and squeezed the triggers. The noise was explosive, rocking the walls. The iron pole struck the left side of his head hard. Blood streamed down his cheek as the lampshade cartwheeled and the pole landed and bounced.

Liz's side erupted in pain. She had been hit. As the assassin shook his head once, clearing it, she snatched the closer gun. And hesitated, dizzy. She collapsed back against the other arm of the chair, taking deep breaths.

Across the room, Dmitri slumped against the wall. A red tide spread across his tan jacket from a bloody shoulder wound. His eyes were large and overbright, strangely excited, as if he had awakened from a long nightmare. Swearing a long stream of Russian oaths, he peeled away and hurled himself at Olenkov.

But Olenkov raised the Glock again. Liz kicked, ramming her foot into his fingers. The pistol flew. His arm swung wide.

Dmitri slammed the heels of both hands into Olenkov's shoulders. The chair crashed backward. As they fell with it, Dmitri dropped his knees onto Olenkov's chest, pinning him. Like a vise, his big hands snapped shut around Olenkov's neck.

Olenkov swung up a fist, but Dmitri dodged and squeezed harder. Olenkov clawed at the hands that crushed his throat. He gasped. He flushed pink, then red. Sweat popped out on his face.

Liz exhaled, fighting the pain in her side. With effort, she focused on Dmitri, a man fueled by years of rage and fear, by terror for Nina's safety. His mouth twisting, he glared down into Olenkov's eyes, cursing him loudly again, his iron grip tightening. He shook the throat, and Olenkov's head rocked. He laughed as Olenkov's eyes bulged.

Liz forced herself up. Resting the pistol on her chair's arm, she pointed it at Dmitri's temple. "Stop! *Let him go.* He can't hurt us now!"

Dmitri gave no sign he heard. He continued to strangle Olenkov, while Olenkov's chest heaved.

"Dammit, *stop,* Dmitri! The sheriff's department

will arrest him. You'll be able to fly to Moscow. You can be with Nina!"

At Nina's name, Dmitri went rigid. His curses turned to mutters. Still, his hands remained locked around the assassin's neck, and his knees crushed the man's chest. Olenkov's eyes were closed, but his raw rasps told her he was alive. The awful sound of approaching death filled her mind. Her husband, her mother and many of her colleagues had died violently. She wondered how she managed to survive. Maybe she was the one in the nightmare.

She clasped her wound and worked to strip the anger and pain from her voice. "You and Nina have a real chance. I'd give a lot to have the chance you have."

At last, Dmitri's shoulders relaxed. As he stood and walked away from the unconscious Olenkov, his upper lip rose with distaste. He did not look at Olenkov.

Sickened by Olenkov, disgusted by her misjudgment, she turned away from Olenkov, too.

In the distance, sirens screeched. Dmitri lifted his chin, listening as they drew near. "When Nina was born, I was in hiding. My wife's parents raised her. She is twenty-three now." He paused. "My fault. I wanted to know about her so bad that I finally wrote her last year. That is probably how he traced me."

Liz's breath caught in her throat. "So Nina is—?"

"My daughter." Dmitri smiled a brilliant smile. "Thank you."

He headed for the door and opened it. Behind him, the night sky that had seemed so drab now shone like ebony. The once-distant stars sparkled brightly.

Gingerly, he touched his wound. "Not bad. How are you?"

"I'll live. Olenkov told me Nina was your wife."

His hand fell from his shoulder. Pain torqued his flat features. "Her name was Natalia. Olenkov terminated her."

"How horrible. I'm sorry." So Olenkov had lied about that, too. "Are you sure my father didn't do it?"

He shook his head. "As soon as the Carnivore found us, Olenkov scrubbed my wife. That pissed off the Carnivore. He said he was hired for wet jobs on criminals—not dissidents. So when the bastard tried to scrub me, too, the Carnivore shot him."

Liz stared. Her father had saved Dmitri? She felt a strange kind of awe. She had always accepted the government's version of the Carnivore's career as an assassin. But then, he had never said anything to make her think otherwise. What else had she missed?

"He sneaked me out of the Soviet Union," Dmitri continued. "We almost got caught twice. We walked three days across terrible ice and snow into Finland." He swallowed and looked away. "They say he was a killer, but he was very good to me."

As if it were yesterday, pieces of her childhood returned. Liz remembered holding her father's hand as they laughed and he led her in a race across the Embankment. Their long conversations as they sat cozily alone to drink tea. The gentle way he brushed away her hair to kiss her cheek. She might have been wrong about him. What else had she missed? For her, the hunt had just begun.

MICHAEL PALMER & DANIEL PALMER

In 1982, Michael Palmer, then a practicing E.R. physician on Cape Cod, exploded on the literary scene with his first thriller, *The Sisterhood*, which made the *New York Times* bestseller list and was translated into thirty-three languages. Since then, he has written nine more thrillers of medical suspense. Palmer attended Wesleyan University with Robin Cook, and the two of them performed their residencies at Boston's Massachusetts General Hospital at the same time. Later, Michael Crichton's work and Cook's success with *Coma* inspired Palmer to write and, between the three writers, the genre of medical suspense became firmly established.

Palmer sees the thriller as distinct from classic detective stories. Two of his favorites are William Goldman's *Marathon Man* and James Grady's *Six Days of the Condor*. In Palmer's thrillers, his protagonists are drawn into the story because of something they do professionally. They are not detectives and are not out to solve mysteries. Rather, their goals are simply to be the best physicians they can be. They're usually pulled into the story against their wills and eventually must defeat the forces impinging on their lives, or be destroyed in the process. Of course, along the way, a catharsis occurs, but what also distinguishes Palmer's work is a frightening aspect that leaves readers wondering if such a thing could actually happen to them.

Palmer has never before collaborated with another writer on a project, but *Disfigured* is co-authored with Daniel James Palmer, the middle of his three sons. Daniel is a professional songwriter, musician and software manager. *Disfigured* was actually Daniel's brainchild. And although Maura, the protagonist, is not a physician, the theme is medical, and like most of Michael Palmer's main characters, she's drawn unwillingly into the story.

DISFIGURED

We have your son. The picture enclosed is not a fake, this is not a hoax, and we cannot be bought. If you want to see your son alive again you will read this letter carefully and follow our instructions precisely.

At 4:00 p.m., on June 23, you have face-lift surgery scheduled on your patient, Audra Meadows, of 144 Glenn Cherry Lane, Bel-Air. During the procedure, you will inject 5cc of isopropyl alcohol around the facial nerve on both sides of her face. The resulting paralysis of her facial muscles must be complete and irreversible. If you fail, if she can lift even the corner of her mouth, you will never see your son again.

A copy of this note and photo has been placed on David's bed for your wife to find. Do not alert the authorities or anyone else. Choose to do so and you have sealed David's fate.

Dr. George Hill, the plastic surgeon to the stars, slumped down onto the cool marble of his foyer, his heart pounding. Just minutes before, the persistent ringing of the doorbell had awoken him. The manila envelope was propped against the front door.

Hill pushed himself up and studied the photo of his son. David's hair was shorter than when he saw him last. Was it two months ago? Certainly no more than three. His eyes, always bright and intelligent, were blindfolded. He was sitting on a metal folding chair holding a sign that read:

June 22
2:00 a.m.

2:00 a.m.—just three hours ago. Shakily, Hill made it to the phone in his entertainment center and called his office manager.

"Hi, it's me," he said.

"Gee, even without checking my caller ID I guessed right," Joyce Baker replied. "I suppose 5:00 a.m. gave it away."

Odd hours and interruptions during her limited personal time were her curse for running George Hill's medical practice for fifteen years. He was at the top of the heap of plastic surgeons in southern California, if not the country, and he was determined to remain there.

"Have you given anyone in our office access to the new appointment scheduling program?"

"No," she replied. "I'm the only one with a log-on password."

"Has anyone asked you about any client's appointment? Anyone at all?"

"Absolutely not," Joyce said. "What's this all about? Which client?"

"Oh, it's nothing," he said. "Mrs. G. is scheduled to have some more work done Sunday night at the surgical center, that's all."

"I know that. I scheduled her."

"Well, she thinks a reporter knows about it."

"Goodness. I really don't see how that's—"

"Listen, Joyce, don't worry about it. I'll see you later."

This had to be an inside job, he was thinking, someone in the office or the surgicenter. The nature of his patient's procedures, let alone the precise time they were to be done, were more closely guarded secrets than the formula for Coke. Although she was not an A-list celebrity, Audra was still special to him—his Mona Lisa, his Sistine Chapel. Unlike with his other celebrity triumphs, he hadn't once leaked to the press that he was the artist behind her remarkable, enduring beauty.

He paced about his Malibu mansion for a time before working up the nerve to call Maura. As his ex-wife, she, above all, would understand the moral dilemma in which he had been placed, and as David's mother, she had the right to share in the decision that could have her son dead in less than two days.

Maura Hill pounded along Overland Avenue, pushing harder with each step. *A few more minutes, baby,* she gasped. *A few more minutes.* After years of all work and no exercise, she had begun running, then running long distances. Now she was hoping not only to run the L.A. marathon, but also to qualify for a number. However, her dream might have to wait. David's grades and his attitude had been slipping at school lately—too much MTV and guitar, his teachers had said, to say nothing of the hormonal chaos of being fourteen. To that list Maura could add: not enough father. She knew David's potential, and was hoping that she might show him by example how hard work and perseverance could pay off. Next year, maybe. Right now he needed a supportive, present parent.

Maura ran along the paved walkway to the three-bedroom cape where she and David lived. The house was quiet. As usual, her kid would take some major prodding to get up for school, but he would have to get up now if he wanted a ride. She had an early faculty meeting at Caltech where she taught computer science.

The ringing phone startled her. George's number came up on the caller ID. "Bastard," she instinctively muttered to herself. She had come to accept the fact that, after he discovered his remarkable talent for plastic surgery, he became totally self-absorbed and a lousy, philandering husband, but having him honestly believe that dinner or a ball game every couple of months equaled being a good father was too much.

"Hello, George," she said coolly.

Maura listened intently and blanched as Hill spoke. Still holding the phone, she sprinted down the hallway toward David's room. *It's not possible,* she thought. She had kissed David good-night before she went to bed. He couldn't possibly be gone. She opened the door to David's room and gasped. The unmade bed was empty, and his window wide-open. The curtains fluttered like ghosts in the early-morning light.

"Who is she?" Maura shouted, bursting into her ex-husband's elegant Beverly Hills office.

Hill, who was slouched on a chair in his waiting room, drinking whiskey out of a tumbler, barely lifted his head.

"Her name is Audra Meadows," he said, finishing the whiskey and pouring another. "She's been a patient of mine for years. David's only been gone for a few hours, Maura. Shouldn't we call the police?"

"You read the note."

"Then what should we do?"

"First of all, *we* should stop drinking ourselves into oblivion so our brains can at least function with some clarity. I want to see that woman's file."

"But doctors are sworn—"

"Jesus Christ, George! Give me her file or I swear I'll trash this office until I find it. This is our son!"

Hill retrieved Meadows's record from his fireproof vault and handed it over. Maura's eyes widened as she looked through twelve years of surgical notes and photos—the usual Hollywood tucks and augments on her body, plus eight or nine procedures on her face. Even prior to the first of those, Audra Meadows was a strikingly beautiful woman. Her naturally high cheekbones were what others craved. Her almond eyes were a deep green, exotic and alluring. She was, quite simply, a version of perfection. And yet with each subsequent procedure, imperceptible unless the photos were viewed in sequence, Hill had preserved and even improved upon her vibrant, ageless visage.

"Why on earth was she a client?" Maura asked.

"Like many of my patients, Audra sees in herself imperfections others don't."

Maura grimaced. Such vanity.

"So, who would want to hurt this Audra person so badly that they'd be willing to kill my son—I'm sorry, I mean *our* son?"

George shrugged.

"Somebody envious of her looks?"

"Or of your skill. Perhaps they're trying to ruin you."

"I've thought about that. This is a competitive business—especially in this town."

Maura's eyes narrowed.

"George, if it comes to saving our son, you are going to do what they're asking, aren't you? You will do the injection."

Her ex hesitated.

"That procedure will paralyze her facial muscles forever," he said. "Even if I do it there's no guarantee they'll let David live."

"But we have no choice!" Maura screamed. "Can't you do it now and fix it later? You're the fucking surgeon to the stars!"

George slammed his hands against his desk.

"What don't you understand about forever? Jesus, Maura, if I do what they want, and I get caught, I'll be reported to the medical board and never practice again. I'll be sued and lose everything."

"You self-centered bastard!"

"I know this is hard for you to understand, but all I've ever wanted since my rotation in med school is to be a plastic surgeon. It goes against everything I believe to intentionally destroy a person's face. I think we should go to the police."

Her eyes flared.

"You do that, and I swear I'll find a way to ruin you myself. Don't worry," she added, scooping up Audra's file, "I'll find David before you're forced to put your precious reputation up against his life."

She slammed his office door with such force the frosted glass shattered.

Maura left George's office aware that somebody might be watching to ensure she didn't involve the police. It was still before rush hour and there were few cars on the street. None seemed suspicious. Shaking from fear and rage, she drove about a mile west before pulling over at a red light. There, she rested her head against the steering wheel and allowed herself to cry. She was an egghead—a usually gentle scholar, not a woman of action. Now she would have to change, and change in a hurry.

Composing herself, Maura peered into the rearview mirror and noticed a gray Cadillac a few cars away. Its lights were on. Hadn't she seen the same car outside George's office just minutes ago? Her heart started racing. Had George's call to her been tapped? Were the kidnappers watching her right now? Maura slowly eased back into traffic. Seconds later the Cadillac pulled out and followed just a few cars behind. It was impossible to read the plates. Fumbling in her purse, she grabbed her cell phone and dialed.

"Hello," answered a familiar voice.

"Hack, thank God you're there."

Taylor "Hack" Burgess was one of her students at Caltech—a Ph.D. candidate specializing in nanotechnology, the creation of submicroscopic electronic sensors with limitless possibilities. A fellow grad student once claimed that the brilliant, spectral, antisocial Burgess put the "eek!" in geek. His potential was infinite, assuming he could keep out of jail. His passion was the source of his nickname, and Maura was constantly chastising him for hacking into supposedly inaccessible systems. Burgess called it research.

"Hack, listen carefully," Maura said urgently. "I can't explain why, but I need you to do some research for me."

"For you, anything."

She gave him Audra Meadows's name, address and date of birth, and added, "I need to know anything and everything you can find out about her. Has she been arrested? Been in court? Chaired fund-raisers? Gotten honored? Anything at all. Get into any system you can think of. It's urgent."

"Aren't you going to tell me to be careful?"

"Do whatever you have to."

Maura checked the rearview. The car remained behind her. The sun, still low in the sky, made it impossible to get a good look at the driver. She stopped at a red light on Wiltshire. Her fingers were white on the steering wheel. *I can't be this close and not know.*

She grabbed her cell phone, took one deep breath and charged out of her car just as the light turned green. Horns blared as she raced back toward the Cadillac. She was able to see the silhouette of the driver now, but couldn't distinguish anything except a baseball cap and possibly sunglasses. As she approached, the Cadillac's tires screeched and the car lunged forward, smashing into an Acura, which spun forty-five degrees and rammed a VW.

Maura froze as the Cadillac then squealed into reverse and slammed into the car behind. There was the sickening crunch of metal and the car's air bag deployed. The Cadillac then made a sharp left into oncoming traffic. Cars spun out in all directions. Moments later the Caddy had disappeared down Wiltshire. Stunned, Maura reached for her phone. Hack answered on the third ring.

"Gray Cadillac. License plate California AZ3 something. That's all I got. Find a match."

From a distance she could hear sirens approaching.

She used the time before the cruisers arrived to concoct a story of a stalled engine in her car, and road rage on the part of the driver of the Caddy.

Over the hours that followed, Maura was constantly checking to see if she was being followed. Finally, she decided to go to a hotel rather than to chance that her home phone or the house, itself, was bugged. She sent a note to George by messenger, instructing him to speak to no one, and to call her on her hotel-room phone from a pay phone. If she was being overly paranoid, so be it.

George had nothing new to report. Maura held her breath and asked again if he was prepared to honor the kidnappers' demand that he disfigure Audra Meadows.

"We can't let it come to that," was all he would say. "We just can't."

She slammed down the receiver and called Hack.

"What have you learned?" she asked.

"A few things. It took a while for me to penetrate the DMV. They must have a new security guy. Their mistake was upgrading their SQL database to SP4 and that gave me the opening I needed."

"Hack, I don't care how you did it, in fact it's better I don't know. Just tell me what you've got."

"Okay. There are over three thousand California license plates that start with AZ3."

Maura's heart sank.

"Damn."

"Of those, I found less than twenty-five on Cadillacs. Half are owned by rental-car companies, the other half are residential, and none in the Los Angeles area."

"We're dead."

"Not so fast. Rather than risk a trace, I used the good ol' phone and dialed Avis and Hertz."

Maura perked up.

"Go on."

"I pretended to be the police, inquiring about a hit-and-run. Anyway, it appears we have ourselves a bit of a coincidence. Yesterday the Avis by LAX rented their 2005 gray Cadillac to someone from Meadows Productions. It's Alec Meadows's company. I checked."

Bingo! Alec Meadows. Infidelity? Audra threatening to leave him? Whatever the reason, he so badly wanted to hurt his wife that he was willing to threaten David's life. But was he willing to carry out the threat?

Maura crouched behind a row of well-manicured hedges and scanned the Meadows estate through binoculars. She had arrived shortly after sunset and was now wondering if she should just chance calling the police. The place was vast, set well away from the main road, and surrounded by dense woods. It was possible David was inside. If not, she was hoping for some clue as to where he might be.

The fieldstone house was like a castle, with a three-car garage that might have once been a carriage house. Hack had given her a profile of Alec Meadows from data he gleaned off of several sources. Meadows made his fortune in entertainment, producing schlock teen horror movies and several successful TV shows. He had no criminal record. The marriage to Audra was his first, her second. They had no children.

We have your son.

We. Could that be significant? Who might be working with Alec Meadows? Had he hired professionals? Maura struggled to make sense of it all. Alec could have just as easily hired a thug to cut up his wife. Why risk a kidnapping? Then it hit her again. Maybe

Audra wasn't the real target after all. Maybe the real target was George.

The glow of approaching headlights pierced the darkness. Hack was prepared to drive out and sabotage the security system so she could get into the house, but now he might not have to. Maura darted across the drive and dived into the bushes nearest the garage. Moments later the center door lifted and a large black Mercedes drove inside. Maura waited until the garage door was almost closed, then rolled underneath it, continuing until she was under the rear of the car. The exhaust pipe singed her arm. She was biting down on her lip to keep from crying out in pain when the Mercedes's doors opened and two sets of legs stepped out.

"Put this on, Audra, you bitch. Come to me when I am ready." The voice was unwavering, commanding, and filled with rage.

"Of course, Alec," she responded in a shallow whisper.

Maura remained motionless until she was certain they had gone inside. Then she climbed the short staircase and inched open the door to the house. She was in a dark hallway from which she could see into the kitchen. A figure opened the refrigerator door, casting an eerie shadow. Moments later, he left. His footsteps echoed through the cavernous home as he walked upstairs. Maura entered the kitchen, her eyes quickly adjusting to the dark.

She moved stealthily into the dimly lit living room. Her plan was to hide until they were both asleep, and then to begin her search in the basement. If there was some sort of motion-sensitive alarm, she would have to improvise.

Suddenly, there were footsteps at the top of the massive staircase. Her pulse hammering, Maura scrambled behind the sofa and flattened out. Alec entered the living room and turned up the recessed lighting over the fireplace. He was no more than ten feet from where she lay. Two paces to his right and he would be staring right at her.

Maura could now see into the dining room through an open archway. The huge table was draped almost to the floor in an off-white tablecloth, and featured a magnificent centerpiece of freshly cut flowers.

"Audra, get down here!" Alec shouted.

He crossed to the base of the stairs.

Now! Go! Maura commanded herself.

Soundlessly, she crawled to the table and slid between two massive chairs and under the cloth. By pressing her cheek against the plush Oriental rug, she could peer out through a three-inch gap. She saw Alec's bare feet enter the room, followed closely by his wife's.

"You look like a little whore in that outfit," Alec snapped. "I like a slut. I like that a lot."

There was a sharp slap, and Audra cried out.

"Please, Alec, not tonight. I can't."

"You love it, bitch. You know it, and I know it."

There was another slap, this one harder than the last. Audra dropped from the force of the blow, landing just a few feet from where Maura was watching. Their eyes actually could have met, but didn't. The woman was clearly shaken.

"Get up!" Alec demanded. "I'm already hard."

"Alec, please."

Every neuron cried out to save Audra from this monster, but Maura remained in a fetal position underneath the elegant table.

"Get on the table," he commanded. "I love the way you look right now. You're beautiful…so beautiful. Tomorrow, after your surgery, you're going to look even better."

Maura covered her mouth and gasped inwardly. Her calf muscle knotted from the tension and strain of staying in one position. The searing pain felt as though it was being stabbed with a dull knife. She bit her knuckles to keep still and quiet, and to blot from her mind the horror of what was transpiring above her.

For an excruciatingly long time there was no letup in the fury of Alec's attack. Audra's simpering cries had no effect. Finally, there were only the sounds of two people struggling for breath. Alec Meadows's rape of his wife was complete.

If Maura could have killed the man without jeopardizing her son, she well might have. When he was ready, Alec pushed away from the table, fixed his clothing and ambled upstairs. Audra remained where she was for a time, whimpering and totally spent. Maura felt deeply connected to her. Both of them were suffering greatly by Alec Meadows's design.

It was nearly four-thirty when Audra finally headed upstairs. Maura remained concealed. After a few minutes, she cautiously crawled out from under the table and stretched her throbbing calf. Then she conducted a fruitless search of the downstairs and located the door to the basement, which was by the kitchen. The vast, poorly lit space was unfinished concrete, dank and creepy. There were scattered boxes and old furniture, but no sign of David, and nothing that tied Alec to his kidnapping.

Disheartened, Maura considered then rejected the

notion of waiting until the house was empty to search the upstairs. She was heading out when she noticed a door at the far end of the basement. It opened into an unfinished bathroom with a small vanity, sink, mirror and toilet. Inside the vanity she found a blue cosmetics kit containing several plastic vials of pills. Valium, Zoloft, Prozac, Xanax, Effexor—all prescriptions, and all in the name of Audra Meadows. Most of them were empty, but there was a good supply of both Effexor and Xanax. Maura knew those medications well. During and after her divorce, she suffered from depression. Effexor made her feel logy, and highly addictive Xanax was just plain scary. Instead, she opted for late-night TV, counseling and rigorous exercise. Still, it was easy to see why Audra might need medication.

The pills gave Maura something to work with. Assuming Audra was in therapy, her shrink might know about Alec. The problem would be getting the doctor to break professional confidence. Perhaps, she thought, smiling savagely, Dr. Simon Rubenstein had a son.

She glanced at her watch. There were nine hours left. Pocketing one of the empty pill bottles with Rubenstein's office address, she slipped outside through the basement door, and disappeared into the cool mist of the early-morning woods.

Hack left a small shoe box, per Maura's instructions, at the Holiday Inn reception desk. He knew David well and had no trouble honoring her request. Once inside her car, Maura transferred the loaded .38 special to her jacket pocket. Hack, always slightly paranoid and as eccentric as he was brilliant, had a small arsenal hidden around his apartment. In addition to the gun, he had information in the form of printouts regarding Alec Meadows.

Meadows had no actual studio or warehouse in his own name or the name of his company, and his office in downtown L.A. didn't sound like a place David would be kept. Also included was a list of twenty properties in southern California owned by people named A. Meadows. One of them, Hack had circled—perhaps a cabin of some sort, he noted, in the Los Padres National Forest north of Ventura. It was owned by an A. R. Meadows—Alec's initials. She checked a map and estimated the drive there and back would be five hours. There were eight left before the surgery.

Dr. Simon Rubenstein had an unlisted home number, but Hack was working on finding it and his home address. Meanwhile, Maura went to the shrink's office in Hollywood, only a few blocks from George's surgicenter. The building was locked. She could hang around and wait for Rubenstein, or go with the only lead she had—the place in the mountains.

She called George at home, at the office and on his cell, but got only machines. Dr. George Hill, plastic surgeon to the stars, was never out of touch. He was avoiding her, and that meant he was still ambivalent as to what he would do when the moment of truth came. She left testy messages on each of his phones, letting him know in no uncertain terms what his life would be like if anything happened to their son because of him. Then she filled up the tank of her Camry and headed toward the freeway.

It took a stop at a Los Padres Forest ranger station, and some blind luck, but finally, nearly two and a half hours after she left L.A., she pulled onto Eagle's Nest

Road, two miles west of Frazier Park. She had just four and a half hours to find David.

Number 14 was painted on a piece of wood nailed to a tree. The house, a cabin, just as Hack had suspected, was a tiny, ramshackle place with junk in the dirt yard—hardly the sort of property the Meadows were likely to own. Maura parked down the drive and approached through the woods. At the edge of the clearing, she took the .38 from her pocket. At almost the same moment, she felt a gun barrel pressed firmly against the back of her neck.

"Drop it!" a bass voice growled. "Now, turn around. Slowly!"

The gun was a hunting rifle with a telescopic site. The man was huge—six-six at least, with a dense red beard. Maura looked up at him defiantly.

"Where's my son?" she demanded.

"Lady, the only son you'll find around here is mine. Luanne?"

A frumpy woman came into the yard, hand in hand with an unkempt two-year-old.

Maura felt ill.

"Is your name Meadows?" she asked, her voice hoarse and shaky.

"*Ambrose* Meadows if it's any business of yours. Now, what'n the heck are you doin' here?"

One hour.

Devastated that she had rolled the dice with her drive to Los Padres and lost, Maura drove back to L.A. in heavy traffic. Her pistol was back in her jacket pocket. Calls to her ex-husband's various lines brought no response except the answering service.

"Perhaps you forgot," the operator said firmly, "but

Dr. Hill doesn't allow any calls to the surgicenter while he is operating."

Maura groaned. It was the great doctor's crowd-pleasing policy that every patient was his only patient. She made no attempt to threaten the woman, but instead cut into the breakdown lane and sped back to Simon Rubenstein's office building and ran up three floors to his office. A man she assumed was Rubenstein, squat and egg bald with a kind, wise face, was just locking the door behind him.

"Dr. Rubenstein?"

"Yes?"

"I have a gun. Please step back into your office or I swear I'll shoot."

If the psychiatrist was the least bit frightened, it didn't show. He turned the key the other way and held the door open for her. Maura escorted him to his back office and closed the door behind them.

Thirty minutes.

"I don't want to hurt you," she said, "but I need help."

"I don't carry any drugs, but you don't look as if that's your problem."

Maura took out the letter from the kidnappers and handed it to him. He read it thoughtfully.

"I snuck into the Meadows estate and found prescriptions with your name on them. But before that, I was in hiding when Alec Meadows raped his wife. He's behind this. Either he wants to hurt his wife or discredit my ex-husband. She's due to be operated on in just a few minutes, and I don't know where my son is."

She had begun to cry.

"Please put the gun down," Rubenstein said with calm force. "Have you gone to the police?"

"It said not to. I…I thought I could find David before—"

"And do you know if Dr. Hill will disfigure Audra as this note demands?"

"I…I don't know, I really don't. Now, please, the surgery's scheduled to begin in just a few minutes."

"I believe I can help you," Rubenstein said, "but first you must trust me and somehow stop the operation. How fast can you cover four blocks?"

Maura knew that George was as meticulous about his surgical schedule as he was about everything else. Stunned by what Rubenstein had shared with her, Maura vaulted down the stairs of his office three at a time, and out onto the street, dodging through dense pedestrian traffic like a halfback.

It was exactly four when she reached the gleaming glass-and- white-brick surgicenter. The doors were locked, the foyer dark. Without hesitating, she kicked in a plate-glass window, punched out the shards and clambered inside. The operating rooms were at the rear. One was in action.

"Mrs. Hill, you can't go in there," a nurse said as Maura rammed through the O.R. door. It was 4:05. Audra Meadows lay draped on a brilliantly lit table, her face prepped with antiseptic.

George, the Emperor, gowned, masked and gloved, stood beside her, a large syringe poised in his hand. There was another, similar syringe on the stainless-steel instrument tray. One of them probably contained some sort of anesthetic. The other?

"Maura!" he cried. "What the—?"

Ignoring him, she raced over to Audra. The woman's eyes were rheumy from pre-op medication.

"Maura, you can't be in here," George said.

Ignoring him, Maura bent low beside his patient.

"You poor baby," she whispered. "I know what's been happening, Audra. I know and I'm going to help you. Everything is going to be all right. Do you understand?"

"Yes, I...understand."

"Okay. Now tell me, where are you keeping my son?"

George shook his head in disbelief.

"I can't believe Audra Meadows would want to do this to herself."

The police had called with reassurance that a SWAT team had picked up David exactly where Audra said he was being held—in a friend's little-used cottage in the hills above Malibu. The man she hired to do the kidnapping and guard David was under arrest, as was Audra, herself, although a judge had already promised Dr. Rubenstein she would be remanded to his service for a full evaluation.

"Her psychiatrist called it complex post-traumatic stress disorder," Maura explained. "Since well before her marriage she's had a pathologic love/hate relationship with her sadistic husband. He's the one who forced her into having all those surgeries. I guess the years of sexual and mental abuse finally pushed her over the edge. She believed if she were disfigured, Alec would reject her, and then she'd be free. Maybe she just couldn't deal with cutting her own face or even hiring someone to do it, or maybe she thought that with your skill, no scar was permanent."

A young detective entered the room, motioning for George. "Dr. Hill, I need to take a statement from you."

George got up to follow the detective and Maura stopped him.

"George," she said, "you had one syringe in your hand and I saw another on the tray. Were you going to go through with it? Was the one you were holding filled with alcohol?"

George smiled. "Well, Maura, what do you think?" He then turned and walked away.

DAVID MORRELL

The Brotherhood of the Rose is a special book for David Morrell. It was his first *New York Times* bestseller. Later, it was the basis for an NBC miniseries. The "rose" in the title refers to the ancient symbol of secrecy as depicted in Greek mythology. Clandestine councils used to meet with a rose dangling above them and vowed not to divulge what was said *sub rosa*, under the rose. The "brotherhood" refers to two young men, Saul and Chris, who were raised in an orphanage and eventually recruited into the CIA by a man who acted as their foster father. Having spent time in an orphanage himself, Morrell readily identified with the main characters.

When *Brotherhood* was completed, Morrell so missed its world that he wrote a similarly titled thriller, *The Fraternity of the Stone*, in which he introduced a comparable character, Drew MacLane. Still hooked on the theme of orphans and foster fathers (Morrell thinks of this as self-psychoanalysis), he wrote *The League of Night and Fog* in which Saul from the first thriller meets Drew from the second. *Night and Fog* is thus a double sequel that is also the end of a trilogy. Morrell intended to write a further thriller in the series and left a deliberately dangling plot thread that was supposed to propel him into a fourth book. But his fifteen-year-old son, Matthew, died from complications of a rare form of bone cancer known as Ewing's sarcoma. Suddenly, the theme of orphans searching for foster fathers no longer spoke to his psyche. Morrell was now a father trying to fill the void left by a son, a theme later explored in several non-*Brotherhood* novels, especially *Desperate Measures* and *Long Lost*.

These many years later, Morrell still receives a couple of requests a week, wanting to know how the plot thread would have been secured and asking him to write more about Saul. When this anthology was planned, Morrell was specifically asked about a new *Brotherhood* story. He resisted, not wanting to go back to those dark days. But Saul and his wife, Erika, returned to his imagination and refused to leave. The plot thread—an unexplained attack on Saul's village—has been tied. Perhaps both Morrell and his readers will now find closure. There wasn't room to include Drew and his friend, Arlene, but fans will sense them, unnamed, in the background.

One other element is included, too—for what would a *Brotherhood* story be without the Abelard sanction?

THE ABELARD SANCTION

At the start, Abelard safe houses existed in only a half-dozen cities: Potsdam, Oslo, Lisbon, Buenos Aires, Alexandria and Montreal. That was in 1938, when representatives of the world's major intelligence communities met in Berlin and agreed to strive for a modicum of order in the inevitable upcoming war by establishing the principle of the Abelard sanction. The reference was to Peter Abelard, the poet and theologian of the Dark Ages, who seduced his beautiful student Heloise and was subsequently castrated in family retaliation. Afraid for his life, Abelard took refuge in a church near Paris and eventually established a sanctuary called The Paraclete, in reference to the Holy Spirit's role as advocate and intercessor. Anyone who came for help was guaranteed protection.

The modern framers of the Abelard sanction reasoned that the chaos of another world war would place unusual stress on the intelligence operatives within their agencies. While each agency had conventional safe houses, those sanctuaries designated "Abelard" would embody a major extension of the safe house concept. There, in extreme situations, any member of any agency would be guaranteed immunity from harm. These protected areas would have the added benefit of functioning as neutral meeting grounds in which alliances between agencies could be safely negotiated and intrigues formulated. The sanctuaries would provide a chance for any operative, no matter his or her allegiance, to rest, to heal and to consider the wisdom of tactics and choices. Anyone speaking frankly in one of these refuges need not fear that his or her words would be used as weapons outside the protected walls.

The penalty for violating the Abelard sanction was ultimate. If any operative harmed any other operative in an Abelard safe house, the violator was immediately declared a rogue. All members of all agencies would hunt the outcast and kill him or her at the first opportunity, regardless if the transgressor belonged to one's own organization. Because Abelard's original sanctuary was in a church, the framers of the Abelard sanction decided to continue that tradition. They felt that, in a time of weakening moral values, the religious connection would reinforce the gravity of the compact. Of course, the representative from the NKVD was skeptical in this regard, religion having been outlawed in the USSR, but he saw no harm in allowing the English and the Americans to believe in the opiate of the masses.

During the Second World War and the escalating tensions of the subsequent cold war, Abelard sanctuaries proved so useful that new ones were established in Bangkok, Singapore, Florence, Melbourne, Ferlach,

Austria and Santa Fe, New Mexico. The latter was of special note because the United States representative to the 1938 Abelard meeting doubted that the sanction could be maintained. He insisted that none of these politically sensitive, potentially violent sites would be on American soil. But he turned out to be wrong. In an ever more dangerous world, the need for a temporary refuge became greater. In a cynical profession, the honor and strength of the sanction remained inviolate.

Santa Fe means Holy Faith. Abelard would approve, Saul Grisman thought as he guided a nondescript rented car along a dusk-shadowed road made darker by a sudden rainstorm. Although outsiders imagined that Santa Fe was a sun-blistered, lowland, desert city similar to Phoenix, the truth was that it had four seasons and was situated at an altitude of seven thousand feet in the foothills of a range of the Rocky Mountains known as Sangre de Cristo (so-called because Spanish explorers had compared the glow of sunset on them to what they imagined was the blood of Christ). Saul's destination was toward a ridge northeast of this artistic community of fifty thousand people. Occasional lightning flashes silhouetted the mountains. Directions and a map lay next to him, but he had studied them thoroughly during his urgent flight to New Mexico and needed to stop only once to refresh his memory of landmarks that he'd encountered on a mission in Santa Fe years earlier. His headlights revealed a sign shrouded by rain: Camino de la Cruz, the street of the cross. Fingers tense, he steered to the right along the isolated road.

There were many reasons for an Abelard safe house

to have been established near Santa Fe. Los Alamos, where the atomic bomb was invented, was perched on a mountain across the valley to the west. Sandia National Laboratories, a similar research facility important to U.S. security, occupied the core of a mountain an hour's drive south near Albuquerque. Double agent Edward Lee Howard eluded FBI agents at a sharp curve on Corrales Street here and escaped to the Soviet Union. Espionage was as much a part of the territory as the countless art galleries on Canyon Road. Many of the intelligence operatives stationed in the area fell in love with the Land of Enchantment, as the locals called it, and remained in Santa Fe after they retired.

The shadows of piñon trees and junipers lined the potholed road. After a quarter mile, Saul reached a dead end of hills. Through flapping windshield wipers, he squinted from the glare of lightning that illuminated a church steeple. Thunder shook the car as he studied the long, low building next to the church. Like most structures in Santa Fe, its roof was flat. Its corners were rounded, its thick, earth-colored walls made from stuccoed adobe. A sign said, Monastery of the Sun and the Moon. Saul, who was Jewish, gathered that the name had relevance to the nearby mountains called Sun and Moon. He also assumed that in keeping with Santa Fe's reputation as a New Age, crystal-and-feng-shui community, the name indicated this was not a traditional Catholic institution.

Only one car, as dark and nondescript as Saul's, was in the parking lot. He stopped next to it, shut off his engine and headlights, and took a deep breath, holding it for a count of three, exhaling for a count of three. Then he grabbed his over-the-shoulder travel bag, got out, locked the car and hurried through the cold downpour toward the monastery's entrance.

Sheltered beneath an overhang, he tried both heavy-looking wooden doors but neither budged. He pressed a button and looked up at a security camera. A buzzer freed the lock. When he opened the door on the right, he faced a well-lit lobby with a brick floor. As he shut the door, a strong breeze shoved past him, rousing flames in a fireplace to the left. The hearth was a foot above the floor, its opening oval in a style known as kiva, the crackling wood leaning upright against the back of the firebox. The aromatic scent of piñon wood reminded Saul of incense.

He turned toward a counter on the right, behind which a young man in a priest's robe studied him. The man had ascetic, sunken features. His scalp was shaved bare. "How may I help you?"

"I need a place to stay." Saul felt water trickle from his wet hair onto his neck.

"Perhaps you were misinformed. This isn't a hotel."

"I was told to ask for Mr. Abelard."

The priest's eyes changed focus slightly, becoming more intense. "I'll summon the housekeeper." His accent sounded European but was otherwise hard to identify. He pressed a button. "Are you armed?"

"Yes."

The priest frowned toward monitors that showed various green-tinted night-vision images of the rain-swept area outside the building: the two cars in the parking lot, the lonely road, the juniper-studded hills in back. "Are you here because you're threatened?"

"No one's pursuing me," Saul answered.

"You've stayed with us before?"

"In Melbourne."

"Then you know the rules. I must see your pistol."

Saul reached under his leather jacket and carefully withdrew a Heckler & Koch 9mm handgun. He set it on the counter, the barrel toward a wall, and waited while the priest made a note of the pistol's model number (P2000) and serial number.

The priest considered the ambidextrous magazine and slide release mechanisms, then set the gun in a metal box. "Any other weapons?"

"A HideAway knife." Modeled after a Bengal tiger's claw, the HideAway was only four inches long. Saul raised the left side of his jacket. The blade's small black grip was almost invisible in a black sheath parallel to his black belt. He set it on the counter.

The priest made another note and set the knife in the box. "Anything else?"

"No." Saul knew that a scanner built into the counter would tell the priest if he was lying.

"My name is Father Chen," a voice said from across the lobby.

As thunder rumbled, Saul turned toward another man in a priest's robe. But this man was in his forties, Chinese, with an ample stomach, a round face and a shaved scalp that made him resemble Buddha. His accent, though, seemed to have been nurtured at a New England Ivy League university.

"I'm the Abelard housekeeper here." The priest motioned for Saul to accompany him. "Your name?"

"Saul Grisman."

"I meant your code name."

"Romulus."

Father Chen considered him a moment. In the corridor, they entered an office on the right, where the priest took a seat behind a desk and typed on a computer keyboard. He read the screen for a minute, then again looked at Saul, appearing to see him differently. "Romulus was one of the twins who founded Rome. Do *you* have a twin?"

Saul knew he was being tested. "Had. Not a twin. A brother of sorts. His name was…" Emotion made Saul hesitate. "Chris."

"Christopher Kilmoonie. Irish." Father Chen gestured toward the computer screen. "Code name Remus. Both of you were raised in an orphanage in Philadelphia. The Benjamin Franklin School for Boys. A military school."

Saul knew he was expected to elaborate. "We wore uniforms. We marched with toy rifles. All our classes—history, trigonometry, literature, et cetera— were related to the military. All the movies we saw and the games we played were about war."

"What is the motto of that school?"

"'Teach them politics and war so their sons may study medicine and mathematics in order to give their children a right to study painting, poetry, music and architecture.'"

"But that quotation is not from Benjamin Franklin."

"No. It's from John Adams."

"You were trained by Edward Franciscus Eliot," Father Chen said.

Again, Saul concealed his emotions. Eliot had been the CIA's director for counterespionage, but Saul hadn't known that until years later. "When we were five, he came to the school and befriended us. Over the years, he became…I guess you'd call him our foster father, just as Chris and I were foster brothers. Eliot got permission to take us from the school on weekends—to baseball games, to barbecues at his house in Falls Church, Virginia, to dojos where we learned martial arts. Basically, he recruited us to be his personal operatives. We wanted to serve our father."

"And you killed him."

Saul didn't answer for a moment. "That's right. It turned out the son of a bitch had other orphans who were his personal operatives, who loved him like a father and would do anything for him. But in the end he used all of us, and Chris died because of him, and I got an Uzi and emptied a magazine into the bastard's black heart."

Father Chen's eyes narrowed. Saul knew where this was going. "In the process, you violated the Abelard sanction."

"Not true. Eliot was off the grounds. I didn't kill him in a sanctuary."

Father Chen continued staring.

"It's all in my file," Saul explained. "Yes, I raised hell in a refuge. Eventually Eliot and I were ordered to leave. They let him have a twenty-four-hour head start. But I caught up to him."

Father Chen tapped thick fingers on his desk. "The arbiters of the sanction decided that the rules had been bent but not broken. In exchange for information about how Eliot was himself a mole, you were given unofficial immunity as long as you went into exile. You've been helping to build a settlement in Israel. Why didn't you stay there? For God's sake, given your destructive history, how can you expect me to welcome you to an Abelard safe house?"

"I'm looking for a woman."

Father Chen's cheeks flared with indignation. "Now you take for granted I'll supply you with a prostitute?"

"You don't understand. The woman I'm searching for is my wife."

Father Chen scowled toward an item on the computer screen. "Erika Bernstein. A former operative for Mossad."

"The car in the parking lot. Is it hers?"

"No. You said you're *searching* for her?"

"I haven't seen her in three weeks. Does the car belong to Yusuf Habib?"

As thunder again rumbled, Father Chen nodded. "He is a guest."

"Then I expect Erika to arrive very soon, and I'm not here to cause trouble. I'm trying to stop it."

A buzzer sounded. Frowning, Father Chen pressed a button. The image on the monitor changed to a view of the lobby. Saul felt blood rush to his heart as a camera showed Erika stepping from the rain into the lobby. Even in black and white, she was gorgeous, her long dark hair tied back in a ponytail, her cheekbones strong but elegant. Like him, she wore running shoes and jeans, but in place of his leather coat, she had a rain slicker, water dripping from it.

Saul was out of the office before Father Chen could rise from his chair. In the brightly lit lobby, Erika heard Saul's urgently approaching footsteps on the brick floor and swung protectively, hardly relaxing when she saw who it was.

She pointed angrily. "I told you not to come after me."

"I didn't."

"Then what the hell are you doing here?"

"I didn't follow you. I followed *Habib*." Saul turned toward Father Chen. "My wife and I need a place where we can talk."

"The refectory is empty." The priest indicated the

corridor behind them and a door on the left, opposite his office.

Saul and Erika stared at one another. Impatient, she marched past him and through the doorway.

Following, Saul turned on the overhead fluorescent lights. The fixtures hummed. The refectory had four long tables arranged in rows of two. It felt cold. The fish smell of the evening meal lingered. At the back was a counter behind which stood a restaurant-size refrigerator and stainless-steel stove. Next to containers of knives, forks and spoons, there were cups and a half pot of coffee on a warmer. As rain lashed at the dark windows, Saul went over and poured two cups, adding nondairy creamer and the sugarless sweetener Erika used.

He sat at the table nearest her. Reluctant, she joined him.

"Are you all right?" he asked.

"Of course I'm *not* all right. How can you ask that?"

"I meant, are you injured?"

"Oh." Erika looked away. "Fine. I'm fine."

"Except that you're not."

She didn't reply.

"It's not just *your* son who's dead." Saul peered down at his untasted coffee. "He was *my* son, too."

Again, no reply.

"I hate Habib as much as you do," Saul said. "I want to squeeze my hands around his throat and—"

"Bullshit. Otherwise, *you'd* do what *I'm* doing."

"We lost our boy. I'll go crazy if I lose you, also. You know you're as good as dead if you kill Habib here. For breaking the sanction, you won't live another day."

"If I don't kill Habib, I don't *want* to live another day. Is he here?"

Saul hesitated. "So I'm told."

"Then I'll never get a better chance."

"We can go to neutral ground and wait for him to leave. I'll help you," Saul said. "The hills around here make perfect vantage points. Will a shot from a sniper's rifle give you the same satisfaction as seeing Habib die face-to-face?"

"As long as he's dead. As long as he stops insulting me by breathing the same air I breathe."

"Then let's do it."

Erika shook her head from side to side. "In Cairo, I nearly got him. He has a bullet hole in his arm to remind him. For two weeks, he ran from refuge to refuge as cleverly as he could. Then six days ago, his tactics changed. His trail became easier to follow. I told myself that he was getting tired, that I was wearing him down. But when he shifted through Mexico into the southwestern United States, I realized what he was doing. In the Mideast, he could blend. In Santa Fe, for God's sake, Mideasterners are rarely seen. Why would he leave his natural cover? He lured me. He *wants* me to find him here. I'm sure his men are waiting for me outside right now, closing the trap. Habib can't imagine that I'd readily break the sanction, that I'd gladly be killed just so I could take him with me. He expects me to do the logical thing and hide among the trees outside, ready to make a move when he leaves. If I do, his men will attack. *I'll* be the target. Dammit, why didn't you listen to me and stay out of this? Now *you* can't get out of here alive any more than I can."

"I love you," Saul said.

Erika stared down at her clenched hands. Her angry features softened somewhat. "The only person I love more than you is...was...our son."

A voice said, "Both of you must leave."

Saul and Erika turned toward the now-open doorway, where Father Chen stood with his hands behind his robe. Saul had no doubt that the priest concealed a weapon.

A door farther along the refectory wall opened. The ascetic-looking priest from the reception counter stepped into the doorway. He, too, had his hands behind his robe.

Saul took for granted that the refectory had hidden microphones. "You heard Erika. Habib has a trap arranged out there."

"A theory," Father Chen replied. "Not proven. Perhaps she invented the theory to try to force me to let the two of you stay."

"Habib's an organizer for Hamas," Erika said.

"Who or what he works for isn't my concern. Everyone is guaranteed safety here."

"The bastard's a psychologist who recruits suicide bombers." Erika glared. "He runs the damn training centers. He convinces the bombers they'll go to paradise and fuck an endless supply of virgins if they blow themselves up along with any Jews they get near."

"I'm aware of how suicide bombers are programmed," Father Chen said. "But the sanctity of this Abelard safe house is all that matters to me."

"Sanctity?" Saul's voice rose. "What about the sanctity of our *home?* Four weeks ago, one of Habib's maniacs snuck into our settlement and blew himself up in the market. Our home's near the market. Our son…" Saul couldn't make himself continue.

"Our son," Erika said in a fury, "was killed by a piece of shrapnel that almost cut off his head."

"You have my sincerest and deepest sympathy," Father Chen said. "But I cannot allow you to violate the sanction because of your grief. Take your anger outside."

"I will if Habib calls off his men," Erika said. "I don't care what happens to me, but I need to make sure nothing happens to Saul."

Thunder rumbled.

"I'll convey your request," Father Chen said.

"No need." The words came from a shadow in the corridor.

Saul felt his muscles tighten as a sallow face appeared behind Father Chen. Habib was heavyset, with thick dark hair, in his forties, with somber eyebrows and intelligent features. He wore dark slacks and a thick sweater. His left arm was in a sling.

Keeping the priest in front of him, Habib said, "I, too, am sorry about your son. I think of victims as statistics. Anonymous casualties. How else can war be waged? To personalize the enemy is to invite defeat. But it always troubles me when I read about individuals, children, who die in the bombings. *They* didn't take away our land. *They* didn't institute laws that treat us as inferiors."

"Your sympathy almost sounds convincing," Erika said.

"When I was a child, my parents lived in Jerusalem's old city. Israeli soldiers patrolled the top of the wall that enclosed the area. Every day, they pissed down onto our vegetable garden. Your politicians have continued to piss on us ever since."

"Not me," Erika said. "I didn't piss on anybody."

"Change conditions, give us back our land, and the bombing will stop," Habib said. "That way, the lives of other children will be saved."

"I don't care about those other children." Erika stepped toward him.

"Careful." Father Chen stiffened, about to pull his hands from behind his robe.

Erika stopped. "All I care about is my son. *He* didn't piss on your vegetables, but you killed him anyhow. Just as surely as if you'd set off the bomb yourself."

Habib studied her as a psychologist might assess a disturbed patient. "And now you're ready to sacrifice the lives of both you and your husband in order to get revenge?"

"No." Erika swelled with anger. "Not Saul. He wasn't supposed to be part of this. Contact your men. Disarm the trap."

"But if you leave here safely, you'll take their place," Habib said. "You'll wait for me to come outside. You'll attack me."

"I'll give you the same terms my husband gave his foster father. I'll give you a twenty-four-hour head start."

"Listen to yourself. You're on the losing side, but somehow you expect me to surrender my position of strength."

"Strength?" Erika pulled down the zipper on her rain slicker. "How's this for strength?"

Habib gasped. Father Chen's eyes widened. Saul took a step forward, getting close enough to see the sticks of dynamite wrapped around Erika's waist. His pulse rushed when he saw her right thumb reach for a button attached to a detonator. She held it down.

"If anybody shoots me, my thumb goes off the button, and all of us go to heaven, except I don't want any virgin women," Erika said.

"Your husband will die."

"He'll die anyhow as long as your men are outside. But this way, you'll die also. How does it feel to be on the receiving end of a suicide bomb? I don't know how long my thumb can keep pressing this button. When will my hand start to cramp?"

"You're insane."

"As insane as you and your killers. The only good thing about what you do is you make sure those nutcases don't breed. For Saul, I'll give you a chance. Get the hell out of here. Take your men with you. Disarm the trap. You have my word. You've got twenty-four hours."

Habib stared, analyzing her rage. He spoke to Father Chen. "If she leaves before the twenty-four hours have elapsed…"

"She won't." Father Chen pulled a pistol from behind his robe.

"To help me, you'd risk being blown up?" Habib asked the priest.

"Not for you. For this safe house. I pledged my soul."

"My thumb's beginning to stiffen," Erika warned.

Habib nodded. Erika and Saul followed him along the corridor to his room. Guarded by the priests, they waited while he packed his suitcase. He carried it to the reception area, moving awkwardly because of his wounded shoulder. There, he used a phone on the counter, pressing the speaker button, touching numbers with the index finger of his uninjured right arm.

Saul listened as a male voice answered with a neutral, "Hello." Rain made a staticky sound in the background.

"I'm leaving the building now. The operation has been postponed."

"I need the confirmation code."

"'Santa Fe is the City Different.'"

"Confirmed. Postponed."

"Stay close to me. I'll require you again in twenty-four hours."

Habib pressed the disconnect button and scowled

at Erika. "The next time, I won't allow you to come close to me."

Erika's thumb trembled on the button connected to the detonator. She nodded toward a clock on the wall behind the reception desk. "It's five minutes after ten. As far as I'm concerned, the countdown just started. Move."

Habib used his uninjured right arm to open the door. Rain gusted in. "I am indeed sorry," he told Erika. "It's terrible that children must suffer to make politicians correct wrongs."

He used his car's remote control to unlock the doors from a distance. Another button on the remote control started the engine. He picked up his suitcase and stepped into the rain.

Saul watched him hurry off balance through shadowy gusts toward the car. Lightning flashed. Reflexively, Saul stepped back from the open door in case one of Habib's men ignored the instructions and was foolish enough to shoot at an Abelard safe house.

Buffeted by the wind, Habib set down his suitcase, opened the driver's door, shoved his suitcase across to the passenger seat, then hurried behind the steering wheel.

Father Chen closed the sanctuary's entrance, shutting out the rain, blocking the view of Habib. The cold air lingered.

"Is that parking lot past the boundaries of the sanction?" Erika asked.

"That isn't important!" Father Chen glared. "The dynamite. That's what matters. For God's sake, how do we neutralize it?"

"Simple." Erika released her thumb from the button.

Father Chen shouted and stumbled away.

But the blast didn't come from Erika's waist. Instead,

the roar came from outside, making Saul tighten his lips in furious satisfaction as he imagined his car and Erika's blowing apart. The vehicles were parked on each side of Habib's. The plastic explosives in each trunk blasted a shock wave against the safe house's doors. Shrapnel walloped the building. A window shattered.

Father Chen yanked the entrance open. Slanting rain carried with it the stench of smoke, scorched metal and charred flesh. Despite the storm, the flames of the gutted vehicles illuminated the night. In the middle, Habib's vehicle was blasted inward on each side, the windows gaping, flames escaping. Behind the steering wheel, his body was ablaze.

The rumble of thunder mimicked the explosion.

"What have you done?" Father Chen shouted.

"We sent the bastard to hell where he belongs," Erika said.

In the nearby hills, shots cracked, barely audible in the downpour.

"Friends of ours," Saul explained. "Habib's team won't set any more traps."

"And don't worry about the authorities coming to the monastery because of the explosion," Erika said.

A second explosion rumbled from a distance. "When our friends heard the explosion, they faked a car accident at the entrance to this road. The vehicle's on fire. It has tanks of propane for an outdoor barbecue. Those tanks blew apart just now, which'll explain the blasts to the authorities. Neither the police nor the fire department will have a reason to be suspicious about anything a half mile farther along this deserted road."

By now, the flames in the cars in the parking lot were almost extinguished as the rain fell harder.

"We had no idea there'd be a storm," Saul said. "We

didn't need it, but it makes things easier. It saves us from hurrying to put out the flames so the authorities don't see a reflection."

Another shot cracked on a nearby hill.

"We'll help clean the site, of course," Erika said. "The Monastery of the Sun and the Moon will look as if nothing ever happened."

"You violated the sanction." Father Chen raised his pistol.

"No. You told us the parking lot wasn't part of the safe house," Saul insisted.

"I said nothing of the sort!"

"Erika asked you! I heard her! This other priest heard your answer! You said the parking lot wasn't important!"

"You threatened an operative within a sanctuary!"

"With what? That isn't dynamite around Erika's waist. Those tubes are painted cardboard. We don't have any weapons. Maybe we bent the rules, but we definitely didn't break them."

The priest glowered. "Just like when you killed your foster father."

Erika nodded. "And now another black-hearted bastard's been wiped from the face of the earth." Tears trickled down her cheeks. "But my son is still dead. Nothing's changed. I still hurt. God, how I hurt."

Saul held her.

"I want my son back," Erika whimpered.

"I know," Saul told her. "I know."

"I'll pray for him," Father Chen said.

"Pray for us all."

CHRIS MOONEY

Deviant Ways was Chris Mooney's first thriller. In the novel, Mooney introduces a secondary character named Malcolm Fletcher, a mysterious, enigmatic former profiler with strange, black eyes who's hiding from the FBI. Another former profiler, Jack Casey, manages to track Fletcher down and convinces him to assist in a disturbing case— a serial killer who murders families in their sleep and then detonates bombs just as the police arrive. Fletcher, Casey discovers, knows the identity of the killer, who happens to be a former patient from an FBI-sponsored behavioral modification program. By the end of the thriller, Malcolm Fletcher is once again on the run, being hunted by his former employer.

When the book was first published, Mooney was surprised by the number of letters and e-mails he received wanting to know more about Malcolm Fletcher. What happened to him? Was he still being chased by the FBI? What other secrets did Fletcher have? More important, what was Fletcher doing? Mooney himself didn't know the answers to these questions. Fletcher had actually disappeared from Mooney's imagination, so the author went to work on two stand-alone thrillers: *World Without End* and *Remembering Sarah*. But the e-mails from readers didn't stop, so Mooney started asking himself those same questions and decided to revisit his popular character. During the process, Mooney discovered he missed Fletcher and the world he inhabited, so he's now exploring the idea of using Fletcher in a potential series.

Here, in *Falling*, Mooney explores his trademark themes of loss, retribution, and how justice so often depends on one's interpretation. He also introduces a new character, a young woman who has been asked to help set a trap to capture the dangerous former FBI profiler.

So what has Malcolm Fletcher been up to all these years?

Time to find out.

FALLING

The airport was busy and hot. Marlena had to walk fast to keep up.

"The transmitter is very small, less than half the size of a pencil eraser," Special Agent Owen Lee said. He had the slender build of a swimmer and talked with a slight lisp. "Your job is to plant the transmitter and walk away, and then you can enjoy a few days of R & R here in the Caymans, courtesy of the federal government."

"I still don't understand why you specifically requested me," Marlena said. It was a valid question. She was a lab rat. Her expertise was in forensics not surveillance.

"I asked for a confident young woman, someone who could think on her feet," Lee said. "She also needed to be exceptionally good-looking and Cuban, because this guy has a thing for Cuban women. That's when your name came up."

"Who's the subject?"

"Malcolm Fletcher."

Marlena felt her legs wobble.

Malcolm Fletcher, one of the brightest minds the FBI had ever produced, was now one of the FBI's Most Wanted. Currently he had a two-million-dollar price tag on his head for the deaths of at least three federal agents.

And that was just what the federal government was offering. For years, Marlena had heard rumors of a reward somewhere in the neighborhood of five million dollars being offered by Jean Paul Rousseau. His son, Special Agent Stephen Rousseau, had been part of a failed attempt to apprehend Fletcher. Now Stephen Rousseau was brain dead and still on a feeding tube.

"Judging by your expression, I take it you know who he is."

Marlena nodded, swallowed. "Is it true about his eyes?"

"No pigment at all, totally black," Lee said. "I hear you've applied for the open position in Investigative Support."

"Yes." Marlena was hoping her lab experience would give her an edge over the other applicants competing for the coveted spot inside the Investigative Support Unit, the section of the FBI that deals exclusively with serial murder.

"Capturing Fletcher and bringing him home to justice—this is the kind of case that makes careers. I hope you take directions well."

"You can count on me, sir."

"Good. Now let's go buy you a dress. You're going to a cocktail party."

Marlena dropped her suitcase into the back of a battered Jeep. Sitting behind the wheel was a man who could have easily passed as a body double for the Incredible Hulk. He wore a Yankees baseball hat and a T-shirt stretched so tight it looked moments away from splitting. His name was Barry Jacobs, one of the members of Lee's surveillance team.

Malcolm Fletcher, Lee explained, was a man with very particular tastes. Everything had to be just right. Lee insisted she model each dress for him.

Each time, Marlena stood in front of him while Lee sat in a leather chair, telling her to turn around or to the side. Lee didn't smile or say much, but she felt his gaze lingering too long over the exposed parts of her body. To get past her discomfort, Marlena focused on the store—the rows of expensive shoes and the glass jewelry cases, the bright smile of the helpful French-woman who kept bringing her different cocktail dresses. Here she came again, holding up a tasteful yet revealing black Gucci.

When Marlena stepped out wearing the Gucci, Lee's expression brought to mind a recent rape case she had worked on—a handsome, Ivy-educated young man who drugged women with Rohypnol and video-taped what he did with them. The way the young man smiled as he unbuckled his belt was a lot like the way Lee was smiling right now.

While Lee paid for the dress and shoes, Marlena excused herself and went outside. Jacobs was leaning against the store wall, smoking a cigarette.

"Can I bum one of those?"

Jacobs handed her a cigarette, then lit it for her. "You nervous about tonight?" he asked.

"Should I be?"

"No. I'll be at the yacht club, but you won't see me. Lee and the other two agents on our team, they'll be monitoring everything from the operations house about five or so miles down the road. That's where we've been staying. Lee's got you booked in a nice hotel."

Having male and female agents sharing the same quarters was now against regulations; too many female agents had complained about lewd behavior and sexual harassment. And after the creepy way Lee had looked her over, Marlena felt relieved to be staying someplace else.

"Fletcher has never attacked anyone in public before. As long as you don't go anywhere alone with him, you'll be fine." Jacobs stubbed out his cigarette. "I'll go get the Jeep. Tell Lee it's going to be a few minutes. I had to park in a garage."

Two doors down, Marlena spotted a revolving display holding rows of bright, colorful postcards of the Caymans. The postcards immediately brought to mind her mother. Ruthie Sanchez took the postcards family and friends had sent her over the years and taped them up on the wall inside her janitor's closet. She'd loved her postcards with their scenic views.

Marlena picked out two postcards she thought her mother would have enjoyed. As she paid for them, along with a pack of cigarettes, she tried hard to push away the memory of her mother trapped on the fifty-sixth floor of the World Trade Center's north tower, the fire and horrifying screams growing louder and closer as her mother stared at the shattered window leading out to a blue sky thick with smoke, her only way out.

Owen Lee insisted on conducting the briefing inside her hotel room. He handed her a folder and excused himself to talk with Jacobs in the hallway. Marlena read the file on the balcony overlooking a crowded beach.

The report was mostly about Fletcher's movements on the island over the past week. Twice he had been spotted talking to Jonathan Prince, a lawyer who owned a private bank on the island. According to an unnamed informant, Fletcher was supposed to meet Prince at tonight's cocktail party to pick up his new identity, complete with passport and credit cards.

Here were four surveillance photos. The first was of Jonathan Prince standing outside a pair of glass doors. He was an older man, with a shaved head and a nose shaped like a beak. The last three photographs were of Fletcher. In each, the former FBI profiler wore stylish clothing and different types of sunglasses. Marlena was wondering about the strange, black eyes hidden behind the dark lenses when Lee stepped onto the balcony and handed her a Prada handbag.

"A Rolex watch and a pair of diamond stud earrings are in there to help you look the part," Lee said. "The transmitters are inside the small, zipped pouch."

Mounted on a rectangular piece of plastic were six transmitters, each one a different color to match whatever fabric color the target might be wearing.

Lee pulled up a chair and sat down. "The top part is made with this Velcro-like substance that attaches itself to any fabric. You barely have to apply any pressure. Go ahead and try it."

Marlena peeled off the white disk, reached around Lee's back and brushed her finger against the collar of his shirt, marveling at the way it so easily stuck to the fabric. The transmitter was so small you could barely see it.

"Good technique," Lee said, and smiled.

Marlena smelled the mint-scented mouthwash on

his breath. His red hair was damp and neatly combed. She hoped to God he hadn't spruced himself up for her.

"You mind if I smoke?" Marlena asked.

"Not as long as you share," Lee said.

Marlena went into the bedroom and came back with her cigarettes. She lit one, then handed the pack and matches to Lee. "I read over the report." She casually moved her chair to give her some distance. "There was no mention as to where Fletcher is staying on the island."

"That's because we don't know. Fletcher's highly educated with surveillance techniques, so we can't use our normal methods. Plus, he tends to move around only at night, which presents its own set of problems. Now, tell me what you've heard about him."

"Mainly that he's brilliant."

"Without a doubt. When he worked for Investigative Support, he had the highest clearance rate on serial murder. Unfortunately, Fletcher crossed a line. Instead of bringing these monsters in, he acted as their judge, jury and executioner. When the bureau found out what he was doing, they sent three agents to Fletcher's home to handle the matter discreetly. One agent is brain dead and hooked up to a feeding tube. The other two agents...we still don't have any idea what happened to them. Fletcher's been on the run ever since."

"How did you find him?"

"The informant mentioned in the report is a secretary at Prince's firm. For years, we've believed Fletcher used the Caymans to shift around his money and change identities. Now we know it's true. She supplied us with the aliases Fletcher's been using, his bank accounts, you name it."

Lee lit his cigarette, tossed the match off the balcony.

"Fletcher's scheduled to meet Prince at ten. The cocktail party will be crowded, everyone holding drinks, trying not to bump into one another. You're going to walk behind Fletcher, touch the back of his arm and say, 'Excuse me'—you know, pretend to bump into him. Go for a casual approach, it always works best."

"And if Fletcher approaches me?"

"Then you talk to him. Be yourself, flirt with him, touch his arm or shoulder like you're interested, and then find a way to put the transmitter on him—and once you do, don't disengage right away. That will look suspicious. Talk to him for a few minutes, and then find a way to excuse yourself. We'll take it from there."

"Why did the secretary give up Fletcher?"

"She's planning on leaving her husband, and two million buys her a new life and a whole lot of distance. Now, to answer your next question—why aren't we using her to plant the transmitter? First off, she doesn't have direct access to Fletcher. He never meets Prince at the office, only in public places where he has multiple escape routes. Second reason is, even if I could arrange some scenario to get the secretary next to Fletcher tonight, the woman is not what I'd call grace under pressure. If I send her in with an agenda, Fletcher will pick up on it right away."

"Why not just approach Fletcher directly? You certainly have the manpower."

"True, but then we'd have to bring in the locals. Prince has many friends on the inside, people who can be easily bought. There are extradition issues and some others that don't concern you.

"Look, Marlena, I can understand why you're nervous," Lee said. "But you've got to trust me when I say I have all the bases covered. The watch in your purse is equipped with a listening device, so we'll all be listening in. If there's a problem or a change in plans, Jacobs will get word to you. And if I think you're in danger, I'll pull you out. We've got a boat standing by, just in case. You'll be fine as long as you remember this rule—under no circumstances are you to go anywhere alone with Fletcher."

"Jacobs mentioned that."

"Head over to the party around eight and get a feel for the place. Your name is already on the guest list. The set of keys on your bed belong to a black Mercedes parked out in the back lot. The directions to the club are under the seat."

Marlena stared out at the water.

"Wipe that look off your face," Lee said. "Everything's going to be fine."

You keep saying that, Marlena thought, wondering who Lee was really trying to convince.

The yacht club was located at the opposite end of the island, a remote and stunningly beautiful spot overlooking a sprawling dock packed with sailboats and yachts. Apparently, this was the place to be if you were in the market for a trophy wife or a sugar daddy. There wasn't a woman here over the age of thirty-five, each stunningly beautiful and wearing a dress worthy of a red-carpet show. Now Marlena understood Lee's obsession about picking out the perfect dress.

It was coming up on ten. For the past half hour, Marlena had been forced to listen to a fossil named William Bingham, aka Billy Bing, the Mercedes King of Fresno, California, talk about sailing the way you'd talk about great sex. As she pretended to listen, scanning the well-dressed crowd for Malcolm Fletcher and Jonathan Prince, her thoughts kept drifting back to the postcards.

This wasn't the first time she had purchased something for her mother after she died—this past Christmas she had dropped two hundred dollars on a cashmere sweater at Talbots. It wasn't like she could take the sweater or the postcards to her mother's grave. Ruthie Sanchez didn't have a grave. Like so many 9/11 victims, her remains were never found—and they would never be found because Marlena had signed away all rights to her mother's remains in exchange for a lucrative settlement that had allowed her to put her severely autistic brother in a special home.

Anyone with a rudimentary understanding of psychology would say her need to purchase gifts for her dead mother was about not wanting to let go. Fine. But there was another reason, something Marlena had told no one, not even her therapist. Every time she held the postcards, the Christmas sweater, the crystal vase she had bought on the first anniversary of her mother's death, the feeling that kept boiling to the surface was outrage. The hijackers and planners, the CIA and FBI bureaucrats and politicians who had ignored the warning signs—Marlena wanted to take these people and, just like in the Bible, stone them to death over a period of weeks. Thinking about the different ways she could punish the people responsible—*that* was the feeling that kept coming to her over and over again.

Marlena snapped her mind back to the present. Billy Bing was still talking; something to do with golf. Thank God, here came the waiter with her glass of wine.

"A gentleman at the bar wanted me to give this to you," the waiter said, and handed her a folded napkin.

Written in black ink was a message: *Use phone on*

top of cooler inside boat Falling Star, *near end of dock. Untie boat, then call and follow instructions. Jacobs.* A phone number was written under his name.

Marlena politely excused herself from the conversation and headed for the docks, remembering Lee's words from this afternoon: *If I think you're in danger, I'll pull you out of there. We've got a boat standing by.*

So something *had* gone wrong, and now she was in danger.

Heart pounding, she stood on the dock in front of the *Falling Star,* an oversized Boston whaler, the kind of charter boat most likely used for deep-sea fishing. The boat was dark and empty, but the one moored next to it, a Sea Ray motor yacht, was lit up and packed with well-dressed people drinking highballs and smoking cigarettes and cigars.

Marlena took in her surroundings. A lot of people were milling around on the docks but nobody was heading this way. *Okay, get moving.* She stepped on board the *Falling Star,* feeling it rock beneath her heels, and set her wineglass and purse on the table inside the cabin. Under the table were two matching extra-large Coleman coolers wrapped in chains and secured by padlocks. A third Coleman sat against the wall behind her, near the cabin door. This cooler wasn't locked; the chains had been removed and lay in a ball on the floor. Sitting on the cooler's top were two items: a cell phone and a set of keys. The top, she noticed, wasn't fully shut.

As instructed, Marlena went to work untying the boat from the dock, glancing up every few seconds to survey the area. People were minding their own business, their laughter and voices mixing with the old-time jazz music coming from the Sea Ray. After she hoisted the last rubber fender onto the stern, she moved back inside the cabin, grabbed the cell and dialed the number written on the napkin.

"Don't talk, just listen," said the man on the other end of the line. His voice was deep and surprisingly calm. *Must be one of the two agents she hadn't met—the ones monitoring from the house*, she thought. "The keys on top of the cooler are for the boat. Drive out of the harbor. Get moving. We don't have much time."

The man on the phone told her where to find the switch for the lights. Marlena started the boat. The twin engines turned over, the floor vibrating beneath her as she increased the throttle and slowly eased the boat away from the dock with one hand on the wheel, the other pressing the phone tightly against her ear.

Something heavy landed on the stern. Marlena whipped her head around, her panic vanishing when she saw Barry Jacobs, dressed in the same dark suit as the waitstaff, step inside the cabin.

Thank God, Marlena thought. Jacobs, red-faced and sweating, yanked the phone away from her and tossed it against the floor. Marlena stared at him, dumbfounded. She opened her mouth to speak, the words evaporating off her tongue as Jacobs shoved her up against the wall.

"What the fuck do you think you're doing?" he demanded.

"You told me to take the boat out."

Jacobs dug his fingers deep into her arms. "Don't lie to me, or I swear to Christ—"

"I'm telling you the truth," Marlena said. "A waiter gave me a note written on a napkin. Your name was signed on the bottom. It said to—"

"And you just came down here?"

"Lee said if there was a problem, you'd get word to me—"

"Where's this note?"

"In my purse."

"Get it." Jacobs released her and took control of the wheel. He increased the throttle, and the boat lurched forward.

Glass shattered inside the cabin. When Marlena stepped inside, she saw that her wineglass had fallen to the floor. The cooler near the cabin door had moved. Drops of blood were leaking around the seams of the cooler's half-opened top. Marlena reached down and opened the cooler.

As a forensics specialist, she had seen her share of dead bodies, the dozens of different ways human beings could be cut, broken and bruised. But seeing the way Owen Lee had been dismembered sent a nauseous scream rising up her throat.

"*Barry*."

Then Jacobs was standing next to her. He slammed the cooler shut.

"Relax, take deep breaths," Jacobs said as he escorted her to the seat. "I'm going to call the command post."

Jacobs held out his cell phone. Marlena stared at him, confused.

Something hot and sharp pierced her skin. Marlena looked down at her chest and saw twin metal prongs attached to wires; Jacobs was holding a Taser. The charge swept through her body, and the next thing Marlena saw was her mother clutching her hand as they fell together through an electric-blue sky.

Marlena heard splashing. Her eyes fluttered open to moonlight.

She was still on the boat, lying across one of the padded seats set up along the stern. All the deck and interior lights had been turned off, as had the engine. A cooler lay on its side, opened. It was empty.

Something heavy bumped against the boat. Marlena had an idea what was going on and went to push herself up but couldn't move. Her hands were tied behind her back, her ankles bound together with the same coarse rope. She swung her feet off the seat and managed to sit.

She was out in open water, far away from the harbor. Zigzagging along the sides and back of the boat were several distinctively shaped dorsal fins. And those were just the sharks she could see.

"There's no need to panic, Marlena. I'm not going to feed you to the sharks."

She turned away from the water and looked up into Malcolm Fletcher's strange, black eyes.

Marlena backed away and fell, hitting her head against the side of the boat before toppling onto the floor. She lay on her stomach, about to roll onto her back—she could use her feet to kick—when Fletcher's powerful hands slid underneath her arms and lifted her into the air, toward the water. She tried to fight.

"Despite what the federal government has led you to believe, I have no intention of harming you," Fletcher said, dropping her back on the seat. "Now, I can't say the same is true about Special Agent Jacobs. Lucky for you I was on board to put a stop to it."

Fletcher's face seemed darker than in the surveillance pictures, more gaunt. He was impeccably dressed in a dark suit without a tie.

"Before I cut you free, I'd like a piece of information—and I'd appreciate some honesty," Fletcher said. "Will you promise to be honest with me? This is important."

Marlena nodded. She took in several deep breaths, trying to slow the rapid beating of her heart.

"Those postcards you purchased earlier, who were they for?"

The question took her by surprise.

"I bought them for my mother," Marlena said after a moment.

"She's dead, isn't she?"

"How did—? Yes. She's dead. Why?"

"Tell me what happened."

"She died on 9/11. She was inside one of the buildings—the north tower."

"Did you have a chance to speak with her?"

"Not directly. She left a message on my machine."

"What did she say?"

"She said, 'I love you, and remember to take care of your brother.' There was some background noise, and then the cell-phone signal cut off."

Marlena thought about the other voice on the tape, a man whispering to her mother. A friend at the FBI lab had enhanced it: *"Hold my hand, Ruthie. We'll jump together."* The crazy thing was how much the man sounded like her father, who died when she was twenty. Or maybe she just wanted to believe her mother hadn't been alone during her final moment.

"I'm sorry for your loss," Fletcher said, and meant it. "Excuse me for a moment."

Fletcher ducked inside the cabin. Water splashed along the back and sides of the boat. A moment later, he came back, dragging a hog-tied Jacobs across the floor. Fletcher propped Jacobs up into a kneeling position directly in front of her. A piece of duct tape was fastened across Jacobs's mouth.

"Remember what I said earlier about confession being good for the soul," Fletcher said to Jacobs, and then tore off the strip of tape.

Jacobs stared at the sharks circling the boat. He swallowed several times before speaking. "I sold you out to bounty hunters working for Jean Paul Rousseau. Stephen, his son, was a federal agent, part of a team sent to apprehend Fletcher."

"Those agents were sent to kill me," Fletcher said. "I acted purely out of self-defense, but that's a story for another time. Keep going, Special Agent Jacobs."

"Rousseau wanted Fletcher captured alive and brought back to Louisiana. That was the condition of the reward. The bounty hunters and people working for Rousseau, they wanted us to disappear. Everyone would assume you were responsible because you have a track record of making federal agents disappear. That way, it would keep the heat off Rousseau."

"I'm afraid Jacobs is telling the truth about the bounty hunters," Fletcher said. "I've been following Lee for the past week. Naturally, I wanted to see what he was up to, so I took the liberty of tapping into his phone conversations—the FBI's encryption technology is woefully out of date. After Lee and Jacobs left your hotel, I followed them back to the house they've been using as a base of operations. You can imagine my surprise when, two hours later, five rather disturbing-looking men emerged from the back doors and carried three oversize coolers to the fishing boat Lee used to transport all his surveillance equipment. I recognized one of these gentlemen from a previous entanglement—a professional tracker, or bounty hunter, who works for Daddy Rousseau. Now tell Marlena about what you had planned for her."

Jacobs didn't answer.

Fletcher whispered something in Jacobs's ear. He looked terrified.

"After you planted the transmitter, the bounty hunters were to move in and take care of Fletcher," Jacobs said, his voice quivering. "They wanted me to take you out on the boat under the guise of meeting up with Lee at the operations house. You were supposed to disappear, out here in the water. The sharks were going to take care of you. No bodies, no evidence, no case."

"And where were you going?" Fletcher said.

"Costa Rica."

"With how much money?"

A pause, then Jacobs said, "Seven million."

"It seems the price on my head has gone up," Fletcher said, grinning. "Jacobs neglected to mention the part where I slipped out of the utility closet and caught him in the act of feeling you up. I think he was preparing to share a special moment with you before dumping you overboard. It's not every day he has an opportunity to be intimate with such a beautiful woman. Did you tell Marlena about your colorful tenure in Boston?"

"I worked as a handler for informants."

"He's being modest," Fletcher said. "Special Agent Jacobs was the handler for two *very* powerful figureheads inside the Irish mafia. In exchange for lucrative payoffs, Jacobs ran interference so these two men could continue committing extortion, money laundering and murder. When his superiors got wind of what was going on, these two men suddenly disappeared. Any idea what happened to them?"

"I was cleared on those charges," Jacobs said.

"You were never indicted because the president stepped in and invoked executive privilege in order to protect a member of his high-ranking staff—a member who once worked as your boss in Boston. The corruption went well beyond Jacobs, and the president wanted it kept quiet. How many people died to protect your secrets, *Special* Agent Jacobs? How many people did you kill?"

Jacobs didn't answer.

"It doesn't matter. I think we've heard enough." Fletcher taped Jacobs's mouth shut.

Then Marlena watched as Fletcher dragged Jacobs, kicking and screaming, to the back part of the boat. The idea flashed through her mind: Jacobs alone in the water, screaming out in pain and horror as the sharks ripped him apart. No part of her rose up in protest or tried to push the thought away.

Jacobs was pinned against the stern, screaming behind the duct tape as he stared, wide-eyed and terrified, at the water.

"Do you want me to cut him loose before I toss him overboard?" Fletcher asked her.

Marlena didn't answer, aware of the intense feeling building inside her, the one she had when holding things like the postcards and the sweater.

"What would your mother want you to do?" Fletcher asked.

Marlena thought of her mother alone in that terrible moment, a woman who worked as a janitor and wanted nothing more out of life than to be a good mother to her two children, now forced to make a decision between jumping to her death and being burned alive.

She spotted a bright light on the horizon. The light belonged to a boat.

"That would be my ride," Fletcher said. "What's your answer?"

She *wanted* Jacobs to suffer. But giving the order to do it was something else entirely.

"I want to bring him in," Marlena said.

"At the moment, you have no direct proof of his involvement with the bounty hunters. Jean Paul Rousseau is not a stupid man. And despite his rather apish appearance, I'm willing to bet Jacobs covered his tracks just as well. It will be your word against his. I don't have to remind you how those cases turn out, especially since Jacobs has connections in very high places."

"I'll work the evidence."

"I doubt you'll find any."

"I'll take my chances."

"Your choice." Fletcher released Jacobs. "Turn around, Marlena, and I'll untie your hands."

The boat that pulled alongside them was a cigarette boat, a bullet-shaped race boat designed for incredible speed. Standing behind the wheel was a pale man with a shaved head and an odd-looking nose—Jonathan Prince.

"Malcolm," Prince said. "We need to get moving."

She recognized the voice as the one she had spoken to earlier on the cell phone.

"You had this whole thing planned out," Marlena said, more to herself.

"I needed to move you to safety, and the only way to do it was to get you on the boat, away from the club." Marlena felt Fletcher's breath against her ear. "Those postcards and whatever other items you've bought since your mother's death? I suggest you bury them."

Her hands were cut free.

"I'll leave Jacobs tied up, in case you change your mind. Good luck, Marlena."

The cigarette boat roared away. She got to work untying the rope around her ankles. She didn't rush. She knew there was no way she could catch up to Fletcher.

During the commotion, Jacobs had managed to rub off part of the duct tape from the corner of his mouth. "I have an account set up here on the island," he mumbled. "I'll transfer the money to you. All I need is a laptop. You let me go, and I'll disappear. You'll never see me again."

Marlena didn't answer.

"Seven million," Jacobs said. "That kind of money can buy you a lot of things."

But it can't buy me what I need, Marlena thought, and went to start the boat.

"Wait, let's talk about this," Jacobs said. "We can come to some sort of agreement."

Marlena drove toward the bright lights of the island. She heard Jacobs screaming over the roar of the engines and wind, pleading with her to make a deal. Marlena drove faster and thought of her mother falling through the sky and tried hard not to dwell on the limitations of justice.

DENNIS LYNDS

Both a literary and suspense novelist, Dennis Lynds is credited with bringing the detective novel into the modern age then, twenty years later—in the 1980s—introducing literary techniques that propelled the genre into its current dynamic form. An award winner, Lynds wrote under several pseudonyms, publishing some eighty novels and two hundred short stories. His most famous pen name was Michael Collins. Under that label he created fiction's longest-running detective series, starring the indelible private eye Dan Fortune. The *New York Times* consistently named Lynds's mysteries among the nation's top ten. One year, it listed two of his titles, each written under a different pseudonym, without realizing he was the author of both. His awards include both the Edgar and the Marlowe Lifetime Achievement.

Lynds also published literary novels and short stories. Five were honored in *Best American Short Stories*. Then, in the late 1980s and into the 1990s, he pioneered the detective form again, writing books in both third and first person and lacing them with short stories, techniques which today's writers employ regularly.

"Powerful and memorable, [these works] indicate Collins has embarked on a new course after some 60 books," wrote critic Richard C. Carpenter in *Twentieth Century Crime and Mystery Writers*. "Truly, he is a writer to be reckoned with." Of his most recent short story collection, *Fortune's World*, the *Los Angeles Times* commented, "To spin tales as intriguing and thought provoking as these for three decades is a remarkable enough achievement. Even more remarkable is the sustained quality.... It takes style to bring that off. Bravery, too, of course."

Iconoclastic, witty and generous, sadly Lynds died August 19, 2005, at the age of eighty-one. Several of his short stories will be published posthumously, including the one here, *Success of a Mission*. This story was first published in 1968. Since then, it has been nominated for several awards and anthologized. The story is still relevant today in both its triumph and its tragedy.

SUCCESS OF A MISSION

The minister of defense stood with his back to the room. He faced a large map on the wall of his office.

"They will attack," the minister said. "If we do not know the locations of their ammunition dumps, supply depots and fuel stores, we cannot stop them."

The minister turned. He was a small man with a round face that would have been kindly except for the hard gray surface of his eyes. These hard gray eyes studied the faces of the other two people in the room the way a scientist would study a specimen on a microscope slide.

"That data would only be at army headquarters in their capital, Minister," the tall infantry captain said.

The minister nodded. "Yes. Our man at their headquarters knows that much, has already located exactly where they are in the building."

"He cannot get the data for us, Minister?" the woman asked.

"No. He cannot get into the building. It would be quite impossible in his disguise, and in any case we need him to remain in his present position. His contacts are too low level, and we have no other reliable agents with the necessary experience at their headquarters for a job of this degree of difficulty, sensitivity and importance. There is no time to place an undercover man in the headquarters now. It will have to be a single swift operation from outside army headquarters. Get in, get the data, bring it back without them being aware that we have it."

The woman paled under her olive complexion. There and gone, the quick fear, but it had been there. She was little more than a girl, despite her officer's uniform. Her face was oval, with a small nose, wide and full lips and soft brown eyes. She had been in the army three years, and had killed four men with a knife in the dead of night, but she paled as the minister described what would have to be done at the headquarters of the enemy's army in the heart of enemy country.

The tall man only nodded. "When do we leave?"

His voice, when he said this, was low, and had a faint trace of an accent different from that of the woman and the minister. There was a long scar on his lean, tanned face. The middle finger of his left hand was missing. His almost-black eyes showed no expression.

"In ten minutes, Captain. All your papers are ready," the minister said. "You, Captain Hareet, will be an American automobile salesman on a long-planned combined vacation and business trip that could not be canceled despite the crisis. We have picked you for this job because of your experience, your colloquial American English and your command of Arabic. With some darkening of the skin, your features will also pass as Arab, if that becomes necessary. You know their army and their city."

Captain Hareet nodded. "Yes, sir. I know both only too well to lose a war to them."

The minister faced the girl. "Lieutenant Frank, you will be his wife. Your home is in Santa Barbara, California. You have lived there, and no special regional accent is required for an educated Californian. Standard American will do. Your Arabic will pass in an emergency, but we hope there will be no need. It is hard for a woman to infiltrate in Arab countries."

"Yes, sir," Lieutenant Frank said. The shiver in her voice was so faint no one but a man as trained as the minister, or Captain Hareet, would have caught it, and it disappeared as quickly as it had come. The two men looked at each other, nodded, and then smiled at the woman.

"You are lovers?" the minister asked.

The captain was silent. Lieutenant Frank hesitated for a moment. Then she nodded. "Yes, sir. Paul and I have lived together for over a year. We were lovers before that. We planned to marry soon, but that will have to wait now until after the crisis has passed."

"I am sorry for that, Lieutenant, but it is good that my information is correct."

"Is such information necessary?" Captain Hareet asked.

"All information is necessary," the minister said. "In this case, it might be vital. You will be posing as man and wife under the most careful scrutiny of every foreign national who arrives in their country at this moment. They will expect us to send spies, try to learn what their plans are. Women who are not married tend to act like coy maidens at the wrong moment. They forget. To act like she sleeps regularly with a man, a woman must be sleeping regularly with the man. Men who are not married don't know how to act with a wife at all."

"Yes, sir," Hareet said, and smiled again at the young woman. "I think Greta and I will be able to act the part well enough to pass any inspection."

"Do we parachute?" Greta asked.

"The sky is too clear. They will be alert. You will fly to Rome, and there you will board a normal commercial carrier. You will be Mr. and Mrs. Rogers of Santa Barbara. Harry and Susan, but he calls her Susy. Your papers are in order. The real Mr. and Mrs. Rogers are in Europe on such a trip with a different order of itinerary caused by a sudden change in plans we managed to arrange, and are being watched by our agents. You look enough like them to pass a cursory inspection."

The minister turned again to the large map on the wall. "I wish we could allow you some time to prepare. We can't. You are the only suitable team we have that can act the part on such short notice. I cannot even tell you how to proceed. Only that we must have the data within three days."

The minister turned once more to look at Hareet and Greta with his hard gray eyes. "In three days, they will attack us."

Mr. and Mrs. Harry Rogers of Santa Barbara, California, U.S.A., passed through Rome customs and immigration without any trouble. The Italian officials were most polite, and more than a little appreciative of Mrs. Rogers's dark beauty. She received all the customary whistles and smiles, and one definite pinch. In the taxi that took them to their hotel, they peered out the windows and exclaimed over everything, as American tourists would.

They checked into the hotel they had booked months ago from the States, showered off the grime of their trip, made love in the ornate Italian bed and went out to see the sights of the Eternal City. They ate in one of the best restaurants in Rome, ordered two bottles of good local white wine, went dancing, threw some coins in the proper fountain and visited the others, and generally had a fine tourist evening in the Italian capital.

The next morning they did not rise early, took the time to have their usual big, leisurely breakfast, then caught a taxi back to the airport for the next leg of their journey. On the jet out of Rome, they had seats just behind the wing. Harry Rogers held a guidebook and pointed out the sights below they had missed on the ground the night before.

"Look, dear," Captain Hareet said to Greta, the perfect eager American automobile salesman on his first trip to Europe. "There's St. Peter's, and the Colosseum, and the Via Veneto. We were standing right down there just last night, honey."

"Did you remember to send the postcards to the Phelps and the Temples, Harry?" Greta said, her mind clearly at home with her social obligations where a good wife's mind should be.

"Ouch, I forgot," Mr. Harry Rogers said, the self-centered American husband. "We'll send some from Athens when we get there, okay?"

When they arrived at the airport of their next stop, the capital of the enemy country, there was the loud confusion normal to Arab countries. The present political crisis and impending possibility of war only heightened the clamor and chaos. They were inspected thoroughly at customs. With the mighty United States Seventh Fleet cruising pointedly at this end of the Mediterranean, Americans were not in the best standing in Arab countries at the moment.

"You will do well to remain safely within the city," a customs official told them coldly. "And I suggest you do not enter the less visited and policed areas."

"We sure won't, buddy," Hareet said, his voice clearly nervous.

The official smiled at the intimidated American. Another man who stood off to the right and watched everyone who passed through customs did not smile. The dark shadows of his Levantine eyes stared at Captain Hareet's left hand. He showed nothing on his face, no particular expression, but his steady gaze followed them as they left.

"He's interested in your missing finger, Paul," Greta said through a wifely smile. "They might have a file on you."

"Possible," Hareet agreed, smiling down at her. "We must go to the hotel, however. The risk can't be avoided, our contact will be made there."

Greta walked ahead of her husband in the American fashion. They took a taxi to their hotel, where she walked in first, left Hareet to pay the cabdriver and run after her.

In their suite of rooms, Hareet remembered to over-tip the robed and surly bellman, and Greta remembered to prepare at once for a shower. They were well-taken precautions. Two maids soon arrived to perform some barely necessary tasks.

"We're being watched, Paul," Greta said.

Hareet agreed. "The question is, are we being watched as their normally trigger-happy suspicion against all tourists at a time like this, or have we been spotted as something special and possibly dangerous?"

"I would say something special." Greta thought carefully. "But not yet certain. They are checking on us."

"So we have some time. A few hours at least. Unless they do have a file on me and have connected it to Harry Rogers."

"How many will come?" Greta asked.

"If they are sure, a squad of soldiers and a vehicle. If they are still only suspicious, two men."

"We can't stay here in the rooms. We wouldn't look much like American tourists."

"No. Are you ready?"

They went out and down to the crowded streets that smelled of the masses of humanity and poor sewage disposal. Streets now crowded more than usual with the local inhabitants, the fellahin and the middle class and even the elite upper classes in their Cadillacs and Mercedes. They were all more excited than normal. There was a high tension in the city, a fever of hate and violence building almost by the minute. In the markets, the merchants hawked and sold frantically. In the shops, shutters were being readied for possible mass demonstrations.

The two Americans were watched with barely concealed antagonism.

Hareet took pictures until it was dark. They went to clubs that throbbed with excited patriotism. The belly dancers appeared overcome with ecstasy, danced specifically for the soldiers in uniform who seemed to throng everywhere. Four Americans sat near Hareet and Greta in one popular tourist club.

"I don't like it," one American said to them. "Time we got out of here."

"The sooner the better," another said.

"It doesn't look so good," Hareet acknowledged, his voice nervous again.

"Dave Spatz," the first American introduced himself. "Where you folks from?"

"Santa Barbara," Hareet said. "Harry and Susy Rogers."

"I was in Santa Barbara once for Fiesta. That's one helluva great town to live in. We're from Chicago."

"August is our best month," Greta said.

The police watched them, listened to them. But the police were watching everyone. They sat through two drinks and three belly dancers, then left and returned to their hotel. The desk clerk was friendly.

"Terrible times," the clerk said. "Even our thieves are too excited to work."

"Thieves?" Hareet said.

The clerk smiled and held out Greta's wedding ring. "Madame forgot her ring after her shower. The maid found it after you had gone out."

"Oh, my, how careless of me," Greta exclaimed, and smiled at the clerk.

She reached for the ring with her left hand. The clerk bowed over her hand to put the ring on. When he straightened up, his eyes had subtly changed, clouded, but he continued to smile as if nothing had happened.

Greta and Paul went up to their suite.

"They searched our rooms," Hareet said. "That's when they found your wedding ring."

"It won't matter," Greta said. "I made a bad mistake, Paul. Did you see the clerk's eyes? He saw it."

"A mistake?"

Greta took off her wedding ring and held up her hand. The ring was a broad gold band. The third finger of her left hand was smooth and unmarked, one single color.

"I'm suntanned, Paul," Greta said. "There should be a pale ring mark on my finger. The clerk knows I haven't worn the ring more than a few days."

"You have a dark complexion."

"Not that dark. Look under my wristwatch. My sunglasses have left a pale patch on my nose. He saw all that, too, Paul."

Hareet looked at his watch. "We'll wait half an hour for the contact."

The knock came in fifteen minutes.

Hareet opened the door. Behind him, the shower was running in the bathroom, the noise coming from under the bathroom door.

The two dark-eyed men who came into the suite wore Western clothes. They both glanced toward the sound of the shower, then back at Hareet.

"My wife can't stand this heat of yours, too muggy," Hareet said with an apologetic smile. "Back home, our heat isn't so humid. Dry and not all that hot except when the Santa Anas blow down the canyons, you know?"

"In Santa Barbara, sir?" one man said. "The sundowner winds, yes?"

The other man walked through the rooms, his hand in his pocket. All the rooms except the bathroom. He returned, shook his head to the first man, and stood near the hall door they had left open.

"That's right," Hareet said to the first man. "You've been to Santa Barbara?"

"If you will ask your wife—" the first man began.

Greta appeared silently in the open door from the hall. The man at the door heard her soft step, turned. She stabbed him twice in the heart before he could move or even open his mouth.

Hareet's knife appeared in his hand. The first man only managed to half draw his pistol. Hareet killed him with a single thrust.

Greta closed the door. They dragged the bodies into the bedroom and pushed them into a closet, moved the furniture just enough to cover the bloodstains on the carpeting. They changed into Arab clothes and left the room. They took nothing with them but their weapons and their second set of papers. They took the back stairs down.

Before they left, Hareet broke the mirror of the dressing table in the bedroom.

In the noisy streets, they mingled with the crowd. As they walked through the packed throngs of the enemy capital, Greta held Hareet's hand once. Her veil hid her face. Then they separated and she walked behind him until they reached the dark and deserted streets in the slums of the city where the fellahin wallowed in filth and misery.

On a particularly dark and silent street they went down four steps into a dank cellar where water ran in a deep trough at one side of the room. Slime floated on the water and rats swam in the slime. Hareet haggled with a one-eyed Arab in ragged Western clothes and a stained fez. Money changed hands. Hareet and Greta found a deserted corner of the cellar. They lay down to sleep as much as they could.

"How long do we have?" Greta said.

"As long as we've always had, Greta. Two more days."

They spoke softly in stilted Arabic. Water spouted in ragged streams from pipes in the walls, human waste reeked through the darkness. The people lay in stuporous sleep, or sat against the walls and stared at the poverty and need and squalor of their lives. No one cared about Greta and Hareet in the darkness and silence of the cellar, no one was suspicious. Patriotism does not run deep among the ragged and starving and diseased of any country, not even here where patriotism was often all they had to make them feel human.

"They have no way to trace us," Hareet said. "The Rogerses are gone for good. They know that two spies are in the city, but they expected there would be spies anyway. Our problem is still the same—to get the data. The only change is that it will be a little harder to get it back and in time."

"There's another change, Paul," Greta said. "We don't have a bed for tonight."

"No," Hareet said. "I'm sorry, *liebchen*."

Greta smiled at the endearment that was far from his stilted Arabic. "I'm sorrier," she said, and lay close against him in the dimness. "Where will we live when we retire, when this is over?"

Hareet stroked her arm softly. "There's a hill in the north. It looks out over orange trees and an olive grove. You can see the border. I own it, and when I can look at that border and know that no danger will ever come across it again, then we will build a stone house and live in it."

They slept for a time, took turns on watch. Greta was awake when the ragged peddler sidled up to them like an apparition from the slimy water of the cellar itself. She touched Hareet, who opened his eyes but did not move.

"The mirror could be mended," the peddler whispered in English.

Hareet took his hand from the pistol under his ragged robes. Greta slipped her knife back up her voluminous sleeve.

"We had to kill two," Hareet said.

"They were found. Fortunately, I had seen the mirror five minutes before. What is your assignment?"

"The ammunition dumps, supply depots, fuel centers."

"Impossible. The maps and information are in General Staff Headquarters," the peddler said.

"I can get in," Hareet said.

"But not out, Captain. No way you can get out. Not with the data in usable form."

"Why?" Greta asked.

The filthy peddler sat against the wet stone walls, seemed to close his eyes and go to sleep. "Because our Arab friends have become modern, Lieutenant. At least at General Staff Headquarters. The documents will have been chemically treated so that no one can touch them undetected, or film them undetected. A sophisticated touch supplied by their friends in the bigger nations. Also, to get out you must pass two ranks of guards and locked gates, and a bank of detectors that detect film or the documents themselves."

"So if we steal them, they would know at once and change the locations."

"If you got them out, the present locations would be changed as fast as they could do it. Perhaps a short delay in their plans, and no help to us."

"And we could only make the attempt once," Greta said.

"No matter how many attempts we made, the data is useful to us only as long as they do not know we have it," Hareet said. "It must be taken and sent to our forces undetected."

"And that can't be done, Captain," the peddler said. "We'll have to beat them head to head, no matter how bad that looks."

"Everything can be done in some way," Hareet said, and sat for a time in the raw stench of the cellar filled only with the sound of running and dripping water. "Our man inside General Staff Headquarters is still there at his job?"

"Yes." The peddler nodded. "But there is no way—"

"The main building with the information we need is inside a courtyard?"

"Yes. And there is a locked gate in the outer wall of the courtyard."

"Where are the detectors?"

"At the door of the building."

"How is the security inside the building in the day and the night?"

"In the day, fairly tight. At night, poor. They rely on the wall and outer gates and perimeter guards. The guards inside make rounds but don't go into the offices. The staff officers don't trust the soldiers with keys to the offices. That's their weakness."

"And we'll use it," Hareet said.

"Can we go in together, Paul?" Greta said.

"Of course not," Hareet said simply. Then he smiled at her. "But perhaps we can find some private place later tonight. A place for us to sleep."

She smiled in return. "Tonight, then."

Hareet and the peddler lay down on the stone. Greta sat up, watching. Hareet and the peddler talked for a long time. It was well past midnight when the peddler left alone. Hareet and Greta pretended to sleep for another hour, then slipped out of the dank cellar together.

"Our peddler gave me another address," Hareet said. "Somewhere we can be alone. It's not far."

They both knew the danger of such a move, every moment on the streets brought the possibility of being stopped, observed, making a mistake. Every new place exposed them to more contacts, more unexpected events. But they both also knew the risks of tomorrow.

The place turned out to be a small room on the second floor above a dark bookshop owned by an old Coptic Christian widow with patriotic slogans in her window. The peddler himself let them in, had a room of his own on the first floor where he had lived for over a year.

"It's as safe as anything can be here," the peddler said, and left them alone in the tiny room with its one bed and some chairs and a cabinet they could barely see. There was no light.

They didn't need a light. After they had made love once more, Hareet held her close against him for the rest of the night as if to build a wall of protection that would keep her safe. He was not a demonstrative man; Greta knew he was afraid for what could happen to her, to them, when the night ended.

The guards paced at the gates in the outer wall of Army General Staff Headquarters far out on the edge of the city. They looked up as they walked their posts to watch their jets fly high above in beautiful formation. The ragged people on the streets cheered the jets and the guards as they shuffled past the front gates.

Among the throngs of people that passed the gates was a tall, dark-skinned man with a pointed beard, thick glasses and a fez. He walked purposefully, with an arrogant bearing. With the tasseled fez he wore a dark Western suit and immaculate pale kid gloves. The crowds of fellahin gave him respectful room as he strode around and through them.

Hareet, in the dark makeup and wearing the gloves to conceal his missing finger, turned into a side street at the corner of the wall and proceeded on his inspection of the headquarters building. The side wall was broken by only another high wooden gate, locked on the inside and outside. In the rear, the wall stretched without a break, and on the fourth side there was only a narrow, barred gate, also locked on the inside and outside and patrolled by a guard.

The building inside the high stone wall was from the last century and only two stories high. The roof had a steep pitch, and the windows of the upper floor were barred and shuttered. Two armored cars slowly patrolled the street all around the building, moving in opposite directions.

Hareet, his study completed, walked to a house a few blocks from the headquarters, and there changed into the flowing and ragged burnoose of an Arab country. He removed the fez and glasses, replaced the fez with a keffiyeh, and rearranged his false beard. He strapped his left arm to his side, and assumed a limp in his left leg.

A crippled fellahin was too common a sight in the streets of the city for anyone to look at twice. The fellahin limped his way to a filthy alley that paralleled the street in front of staff headquarters, and entered the rear of a building. He climbed to the second floor and slipped into an empty room at the front. He locked the door behind him, crossed quickly and without a limp to the front window with its clear view of the guarded gate into the headquarters.

Hareet sat in a chair some three feet inside the window so that no sun would glint on the powerful binoculars he took from beneath his burnoose. He sat on the chair for six hours without moving, except to rest his

eyes now and then, and to light a cigarette. He scruti-
nized the building, and the officers who went in and out.

Late in the afternoon, a slight scratching came at the
door of the room. Hareet listened from his chair. The
scratching was repeated in a definite pattern. He
opened the door. The peddler came in.

"Have you found your man, Captain?"

"A colonel of artillery," Hareet said. "He looks
enough like me to pass. He's in there right now. He is
arrogant, the soldiers do not seem to like him, and he
drives himself. His vehicle indicates that he is a field
commander, not a staff officer. He is unusually tall, has
slightly Sudanese features, wears a monocle and
strides much as I do. He also wears gloves. He carries
a swagger stick and is annoyed at having to present
credentials every time he goes in or out of the front
gate. When does the guard change?"

"In an hour."

"Where are all the supply, fuel and ammunition
depot documents we need?"

"In a small vault. It's an old key-locked type left by
the British. With all other precautions supplied by
their more modern friends, they don't feel a need to
spend what a new vault would cost. It won't be hard
to open, and it's located in a file room connected to
the office of the chief of supply. They may work
around the clock tonight."

"No, not an Arab army. They will be in conferences
or with their mistresses. Come."

Hareet and the peddler left the room, and went
down to the alley. Greta stood in the shadows of the
alley dressed as a street boy.

Hareet described the colonel of artillery. "Watch
for him. If he comes out, don't lose him."

Hareet and the peddler returned to the building a few blocks away where Hareet had changed from the gentleman in the fez to the crippled fellahin. There the peddler opened a large dossier, and Hareet found the picture and official history and designations of the artillery colonel he had seen go in and out the main gate of General Staff Headquarters.

The peddler read the details. "Colonel Aziz Ramdi. Forty-two years old. Unmarried. Sudanese mother. No foreign posts or training, no staff time, but many commendations for bravery in the last war with us. Commander of the Hundred and Twelfth Field Artillery. They're part of the city defense. Only recently transferred to the city from service on the southern border. He hasn't had the plum positions, doesn't sound like he's made any good connections. Probably because of that Sudanese mother. Hard to say how well-known he could be at staff headquarters."

"I won't need long," Hareet said. "It's reasonable to assume that a line officer who's been out in the field and far from the capital won't be all that familiar to the staff here. He's my best chance, we don't have a lot more time."

The peddler nodded, and with the picture of the artillery colonel in front of him, Hareet worked on his face until he looked as much like Colonel Aziz Ramdi of the Hundred and Twelfth Field Artillery as he could.

"The film could be shot over the wall from a top window," the peddler said. "I have the equipment."

"They would know," Hareet said.

"You could copy and not photograph, then the light would not sensitize the chemicals on the documents."

"There would not be time. I would have to touch

the papers. The data must be secured without their knowing that we have it," Hareet emphasized.

Hareet completed his disguise. With the peddler shuffling far enough ahead of him that they could not be considered in any way together, he walked back to the alley and the room across from the headquarters. It had grown dark in the city, and large floodlights illuminated the headquarters wall and building.

"He is still inside," Greta said from the shadows of the alley.

An hour later, the colonel of artillery came out, got into his Jeep and impatiently presented his credentials at the front gate. He drove off to the left and made a right turn onto a narrow street that was the direct route to his unit.

A fellahin woman dashed out of the shadows directly into the path of his Jeep. A ragged peddler pursued her. The peddler caught the woman in the street in front of the colonel's Jeep, struggled with her amid a torrent of loud screams and curses. Ramdi jammed on his brakes, and added his own curses to the loud Arabic.

The colonel barely felt his Jeep sway as someone jumped into it behind him. His pistol was still under its flap when the thin cord tightened around his throat.

Colonel Aziz Ramdi glared angrily at the officer of the guard at the gate into headquarters. The officer of the guard was nervous as he inspected the colonel's credentials. Only fifteen minutes ago he had checked the colonel out, and he felt ridiculous going through the entire routine again, but he knew he would have been even more nervous if he hadn't. In an Arab army, independent thought and decisions are not encouraged. Another weakness Hareet had exploited before.

The colonel made no explanation for his sudden return, sat in stony silence through the entire careful process. But his arrogant eyes bored through the junior officer with the clear implication that the colonel would remember this insult. The status of recognition is also part of an army too rigid with class and privilege.

"A thousand pardons, Colonel," the officer of the guard said, and returned the credentials with a smart salute.

Hareet drove on into the courtyard without even returning the salute. The junior officer swore under his breath at the back of the arrogant colonel.

Hareet parked his Jeep as close to the main entrance of the headquarters building as he could—a senior officer does not walk far. He jumped out as if impatient to get to some important task, strode rapidly to the entrance. Two majors reached the entrance a hair before he did—which he had arranged by slowing his pace. The majors both stopped and deferred to him. He waved them ahead with an impatient gesture of his swagger stick: asserting his rank, showing democratic largesse and distracting the guard at the front door.

The two majors hurried on into the building so as to not keep the colonel waiting. Not much more than an inch behind them, Hareet merely flashed his credentials to the guard. The guard, hurried by three credentials almost together, and the need to give three fast salutes, barely glanced at the tall colonel's identification.

Hareet was inside the building.

The long corridors were dim, cool and high-vaulted. Hareet strode loudly along the corridors until he located the office of the chief of supply. There was light under the door and the low sound of steady activity inside. As the peddler had predicted, the office of the chief of supply was working long and late this night.

Hareet walked into a lounge for officers only. He entered, went into the lavatory, and then into a booth. Inside the booth, he removed all his makeup. He changed his rank to major. He changed his insignia to that of an artillery unit stationed far to the south. He tore all the credentials of Colonel Aziz Ramdi into small pieces and flushed them down the toilet, removed the credentials for a major of a tank unit in the south from a thin pouch under his clothes. He flushed the pieces of the pouch. He remained in the lounge for an hour, absorbed in reading some important report.

Each hour, he walked back to check the office of the chief of supply. Twice, he went into the officers' dayroom and read a magazine. He drank the thick Turkish coffee the orderly served. In his normal appearance, there would be no one who could know him, as far as the peddler knew there were no officers from the distant artillery unit in the capital at this time, all field units being on twenty-four-hour alert.

At midnight, the office of the chief of supply was as dark and silent as all the other offices. As Hareet had been sure they would, all the officers from the chief of staff on down had gone to rest or party. Tomorrow would be a great day, tonight the building was quiet. Only the guards moved in the corridors of the headquarters.

Hareet waited until a guard had made his rounds of the corridor outside the office of the chief of supply. The corridor silent and empty, Hareet opened the door of the office with a picklock, slipped inside, his knife ready on the remote chance someone had been left behind, perhaps asleep.

No one had.

The door into the windowless file room was open. Hareet fitted a small light to his head and crouched to inspect the vault. It was a simple key-locked vault from British days such as the peddler had reported. Hareet picked the lock with no trouble, swung the door open.

The documents he needed were neatly filed in their proper places. The folders were sealed with a wire-and-plastic seal that had to be broken to open the folder. Hareet broke the seal and removed the documents. They felt faintly slippery to his touch. Tomorrow, ultraviolet light would reveal Hareet's prints, but that would not matter.

He photographed the documents with the miniature camera that had been hidden in the built-up heel of his boot. There were ten lists with maps and dated overlays. The overlays were all new and dated that day. Hareet photographed each document. They became faintly darker under the heat of his intense light. He unloaded the roll of microfilm and placed it in its container in his breast pocket.

He took a second roll of film from his other heel, reloaded the camera and took a second set of photographs.

He returned the documents to their files, resealed the folders as best he could, replaced the folders in the vault and relocked the vault.

He left the file room.

Behind the door of the dark office he sat at the general's desk, smoked a slow cigarette, looked around this high-level office of the enemy and waited for the guard to make his next round. It took a second and a third cigarette. He smoked deeply, enjoying the relaxation.

When the guard had passed, he slipped out of the

office of the chief of supply, relocked the office door and walked openly again to the lounge for officers. Inside a booth once more, he sat and went to sleep with his head against the wall.

Dawn arrived soon after five o'clock that morning. The building came slowly to life. Vehicles drove up and parked outside. Orders were shouted all through the courtyard and at the gates. The corridors echoed with the smart clicking of heels, and the morning greetings of the elite officers. Heavy-booted footsteps rang all through the building. Office doors opened and closed like the ragged sound of small artillery.

Hareet waited until just after six o'clock when the initial chaos had slowed to a steady sound of routine.

Inside the booth he took a large piece of wrapped halvah from his pocket, unwrapped it, and embedded the second roll of microfilm inside until it was completely covered with the soft confection.

He left the booth, went out into the lounge that was still empty at the early hour and returned to the corridor.

Hareet walked calmly toward the front door. Visiting officers were being checked in by the sleepy nightshift guards. Excitement and confusion were high at the door—the fever of impending war in any army. The day-shift guards were forming in the courtyard. The ragged fellahin servants were sweeping the courtyard, watering it down in preparation for the heat of the day to come.

Already the sun was up. It was going to be a dazzling day. Far across the courtyard at the front gate, Hareet could see the night-shift guards stretching the weariness from their bones, waiting for their relief. Vehicles coughed and sputtered in the morning air. The officers continued to pour in. No one was going out.

Hareet waited until the day-shift guards forming outside began to march to the posts to make the official transfer with the night-shift guards. He placed his pistol in his pocket, checked the film in his breast pocket, and when a large group of officers came across the courtyard and approached the front entrance, strode out and walked straight up to the door.

The officers thronged in the entrance.

A guard turned around to check Hareet's credentials.

There was a faint click somewhere in the wall, and an alarm began to sound, echoing through the building and out across the courtyard. The guard at the door stared at Hareet.

Hareet stabbed him in the heart, held the man's body close against him, and walked out into the courtyard through the confused group of incoming officers.

For a long moment, as the alarm continued to sound through the headquarters and over the courtyard in the bright morning, the officers and guards milled around and shouted and no one noticed Hareet walking across the courtyard away from both the building and the front gate still carrying the dead guard upright against him as if they were hurrying together toward some important official duty.

Then the officer of the guard saw them out there all alone and going in the odd direction, saw that one man was holding up the other. He ran after them, shouting, "You out there! You, Major! Stop where you are! Stop—"

Hareet dropped the dead guard, drew his pistol and shot the running officer of the guard. Then he turned and ran on across the courtyard toward the small barred side gate where he knew there was only one guard.

Pandemonium flowed through the building and the courtyard as the guards and officers all grabbed for their weapons. Quickly the day-shift and night-shift guards all spotted Hareet and began to converge on him. The guard at the side gate fired and missed.

Hareet shot the guard down.

He leaped for the wall. A bullet hit him in the leg, buckled it. He collapsed, rolled, and struggled up again. He grasped the bars of the gate and hauled himself up toward the top of the wall. Outside the wall, the two armored cars on patrol both careened into the street. Hareet reached the top of the wall.

A burst of fire struck him in the back. The machine guns on the armored cars cut him in two. Two rifle bullets exploded in his head. His body, at the very top of the wall, fell back to the stones of the courtyard.

The night-shift and day-shift guards stood all around Captain Hareet's body, uncertain what to do, perhaps awed by the daring escape that had failed.

A colonel of military police pushed through the guards and shot Hareet in the head again.

The colonel bent down, searched, and found the microfilm in Hareet's breast pocket. The colonel laughed and kicked the dead body. Some soldiers laughed now, spat on Hareet's lifeless eyes.

"Cut his head off," the colonel of military police ordered. "Hang it on the gate with a sign: Pig of a Spy!"

A general of the staff walked slowly up, and the soldiers and other officers gave way. The general looked down at Hareet's body. The colonel of military police handed the general the roll of microfilm.

"Take his body and identify it, Colonel, before you cut off any heads," the general said. "A very stupid attempt, but well done. He very nearly escaped."

"A desperate attempt," the colonel sneered. "A hopeless attempt. They are afraid of us, General."

"Of course they are afraid of us, as we are afraid of them," the general said almost wearily. "Find out what it was they wanted, Colonel, what he has on that microfilm. Not that it matters now, but they might try again."

"They will always fail," the colonel insisted. He did not like to be told he was afraid of the enemy. That was weak, defeatist talk. He would watch the general. But now he looked down again at the dead body. "The fool never knew it would have done him no good to succeed. We would locate what he took even if he had escaped, and instantly change our plans."

The colonel laughed. Hareet's body was taken away. The chief of supply quickly identified the enormity of the theft and posted a twenty-four-hour guard at his door. Even though, he explained to the army commander, there was no way anyone could get that data without the chief of supply knowing it instantly and changing it. In any event, the chief of supply assured the army commander, the data was still secret and safe, there was no need to change the vital plans with so little time left. The army commander was relieved, such a change could have delayed them for days.

Captain Hareet was soon identified, and his head cut off and hung on the gates for the fellahin to jeer at.

The headquarters returned to its routine. Officers came and went in a steady stream. The fellahin servants cleaned the courtyard while the officers prepared for war. The hardworking, important and excited officers ignored the ragged peasants. One of the fellahin swept up a large piece of discarded halvah. He dropped the halvah into his trash sack. Eventually he took the sack to a trash box near the small barred gate in the side wall where Hareet had died.

Soon, a truck picked up the trash boxes and drove them to the city waste dump. Out at the dump, a ragged peddler scraped among the boxes. Later, the same peddler hawked wares in front of a hotel near the eastern edge of the city.

A pretty Italian tourist woman bought a small urn from the peddler.

That evening, the pretty Italian tourist checked out of her small hotel and drove from the city to a deserted beach. On the beach, she stripped down and swam out to sea.

Thirty-six hours later, the attack was launched. Ten hours after that, the war was essentially over. All the supply depots, ammunition dumps and fuel centers of the attacking army were destroyed within ten hours of the initial attack.

Some weeks later, Lieutenant Greta Frank sat alone on a hill in the north of her country and looked out toward the border beyond the orange trees and olive groves. The border was quiet. It was not yet safe, but it was becoming safer.

Greta cried.

The minister came up the hill and squatted down in the dry dust. His hard gray eyes looked out toward the border.

"There was no other way," the minister said. "They had to be convinced that he had tried and failed. They had to catch him—and not alive. He knew it was the only plan that would work."

"And you knew," Greta said.

"I knew."

"You knew before we went."

The minister drew patterns in the dust with his walking stick.

"Why didn't you go there and do it yourself?" Greta asked. "The great minister who won the war."

"I could not have done it."

"No, you could not have done it, and I could not have done it, and the peddler, whoever he really is, could not have done it. Only Paul could have done it," Greta said. She studied the patterns drawn in the dust by the minister. Ancient patterns like the sun and moon of cavemen, hieroglyphics. "He knew he was the only way."

Below, among the orange trees, two young boys ran and shouted, played soldier.

JOHN LESCROART & M. J. ROSE

John Lescroart is a bestselling writer of legal thrillers. M. J. Rose is an international bestselling writer of thrillers about a sex therapist and her patients. Intersecting those two variations seemed like a difficult challenge, but that's exactly what *The Portal* does. Via e-mail from one coast to another, Lescroart and Rose explored the psyche and actions of Lucy Delrey, a young, disturbed woman who, at different points displayed facets that surprised both authors. For Rose, Lucy's therapy is the portal itself: a door that opens into a darkened room, which is all Dr. Morgan Snow (from Rose's thriller *The Halo Effect*) can see. Consequently, the therapist's advice, which Lucy takes to heart and which propels the story forward, is based on elusive shadows. For Lescroart, the story represented an opportunity to revisit the legal world from which he drew his bestselling thriller *Guilt*. Lucy's trip to exorcize her demons takes her straight to San

Francisco (Lescroart's main stomping grounds), where sophisticated professionals eat in fine restaurants, stay in fine hotels and mingle within a society that, for all its surface appeal, hides many a dark secret.

THE PORTAL

"I think there is something wrong with me, emotionally."

I nodded. She'd said this before. In almost every session. Lucy Delrey had been in therapy with me for two months. Every Tuesday evening at 6:00 p.m. she arrived at my office on Manhattan's Upper East Side, sat opposite me, and we chipped away at her defenses.

"Why do you feel there's something wrong?" I asked her.

"I just don't feel anything, Dr. Snow. Not even in the most extreme circumstances."

"What are the most extreme circumstances?" The conversation we were having was almost identical to the conversation we'd had last week, and every week before that. We always got to this point when Lucy would shut down, sit silently for a few minutes, and then change the subject and talk about how as a child she'd wanted to be an artist and about the man who had inspired her.

Tonight she answered me, for the first time.

"When I destroy someone. Even then, Dr. Snow. I don't feel anything."

She paused. Looked at me. Waited. Tried to read my face. But I was sure I hadn't shown any shock or surprise. I was used to confessions. Even overly dramatic ones, like this.

I persevered. "What do you mean, destroy someone?"

In the few seconds it took until she answered, I anticipated she meant that she was speaking of destruction metaphorically. I waited, curious.

"Destroy. You know. Assassinate." Her voice started out as a whisper and became softer with each additional word. "Annihilate." And softer still so that the last word, "Kill," was barely audible.

There was no change of expression while she spoke, but as soon as she finished, a look of exhaustion settled on her face. As if just saying the words had been tiring.

It was this expression that made me wonder for a brief second if it was actually possible that she was— no. In all the time she had been in therapy, nothing she had ever said suggested she was capable of killing anyone. She was using these words as a metaphor for the psychological destruction of people she loved.

"I should feel something. I should be upset." Her voice was back to its usual timbre.

This was the longest Lucy had ever gone without mentioning Frank Millay—the artist she had known when she was a child—who had painted watercolors on the boardwalk in Brooklyn Heights.

Some sessions she described the paintings: how they captured the essence of the river and the cityscape, how they moved her and made her want to learn how to use the brush and the pigments to create washes that would mean something. Other nights she told me about the painter himself and how it had taken her, a girl of seven, months to get him to talk to her and then finally to show her how to use the brush on the thick paper that had a texture created to capture the merest hint of color.

During all those sessions I had become aware of my patient's attention to detail. Her obsession with color. Her memory that retained every nuance of those days.

But even after all those months I did not know why Lucy had come to me.

Oh, I knew she was troubled by what she perceived about her lack of emotion. But we never got further than the fact of it. The only real emotion she ever exhibited was when she spoke about the painter and the paintings and her impression of them.

Now, finally, she had broken the repetition of her childhood memories with a revelation that caught me off guard.

"What do you think about when you are—while you are destroying someone?"

"Just that it's a job. I'm concentrating on the steps. On the work."

I still didn't believe that she was serious. Nothing in her character suggested it. I had worked with men and women in prison. I'd listened to descriptions of cold-blooded murders and crimes of passion. I'd watched patients' faces contort with anguish as they described breaking out of a fugue state and finding a knife or a gun in their hand or their fingers around someone's throat, the skin a milky blue-white streaked with finger burns.

"I'm sorry, Lucy. I'm not sure I understand. 'It's a job'? Do you mean that literally? I thought you were a photographer."

"I am. But in addition…people hire me…" Lucy's words trailed off.

I nodded, encouraging her to go on.

"It's not something I talk about in polite society. I'm not used to talking about it. But I think you need to know so that you understand me better. So that you can help me figure out why I don't even care about how I fuck up people's lives. Destroy them."

I put my right foot out in front of me instinctively. To press down on the panic button.

But there was no such button in my office—it was in the small room where I used to conduct therapy sessions at the prison. Lucy was so convincing that she actually was a killer that I'd responded the way I would with a criminal in prison and extended my foot to call for help. This prickling realization—that Lucy might indeed be a killer and not just speaking in metaphor—chilled me.

But I didn't have the luxury of focusing on how I was feeling. I had to say something. To get Lucy to keep talking. To get more information from her. To figure out what I was going to do because the one time a therapist can break a client's confidentiality is if a life is in imminent danger.

The one time.

"I don't believe that you don't have feelings about what you do," I offered. "Usually when we don't feel it's because we are blocking our emotions."

"Why would I do that? It's how I make my living. I'm not ashamed of it. I kill them with their own passions."

"What do you mean?"

"Do you know that if you offer a man sex he won't pay a whole lot of attention to who you are? The same man who would run a Dun & Bradstreet before he'd take your business call will take a woman to bed without even knowing her last name. It's that lust that I count on. That hard-cock need that makes what I do so easy. Too easy really. I don't think that a man should be that easy to murder. He should fight. He should be scared. He should know his life is in danger—not just be lying there bare-assed and spread-eagled with a blonde giving him head. They don't even know…" Lucy stopped here to take a sip from the coffee cup she'd brought in with her.

My own hand was shaking slightly. I hoped Lucy didn't notice.

Yes, I'd heard confessions like this before, but always before in the prison, with guards watching. Not here in my offfce.

"Does it give you pleasure?"

She nodded. "If I know enough about the man. And if he's enough of a scum. Yes. You could say I'm some sort of avenging angel. I only kill men who deserve it. Who have done the unforgivable. Who need to be punished."

I was watching for any sign of psychosis, still trying to tell if this was fantasy or reality. But her pupils were not dilated. Her breathing was regular. There was no sweat on her upper lip or forehead. No sheen to her skin. Her fingers did not twitch in her lap. Her feet did not tap. She spoke in the same even voice I'd heard for a long time. She seemed in full control and connected, very much in the present moment.

"The painter," she said. I nodded. "When I was a kid, he made me realize that anything could be made into something else. He'd look at that water that I just saw as some stretch of muddy blue and he'd find a hundred colors in it. Some of them brilliant."

"Did the painter die?"

"I don't know. He moved away. He didn't tell me. One day, he was just gone. I went looking for him. But no one knew what happened. I look in galleries when I can. He'd be about fifty now. Fifty-year-old men are easier to fool than thirty-year-old men. The younger men aren't always sure. They succumb but they can be a little suspicious at first. Like, why is she coming on to me? *To me?* But the older guys are so damn flattered you can see their eyes getting erections. They are too damn easy."

I nodded. "Maybe the painter died. Maybe he didn't move away."

She didn't say anything. But suddenly her eyes filled with tears. One rolled down her cheek and she reached out to brush it away. Her surprise at her tears was clear.

"I never thought about him dying."

"Why not? Why did you assume he moved without saying goodbye?"

She shook her head as if she were getting rid of the question I'd raised. And then she changed the subject. "I should be upset about what I do. I know I should. But it's like these guys deserve it. I mean most of them are doing something to someone. They are abusing someone somehow. It's not like they are all nice guys. But I give all of them a chance. Before I take them back to the room, I give them a chance to turn me down. I ask them if they are married or if they have a girlfriend. And then ask them if they really want to do this. If they really want to hurt the women they are with."

"Some of them must say no."

"Not very many. Maybe two."

I wanted to ask her out of how many. But I didn't want to stop her.

"One man stroked my skin. His fingertips were as

soft as a woman's. He had blue eyes. I remember his eyes. Because of those damn fingers that ran up and down my arm making me shiver. Usually, I don't feel anything. That's what I meant. Before. I don't feel anything when they touch me. Or when I pull the trigger."

"You use a gun?"

I hadn't meant to ask that bluntly—as if I doubted her. It was unprofessional. I'd wanted to ask her how she killed them, not blurt out the worse-case scenario I could imagine.

She looked at me as if I were the one who was crazy and needed help. "A gun?"

"When you kill them?"

"Dr. Snow, I set them up. I pump them up. I am a hired assassin. I expose them and ruin them. My whole apartment is a camera. I destroy them by taking pictures of them and then turning them over to cops or detectives or the tabloids. Character assassin." She smiled.

And for a few seconds there was no question in my mind that a man would go with her and not think twice.

"Do you think I should try to find him? Find Frank Millay, finally?"

It was the end of the session, but I didn't stand as I often did to signify that Lucy's time was up. She had arrived at a crucial point in her therapy and I didn't want to cut her short.

"I think you want to find him. And that's what's important."

Typically, I preferred to ask, not to answer, questions. In fact, I'd told Lucy, the same way I told all my patients at some point, that only by answering one's own questions could one come to terms with personal truths. But she had finally expressed a need, a desire. And that was a breakthrough for her. From everything she'd described, she hadn't given in to any real emotion since that last time she was with him. She called him the portal. After he was gone, her emotional life effectively stopped.

"There's one thing, Lucy. We need to make sure that if you do go find him it's to understand. Not to act out."

She smiled, slyly, seductively, slipping into the pose she used when she needed to hide from me. From anyone, I guessed. I'd witnessed her do this in almost every session. We'd get close to something critical and she would shut down.

Was Lucy ready to go find Millay?

Was it within the realm of my responsibility to hold her back?

"I'm sure that I'm going to understand. Not to act out. Aren't you sure, Dr. Snow?"

"While we've considered that something may have happened with Frank Millay that both closed you up emotionally and caused him to disappear, I wish you would give it some more time here. But I understand your frustration. How long are you going to give yourself to find him?"

"I don't know. Maybe a couple of weeks?"

"Would you think about coming in for another session? Or two? So we can make sure that if you find out what happened, you will be prepared."

Lucy grasped the implication immediately. She sat with her back pressed into her chair, all defensiveness now, her legs tightly crossed and turned sideways. "I've already done regressive-analysis hypnosis with my last therapist," she said. "We didn't uncover anything like that."

"Like what, Lucy?"

"Like rape."

"But that doesn't mean you haven't buried the bare facts."

"The bare facts." Moisture was evident in Lucy's eyes and her voice came hot with anger, although she, too, modulated her volume. "Frank Millay did not rape me."

"All right."

"Please don't 'all right' me, Doctor. I would remember that. I promise you."

I nodded, drew in a breath. I couldn't hold her here.

"You're searching for something that you've lost, and whatever that is has had a profound effect on your ability to feel things. If you can find that something in the real world, rather than in my office, or with some other psychoanalyst, yes, Lucy, yes, it might start the healing."

"Law offices of Bascom, Owen, Millay."

"Oh. Could I speak to Frank Millay, please?"

"Certainly," the cultured female voice said. "Can I tell him who's calling?"

"An old friend. I'm not sure if he'd remember me. My name is Lucy Delrey."

"Just a moment."

On the one hand, it had been too easy; and on the other hand, impossible. Before Dr. Snow's suggestion that she try to physically locate Frank Millay, Lucy had looked in a haphazard fashion through gallery openings in the newspapers, or stopped in at galleries when the art struck her in some way that seemed vaguely familiar. She never consciously considered the fact that the street artist had given up on his first love and entered another field. Similarly, she had never before considered Googling the name Frank Millay.

Where the name came up in two seconds.

An attorney in San Francisco.

It couldn't possibly be the same man. But she had to call and find out. She had to be sure.

"This is Frank Millay."

For an instant, she found herself tongue-tied. But then, afraid that he'd hang up if she didn't speak, she found her voice. "Is this the Frank Millay who used to be an artist in New York?"

Now the pause came from the other end. "Who used to paint anyway. Yes." Another hesitation. "I'm sorry. My secretary gave me your name, but…"

"Lucy," she said. "Lucy Delrey. I was a little girl…"

"Oh my God," he said under his breath. "Little Lucy, of course. How little were you then?"

"Seven. I'm thirty now."

"Thirty? God. Thirty is impossible."

"Not if you're about fifty. That would be about right." She couldn't hold back a small, nervous laugh. It was *his* voice. She'd have recognized it anywhere. Although it had an unaccustomed seriousness to it, an adultness that she thought befit his new profession. "You're a *lawyer* now?"

"Only for the past twenty years," he said. "Wow, Lucy." Words seemed to fail him. "You looked me up?"

"Googled you actually, yes."

"But…what are you doing? Where are you?"

"I'm home, still in New York. I'm a…" But her business didn't lend itself to easy explanation. "I'm a photographer," she said.

"So somebody's still doing art," he said. Then, in an awkward tone, filling in the space, "That's good to hear."

"Yeah, well…" A silence settled for a minute, until Lucy surprised herself. "Listen, Mr. Millay," she began.

"Frank, please."

"Okay, Frank. It just happens that I'm coming out to San Francisco next week on some business. Would it be too weird if I came to see you? If we had lunch or something?" Sensing his reluctance over the line, she pressed on. "I wouldn't blame you if you said no, but in spite of this call, I promise I'm not a flake or a stalker or anything... I just still remember what an incredible impact your paintings had on me. Still do, as I remember them. It...it would mean a lot. I just feel like I need to see you."

Silence for a long beat. "I'm married now," he said. "I've got three children. I don't know if my wife..." He let the sentence hang.

"Please," she said. "She doesn't have to know. It's so important. We need to talk, that's all."

"You know I don't paint anymore, Lucy. I haven't touched a brush in twenty years."

"No, it's more than that. It's you, who you were." Then, unsure of exactly what she meant, she added, "It's not just that, either."

"No," he said. "No, I suppose not." Finally, when he did speak, his voice was nearly unrecognizable, constricted with that *adult* quality. "I'll find some time," he said. "What day next week?"

She didn't sleep well over the next five days.

Frank Millay's colors, particularly that muddy blue, seeped into her dreams and woke her over and over again. It was a cold blue under a cold sky and she woke up, paradoxically, dripping with sweat. And sexually aroused.

All the dreams had the same setting. Millay's whole room was a womb enclosed in that dark, muddy blue—the river as he'd painted it endlessly flowing along the windowless walls over the bed.

Which made no sense.

She had no memory that she had ever been to his bedroom. She had never seen his bed.

But something was stirring things up.

The last dream was different. It started with the smells of must or animal or mold, and there was a bright light at the end of a dark green tunnel. Then she turned and walked through a red door and suddenly was in Millay's muddy blue room. She felt the skin on her thighs rubbing together and realized that she didn't have any clothes on. She was standing on a golden storage box and he was painting her picture, although she could only see his head behind the canvas. He had a blond beard that looked wet somehow. He kept saying something in a deep voice that seemed to echo in her bones and make her weak. Stepping around the picture, he walked right up close to her. He smelled like that other smell, and now she recognized that it was semen. He wore an orange tie-dyed T-shirt, but no pants and no underwear. Because she was standing on the storage box, their faces were at almost the same height and he held her eyes while he put his hand between her legs. Then she looked down and something muddy and blue was coming out of his penis and he was painting her with it. Stroke after stroke after stroke.

She woke up, sobbing, in the middle of an orgasm.

And finally it all came back.

She knew now that in a fundamental way, she had at last begun to heal. The recurring waves of what had been repressed memory now throbbed with the persistence of a bone bruise, painful enough on two more occasions to bring her to tears, but at least she was no longer numb. She almost called Dr. Snow to tell her that she'd begun to feel things again. If much of it was negative and painful, that was okay. It was the price to get back to normal. But she knew that she wasn't quite finished yet. To complete the recovery, she would have to assassinate one last man. The one who'd all but destroyed her so many years ago.

Frank Millay clearly didn't want her to come to his office. He'd e-mailed her to say they should meet at the Slanted Door, a terrific and easy-to-find Vietnamese restaurant located in San Francisco's newly renovated Ferry Building, at the foot of Market Street. He had one o'clock reservations there under the name York. He'd explained that it wasn't a place where they were likely to run into too many of his colleagues on a weekday afternoon. She realized with a bit of a thrill that he was already afraid of exposure, even of being seen with her. And this led to the understanding that he only could have agreed to the meeting with her for one of three very different reasons—to somehow try to explain what he'd done, to beg her to forgive him, or to get the details of her blackmail.

But Lucy knew fifty-year-old men. Once she started coming on to him, in spite of what he'd done to her, he would never suspect her true motive. He would believe that, sick as it might be, she was still, after all, attracted to him. She had her story down, her cameras and microphones hidden and primed in her hotel room at the Four Seasons a couple of blocks away.

She was ready.

Lucy, braless, and further turned out in a black slit skirt, low heels and a tightly fitted red silk blouse, arrived and got seated at their table—tucked away in a corner—twenty minutes early. It was a cool day, and cool in the restaurant. It calmed and somewhat gratified Lucy to realize that no man who looked her way seemed to be able to avoid a glance at her erect nipples.

When Frank Millay came to the greeting station, she recognized him immediately, even though he was now the quintessential lawyer—clean-shaven, short-haired, dressed in a three-piece suit. He was still trim, still handsome, although slightly gone to gray. But the face had no slackness to it, the jaw was firm. Close up, she could see that the deep blue artist's eyes still might have the power to captivate. But not her. Not anymore.

When the hostess left him, he sat, assayed a bit of a worried smile and said, "My God, you're beautiful."

"Thank you."

A waiter came by, introduced himself and presented menus, saying he'd be back in a couple of minutes. A busboy poured water. Out the window, on the Bay, the Sausalito ferry with its complement of screeching sea-gulls steamed out from its mooring under the scudding clouds.

Millay's eyes darted down to her breasts, then came back up to her face. He sighed. "This is awkward."

Lucy reached out her hand and placed it over his for an instant, then withdrew it. "It's all right," she said. "I guess I should have told you on the telephone. I contacted you because I wanted you to know that I forgive you."

"I don't know why…" he began. "It's why I left New York, to get away from what I was doing. It was all getting out of control, what I did to you was just part of it. I was going through a crazy time." He brought his hand to his face, rubbed the side of his cheek. His look was something more than chagrin, touched by a brush—still—of fear. "I can't explain it."

"You don't have to," Lucy said. "We all make mistakes."

"Not like that. I've got a seven-year-old daughter right now. The thought of what I did to you still makes me sick. I'm so sorry. So sorry."

"Were there others?"

"No!" Frank Millay nearly blurted it out. "No," he said again. "It was just you, the pretty little girl who loved my paintings. The only one who loved them, to tell you the truth. And who made me take her up to my room one time to see them."

"Was it only once?" Again, she touched his hand. "I really don't remember."

"Just once," he said. "Once was enough."

The waiter arrived and took their order. She said she'd like to have some wine, but only if he'd join her. By the time the waiter left, Frank Millay had visibly relaxed. Pushed back from the table, he sat with his ankle resting on the opposite knee. He wore stunning black shoes of knitted leather, black socks that disappeared into his pants leg. Lucy, fidgeting now as though she were slightly nervous, managed to undo the second button on her blouse.

"So," she said, "you're married now?"

"Yes."

"Happily?"

"Well, seventeen years. We're okay."

"That doesn't sound very romantic."

"It's really not very romantic."

"Do you miss it? Romance?"

"Not really," he said. Then, "Sometimes, I guess. Who wouldn't?"

"That seems a shame. You're still a very good-looking man. You must know that. You must hear it all the time."

A small embarrassed chuckle. "Thank you, but I wouldn't quite say that I hear it all the time. And I for damn sure wouldn't call me good-looking anymore."

She put her hand on his again, and this time she left it there as she met his eyes. "I would," she said. "Why do you think I've remembered you after all this time? Do you think, that day, it was all your idea?"

After that, it was easy.

At the Four Seasons, they went straight up from the hotel entrance to her two-room suite. As soon as they were inside, Lucy excused herself for a moment, leaving Frank Millay in the living-room section while she went, ostensibly, to use the bathroom. One of her cameras that looked like a pen she had arranged on the dresser—it would automatically snap a picture every minute until she turned it off. The video camera was her cell phone, which she arranged and propped on one of the bed tables.

In the bathroom, she flushed the toilet for verisimilitude's sake, then stepped out into the bedroom, undoing her blouse now, taking it off, laying it on the bed. "Frank," she said, "aren't you going to come in here?"

"Sure."

He appeared in the doorway and stopped, taking her in.

She saw the hesitation now. He still had his coat and tie on. And it was one of her inviolable rules—she would give each of her victims one last chance to save themselves, to prove to her that they were better than they appeared. Even Frank Millay might still escape, although she didn't want that to happen.

She gave him what she knew was her finest smile. Winsome and seductive at once, playful but with a serious edge of promised passion underneath. "Are you sure you're comfortable with this?" she asked him. "I don't want to force you to do anything you don't want to do."

He broke a small smile that seemed to mock himself. "If you hadn't wanted to force me," he said, "you would have left your shirt on."

She unclasped the hook on her skirt and let it drop to the floor. "Well, then," she said, stepping out of it, sitting on the bed where she knew the cameras would capture everything. She patted the mattress next to her. "Why don't you come over here?"

Still, he seemed to hesitate for one last moment before he started moving toward her. When he got in front of her, she reached for his zipper, traced her finger down the bulge in the front. "Oh, my," she said.

She felt his hands in her hair, traveling down the sides of her head to cup her face, which he lifted so that she looked up at him.

"I'm so sorry," he said as his hands slipped lower.

"No. You don't need—" But suddenly she felt the hands pushing down on her shoulders, holding her where she sat, then slowly, almost as though he were caressing her, closing around her neck.

"Don't you see?" His face suddenly inches from hers. "I can't take the risk. Someday you might tell."

"But no, I—"

And then there was no way to make any more sound. She tried to call out, to straighten up off the bed, to kick at him, but he was nearly twice her size and now seized with an irresistible power. He pushed her back onto the bed and fell upon her, his hands closing tighter and tighter around her windpipe.

Her vision exploded into yellows and purples and greens and then they all blended to a muddy blue, then a darker, colder blue.

And then no colors at all. Only black.

I hadn't heard from Lucy for two weeks when I turned on the news late one night and watched her face appear on the screen while a reporter described the brutal murder that had taken place in San Francisco.

"The killing was recorded on Lucy Delrey's cell-phone camera, which the police discovered at the scene."

Immediately in the hours, days and weeks afterward, Millay's PR machine went into action and it was clear that by the time the case went to trial, his attorneys would have spun it so that the world at large would perceive Lucy Delrey as a psychotic nymphomaniac who got pleasure from setting up men sexually in order to destroy them. Frank Millay had been her hapless victim.

The sympathy would be with him by then, but I've got to believe that even in San Francisco, if you strangle a woman on videotape, you're looking at some kind of a stretch in prison. Millay's career—his entire life—would be ruined. It could never be the same.

And the strange thing was, just as I had asked her to, Lucy had found the complicated truth. No matter what had happened in those final minutes, she had gone out there to destroy him and she'd done it.

DAVID LISS

David Liss's first novel, *A Conspiracy of Paper* began with what may have been an unlikely inspiration for a thriller: his ongoing doctoral work on the 18th century British novel and its relationship to emerging modes of finance. Liss succeeded by showing how the rise of paper currency was surrounded by an air of mystery, danger, urgency and cultural paranoia, but he also succeeded because of his intrepid protagonist, Benjamin Weaver, a daring and reckless thief-taker—roughly a combination of modern-day private eye, police-officer-for-hire and hired muscle. Weaver's fearlessness on the lawless streets of 18th century London, and his willingness to meet danger head-on, won the character many fans, and he returned in *A Spectacle of Corruption* and will be back again in *The Devil's Company*.

Liss has stated in interviews that he tremendously enjoys writing about Weaver and the violent and colorful world he inhabits, but he feels the need to divide his time between that character and his stand-alone thrillers, *The Coffee Trader* and *The Ethical Assassin*. Unfortunately, between writing more tales of Weaver and the time required to explore other interests, Liss has had no time to pursue a project that has interested him since completing *Conspiracy*—a story set in the same world inhabited by Weaver but focusing on other characters—with Weaver occupying the role of secondary figure.

Until now, that is.

The Double Dealer has at its center an aging highwayman who wants to tell one last story before he dies, the story of an encounter years ago with the young Benjamin Weaver, once a highwayman himself. The fun in a project like this, according to Liss, is to rethink some of the most basic ideas of a recurring character in order to see him anew. Liss enjoys writing about flawed protagonists and sympathetic villains because in real life no one is perfect or perfectly bad, and everyone is the hero of his or her own story.

The Double Dealer has given Liss the chance to present his ongoing hero as the villain of someone else's story.

THE DOUBLE DEALER

I'm old and like to die soon, and no one will care when I do, and that's the truth. But I've a story to tell before I go, and I've paid this here gaunt scholar fellow with a face of a rotten apple to write it down. I aim to make him read it back, too, as I don't trust him and I'll not pay a penny until I like what I hear.

It ain't often I like what I hear. Them newspapers are full three, four, maybe five times a year of the great deeds of that worthless Jew, Benjamin Weaver—that great man, what done this favor for the ministry, or that for the mighty Duke or Arse-Wipe or good Squire Milksop. Old as he is, he's still at it. They forget, they do, but old Fisher don't forget. I recollect it all, as I crossed with him when we was both young and he was no better than me—maybe worse, for his being a Jew withal.

It ain't no secret, but not oft spoke of neither, that time was this hero, a "thief-taker," claims to make streets safe for the likes of what calls themselves ordinary man. No better than one of my number, a prig and one of the highway, and he'd have been at ease with the shitten likes of any blackguard cutpurse.

The world remembers that he was once a pugilist, and lived by his fists. They know him now as some kind of do-gooder, but there was a time between that, when his fighting days was done, and he ain't yet figured out this thief-taking lay. I know all about it, and I aim to make it public.

So, I begin with a piss-rainy autumn day, maybe 1717 or '18—maybe '19 or '20. Can't say as I quite recall, being as I said old and having blood come out both me lungs and me arse. But that ain't your concern. Yours is that when I was young I come 'pon a handsomely dressed spark finishing his business with a mighty fine-looking equipage—lonely all of them, on a nice, ripe deserted stretch of highway. He had in his hands a sack full of coins and jewels and mighty pretty things, and then said his farewells to a pair of ugly bitches, past thirty, and so good for nothing. He charmed them, though, as he called himself Gentleman Ben, and they blushed and bat their eyelashes like he were a spark at a dance and not the man what bound up their coachman and took their precious dainties. His partner, a fellow called Thomas Lane, were some twenty feet down the road, keeping his eye sharp for trouble.

These two were like brothers, never thinking to do a lay, one without the other. They even looked alike, with their dark hair, tall stature and wide backs, both. And that's the thing, ain't it? You don't want to mess with these sorts of prigs, these coves what are never one without the other, these sparks what come to be like blood, for you do wrong by the one, you must surely face the other.

So it was that I rode close to Thomas Lane (though I didn't hear his name 'til later). The other one, what I learned was Weaver, was at the equipage, making pretty talk to the ladies. The sun, peeking through them clouds, were before me, and I couldn't see Lane's face all clear, but I could see it crumpled well enough and I knew he'd had enough and more of Weaver's fripperies with these hags. He were looking back 'pon Weaver and not forward to me, so that he never heard me nor saw me neither, and I rode real quiet, as I trained my horse to do, and snuck up to him all silent like and pummeled him hard in his head. He fell over but not down, and so I struck him in the head again, and once again in that very same pate to make certain he stayed quiet, and this plan worked well enough, for this last blow, I later heard, quite killed him, but I didn't think so then. All I knowed was that he made not a sound more, and that contented me.

I had no plan to kill him. He weren't no friend of mine, but he was a brother prig, and I meant no more but his silence. Still, once it were done, there could be no helping it. No tears will squeeze the breath back into him, will it?

Now, coming from the other way were my friend and partner in these affairs, a spark called Ruddy Dick. There were some three or four fellows I regularly engaged with for my adventures, but none were more trusted by me than old Dick, an aged fellow, as I thought then, though some twenty years my junior to where I am now. So, I catch old Dick's eye, and we know at once the lay, for we were longtime friends, like I said.

This Weaver might have not been keeping his wits about him, but those what he robbed were, and they saw the freaks I played 'pon Thomas Lane. They pointed and cried out, as though these two highwaymen were friends and I the enemy. Never once did they presume I come to save them, but that's the curse of this here face, even more terrible when I was young, if you'll credit that.

With the hags crying out and then taking shelter in their coach, I turn to this gentleman bandit, and I shout to him. I say, "Ho, my spark, I'm afeard I've quite bludgeoned your fellow, and I'm afeard you're next."

Weaver—though, as I says, I knew not yet his name—turns to me and stares not with surprise or horror or sadness, but with a rage burning in those dark eyes, clear enough through the misty rain. In the time it takes between you cut yourself and the blood starts its flowing, he understood all. He observed the scene, observed what I intended, and I knew then that I'd made an enemy.

That were the bad news, as they say. The good news were that I didn't expect he'd live long, not with Ruddy Dick coming down 'pon him hard. He'd spurred his horse to a good gallop and drew his blade, ready to take off the distracted Jew's head as though it were the foreskin 'pon a privy portion.

Now, there's Weaver, staring at me with those hateful eyes, and there's me, holding his gaze, keeping him distracted while Dick rides hard. It's but a tick of the clock, or less even, before this angry fellow is a headless angry fellow, but all at once, like he's got eyes peeking through them locks behind him, he turns. He drops his sack of goodies, and in an instant his blade is out and swinging, and it's at Dick before Dick's blade is on him. Nothing quite so colorful as a beheading, but the blade swings and opens Dick's throat, and the blood's all ruddy fountainish. That was it, then. The death of Dick.

Right tragic it was, a good friend such as he, who I shared my victuals and coin and whores with. Still, life must march forward, and Weaver weren't the only one who could see all clear and easy in the blink of a rat's eye. I spurred my horse, and make like I'm like to take a swipe at Weaver, all revenge-ish, but instead I reach down, grab the sack of plunder as was dropped, and I speed away, leaving behind me a pair of corpses with their puddles of blood.

It was but a matter of weeks before I learned that the one I pummeled never lived after. The other one, the cove yet alive, I now heard were called Benjamin Weaver, and that he had vowed to be revenged for what I done. So a month or two I stays on my guard, but nothing transpired. I heard no discussion of Weaver nor of his exploits, and I began to wonder if he might be dead or gone into hiding. That, I told myself, were the end of it. But it weren't the end, and though I talked a mouthful and been through two pints, it ain't but the beginning of this tale.

So, a year or more later, I'm on a fresh lay. I wished I could hole up as men was being nabbed all regular like, sent to the gallows like chickens to the butcher. I planned my lays careful, and didn't like to do many and take the chance of being 'peached. This one was no more than a month since the last because the last ain't quite worked as intended. I'd been led to believe that a particular coach would contain a great fortune, and for what I knew it did, but all were contained within a strongbox. This particular box was made by some German named Domal, said to be the cleverest maker of such things in the world. It were too strong for breaking, and too intricate for picking. All that work had brought wealth, but wealth I could not reach. I still had it hidden away, in my secret spot in my secret rooms—for I told no one where I lived, not even my closest friends, for it's best to trust no one, in particular your friends.

Instead of this box, which I can't open, I now set my eyes 'pon a coach to return Londonward for the season from the summer in Yorkshire. These things are ordered just so, and there would be trunks and ladies and jewels—silver buckles and fine handkerchiefs, and linens and all manner of goods. It's somewhat dispiriting, as a prig can take three or four hundred pounds of swag, and not get more than three or four pounds from the fence, but there it is. Now, these rich folks, they would never have been so foolish as to travel the roads without escort, and an escort they could trust, too. But what signifies that? They were to have two, and a manly, strapping, all burly coachman besides. This coachman was a handsome fellow named Phillip, what name means "lover of horses." I tell you that only so you understand I'm a scholar on top of all else.

This Phillip showed himself a liking for a kitchen girl, a pretty little thing, slim of form but fiery in humor. Maggie, she was called, and she loved me hot and mighty well, which was how I entered into this lay. I convinced her to shine her favors on poor Phillip, and so she done. Maggie worked her wicked charms, and he come up so gasping for breath, so clouded with the stink of love, he would do anything she might ask. So it were he consented to aid us for a share of the treasure and a share of pretty Maggie, too.

So he thought, but I'd taken to myself the role of the double dealer.

That's how we begun, me with my partner by my side, for as I said, I had not come so far and done so much without a few good fellows to aid. Here was a spark called Farting Dan, and aptly named he was. But beyond his farting, he was one of them thinkers, which was the good of him. The bad was his stench.

Many's the time I thought the men in pursuit should find us by his fragrance, for it weren't any ordinary farts he offered, but the kind to make your eyes water and your head feel strange. For all that, Dan earned his keep, he did, stench be damned. Not quite so daring or adventuresome as old Ruddy Dick, but a dependable man, who knowed more about pistols than any other spark I'd encountered. With his aid, I could be as certain as ever a man could hope, that my pistols should not misfire. Besides, once we divvied up the spoils and went looking for our fun, never once did the choicest ladies prefer him to me, even with my face being what it is.

So the day comes, and we wait among a copse of trees until our mark passed us, a fine equipage 'twas, all turquoise and gold, with black trim. It looked to me like money bags pulled by two stout horses. Before it rode one tough, and behind it another, and both these fellows burdened by the tedium, which was how I liked them.

Farting Dan begins it, riding hard up to the rear guardian and unloading a pistol directly into his chest. There's a burst of powder and flame, and this fellow slumps over onto his horse.

This were by no means the way I was accustom to do business. No need to kill a spark who might as well be knocked down. Still, best never to fret, and I go to take care of my guardian to the front, but Farting Dan is on it before me, galloping hard and now firing a second pistol right into this fellow's back.

I'm close now, and for an instant I'm blinded by the flash, but when it clears I see the horse with no rider, and a body 'pon the ground.

I give him a look, and he shrugs in answer. Fair enough, I thinks to myself.

Screams and cries now filled the air, for the sorts of folk in the equipage were by no means prepared for such bloodshed as now was unleashed. In truth, these dandy highwaymen had made our job easier, for the ladies were inclined to believe that being robbed should be the most romantical of experiences, so when they saw it up close, with its blood and gore and the stench of death and shite they were all the more like to obey our commands.

Farting Dan let loose with one of those stenches for which he was known and rode hard to the coach. I'm behind him, making ready with a pistol, wiping at the stink-full air, for the equipage must be stopped. Phillip were supposed to make a good show of attempting to outrun us, and he's making wild with the reins and the horses are at full gallop, maybe a fuller gallop than I'd like, and by all appearance, the two dead toughs inclined Phillip to feel all mistrustful and switch allegiance.

The way we'd planned it, I'd be the one who made as though I was dealing with Phillip, but that Farting Dan had another scheme, and like a trick rider at Bartholmew Fair, he's on the back of his horse, and then leaping in the air. Always thinking, that Farting Dan, and now he thinks to come down 'pon that coachman

Phillip, the very one what's supposed to aid us. Farting Dan knowed that well, but he showed no sign of caring, for I look over and see he's got a pistol out and he's using it as a club. He swings it and swings it again. A third time and a fourth. I hear grunts and moans, but the struggle is out of my view. When I come again into the view, the coach is still, the coachman is slumped over, the ruins of his skull are bathed in blood. Farting Dan has that terrible redness all over his hands, splattered upon his shirt, sprinkled upon his face. He grins at me something terrible and then licks the blood off his lips.

I ride now up to the still coach. A quarter mile down the road are two bodies and two horses. I don't like to leave a trail such as that, but the road is not so traveled that we can't presume a quarter hour's isolation. Most like we'd have an hour, but I don't care for presuming. A man remains cautious or he gets nabbed. Nothing simpler.

Farting Dan jumps down, letting loose with an arsey trumpet blast. I breathe through my mouth and dismount. Now's the time to conduct the business.

Whimpers come from the guts of the equipage, but I could see nothing with the curtains drawn, as though they might hide behind their flippery. Still, a man is wisest to exercise caution, so I wave my pistol and point at the door. "Out, you bitches!" I shout. "Nice and slow, with your hands high and not near nothing. Any man what don't do as I say gets himself shot, his privy removed, and placed in the mouth of the nearest lady."

You shock 'em to their core. None of this pleasantry crap. *My, what a pretty string of jewels. Would you mind ever so much placing it 'pon my hand?* I'd as soon swive a barnyard pig as say such shite. I've done one in my time and not the other, and I shan't tell you which.

The door then opens a crack, and then all at once, and a great man with a great belly, dressed in a suit of sky-blue cloth, all lace and gold thread about him, stumbles out. His wig is askew, no doubt knocked about from his terrible trembling, and his face is slick with perspiration, despite the chill in the air. Hard by fifty years of age, and there are tears in his eyes; he's crying like an infant what been ripped from its mother's teat and hurled against the wall.

"Please," he says, all snotty weepful. "We'll do as you say. Don't hurt anyone."

"Don't hurt anyone?" I bark. "Why, look about you, my blubberer. Your guardians are dead, your coachman smote. Mean you that I should not hurt anyone above the station of a servant?"

I think to add more, but time is of the most importance, and a man of the highway ought not to comport himself as though he were a comedian. "Out of the coach, the rest of you," I says.

"There's no one in there but my wife," the weeping fat man tells me.

"Out with her, or there shall be no one in there but your widow," I answer. Mighty clever, I was in those days.

Out she comes, as pretty a thing as I've ever seen. Not more than eighteen, with white skin, a swan's neck, eyes so green they're like the brightest leaves on the sunniest day of the clearest summer. She's got one of those fancy gowns on, and the bodice makes visible a fair portion of her massive bubbies. She has her eyes cast downward, and, like her husband, her lips are all atremble, but these lips are red and moist and waiting to be kissed.

Farting Dan gives a right lascivious look, and neither the woman nor the husband can guess if he means to blow a hole through her or to make use of the ones she's already got.

I toss the fat man a sack. "Start filling it. Your coins, your notes, your jewels, aught of import. I plan a search before we go, and I mean to cut off one of your fingers for everything I find that you ain't included."

I've still got my pistol trained on them when Farting Dan says, "I believe we must tarry a few minutes longer than planned."

He's looking at the wife, so there is no mistaking his mind, but I wish to make it clear that this ain't the time for frolicks. "Spend your share with the whores," I say. "I'll not take chances here."

"I'll wager you will." He gets onto his horse so as say he's no concern for my preferences.

The sods, meanwhile, are putting into the bag what I ask. The fat man has put in his purse and is taking the buckles off his shoes. The lady is taking off her rings and her necklace.

I send the husband up top to throw down the trunks what's stationed up top, a pair of fat ones they've got. They crack open egglike when they hit the dirt, and out spills a mass of clothing and trinkets. I make the pretty lady collect the trinkets, and put them in the bag, and as she pushes things this way and that, I see something bright and shiny, all glistening in the sun. It can't help but draw my attention.

It's a lock box, very like the one I have back in my rooms, the one I schemed to get, the one containing a fortune which might as well not exist since I can't get at it. It's the same sort, with the very same filigree design on the steel of it. This one is a great bit smaller, about twice the size of my fist, but the lock seems to be exactly the same size, looking unusual large on this piece. So now there's something on my mind more important than the pretty wife.

"What's in the box?" I ask the husband.

"Banknotes," he tells me. He clearly don't want to, but he does it anyway. Good fellow. Deserves a pat on the arse, he does.

"Give me here the key," I order.

He only shakes his head, and tells me, "I don't have it."

"Where is it?" I demand.

"There isn't one. The notes inside are too valuable, so I destroyed the key."

"Then how the deuce do you get them out?" I roared, for it was a mighty reasonable question, and worthy of being asked loudly.

"I have the one man in the world who can pick a Domal lock," he says. Thus it is that he points to the crumpled heap of Phillip the coachman, bloody, glistening in the sun almost so much as the metal box.

This is what they call an irony. Farting Dan has bashed the brains out of the one man who could help me get into this box, and the one I got hidden in my rooms, too. I stare at the heap, and then something happens that don't look like it should. Phillip, like as if on cue in a stage play, twitches.

With the pistols still on the happy couple, I take a closer look at him. There's blood all matted in his hair, but his skull ain't bashed in at all. For all his wild swinging, it don't seem that Farting Dan done very much damage.

What I need to do is get Phillip back to my rooms and tend to him until I can ask him to get my box open. That's as much as anyone would conclude.

Farting Dan's been gone for a bit longer than perhaps he ought to've been, so I glance about, and see nothing. Then, with pistols held steady, I take a fleeting look behind me. If those two had been of a mind to overpower me, they could have done then, for I gazed at the scene longer than a wise prig ought.

What was it that so caught my attention? It was Farting Dan. He was behind me, all right. Behind me, and tied to a tree. His eyes were open, his mouth was open. And though I was a good hundred feet away, it looked to me for all the world like his throat was open, for it was much streaked with blood, as was his shirt and jacket.

Such cruelty. Such malice. Anyone casting his eyes to it would see that this weren't meant to hurt Farting Dan, though it appeared to have done that plenty, but to put the scare into those gazing 'pon it. It felt a whole lot like someone getting even, and in that moment I knew full well that there could only be one man behind it all. Benjamin Weaver, and he meant to even things up.

"Why didn't you open your gob?" I demanded the fat man.

"I didn't see it," he whimpered. "I was too busy collecting the articles for you."

"Then you'll die for it," I said, for this was the sort of outrage that demanded someone die, even if it were not the person what done it. My hand was calmed, however, by a voice.

"Leave him be, Fisher," I heard. "Face me like a man, if you dare."

I turned and there he was, astride a horse, about halfway between Farting Dan's body and myself. I was far away, and it had been more than a year, but I recognized the face all the same. Sure 'nough, 'twas Weaver, the man what had struck down Ruddy Dick. He held pistols in both hands, and they was trained upon me.

At that distance the guns should be entirely worthless, so he prods his horse forward. "It's time for you to pay for what you did to Thomas Lane," he says.

I was determined to show no fear, though I was fearful plenty. "What about Farting Dan there? He didn't have nothing to do with your precious pretty fellow."

"I see the damage you've done," he answered, arrogant as a lord. "He deserved to die, and so do you."

He had his pistols trained on me, and I had mine on him. He had two, and I had one, but mine had been tended to and loaded by the great and deceased Farting Dan, and that gave the advantage to me. I would be able to fire before he dared, and lucky shot would do the business.

He was about five feet short of what he must have considered being in range when I fired my pistol. He fired his in almost instant response, but my shot had been true, his false. Not so true as a man in my state should have liked, for it only hit his shoulder, but he lurched backward, and his pistols fired upward.

Weaver tumbled backward off his horse, and this, I knew, was my moment. "You!" I shouted at the fat man. "Get him on my horse." I gestured with a fresh pistol toward the still, slumped body of Phillip.

The fat man obliged, and in less than thirty seconds, I had him on the horse, and myself besides. Weaver was still struggling to get to his feet. He clutched at his shoulder, and there appeared to be a great deal of blood. It seemed I had hit him in his blood tubes, a wound that would make my escape all but certain, but I would take no chances.

I passed him quickly on my horse, emptied a pistol shot into him and rode on, my still prisoner balanced on the horse like a big bloody sack of shite.

It was a hard three-hour ride to my rooms in London. I could have not have planned this better had I tried, for it was full dark by the time I arrived, though not so dark that my presence on the street should draw attention from. And London, though it has many faults, at least enjoys the marvelous trait of being a city where no one will wonder why you ride about with a slumped man over your horse. There were, after all, too many other distractions. The cries of women selling shrimp and oysters, the pie men, the whores and traders in nefarious goods. Fools ran their coaches down the narrow streets too fast, farmers led their pigs this way and that. The streets were full of emptied chamber pots and kennel and dead horses carved up by beggars for their dinner. The skies in London were full of smoke and coal, the people rushed and angry and afraid. I may as well have been a buzzing fly for aught anyone gazed upon me.

I kept my rooms in Hockley in the Hole, and in that maze of makeshift buildings without addresses, sometimes without streets, no one could find me who was not led there by myself. And my landlord, who observed me dragging Phillip upstairs—he would say nothing. I paid him for his silence. He even helped get Phillip to my rooms, where we dropped him on the floor. To best make sure all went as it should, I gave the landlord a coin and sent him on his way.

I didn't live richly in my home, for it were only a place to rest; I lived in taverns and bagnios and with the ladies of the streets. Here I had my poor bed, a few furnishings upon which to sit and rest my food when there I ate. I hung nothing on the walls, covered the splintering floor with no rugs, put no dressings 'pon the cracked windows.

On our journey home, I had observed that this Phillip's head was no longer bleeding, and his breathing appeared to me fairly normal, all of which gave me hope. I lit a few oil lamps to allow me as much light as I needed. Then I took a bucket of water, what I used for washing that morning, and threw it upon Phillip. He stirred at once. He groaned and coughed and sputtered. He opened his eyes.

I trained a pistol on him. "Sit up."

He done it and put a hand to his head and then drew it away sharply.

"I hears you can open a Domal box."

He nodded, and it looked to me like the effort almost made him tumble over, and for all the world it seemed like it should take a miracle for this hurt bastard to open the box tonight.

With some difficulty, for I was very tired, I pushed aside a large and uncommon heavy chair I kept by the wall, and then opened the secret compartment in which I stored my most precious valuables. Included among these, and indeed almost alone among these, for I had little of value at the moment, was the box. Unlike the one I had in my loot bag, this one was near the size of a man's torso, and heavy, though from its frame or contents I knew not.

I set it down on the floor next to him, and he gazed 'pon it groggily.

"Open it," I told him.

"No," he said in a voice surprisingly steady.

I trained my pistol on him. "Do it."

"Killing me won't get it open," he said.

"True," I agreed. "But lead in your leg might encourage some cooperation."

Then he did something most unlike a man with a bashed head. He pushed himself to his feet and stood facing me, gazing at me with unclouded eyes, standing steadily and strong. His injuries were perhaps not so severe as they appeared, not so severe as he'd led me to believe.

Not ten feet from him, however, with a loaded pistol, I was the master, and if he would not believe it, I would be forced to explain it in terms he could not ignore.

"Open it," I told him, "or you will regret it."

He smiled at me, and it was a smile full of confidence and, yes, pleasure. Here was a man enjoying himself not a little.

"I don't know how," he said.

"Then I will remind you," I answered, and fired the pistol directly at his knee. An injury of that nature might cause him so much pain that he would be unable to do his business, but I have observed, and more than once, that a man with one knee shot will go to great lengths to avoid having the other served with the same sauce.

Through the smell of powder and cloud of smoke, I noted that a man who ought to have collapsed remained still standing. From so little a distance, I could not have missed. There were no marks upon the floor, yet he remained unscathed, and had not even flinched during the firing.

"Your pistol is spent," he said. "Mine, however, is not." From his pocket he withdrew an imposing piece, which he aimed at my chest. "Sit." He gestured to my great and heavy chair.

Make no mistake, I had my wits about me. I saw no reason to lose heart, but with no choice but to obey, I sat. From his pockets he then withdrew a length of thick rope.

"Tie yourself to the chair," he said. "And no deception, if you please. I have my eye 'pon you, and I know a fine knot from a poor."

My hands fumbled with the rope. "Look here, Phillip. I have a great deal of money about me, and rather than be enemies, let's come to what they call an understanding."

He said nothing until I had secured myself tight to the chair. I meant to create a loose knot, but his eyes never left me. I must now operate under the belief that he could not kill me in cold blood—and that I could buy my freedom with the promise of silver.

Once I was bound, he smiled at me, a devilish sort of smile. "My name is not Phillip," he said to me. "I presume you did not see my face when you knocked me down a year and a half ago, and so it is you who do not recognize me today."

A sort of stillness overtook the room. It was the stillness that came over the theater when a great revelation was made. Even the rabble of the pits would pause in their nonsense to look up and see what secrets were being said. Here it was, in my life, such a moment. A moment of the theater as things that had been hidden revealed themselves.

"Thomas Lane," I said. "I thought you was dead."

"No, Thomas did not die, though I am not he. You mistook the one for the other, as you were meant. I am Benjamin Weaver."

"Then, the man I knocked down…" I began.

"That was me who you mistook for Thomas Lane

during our last encounter. Thomas had some unfortunate bounties upon him, and he thought it useful to let the world believe he died by your hand. It was therefore spread about that you had killed him, and to give the story the credibility Thomas required, it was also spread that I sought revenge for a death that never was."

I began to sputter, for now this story was all confusion. "If I did not kill Lane, why all the trouble to take revenge upon me?"

He smiled again. "It is not revenge, Fisher. It is a matter of business, as I have found a better way to earn my bread. I am no longer a man of the highway, but a thief-taker. The owner of this box employed me to retrieve it. As you would tell no one, not your closest confederates, where you kept your goods, I had no choice but to encourage you to bring me to it of your own free will. Your attempt to rob us 'pon the highway was my scheme. I permitted you to believe you manipulated me, when I was the one who manipulated you."

"You're nothing but a double dealer, and a more ruthless bastard than ever I was," I told him. "You let all those people die so that you could retrieve this box?"

He laughed. "No one has died. No one has been hurt. Did you not wonder how you missed me when you fired 'pon me? Your companion neglected to include balls in the pistols. We deceived you with empty firearms and false blood from the stage."

It was then, over the stench from the discharged pistol, that I began to smell something else. A stench like rotted eggs—and rotted meat and rotted teeth. Then, into the room walks Farting Dan, Thomas Lane by his side.

"I knew you had the box in your rooms," Farting Dan announces, "but as you would tell no one where your rooms were, I could not sell that information. I knew the way you'd have to pass, though, so Thomas and I rode ahead of you and waited for you to glide by. You were so intent in getting home, so certain you were now safe, you did not notice us behind you."

"You've betrayed me," I shouted at Farting Dan. "Why?"

"For money," he said with a shrug.

"It's a good reason," I answered, "and I'll not fault you for it."

"Now," Dan says to Weaver, "take the box and be off with ye. That was our bargain, and I expect you'll honor it."

Weaver nodded. "I should like to bring you to justice, Fisher, but I will honor my word. You'd be wise not to cross my path in the future, however."

And so it was that he lifted the box in his arms, and he and his companion left my rooms.

In silence we waited as we heard their heavy steps down the stairs, then the slam of the front door. Farting Dan went to the window and watched for some minutes, and I watched him. Then at last he turned to me and broke the silence. "Not too tight, I hope, them ropes?"

"I done it myself," I says.

"You comfortable?" he asks.

"Shut your gob and untie me," I says. "You get the last payment?"

He cut through the ropes with his knife. "Ten more guineas, as promised."

With my hands free, I stood and rubbed my wrists. "A lot of nonsense for twenty guineas," I says. "Particularly since the contents of that box must be worth a hundred times that."

"Twenty guineas is better than nothing, which is what the box was worth to us if we couldn't get it open. And we got it without fear of a hanging, or having to do business with a fence. Not bad in my thinking."

He was right, too. That Farting Dan was a practical fellow, and a clever one. I'd have never thought of this plan on my own. But that was Dan. Always thinking. And always farting.

GREGG HURWITZ

As a deputy U.S. marshal tasked with transporting inmates and hunting down fugitives, Gregg Hurwitz's protagonist, Tim Rackley, finds himself in and around prisons on a daily basis. *The Kill Clause*, Rackley's first thriller, begins with Rackley learning about his seven-year-old daughter's murder. From there, he's drawn into a shadowy commission of men seeking justice outside the law. *The Program* brought Rackley inside a deadly mind control cult, when he was tasked with retrieving the missing daughter of a powerful Hollywood producer. For research, Hurwitz went undercover into mind control cults and submitted himself to cult testing.

Troubleshooter, the next Rackley thriller, opens with the leader of an outlaw biker gang pulling off a daring freeway escape while being driven from sentencing to prison. Clearly, the Rackley series grapples with issues of vigilantism—justice versus the law—each book offering Rackley's ever-evolving perspective. In the course of researching each of the Tim Rackley books, Hurwitz himself spent time behind bars, getting to know the men and women who keep the prisons running.

Dirty Weather was inspired by them.

DIRTY WEATHER

He was handsome in a dirty sort of way, lank hair shoved back over his ears, muscles firm beneath a white button-up shirt he wore untucked with the sleeves cuffed past the forearms. He'd slipped into Frankie's Furlough quietly, a swirl of biting wind from the still-closing door conveying him to the far end of the bar. The rickety building stuck out from a snowdrift off the interstate as if hurled there. The interior smelled of sawdust, which layered the floor, soaking up spilled booze and the melted sludge of tracked-in earth.

Home to truckers, twelve-steppers who'd fallen off the staircase, and most often, correctional officers, the Furlough had been something of a roadside institution ever since Frankie had taken his pension from the big house and parlayed it into four walls, a roof of questionable efficacy and a red-felt pool table. He'd done well for himself, too, though it wasn't apparent from the looks of the place.

The surrounding landscape had been stripped bare

by winter, trees thrusting like forked sticks out of gray rises of snow. Few signs of life persisted in the stretch of Michigan freeze: a liquor store across the frontage road, a long-closed diesel station, a sloped gravel turn-off for runaway semis. And then a stark ten-mile crawl north to the only employer of significance in the county, the Upper Ridgeway State Men's Correctional Facility, which rose from behind a stark shelf of white cedars like a secret no one had bothered to keep secret.

Laura finished twirling a pint glass on a towel, her attention drawn back to the stranger at the end of the bar. He'd walked with a slight limp, which interested her. Also, he kept his gaze on the lacquered birch veneer instead of on her breasts (her most attractive feature were she to judge by the eye traffic of Furlough's fine patrons) or her rounded but still-firm thirty-six-year-old ass. Her face wasn't bad either, this she knew, but it had collected age around the eyes and at the line of her jaw. And the skin of the neck. Nothing to be done there. His face, by contrast, was more youthful—she put him in his late twenties—but it was quite pale, almost unhealthily so, as if he were used to living in a warmer climate.

Between small, measured sips, he turned the bottle in his hands as if he'd never seen a beer before. Contemplativeness, in Frankie's Furlough, was something of a rarity. In contrast, Rick Jacobs was all swagger, shooting solids against Myron's stripes. Barrel chest, thermal undershirt, beard, weekend game-hunter— Rick was a carbon copy of a carbon copy. Ever since he'd joined up with the Asphalt Cruisers, Rick asked people to call him Spike. Despite his efforts, the nick-name hadn't taken. He had a penchant for racist jokes and loud belching, and the tremors hit him if he got forty waking minutes from a bottle of Glenlivet. That's why he was here, even during a blizzard that kept the entire county shuttered in except for Laura, who would've burrowed through snow with her bare hands to get some fresh air after playing nurse, and Myron, who Rick had no doubt bullied into playing sidekick. Just good country people, Rick and Myron, quick with a grin and a left hook.

Rick paused, his ass in front of the fire that Laura persistently kept going. Her father had built the brick hearth with his own two hands, an act of masculine creation he reminded her of at least once a week, even though he'd rarely gotten around to using it when he was running the show. He didn't believe in burning resources; this was a hewn-featured man, powerful even in his decline, who still banged about the house wearing the Shetland wool sweater he'd bought on a trip to Montreal during the 1967 Expo.

The stranger caught her next glance and flared a finger from the bottle. She headed over, trailing a soft hand along the bar. "Another?"

"Nah, just a pack of Reds, please."

"No boozing and cruising," she said, sliding the cigarettes across the bar. "Smart choice. You'll wind up on the *other* side of the bars."

He leaned back, a faint grin etched on his face. "Is it that obvious?"

She leaned over the bar (giving him a chance for an eyeful of cleavage, which she was pleased he didn't capitalize on) and peered at the baton ring protruding from his belt. "Plus the Galls boots. Dead giveaway. I been working here a long time. And though you're cute"—this widened the smile—"I know the template. Newjack or transfer?"

His eyes, faded blue, took on a hint of playfulness. "How do you know I'm new here?"

"Because I haven't seen you. Hell, we *are* called the Furlough. Even the prisoners know about us. That's what we get for being on the thoroughfare." She tossed the stale popcorn into the trash and slotted the wooden bowl back into the cupboard. "So, I'll ask you again, hotshot—Newjack or transfer?"

"Newjack." He extended a callused hand. "Brian Dyer."

"Laura Hillman." She pointed at the neon sign hanging over the rust-stained mirror. They hadn't had it serviced in years, so it read, *F nk e Furl gh.* "Frank's daughter. Been around a few blocks a few times." She cocked her head, letting a tangle of hair cross her eyes. "Still embarrassed?"

"Why would you say that?"

"No blazer, no bad maroon tie, no gray slacks. You changed after shift in the lockers even though the draft in there can make your"—a delicate tip of her hand—"retract inside your body. It can catch you a lot of static in the world, being a correctional officer, so you'd rather leave the uniform behind the gates."

Again he smiled, and she felt something inside her warm. A part of her that hadn't felt comfort—or hope—in a long time. Though the fire was a good fifteen feet away, a drop of sweat hung at his hairline. She liked that he sensed the heat so keenly.

He bobbed his head. "What else? I mean, aside from the fact that you're clearly smarter than me. Is there a Mr. Laura?"

Rick strolled to the near side of the pool table, over-chalking his cue. Myron had stumbled out, heading home to get his nightly tongue-lashing from Kathy over with, so Rick was burning his remaining quarters chasing trick shots. He'd started staying right up until last call ever since Laura, in the wake of her father's latest heart attack, had taken over weekends.

A loud click of the pool balls and Rick cheered himself heartily.

Laura leaned forward, lowering her voice. "I look bad in blue, so I married into the family tradition instead. Fresh out of high school. Mr. Laura had just graduated the Academy. And you know what they say are the first three things you get when you become a CO."

"A car, a baton and a divorce," Brian replied.

"We gave it the obligatory two years. Since then, I've been a lonely girl."

"Not so lonely," Rick offered from where he was leaning over the thirteen, which had evaded the corner pocket for three shots running.

"Thank you for that, *Spike*."

He grumbled something and got back to chalking.

"What's with the tattoo?" She rested a hand on the faded blue ink on Brian's forearm, and he jerked ever so slightly at her touch. His skin was warm and soft, and the feel of it against her palm was inexplicably thrilling.

Behind them, the pool cue clattered to the worn velvet, and Rick said, "Fuck this, then." A brief howl of wind as the door banged the chimes, hard, and then they were alone.

"The tattoo," Laura said, tracing the dip of the inked woman's waist with a thumb.

"I don't remember getting it."

"Sounds like a sailor story."

"Not quite." Brian looked away, his mouth firming, and she sensed sadness there, and anger. "It was during an eight-day drunk…"

Her voice was quiet and a touch hoarse with the premonition that she might regret her flippancy. "After what?"

"My wife. Three months pregnant. Drunk driver. High-school sweetheart, for what that's worth. We'd been together four years, were just starting to really fight good—you know, baby'll help things—but she was part of me." He tilted his beer bottle to his lips, but it was still on empty. "Another sob story. Just what you need in a place like this."

Her hand still rested on his arm and it felt awkward to withdraw it now. She liked the feel of their touching, the feel of him. The seam of their skin was slightly moist, their sweat intermingling. She struggled for words that wouldn't sound trite. She thought about fetuses, the crunch of car metal, Brian's faint limp. "How do you get back from that?"

"Am I back?" He laughed a real laugh, like he was enjoying himself. "It put me down for a good while and when I got up, I enrolled in the Academy. You can go either way after a thing like that. The line is—" he held up his hand, thumb and forefinger, measuring a quarter inch. "I thought a little order would help me pull it together and I was right. So order I've got. I spend my time in a place where guys keep Clubs locked on the steering wheels of their cars that they park in the shadow of a wall tower. Guy I work with—Conner?"

"Sure, I know Conner."

"He welded a hasp to his lunch box so he could keep a tiny lock on there. No shit."

"Sounds like Conner all right."

"It's being locked in paranoia. But you know what? I'd be lying to say I don't take comfort in the metal. All those right angles. And the bells, set your watch to them. I'll leave someday, I'm sure, head somewhere warm, and I bet I'll miss it all. It's like…armor, almost."

"And you needed armor."

"Yeah," he said. "Yeah, I did."

She found herself close to him, a foot maybe—he'd been speaking quietly and drawn her in, and there was an instant where she thought she'd just keep leaning until their lips met. His heaviness seemed to match the weight of her disappointments. A single child raised motherless in a frozen plain. She'd tried to get out, even to Detroit, but she'd chosen young and then her marriage had dissolved, leaving her mired like a shot bird. Twenty years old then and she'd never found it in herself to risk again.

She'd gone to Florida once—Disneyworld with Sue Ann—but as for spreading her wings, well, she'd always stayed in her childhood bedroom, except for during her brief marriage. And even then she'd made it not ten miles, just across the gully. A decade and a half ago, now. And so she'd spent her years since laughing with the truckers, shooting stick with the COs and taking the occasional roll in the sheets just to get some warmth inside her. Her indiscretions bought her snickers in church and criminating looks from her father, exaggerated into a kind of horror now by his palsied left cheek and the white film ringing his lips. It stung her deep and hard, the murmur that preceded and followed her, but she'd long resolved herself to getting what sustenance she could where she could, and to hell with the rest of them.

She'd been saving up though, a few years now, and maybe that money would get her out of Upper Ridgeway or at the very least out of her father's house. Or maybe—a notion almost too painfully hopeful to entertain—it would help her get a house with someone else someday. But her radar was off, as her father liked to say. She saw what she wanted to see in men and sometimes these days she didn't even see that.

Brian raised a hand to her cheek (impossibly, impossibly warm), his elbow braced on the bar so she could give his palm the full weight of her chin and then the door smashed open and a man with a gun charged them, screaming so loud flecks of saliva dotted the bar.

"The safe—I *know* there's a fucking safe get it open *now*."

Laura backed against the glass shelves, a bottle of Triple Sec bouncing twice on the floor and clattering to a quiet roll. Brian remained on his stool facing forward, enveloped in an intense calm that spoke of experience, his hands spread in view on the bar. His eyes stayed straight ahead; he seemed to be tracking the man's movement in the mirror behind her.

The gunman wore several long-sleeved T-shirts, one on top of the other. Snow and sweat had matted his wispy blond hair to his skull. He fumbled a credit-card-size block of what looked like beige Play-Doh from his pocket, his stare level on Laura.

"You'd better move, bitch." The gunman shoved Brian's shoulder with his gun. "And you, get up against the—"

Brian pivoted on the stool and drove his fist into the man's gut. The gunman doubled over and the gun barked once. Brian grunted and staggered forward.

The man shuffled backward toward the door, screeching, "Dammit, God*damm*it. You stupid idiot," and then the bells shivered, the wind rushed, and he was gone.

Laura vaulted the bar. Gritting his teeth, Brian

fought off his boot and hurled it into the fireplace. His sock, drenched with blood, made a peeling sound as he slid it off. This too went the way of the flames.

The bullet had pierced the outside of his right foot, two inches back from his little toe. The shock had just caught up to Laura, moistening her eyes. The comforting smell of the fire drifted in, further disorienting.

"You're okay." Disbelief tinged her voice, and not a little relief. "You're okay."

"It's fine. Passed through the side, here."

"I'll bandage it and we'll get you to the hospital. I have a first-aid kit…"

"Lock the door first. And check the parking lot, make sure he's gone."

She did, bending the cheap venetians over the window. The interstate was an oblivious white strip. A wall of snow encircled the empty parking lot, white fading into the white trunks of the firs. A white Subaru was parked at the side of the frontage road, though she had to press her face flat to the glass to see it. The headlights shot twinning beams into the snowfall, but the car was apparently empty. "No one. But there's a car still there. Lights on."

"It's gotta be his. No one else out here. And he's not going far on foot."

"He could be hiding in it. Or in the trees."

"Call 911."

She ran behind the bar and snatched up the phone. Dead. "He cut the line."

"Okay. We're isolated here. You have a gun?"

"No. You think he'll come back, this guy?"

"Looked like he had C4 with him. For blasting a safe."

"Jesus Christ," she broke in, "C4, like action-movie C4?"

"I spooked him, but maybe he settles himself out in that car, realizes that we're holed up and injured. Plus, we're riding the aftermath of a blizzard—not exactly the best time for a speedy police response even if he *hadn't* cut the phone line. I say we split."

"Not before I stop the bleeding." She was pulling bowls and plates from the cabinet. She found the first-aid kit and returned to him. He was sitting, arms braced over his knees, smiling at her in the orange glow. She felt his stare as she worked. He seemed oblivious to the pain. She didn't really know what she was doing, but she cinched a tourniquet midway up his foot and wound an Ace bandage over some sterile pads, applying pressure on the entry wound.

"That happen a lot around here?"

"A correctional officers' bar? You kidding me? A normal night, someone came in here, they'd get beaten within an inch of their lives."

She finished and patted his calf. She could see the fire's glow reflected in his eyes and she touched his face, gently, letting her fingers drift down over his lips.

His face darkened, his gaze shifting nervously to the window. "Let's get going."

"My Bronco's out back." She helped him up.

He leaned on the walls, making ginger progress. "What are you doing?"

Laura was on her knees, rolling back the shitty carpet by the jukebox. She worked the dial of the floor safe until the gears clanked. She withdrew three tight rolls of hundred-dollar bills and stuffed them in her pockets. "There's fifteen grand here. My life's savings. If that guy comes back, he'll have plenty of time to tear the place apart. If he doesn't already know where the safe is."

"Let's go, let's go."

She put an arm around his waist and kicked through the back door, waiting for the gunman to fly out of the white haze at them. But it was just the wide swath of alley, the soggy stack of Budweiser cartons under the overhang and her truck. The wind hit them hard, whipping flecks of snow into their faces. It tore at her collar, the cuffs of her jeans. She deposited Brian in the Bronco and waded around to the driver's seat, her eyes holding fearfully on the Subaru. The gunman's car remained maddeningly motionless, its headlights beaming forward like a dead man's gaze.

Brian was shuddering by the time she got the engine turned over. She'd left the heat blasting and the radio on—Don down at KRZ was spinning the Highwaymen, Kris Kristofferson as smooth as good scotch, save for the pulses of static from the weather. She blasted the heat. The Bronco bucked over drifts of snow past the Subaru, its shadowed interior drawing briefly into view through ice-misted windows, and then they were skating on the frontage road, heading for the interstate entrance. She studied the rearview, frightened. As if on cue, the radio went to fuzz, then warped into silence.

The windshield of the Subaru continued to stare after them, but the car didn't pull out. She watched it recede, her heart pounding.

Barely visible up ahead through the snow were two sets of flashing red lights. Laura eased up to the saw-horses, fighting down the window. Four deputies blocked the overpass.

Before she could say anything, Earl leaned in and shouted over the wind, "We just got word there's been a break at the prison. Miguel's dead—bastard caved his head in on the escape. That's all we know except to lock down the road."

"I just had a guy try to rob me. His car's still back at the Furlough. We think he's still around there." She brought a trembling hand to her face. "My God. Miguel. I just saw him over at the garage yesterday, getting a new radiator in his…" Her eyes welled. "Has someone told Leticia?"

"Thinning blond hair," Brian shouted past her. "Five-eight, five-nine, maybe. Skinny."

Earl's brows rose as his eyes shifted. "Who's this?"

"Brian Dyer. He's a CO up at the big house. He got shot protecting me. I gotta get him to the hospital."

"Okay. Go. Go. We'll take the Furlough." Earl squinted through the falling snow. The Subaru's headlights were barely visible. "That car up there?" He turned to the others. "Move it, let's move." He rapped a gloved fist on Laura's hood and she pulled past the roadblock, coaxing the Bronco back to speed.

They crossed the overpass, veering toward the south entrance, and started the long curve around to the interstate.

The radio crackled and Don's distorted voice came audible in waves. "—deadly escape from the prison…Miguel Herrera's body found stripped and frozen in the east yard…"

Blocking the bottom of the on-ramp, just before the merge, was a felled tree. Brian shouted and Laura hit the brakes, sending the Bronco sideways. They coasted peacefully to a stop, an upthrust branch screeching up Brian's door. She let out her breath in a rush, and he laughed. Up ahead, on the interstate, was a furrow where some poor soul had trudged across from the frontage road, probably a half-frozen construction worker seeing to the sewage drains beneath the overpass.

"I'll steer us around," she said.

Brian leaned forward and punched the cigarette lighter. His other arm was up around her headrest and he dropped it to the back of her neck. His hand was warm, so warm—he'd been holding it over the dashboard vent. The backs of his knuckles drifted down, grazing her cheek, her chin. She felt her neck muscles unclench, her body softening to his touch.

The radio reception came back in, if barely. "—security tapes show…used a starter pistol in their escape…one of the inmates shot in the foot going over the…"

Laura's eyes widened. Her gaze jerked to the base of the tree—ax marks, not splinters. A mosaic of images pressed in on her. Miguel's wife's Subaru. The Furlough's empty parking lot even after Brian had arrived. His limp as he'd entered. The belt with the baton ring, poking out from the bottom of his state-issue button-up shirt. His face, already pale from the injury. The sweat on his brow—pain suppressed. And his stolen boot, thrown in the fire after the ruse so she wouldn't see that it had no bullet hole.

Brian's hand continued to play across her face. Trembling, she lifted her gaze but the stare looking back was unrecognizable. The snow beat against the window behind him, the branch scraping against the door. And then she saw the pale hand reach up over the tree trunk outside like something from a horror movie.

Brian's hand tightened and he drove a fist down across her chin. Her head smacked the window, her head lolled, and she slumped against the door. Digging in her pockets, he removed the rolls of cash. Then he reached past her ample breasts, tugged at the door handle, and shoved her with his good foot out into the snow.

Teddy slid down off the tree trunk, stamping his feet and rubbing his arms. Bits of ice stuck to his thin wisps of blond hair and his lashes, which framed bloodshot eyes. Brian fished the pack of Marlboros from his pocket, tapped out a cigarette and extended it between two fingers across the console. Teddy stepped over Laura's limp body and climbed in, his breath clouding against the wheel as he slammed the door against the cold. He took the proffered cigarette and set it between quivering lips. He removed the beige rectangle from his pocket—a carefully shaped block of used chewing gum—and tossed it into the back seat. Then he cranked the heat even higher, shivering violently and pressing his white fingers against the vents.

The cigarette lighter popped out and Teddy pulled it from the dash and tilted his head, inhaling the warmth.

Brian made a gun with his hand and pointed south. "To the sunshine."

Teddy maneuvered the Bronco through the soft snow of the shoulder, forging a path around the tree. As they pulled out onto the interstate, sheets of snow began to layer Laura into oblivion.

DAVID DUN

Technology and its ills, together with Native American mysticism, contrasts two worlds often at war—science versus back-to-nature values. In his first thriller, *Necessary Evil*, David Dun spun an action-driven tale of wilderness survival that highlighted this war of the worlds, pitting Kier Wintripp against a ruthless corporate personality using human cloning to achieve medical cures.

Kier Wintripp is part of the Tilok tribe. Most of Dun's novels have involved characters from that tribe, which, although fictional, is in many respects based on various factual accounts of Native American life, lore, myth, history and religion. One aspect of Tilok culture is the Talth, a medicine person, part psychologist, part political leader, part judge, an expert on forest-survival arts. The pinnacle of the Talth is propounded by Spirit Walkers. These men come along only once a century and are recognized by their profound intuition concerning the affairs of men and nature. Kier was Dun's first, and perhaps most striking, Tilok character. A superb woodsman and tracker, a guide to youth, a teacher of the forest arts, he's also a doctor of veterinary medicine. Science being the ultimate rationalism, in Dun's novels Kier has many times sought, often unsuccessfully, to find peace in reason.

This is the story of how he became a Spirit Walker.

SPIRIT WALKER

The old people said it was the spirit of a man unloved as a child, roaming the deepest forests of the mountains, but Kier Wintripp didn't believe in spirits that did the work of psychopaths.

He stood beneath the big conifers in front of his cabin picking huckleberries as Matty arrived with Jack Mix. A very curious combination. She an old woman, and he a former FBI agent. Matty approached and Kier sensed the tension in her frail body as she gripped his wrists with a grandmother's love. Mix kept back a respectable few paces.

"Jake, my grandson, has gone off into the mountains, to the caverns, with Carmen," Matty said. "They left three days ago before daylight and were returning late the same day." She stared at her feet. "And there's another thing."

He waited for her to explain.

"Jake was going to the cliffs, at the top of the caverns."

"Below Universe Rock? The sacred place?"

"It's wrong. I know."

"And they were to return the same day?"

She nodded. "The next day was my birthday. Jake would never miss his grandmother's birthday."

He knew that was true.

"You will go?" Matty said, desperation in her voice. "Everyone knows you're descended from the last Spirit Walker. It's in you. You can find them."

His grandfather had indeed been a Spirit Walker, one of the tribe's mystics, revered men who came along once in a hundred years. They guided the Talth, advised the tribe, communed with spirits and discerned the hearts of men. Kier intimately knew the forest and taught the young its secrets. He was an ordinary man, half Anglo, half Tilok, but also a veterinarian trained in science, so part of him required the comfort of reason.

"You'll go get them," Matty said again, her voice breaking. "Please."

"I'll go," Kier assured her. "Spirit Walker or not."

"It's where the ghosts are. Raccoon says he saw a ghost. Robes white as bleached sheets. Jake and Carmen thought maybe Raccoon would be there with the ghosts. That's why they went."

Kier had heard the rumors of ghosts and murder. Fantastical stories that grew under their own weight.

Mix seemed to be waiting for Matty to leave, but she didn't. So they walked up on the porch and Kier invited them both to sit. Kier was curious about Mix. He seemed to be hanging around a lot lately. Under the eave, Mix removed his straw hat, revealing cropped brown hair that matched a neat mustache. Mix had made a fine transition from law officer to owner of a local feed store and wildlife photographer, even if he had never quite fit socially with the stranger-shy locals. Like Kier's wife, Jessie, also an ex-FBI agent, Mix had gladly given up the big city for the backcountry.

"Some of my friends from the FBI called," Mix said. "I recommended that they ask for your help. You're the best forensic tracker around."

He caught Mix's real message. "The FBI isn't looking for Jake and Carmen. Or ghosts."

"You're right," Mix replied. "They want to talk to Raccoon. Just yesterday they spoke with me. The couple over in Lassen County a year ago, they never found the girl, and the boy was a cooked pile of meat. That boy's father was a state senator. Then we had a couple from Humboldt just disappear off the face of the earth. The press is starting to use the words *serial killer.*"

"That's got nothing to do with Raccoon."

"Maybe. Maybe not. What can you tell me about him?"

"We call him Kawa We Ma. A gentle man inside a big body." He pictured Raccoon as he'd last seen him, wearing a leather flight jacket over deer hide. The man had been born Josiah Morgan, a part-Tilok orphan adopted by the tribe. The nickname came from the port-wine stain on his face that gave him the look of a raccoon's mask.

"The tracks the sheriff found, and some other things, were suspicious," Mix said. "Raccoon disappears for days."

"You disappear for days in the woods, too, with your photography."

"I come back out. Talk to people. Run a store."

"Raccoon talks to the forest," Kier said. "People don't understand him, so they fear him. You and I have no idea what it would be like to see a miracle in every blooming flower. Raccoon is a man distracted by miracles. He's incapable of hurting anyone."

"If he isn't doing anything, then why not track him for them?" Mix asked.

"Because I don't want to."

Matty faced him. "Raccoon told Carmen that above the caverns, in the cliffs, there's a cabin with a ghost. Right above Man Jumps."

Carmen was Raccoon's daughter, whom Kier knew the man worshipped. So he believed the information.

Mix produced a bag of shelled pistachios and offered some. Kier scooped a few, as did Matty. "A cabin would show up on aerial photos," Mix said.

Kier shook his head. "It wouldn't be visible in a cave or hollow. And since it is sacred, no one goes there. Not even rock climbers."

"Who would you say Raccoon really cares about?" Mix asked.

Kier smiled. "That's a perceptive question for an ex-bureaucrat who sounds like he's returning to his old ways. My grandfather used to say the difference between a good and an evil man is what he loves. I'm not sure what Raccoon loves, other than Carmen. But, like I said, Raccoon is not a killer."

There were more questions, but Kier found that in answering he was repeating himself in a manner he disliked. Finally he said to Mix, "I thought you gave the FBI a flunking grade. Said they didn't protect the country the way they should. 9/11. The anthrax killer, and all that."

"I've got my beefs with them, but when it comes to a psychopath, I figure everyone has to pitch in."

Kier nodded, as if he understood.

* * *

Kissing Jessie and his children goodbye, dispatching hugs all around, and receiving the benedictory "be careful," Kier left for the woods. Three hours later he studied the tracks of Jake and Carmen, which told him a story. From their separation and angle he was certain these two were friends, not a couple. But it was the third set of prints, following theirs, that consumed his attention. They were made by a heavy man in good physical shape. Given the weight, the tireless stride, the smooth of the sole and the way it rounded at the toe, they could have only come from a handmade hide boot. Only a few Tiloks wore them and none were this size, except perhaps for Raccoon and himself.

The wind molesting the trees made him uneasy. He wondered if the murmur was more of Grandfather's sense of the presence of another life.

He allowed his mind to manipulate the puzzle engulfing him. More unease crept through him. Around him rose the towering rock faces of Iron Mountain with its caverns and Man Jumps, a hole in the cliffside. A slow, 360-degree turn brought his senses to high alert. Something man-made, a patch of cloth on the ground, just visible through the trees, caught his attention.

He inhaled deeply and noticed a strange, meaty smell, something like pot roast.

Hair rose on his arms.

He waited, not moving, listening, looking. Then he silently slipped forward and repeated the exercise. Thirty minutes later, after steadily creeping forward, he concluded that no one alive waited for him ahead. The sense taught by his grandfather confounded him. It would not leave him. But he overruled the sensation and entered the camp.

The first thing he saw was the charred remains of Jake.

A groan escaped his lips. He tried to divorce from his thoughts the agony that must have been Jake's last experiences on earth. He searched for signs of Carmen, imagining the terror she'd be feeling. Anger rose in him, forming a familiar determination.

He studied the fire pit where Jake lay. Given the depth of the ash, the remnants had burned maybe five hours. Probably the killer had watched the campers for a while to savor what was coming. So Kier knew what to do.

Find the watching spot.

He backed away from the fire and soaked in the scene. Quickly, he discovered where the killer had waited. Near the stream. And a fishing rod, probably Jake's, still leaned against a tree. He stared at the prints in the earth. Discernible, but blurred. If he hadn't seen the same blurs elsewhere in the camp, he would have attributed it to the movements of impatience. If he didn't know better, he would have said there were two large men making similar tracks.

Raccoon was here.

But Kier knew he wasn't the killer.

He surveyed the surrounding ground.

Something small and white caught his gaze. He bent down to examine it. A tiny flake. No. A chip of something. Not really. Much more.

A piece from a pistachio nut.

One thought rushed through his mind. Jack Mix.

He reeled off the possibilities. Mix could have easily made a print that size. He possessed the requisite weight, but to make either he would have been forced to stretch his stride to emulate Raccoon.

What did this mean?

He returned to the camp and searched for a sign of struggle or a spot where Carmen might have been tied down, but found nothing. He discovered a blood spatter at the base of the cliff. Fifty feet up the rock wall he spotted a blood smear. He knew what both meant. Jake had tumbled down the cliffs. Then he'd been cooked, like the boy in Lassen County.

But why?

To mask something.

Grandfather's sense of another life dogged him. But his scientific training reminded him that superstitions achieved nothing. So he circled the camp, searching for an exit track. On the far side lay a tan sheet of paper. He bent down and saw that the sheet was a map. Beneath it laid a Polaroid photo of a woman in her mid-thirties.

It was Jessie.

His wife.

And in her engaging smile he saw the inherent goodness that would incite any killer to want to destroy her. Fear threatened to overwhelm him. The message resonated clear. The killer had known he'd be here and had seized his vulnerability.

Ignore it.

He stuffed the picture in his pocket and studied the map. The area depicted was the Wintoon River, with an X marking the location of his cabin. He shuddered, but hesitated. Too obvious.

Something flashed in the corner of his eye.

Movement.

He gazed through the foliage.

Someone was there.

He dived into the brush, but a thump knocked him

sideways, slamming him into the ground. Crawling on one side, a great river of pain swept down his spine, shoulder and arm. His breath came in gasps. Pain screamed through his mind. A crossbow bolt protruded from his flesh just to the left of his chin. It had traveled upward from behind, piercing his left trapezius muscle between the shoulder and neck, exiting just above the clavicle.

He struggled to escape the thickets and developed a sort of sliding crawl that enabled him to keep his shoulder rigid. Any movement produced unbearable pain. Finally he slipped into the forest, away from the camp.

More arrows sliced through the foliage.

He freed his belt and wrapped it around his hand, forming a leather sheath.

Reaching above the razor-sharp blades of the arrow, he nestled the leather against the bottom edges, then yanked. The stiff feather fletching ripped through the meat of his trapezius and came away clean. For several minutes he did nothing but hang on to reality and fight nausea. Then his mind started working. He removed some sterile gauze from his backpack and applied it to both wounds.

The bleeding slowed.

Thank the Great Spirit.

He grabbed hold of his emotions, palmed a compact semiautomatic Ruger .22 pistol from his pack and eased twenty feet away.

The killer was here.

So he waited.

But no one came.

Sweating and in pain, Kier finally slipped warily out of the bushes and found tracks exiting the camp. One set of large prints, blurred, and smaller ones—Carmen's, which showed significant weight on the front of the foot, an indication that the killer might be pulling her. No toe tics, tripping, staggering or the like. She kept up a good stride on a steep incline and the implications were clear. The killer was forcing her deeper into the mountains.

His injury slowed him, and the notion that he might catch up to them vanished. He found that by keeping his upper body rigid, the muscles in his back bunched and naturally splinted the wound. But the side effect was cramping, and soon muscle spasms forced him to adopt an awkward gait.

The trail widened.

He stared down at the prints, but the ground spun from the blood loss. He blinked and steeled his mind, then tried to focus again. Carmen and her captor now walked side by side.

Clearly, Carmen was now accompanying the killer voluntarily. Without Carmen's tracks overlapping his, the big tracks became easier to read and they indeed appeared large, like Raccoon's, but blurred and overlain at times with another track.

What had his grandfather said?

Our eyes are guided by our mind. We need both but either can trick us, so we must rely completely on neither. This is why sometimes we must know without thinking and without seeing.

His mind balked.

To know was to understand.

He wanted to argue with the old man, now gone to the land of the dead, but knew that was impossible. He forced the pain from his mind. What was deceiving him? What was he to know?

Two men, one track.

But maybe the second man came a day or two later. He moved ahead.

At a fork, a third set of tracks stepped *out of* Raccoon's, leaving both men's tracks unblurred. He kept his balance and fought the shock.

The killer's tracks matched his own.

But they were fresher than the others.

What was happening?

He felt like he was living a nightmare. His boot and Raccoon's boot were nearly the same. Both were made in the traditional Tilok method. Both were large, like back at the camp. Raccoon had apparently come, then later perhaps someone else with a boot perfectly matching. If the killer could copy Raccoon's boot, he could also copy Kier's.

Raccoon was here. But so was Mix.

He followed tracks that looked like his own for a couple of hundred feet until he hit a dry creek bed. He knew it was a straight shot to Jessie and their cabin two thousand feet below. If the killer traveled by creek it would lead to a falls and a sheer drop, with a treacherous trail. So he eased his wracked body down the rock waterway, through heavy brush, looking for a print. Spasms played through his body while blood loss sapped him.

He stopped and tried to think.

Sometimes we must know without thinking or seeing.

Something nagged at him. His grandfather's superstitions seemed to beckon him to the sacred place.

If a man listens to such nonsense he won't even be able to put his socks on in the morning.

He had to think. Foolish people believed without their minds.

Jake chose to stay alone. To fish? No. He fell or was thrown down the cliffs. So what of the rod? A plant? The killer wants us to believe he was fishing. Because he wants to distract us from the alternative.

The torture was staged.

After death.

The picture of Jessie and the map now, more than ever, smelled like bait. *A man is made by what he loves.* His grandfather's words were a drum in his mind.

Suddenly he realized that he had wandered into danger. He gripped the pistol with a tight embrace.

Be a tracker, let the earth speak.

Then he saw it.

A dusting of white powder on the brush in the creek just ahead. None immediately to his right or left. Just ahead. He turned, searching for any sign of powder behind him and found nothing.

The sounds of dogs echoed along the mountain.

He pushed himself up the creek bank, ducked behind a tree and waited. His eyes lighted on a sandy area and he spotted footprints like his own, moving *up* the hill, not down to his cabin where Jessie nurtured his children. He stared, not believing his eyes. If he'd stayed on the killer's trail, or fled to the cabin to save Jessie, he would have passed straight through the white powder.

Behind him, the dogs arrived, bloodhounds, straining at their leashes.

He stopped and held his breath.

Following the dogs were men in self-contained Hazmat-equipped outfits with filters for breathing. The dogs leaped forward, but the white-suited men reined them back. Near the white powder the dogs bayed and wagged their tails, not seeming to care about the scent of Kier or the killer.

He turned and resumed his climb. Grandfather's voice had warned him away from the camp, to the caverns. Following logic would have placed him in danger.

Yet he still wanted to argue with the old man.

The cavern network high on the mountain spread out before him. The miles-long labyrinth hid Grandfather's pool and the rock floor allowed no tracks. It took forty minutes for him to make Man Jumps, the hole that opened out onto the seemingly endless wilderness of the Marble Mountains. A narrow ledge led away, making a trail for only the brave.

The opening from the caverns Matty mentioned would be several hundred feet above. There he might find a small cabin, in the sacred place, built against the rock wall, occupied by Jack Mix. The most practical route was through the caverns. So he lit a small Techna light and entered the cave.

His body was now feverish and he could barely stand. To continue forward on the largely vertical and shoulder-tight path was suicide. He thought of Grandfather. Straight as an iron pipe. Eyes seeing everything. *What would he do?* He felt no inner strength, only will, and even that was failing.

I can still go home and try to explain.

Another memory of Grandfather at the cavern pool became clear.

"Someday you will have to decide if you want to put in with the Tiloks. You can do well in the white man's world."

"But I've already decided."

"No. You must decide when it counts."

A small shaft rose before him at a 45-degree angle. He struggled out of his blood-soaked jacket, then removed his pack. He grasped the tiny ledges and maneuvered up the tube. Spasms reignited from thigh to back and he cried in silent anguish. He pressed his back hard against the rock, the cool radiating through his shirt, which offered some respite from the fever.

Then pressed on.

The claustrophobic sense of being trapped became unavoidable. His progress was only a couple of inches at a time, his broad shoulders catching on the rock again and again.

Three minutes of mind-bending pain and contortions were needed to negotiate the narrowest spot. Once past, the passage wasn't much larger.

Finally, he found a ledge and reached daylight. Natural light illuminated ancient Tilok rock paintings. One painting was familiar. A hunter with an antlered crown.

The sign of the Spirit Walker.

One more ledge remained above him. He sucked in a breath and blindly grabbed hold, only to feel a crushing pain in the fingers of his right hand. Standing above him was a man wearing a mask with bulbous filters, gloved hands pointing a crossbow downward.

"I didn't think anyone could get up through there, until Jake did it day before yesterday," Mix said, his voice distant and muffled. The mask shook its head. "What you did is crazy, but maybe convenient. You're supposed to be down at your cabin getting arrested. I explained to the agents how you tried to kill me when I discovered your anthrax-manufacturing operation."

Kier fought both the pain in his fingers and his trapezius wound, which was slowly separating as he hung, fresh blood trickling down his back. He wanted to yank out his fingers and fight, but he saw the antlered crown on the rock wall and knew that his grandfather would wait.

Damn the old man.

"I told them every man, woman and child in the country should be vaccinated against anthrax," Mix said, keeping his crossbow aimed. "A guy like me with no technical training could make anthrax in the basement. I told them anyone can do it, Arab, Jew, black or white. They thought I was nuts. Then I made it and mailed it to Congress and the media. The bureau still wouldn't listen. Oh, they interviewed me about terrorism. Sweated me. But I knew all their secrets. I told them I'd find the real anthrax killer. Now I'm delivering."

Mix pressed his weight more on Kier's hand, grinding it with his heel. The agony released a cold sweat from every pore in his body.

"Why'd you kill the boy?" Kier gasped.

"Let's not play games."

"It started when? The couple…a year ago—"

"I couldn't help that. They broke into my cabin, where I stored the anthrax. They were going to die anyway. One whiff of that stuff and—" He made a throat-slitting gesture. "I decided a year ago to make you the anthrax killer. Then two days ago Jake came and rushed the program."

"We welcomed you—" Kier said.

"Jake saw the cabin. Mouthed off that it was a sacred area. I was going to shove him off the cliff. Strong bastard, though. I had to put an arrow in him. And I couldn't let that be discovered. So I remembered the guy in Lassen. The bureau believes you're the anthrax terrorist, but I knew that convincing them you killed Jake might be stretching it."

Kier fought the pain, begging his muscles for the strength.

"They're desperate for the anthrax terrorist, so I'm

delivering." Mix chuckled. "Ex-renegade survivalist. Rebellious Indian. And you can come to the holy place." He laughed. "The Spirit Walker." Mix pointed. "Cabin's right out there. I made your tracks. A trail straight here. Did you notice around your cabin? The bureau taught me footprints and all the forensics. Ironic, isn't it?"

"The tribe will never believe it."

"There's anthrax hidden in your cellar at the summer cabin. After following my trail now, you've got it on you. If you hadn't seen me there at the camp, I might have just let you die of anthrax while under arrest."

But Kier knew he'd stopped short of all the anthrax. Even to his pain-fogged mind, it made sense. Raccoon followed Jake and Carmen into the camp and took Carmen. Mix killed Jake and then later came down to the camp from the cliff.

"Jessie," he choked out.

"FBI is getting a warrant to search the cellar of your cabin, if they haven't already."

"Lassen?" Kier said, even as his mind was sinking under the weight of terror for his family.

"Why would I murder some couple in Lassen? All that would bring is more cops. But we need to shut that senator up. People need closure. Raccoon will make a fine serial killer. The story of Raccoon, the serial killer, and Kier, the anthrax terrorist. Maybe I'll write a book." Mix went silent, aiming the crossbow at the base of Kier's neck. "I gotta finish you and get busy. Carmen and Raccoon are up here somewhere."

"Profit?" Kier breathed. "That the plan?"

"Book royalties. Some stock shares in the right vaccine company. But this isn't about that. It's about protecting this country when its leaders won't."

Kier couldn't talk anymore. The threat to his family became a hot knife in his mind. He closed his eyes and replaced the pain with an image of Jessie and his children. Then he gained strength from an image of his grandfather's face.

He sucked a deep breath and yanked his broken fingers from under the boot. But before he could do anything, a raging scream blared from several feet away.

Raccoon's massive frame flew at Mix.

Kier's left hand struck like a snake, his fingers wrapping around Mix's ankle and yanking the man down.

Mix fired the crossbow and Kier heard the bow string snap. Then he saw a spray of red from where the bolt sank into the base of Raccoon's neck.

Mix slammed against the cavern's painted wall, and fell into the hole with Kier. With his good hand, Kier pounced and ripped off the mask. Then he focused all his energy in the thumb of his ruined hand and rammed it into Mix's eye, going all the way through the cornea, the meniscus, and into the brain. Mix groaned and clamped his hands over the eye socket. His body began to shudder.

Carmen appeared, standing over Raccoon, screaming, trying to stop the blood. "No. Daddy, no." She was sobbing.

Raccoon took her hand as if he knew the blood would not be stopped.

"Stay with us," Kier said to his friend.

Mix's remaining eye went vacant and still and the body stopped twitching. He was dead. Kier crawled closer to Raccoon and gazed into the eyes of the man who'd saved his life. "You took that arrow for me."

"Spirit Walker," Raccoon said, using his free hand to take Kier's. "Carmen."

Kier watched Raccoon suck in a shallow breath, then the chest became still. He watched the Spirit leave his friend and struggled to raise his hand, wanting to call him back.

There were no words. Only anguish.

"My father's gone," Carmen said in a whisper. "The moment we got here he saw you were in danger. No time to say goodbye."

He wondered if Raccoon could see them from wherever he was.

Carmen went silent and simply stared at her father. He, too, said nothing. Finally, she asked, "How can you not be a Spirit Walker?"

"I've decided," he said. "I am."

And he closed his eyes.

Sitting straight and strong by the reflecting pool, his grandfather nodded and smiled.

DENISE HAMILTON

These days, to her family's great relief, Denise Hamilton stays home in Los Angeles and writes the Eve Diamond crime novels. But in the bad old days before she turned to fiction, Hamilton was a staff writer for the *Los Angeles Times* and roamed the globe, filing dispatches from Asia, Eastern Europe, the Balkans and the former USSR.

In 1993, Hamilton was awarded a Fulbright Fellowship to teach journalism in Macedonia. The Bosnian war was in full swing, and she went with the full knowledge that if the fighting spread to her part of the Balkans, she'd go overnight from college professor to war correspondent. But Macedonia never blew up and Hamilton widely toured the South Balkans and fell in love with the small, quirky nation of Albania, which at that time was just emerging from fifty years of communist isolation. As Hamilton writes in *At the Drop of a Hat*, there were few ways in and out of Albania but she managed to hitchhike into Tirana with some Albanian journalists she met at a conference on beautiful Lake Ohrid, at the Macedonia-Albania border.

Hamilton hadn't been planning such a trip and had only two hundred dollars and one change of clothes in her backpack. But she knew a good offer when she heard it, and being an adventurous sort, arrived in downtown Tirana in the late afternoon and immediately began calling U.S. Fulbright scholars in Albania, hoping to find somebody with a spare couch where she could crash. Luckily, she reached another Fulbrighter before dark and he took her to eat at what was then Tirana's only French restaurant, where they met the proprietor, a handsome and cultured Albanian man.

The restaurateur eventually offered Hamilton a ride back in his Mercedes to Skopje, where he often traveled for business. Due to scheduling conflicts she never took him up on his offer, and it wasn't until much later that she learned the full story of this man's life. In *At the Drop of a Hat*, Hamilton uses that knowledge and takes readers on a thrill ride of Balkan intrigue, providing along the way a taste for the sights, smells, textures and landscape that few Westerners have seen.

A tale from one who lived it.

AT THE DROP OF A HAT

Jane looked out the passenger window and told herself that everything was fine. Bashkim was driving, the Mercedes hurtling along the Albanian highway at a hundred kilometers an hour. The air inside the car felt tight and crackly. Outside, greenhouses stood in untilled fields, their shattered windows gaping empty. A black-clad woman followed a herd of goats up a rockstrewn hillside, spinning wool on a hand spindle. Anything could happen out here, Jane thought, and no one would ever know. The wind would shred her clothes and rain would bleach her bones and when spring came, the goats would crop the earth around her.

This has to stop, Jane scolded herself. She was a sensible girl, not one of those high-strung ones that fell apart at the drop of a hat. She just needed to rekindle the excitement she had felt last night.

She and Paul had been in their favorite Tirana restaurant, arguing because he refused to tap his diplomatic contacts to get her a ride across the border to the former Yugoslav republic of Macedonia. A conference on Balkan literature was taking place in the capital and she really wanted to attend.

"What's the big deal?" Jane had protested. "Your embassy courier does the Tirana-Skopje run twice a week."

But Paul had suddenly grown engrossed in photos of the Eiffel Tower, the Arc de Triomphe and the French Alps that decorated the walls. Over the sound system, Edith Piaf sobbed about love and betrayal. *Omelettes* and *salades niçoises* sailed out of the kitchen. This had been their sanctuary, a little piece of Paris that shut out the chaos outside that was Albania. But now Albania had followed them inside.

"I can't put a civilian on that route, it's strictly for consular business," Paul said at last.

Since when am I just a civilian? she fumed, recalling other, more fevered words he had whispered in the three weeks they'd been together. He was a low-level attaché at the U.S. embassy and she was a Fulbright scholar. They'd met at an embassy reception her first week in Tirana, bonded over too much Albanian merlot and hadn't been apart since, though in her weaker moments she wondered if it was just an expat thing.

"What do you want me to do, hitchhike? There aren't a lot of options going east."

There weren't a lot of options because the delusional Commie who had ruled Albania for almost fifty years had torn up the rail lines and sealed the border out of fear that the Yugoslavs, America *and* NATO planned to attack his backward and impoverished nation. Years after Enver Hoxha's death, it was still a logistical nightmare to get in and out. No trains or regional buses. The only planes went to Western Europe, then you had to double back. Taxis were cheaper, but she was a student and didn't have a hundred and fifty dollars to spare.

"Excuse me," said a low, melodic voice. "I don't mean to eavesdrop, but your voices…perhaps I can be of help."

The proprietor, Bashkim, stood before them, sleek in an Italian suit, hands clasped deferentially. He had toiled for years in Parisian restaurants, then come home to show the natives the glories of French cuisine. Except that Albanians, at their salaries, couldn't afford even one *frite*, though the brasserie had caught on immediately with the expense-account NGO and diplomatic crowd.

Paul fixed the restaurateur with a pensive gaze. "Really?" he said, a strange light flaring, then banking behind his eyes.

Bashkim gave a modest smile and bowed in Jane's direction. "I must go to Skopje on business tomorrow," he said. "I would be honored if you would accompany me. There is plenty of room."

"I'm not so sure that's a good idea," Paul said slowly.

But Jane had seen the shiny blue Mercedes out back and was already imagining the smooth ride, the lively discussion as first the countryside, then the desolate mountain passes, soared by. Bashkim had exquisite manners, spoke five languages, understood civil society. His wife, a beautiful Albanian with green eyes, kept the restaurant books while their little girl, immaculate in frilly dresses, played with dolls in the back. Jane could tell they were in love. Unlike many of the men who stared with hungry, medieval eyes, Bashkim never gave her a second glance. She'd seen how the expat community embraced him. She'd be safe. Plus, it would end the dreary row, her nagging suspicion that Paul didn't care enough to pull this embassy string for her.

Feeling a sudden need to assert herself, Jane said. "I *am* sure. I'm going."

Paul threw up his hands in mock horror, winked at Bashkim. "These Western women, they have minds of their own."

She had kicked him under the table, but later that night, they'd fallen into bed with their usual frenzy, all the sweeter for her impending absence. Afterward, Jane was touched that he shoved his cell phone into her backpack and insisted she keep it on until reaching Skopje, at which point she was to call and announce her safe arrival.

And so it was that Jane had set off from Paul's apartment this morning. The streets smelled of wet earth and sewers. Deformed Gypsy children writhed on cardboard, begging from passersby. Housewives leaned over balconies, beating carpets with red-faced fury. Four stories up, a cow mooed indignantly. The sight of livestock in apartments had startled her initially, but Jane soon learned you couldn't leave a cow out overnight in Tirana any more than you could a car.

Bashkim was tossing a suitcase into the back seat when she arrived. The Mercedes seemed low to the ground, like it was carrying a heavy load, but Jane thought that unlikely. Albania exported little but its own people.

Standing in the clear Adriatic light, she sensed Bashkim checking out her hiking boots and Levi's, the fleece-lined vest she'd thrown over a red ribbed turtleneck, and felt something shift. A flicker of apprehension went through her. Had she misjudged him? Then, he broke into a familiar smile and her misgivings evaporated.

"You ready?"

She climbed in. As the apartment blocks, then the dismal shanties on Tirana's outskirts gave way to farmland, they chatted about Albanian literature and culture. Then talk turned to the present day.

"It's wonderful, what you're building here. There's so much opportunity."

"There was more opportunity in France," Bashkim said. "But I couldn't get residency."

"But the West is so sterile. Everyone's obsessed with money, getting ahead. There's no sense of family, of what's really important."

"You think people here aren't obsessed with money?" he said, jabbing the gas. After that they sat in silence. The Mercedes jostled with donkey carts and tractors, passing so close that Jane could have plucked wisps of straw from a farmer's hair. An olive-green truck of Soviet vintage emblazoned with the letters STALIN passed them, stuffed with young Albanian men who hooted and hollered. But other vehicles fell into line behind them, content to let the Mercedes lead.

Bashkim punched in a CD and the strains of Mozart wafted through the car. The pleasant odor of his cologne hung in the air.

"I'm really lucky you were going to Skopje this week," Jane said, trying to recapture their earlier ease. "How often do you make the trip?"

A smile curled around the edge of his mouth. "Whenever business requires it."

She studied him. He was blond, with blue eyes. This, too, had surprised her. He could have been a surfer from her college back home, if not for his pallid skin and something ineluctable in his profile that, framed against the raw landscape and crumbling stone buildings, she suddenly saw as quintessentially Balkan.

"Do you go to Skopje for restaurant supplies?" she asked.

There was a pause, an intake of breath. Then, "You are very curious."

Jane shrugged. "Just wondering."

"Sometimes it's best not to wonder too much." He let the words hang in the air and she felt it building again, an odd pressure in her head, the tingling of individual hairs on her nape. For a long time, she studied the scrubby landscape, bereft even of litter.

"Look," he said after a time, pointing to a fortress atop a hill, and she knew he was trying to make nice. "Skanderbeg's castle. Our national hero. He was a janissary, a viceroy in the sultan's army. But he rebelled in 1569 and led an uprising of the Albanian people against the Ottomans. He was never captured."

At the turnoff, a crowd of ragged boys appeared, bunching their hands in front of open mouths.

"They're hungry," Jane cried, reaching into her backpack for dried fruit, nuts.

Bashkim pressed harder on the accelerator.

"They have become accustomed to begging," he said tersely. "The foreign-aid workers throw out sweets and they scrabble after them like dogs."

The lack of sympathy struck Jane as harsh. When Bashkim got off the highway in Elbassan, a town dominated by a hulking factory that belched out black smoke, delicate tendrils of unease bloomed inside her.

"Why are we stopping?"

Bashkim's voice was light, nonchalant.

"To drop some medicine off with a friend." He grew apologetic. "It's for his sick mother."

He braked for a herd of sheep and something slid from under her seat, hitting her heel. She looked down and saw the barrel of a machine gun. Bashkim saw it, too. He lunged between her legs, grabbed it. His arm slid against her inner thigh. Then he shoved the gun firmly under his own seat.

"Sorry about that," he said, his voice thick.

Jane gripped the leather edge of the Mercedes seat, her palms slick with moisture. She wanted to scream. Had she only imagined that his arm had lingered? And what if the gun had gone off?

When he tapped her, she jumped.

"It's to protect us," he said. "Just in case."

She tried to still the thudding of her heart against her rib cage, convince herself it made sense. This was still a land of brigands. As for the other, it was just a clumsy accident.

Bashkim wheeled the car into a driveway and the gate to a compound swung open. Jane's unease spiked higher. Why hadn't he told her earlier about the stop? What if it was all a ruse? A trap? The car moved forward. She thought about turning the door handle and hopping out. But then what? The streets were filled with tough-looking, idle young men. And she'd be stranded with little money and no way back. She'd heard whispers about what happened to women found alone after dark, especially outside the capital. The gate clanged behind them and three men with hawk faces materialized. This was where it would happen, she thought.

"I'll wait in the car," she said.

"You should use the facilities," Bashkim said firmly. "There will be no other opportunity."

Then a door to the house burst open and a plump lady waddled out. When Bashkim pulled out a container of pills and handed them to the woman, Jane could have cried with relief. The woman came around to Jane's door, grabbed her arm and tugged her toward the house. Oniony gusts of sweat, overlaid with a yeasty smell, came from her. When Jane glanced back, the men were clustered around the car trunk.

Inside, Jane was plied with tea, orangeade, cookies and raki, a potent and raw grape brandy. When they walked back out half an hour later, she noticed that the car sat higher. The men were examining a stack of boxes, and she thought she saw the glint of sun on metal. Then Bashkim stepped in front of her, blocking the view, and they left. Her mind afloat from drinking raki on an empty stomach, Jane leaned back in her seat. She told herself to stay vigilant, but instead dozed off, waking an hour later with a sour taste in her mouth, acid in her stomach.

They were in the mountains now, the tall, fierce peaks that dominate Albania, leaving only a sliver of arable land. It was afternoon. Just ahead, a bridge spanned a deep chasm. As they shot onto it, Jane looked and saw white water rushing down. She remembered Paul saying that the bridge was near the border. Then for a while the road would skirt Lake Ohrid, a deep body of still water that formed a natural border between Macedonia and Albania. Coming off the bridge, Bashkim executed a sickening curve around a precipice without a guardrail. Hundreds of yards below, Jane saw the rusting skeletons of cars that had misjudged the turn. Jets of saliva shot into her mouth and she thought she might be sick.

They were on a straightaway when Jane saw an accident ahead and a man waving a white shirt tied to a pole. Bashkim swore and slowed. As they drew closer, Jane saw it wasn't an accident but two Albanian army trucks, blocking the road. A pimply-faced soldier with a rifle waved them over to the side. Bashkim stared ahead with a fixed intensity. The car surged forward, and Jane thought he meant to gun the accelerator and try to blast through.

At the last possible second, he hit the brake. The cars behind him careened into a ditch, bumping along on a cloud of dust and then accelerating past the roadblock. Jane wondered if the authorities might give chase, but they seemed supremely uninterested.

A soldier walked up to Bashkim, rifle pointed at his head, barking orders in Albanian. Jane saw the restaurateur's knee tremble but his voice stayed calm. She heard the words *Amerikane* and *Skopje*. More soldiers came, ordered them out of the car. Jane felt unreal, stiff and jerky with fear. She'd heard about Albanian bandits who set up roadblocks and robbed Westerners of cars, clothes and even shoes, leaving them stranded in their underwear. In years past, tractor-trailer trucks had convoyed to the Yugoslav border without stopping. Jane thought about offering the soldiers money.

She pulled out the cell phone, thinking she'd call Paul at the U.S. embassy in Tirana. "Help," she'd say. "We've been stopped at a roadblock by Albanian soldiers and I think we're in trouble. Now aren't you sorry you didn't let me ride with the courier?"

The soldiers shoved Bashkim and screamed questions at him, ignoring her. Jane took several steps away. Nobody noticed. She drifted around one truck, moved along the tarp to the other, then froze in disbelief.

In the cab, hunched over a laptop, sat Paul. Another embassy guy with a crew cut that she remembered from a Tirana dinner party leaned against the door, peering intently at Paul's screen, a cell phone pressed to his ear. Jane checked her first impulse to dash over and throw herself, sobbing, into Paul's arms. Instead, she ran through all the possible reasons her lover might be sitting in this desolate mountain pass with a passel of Albanian soldiers, and why he hadn't told her he was coming or offered her a ride himself. The answers she came up with made her shrink back into the shade of the tarp. But it was too late.

Sensing her presence, Paul looked up. "Jane," he said. "Oh my God. What are you doing here?"

Like it was a big surprise. She thought back on the argument at the restaurant. Paul announcing in a loud voice that he couldn't allow the embassy courier to drive her to Macedonia. His look of near gloating—she now realized—when Bashkim had offered a ride.

"You planned this," Jane said. "You set him up."

"That's ridiculous," Paul said, but his voice was as hollow as his eyes.

He glanced over her shoulder, and grim satisfaction spread across his face. She turned and saw the soldiers unloading boxes from the trunk of Bashkim's car. They had found the machine gun, too. Over to the side of the road, Bashkim lay spread-eagle on the ground. One of the soldiers kicked him as he passed and the prone man gave a strangled cry.

"Stop it, you bastard, we need him for questioning," the crew-cut man called.

Paul cursed and jumped out of the cab. He walked toward the soldier and in the moments that followed, Jane saw a different man than the one she had known. His bearing, even the tenor of his voice, changed. He was self-assured, in charge, bristling with power. The soldier cowered as Paul dressed him down in perfect-sounding Albanian.

Jane listened, astounded. Paul had told her he was hopeless with languages. Now this stranger walked back to her and said, "I'm sorry, Jane. But you were never in danger. We were tracking you with the global positioning device." He nodded smartly at the cell phone, which she still clutched impotently in her hand. "Led us right to the safe house."

Realization bore down like an oncoming train that would smash her into a thousand pieces. She had been the decoy. A nicely turned-out Western woman. Each side had used her. Something did break in her then. But to her surprise, when she examined the sharp and deadly pieces, she found that they had their own terrifying beauty and usefulness.

"What did Bashkim do?" she asked, willing her voice not to tremble.

"Our pal over there is one of the biggest smugglers in Tirana. Remember when the country rioted and looted the armories? He's been trading machine guns to al-Qaeda for Afghani heroin. We've been watching him for months."

"We? Since when does the embassy track smugglers?"

"The embassy works hand in hand with Interpol."

"You're not some lowly attaché, are you, Paul?"

He ran his hands through his hair and looked away. He didn't say anything. He didn't have to.

She felt that sanity was a thin membrane, stretching ever tighter. If she moved even a fraction, it would snap and she'd slip under. Yet she had to know one thing.

"Did you plan this? I mean, from the beginning? Because I thought…it felt…"

She shook her head, blinking back tears. She had been played for a fool.

A shadow crossed Paul's face.

He licked his lips. "I never meant…" he began.

He didn't get a chance to finish.

Two cars came roaring down the highway from the east, machine guns blazing. As she threw herself to the ground, Jane thought she recognized the vehicles that had peeled past the roadblock. Had they also been in the convoy that had trailed them from Tirana? Gunfire erupting around her, Jane clutched her head and crawled on her belly toward the nearest truck, expecting at any second to be hit and feel no more. Reaching the undercarriage, she rolled beneath it and listened to the shouts, the guns, then the groans of dying men. She prayed no bullets would pierce the gas tank.

After what seemed like hours, the shooting stopped. For a long time, there was silence. In the distance, a bird screamed, the exultant cry of a carrion feeder that spies dinner. Then she heard footsteps. She cowered and curled herself into a ball, wishing she might disappear. A shadow fell on the highway, and she saw a polished leather shoe.

"Come out," said an Albanian-accented voice in English. Bashkim.

She didn't answer.

"If you don't come out, I'll shoot you."

Still she stayed silent, wondering if he was bluffing. She heard the crack of his knees as he squatted. A hand with a gun appeared, angling to and fro, then settling its muzzle blessedly far from where she lay. Jane held her breath as he pulled the trigger. One of the truck's tires exploded with a loud pop and began to deflate. She gave an involuntary scream.

"I knew it." His voice was triumphant. "Last chance, Jane. Next time I aim for your voice."

"Okay," she said. "Don't shoot."

She crawled out and they stared at one another.

"Please," she said. "I didn't know it was a setup."

Bashkim's lips pursed. He looked at where Paul's body lay, eyes staring glassily at the sky. Near his head was a pool of blood. All around her were other crumpled bodies. One of the cars that had shot at them lay on its side, smashed and burning. She looked for the other.

"It went over the edge," Bashkim said. "They couldn't have survived."

"Wh-who were they?"

Bashkim grimaced.

"My bodyguards. Don't you know it's dangerous to travel in Albania?"

"Jesus," she said, seized with an uncontrollable bout of shivering.

Bashkim stared at her, and Jane thought he might be trying to decide whether to kill her now or later. They both knew she'd seen too much to live.

"He betrayed me, too, you know," Jane said.

He examined her indifferently. "So I heard."

He walked to where her cell phone had fallen and smashed it with his heel, grinding it into the asphalt like a cockroach.

"Don't kill me," Jane said. "I'll help you. I've got an American passport, money."

"Yes," Bashkim nodded. "With your passport, we'll breeze through."

He prodded her with the gun, back to the Mercedes. All the tires had been shot out, and smoke was rising from under the hood. She wondered if it might catch fire while they stood there. The trunk stood open, white powder seeping out of bullet-riddled boxes.

More boxes were scattered along the road, next to Bashkim's machine gun, which had been reduced to twisted metal. Bashkim told her to empty her backpack and hand over her passport and wallet, which he put in his pocket. Then he made her tear open the boxes and fill her backpack with the sacks of white powder. Pulling an old rucksack from his trunk, he ordered her to fill that, too. Then, he loaded her up like a pack mule and marched her off the highway, into the rocky countryside to a dirt trail pounded hard by animals.

"The border's about ten miles away. We'll have to stay off the road."

They set off, moving like ghosts through the denuded landscape.

"Let's stop here and rest a moment," he said when they reached a rock outcropping. His tone deliberate and unsettling. Bashkim eased himself down. He stared at her and she looked away, thinking about escape and when she might make a break for it. She needed cover. Bashkim stood up, laid the gun on a rock. He walked toward her as she scrambled to her feet. Suddenly he flung himself at her, knocking her to the ground. Jane tried to wriggle free but he was strong and his weight pinned her. She saw the look in his eyes. Perhaps the day's events had awakened something atavistic in him. Perhaps it had always been there. But she knew she was of no consequence to him anymore. He was going to kill her once they crossed, so it didn't matter what else he did in the meantime.

"Get off me," she panted.

He shoved a hand down her pants and tugged.

"Fucking get off."

"Fucking. Yes, that's what all you American girls like. I knew it the first time I saw you."

"You're wrong. Get off."

She tried to brace one hand against the dirt so she could twist aside and knee him. Instead, her fingers glanced off a large rock. She groped for it. It grazed the edges of her fingertips, just out of reach. Bashkim unzipped his fly.

Jane squirmed backward and flexed her fingers toward the rock. Her fingers nudged it, slid along the rough, granular edges, searching for where it might taper, afford a grip. There. Her hand closed tightly.

Bashkim tore at her underwear and rose up, wedging her legs open with his knee. A bloodlust burned in her. She'd get only one chance. The rock was in the air. Jane shoved her knee into his groin and screamed as she brought the rock down hard against the base of his skull.

He gasped, then was still. She rolled the inert body off of her, scrabbled up. Bashkim was unconscious. Bleeding. She looked at him and felt only a mounting need to zip up her jeans and flee.

She still held the rock, now slick with blood. Forcing her fingers to relinquish it took awhile. Jane panted shallowly, and the enormity of everything that had happened overwhelmed her. Leaning over a thornbush, she retched, cursing her weakness. She had to get to the border before night fell, stranding her. Already, the temperature was dropping. She knew the road below led to the frontier, but she had to stay out of sight. Prodding Bashkim's body with her hiking boot, she pulled out her passport, her money and his wallet. She also took a small black notebook with notations in Albanian and Arabic. Lastly she got the gun. She had never touched one before, but she knew they had safeties. She clicked it on and off a few times to familiarize herself with how it worked, then shoved the gun into her waistband. The cold metal felt reassuring against her skin. For two hours she marched uphill, crouching behind rocks whenever she heard a car. She didn't dare stop, terrified that her legs might lock up for good.

In the long gaps between vehicles, Jane kept her mind rigidly focused on the moment she'd hand the guard her passport and slip across to safety. She didn't see the olive-green truck that said STALIN until she was right above it, in full view of the road. The truck was parked and the young men from earlier were arrayed around, eating. Jane froze, then instinct kicked in and she darted off. With any luck they wouldn't follow. Instead, she heard excited voices, then the truck wheezing into reverse as it began backing up to a spot where it could turn off the highway and come after her.

Jane ran, adrenaline powering a burst of speed, her breath coming in great gulps of despair. She'd never outrace them. But she couldn't let them catch her. She'd seen the sporting look in their eyes, knew how the game would end. She had to hide before they came into view and hope they'd barrel past, consumed by the chase. She folded herself behind an insubstantial rock, praying the afternoon shadows would conceal her, and watched the truck bounce by just twenty feet away, ribald laughter erupting from within. Slipping from bush to rock, she followed them, until the truck turned and headed back to the road, figuring she had doubled back and they'd catch up with her before passport control. That meant she'd have to go cross-country. She was so weary but she forced herself to keep going. Another half mile and she reached the saddle between two summits. Below her stretched the water, dark and gloomy. Lake Ohrid. On the other side of the lake was Macedonia, and freedom.

She scanned the shore, looking for a boat, anything to carry her across. It was too far to swim. In the blue dusk, she made out a solitary figure mending a net. She heard the roar of the truck, the shouts of the Albanian men, and knew they had spotted her once more. But they'd have to follow the road's hairpin curves down to the lake, whereas she could plunge straight down the mountain. The lake stretched for miles, most of it unguarded. It was her only hope. She ran, dislodging avalanches of pebbles and dirt, sliding on her ass and once somersaulting head over heels to plow the ground with outstretched arms before righting herself and continuing her descent.

She could see the figure on the shore now. It was an old man. She felt the steel against her skin and knew she'd kill him if she had to. He watched her. As she drew closer, she saw a head of white hair, blackened teeth, a map of brown wrinkles. His face betrayed no surprise, as if deranged Western women tumbled down the mountain every day.

"Please," she said, sliding to a halt before him, scraped and bleeding. "You must take me across." She gestured to the other side of the lake. "I can pay. *Valuta.*" She pulled out Bashkim's wallet, thrust greenbacks and euros and Albanian dinars at him.

"For you."

To her surprise, the fisherman shoved the money back at her. She panicked, screaming at him in fragments of four languages. Ignoring her, he shuffled to a bush and pulled out a rowboat that lay hidden underneath. An ancient, frayed rope lay curled inside.

He began dragging it to the lake and she ran to help him, thanking him in every language she knew.

"But we must hurry," she said, looking over her shoulder to pantomime running and pursuers.

"*Ska problema*," the old man said. "No problem."

"*Besa?*" she asked. The *besa* was a solemn promise, or oath, handed down from feudal times. Albanians would die before violating a *besa*. But did the old ways still hold?

The Albanian side of the great lake was moving into twilight. The few houses clinging to the slopes had never known electricity. Across the water, the Yugoslav coastline sparkled in warm, inviting twinkles of red and yellow.

She helped him push off and scrambled in.

They were about a hundred yards out when the truck came bouncing across the side of the mountain, the men angry as a swarm of bees. Several had already loosened their clothing. They ran to the water's edge and waded in, firing. She and the old man ducked, bullets sizzling past, skimming the water. The old man grunted and kept rowing, the ropy muscles of his arms straining against his skin.

Jane had the gun ready, just in case, but the fisherman seemed oblivious to her, lulled by the repetitive strokes, the plash of the oars in water. The cries and shouts grew distant, then ceased altogether. The wind kicked up and she shivered. They were suspended in nothingness, floating between worlds. Then the lights began to draw nearer. She watched in greedy hunger as the resort hotels and vacation homes appeared in the twilit murk. Then she heard a *scritch* as the rowboat hit the pebbly bottom.

"Bravo Yugoslavia," the fisherman said. Again she

tried to press money on him but he waved it away, then placed his hand over his heart. The *besa* fulfilled.

The old man helped her clamber into the icy, thigh-deep water. She waved goodbye and stepped onto the shingle, legs like jelly, and watched the rowboat already easing back into the inky depths. Then she hiked up to the nearest hotel, got herself a room and ordered *cvapcici* and rice from room service.

The knock, when it came, startled her.

"Who is it?" she called.

When a Slavic voice answered, she cracked the door and saw a waiter with a tray. She opened the door wider for the food and out stepped two men in windbreakers. Before Jane could slam the door shut, one of them had his foot inside. The other passed the waiter a bill. "Thanks. You can go now," the man said in American English.

They came inside and closed the door.

"You did very well, Jane," the first man said. "We were watching from this side, in case anyone made it across. You understand, of course, why we couldn't risk an incident in international waters."

"Who are you? How do you know my name?"

"It's safe to stop running now. Paul was online with us, right before the connection went dead. Why don't you tell us the whole story."

He turned to his companion. "Nick, please relieve Jane of her burden. It must have been so heavy. Where is it, Jane?"

But she had left the bags of white powder behind on a desolate Albanian mountainside, next to what she feared was a corpse. How could they be so stupid to think she'd cross an international border with millions of dollars' of heroin stuffed into a backpack?

Jane fingered the gun at her side and considered her options. She was a sensible girl. Not one of those high-strung ones that fell apart at the drop of a hat.

"There's a lot you don't know," she said evenly. "And I'm the only one who can fill you in. But first I need a square meal and a shower. Then we can cross back over and I'll show you where the drugs are. There's also a notebook that may interest you. Once we take care of business, I'd like one of you gentlemen to drive me to Skopje. There's a conference I really don't want to miss. But I'll be graduating soon. And I can't see myself teaching Balkan literature in some U.S. backwater the rest of my life. So I think we should talk about a job. I understand you have an opening in Tirana."

ERIC VAN LUSTBADER

When Eric Van Lustbader was asked by the estate
of the late Robert Ludlum to continue Ludlum's
series of thrillers featuring Jason Bourne, he told
them he wanted free rein to take the character in
new directions. At the time, Lustbader was grap-
pling with the loss of his father. So, understandably,
the basis of *The Bourne Legacy* revolved around the
thorny relationship between Bourne and the son
he'd for many years assumed to be dead.

Similarly, in Lustbader's latest novel, *The Bravo
Testament*, a father-son relationship fuels the high-
powered action and emotional responses of the
main characters. This familial emotional resonance
will be familiar to Lustbader's fans, as it stretches all
the way back to his first thriller, *The Ninja*.

The Other Side of the Mirror deepens and broad-
ens this theme, but in other ways it's a departure
for Lustbader. He wrote the story after one day re-
discovering *The Outsider*, by philosopher/novelist
Colin Wilson, in his library. *The Outsider* had been

a seminal book, one Lustbader had devoured during his college days. Reading it again he found new meaning in his own work, which is reflected in *The Other Side of the Mirror*, a story about a spy—an outsider, if ever there was one—and the terrible toll secrecy and lies take on him. Lustbader, who thinks of himself as an outsider, seems drawn to his sense of apartness. If you've ever wondered what it would be like to be outside society, or if that's precisely how you feel, this story is for you.

THE OTHER SIDE OF THE MIRROR

He awakens into darkness, the darkness at the dead of night—but it is also the dread darkness of the soul that has plagued him for thirteen weeks, thirteen months, it's impossible now to say.

What he can say for certain is that he has been on the run for thirteen weeks, but his assignment had begun thirteen months ago. He joined the Agency, propelled not so much by patriotism or an overweening itch to rub shoulders with danger—the two main motivations of his compatriots—but by the death of his wife. Immediately upon her death he had felt an overwhelming urge to hurl himself into the dark and, at times, seedy labyrinth in which she had dwelled for a decade before he had discovered that she did not go off to work in the manner of other people.

And now, here he is, twenty-three years after they had taken their vows, sitting in the dark, waiting for death to come.

* * *

It is hot in the room what with all the piles of magazines he's amassed, ragged and torn, beautiful as pink-cheeked children. Joints cracking, he rises, pads over to the air conditioner, moving like a wader through surf of his own making. It wheezes pathetically when he turns it on, which isn't all that surprising since even five minutes later nothing but hot air emerges from its filthy grille. Not that Buenos Aires is a Third World city, far from it. There are plenty of posh hotels whose rooms are at this moment bathed in cool, dry air, but this isn't one of them. It has a name, this hotel, but he's already forgotten it.

In the tiny bathroom, full of drips and creeping water bugs the size of his thumb, he splashes luke-warm water on his face. Cold is hot and hot is cold; does anything work right in this hellhole? He wants to take a shower, but the bottom is filled with more magazines, stacked like little castles in the sand. They comfort him, somehow, these magazine constructs, and he turns away, a sudden realization taking hold.

Curiously, it is in this hellhole that he feels most comfortable. Over the last thirteen weeks he has been in countless hotels in countless cities on three continents—this is his third, after North America and Europe. The difference, besides going from winter to summer, is this: here in this miserable, crumbling back alley of Buenos Aires, death breathes just around the corner. It has been relentlessly stalking him for thirteen weeks, and now it is closer than it has ever been, so close the stench of it is horrific, like the reek of a rabid dog or an old man with crumbling teeth.

The closer death comes, the calmer he becomes, that's the irony of his situation. Though, as he stares at his pallid face with its sunken eyes and raw cheek-bones, he acknowledges that it very well may not be the situation at all.

He stares for a moment at the pad of his forefinger. On it is imprinted part of a familiar photograph—from one of the magazine pages, or from his life? He shrugs, uses the forefinger to pull down his lower lids one at a time. His eyes look like pebbles, black and perfectly opaque, as if there is no light, no spark, no intelligence behind them. He is—who is he today? Max Brandt, the same as he was yesterday and the day before that. Max Brandt, Essen businessman, may have checked into this dump, but it was Harold Moss, recently divorced tourist, who had come through security at Ezeiza International Airport. Moss and Brandt don't look much alike, one is stoop-shouldered with slightly buck teeth and a facile grin, the other stands ramrod straight and strides down the street with confidence and a certain joie de vivre. Gait is more important than the face in these matters. Faces tend to blur in people's memories, but the manner in which someone walks remains.

He stares at himself and feels as if he is looking at a painting or a mannequin. He is Harold Moss and Max Brandt, their skins are wrapped around him, in him, through him, helping to obliterate whatever was there before he had conjured them up. His facade, his exo-skeleton, his armor is complete. He is no one, nothing, less—far less—than a cipher. No one glancing at him on the street could possibly guess that he is a clandestine agent—save for the enemy against whom he has labored tirelessly and assiduously for thirteen years, and possibly longer, the enemy who is no longer fooled by his periodic shedding of one persona for another, expert though it is, the enemy who is now curled on his doorstep, having finally run him to ground.

He returns to the rumpled bed, flicking off more water bugs. They like to gather in the warm indentations his body makes, no doubt feeding on the microscopic flaking of skin he leaves behind in sleep, like fevered nightmares sloughed off by the unconscious mind. He moves the bugs out of necessity only; really he has no innate quarrel with them the way most people do. Live and let live is his motto.

His harsh laugh sends them scattering to the four shadowed corners of the room. Some disappear behind the closed wooden jalousie that covers the window. They have all too quickly come to know him, and they have no desire to be eaten alive. Flopping down on the thin mattress in a star position, he gazes up at the constellations of cracks in the plaster ceiling that at one time long ago must have been painted blue. They seem to change position every time he takes this survey, but he knows this cannot be true.

I know, I know… A singsong lullaby to himself. *What do I know?* Something, anything, who can say with the fissures appearing inside his head?

It never fails, the color blue makes him think of Lily. The azure sky under which they picnicked when they were dating, the aquamarine-and-white surf through which he swam, following her out to the deep water. There were bluebirds in the old sycamore that dominated the front yard of their house in Maryland, and there was a time, early on in their marriage, when Lily cultivated bluebells in her spare moments. She liked to wear blue, as well—powder-blue sleeveless blouses in summer, navy cardigans in autumn, cobalt parkas in winter, denim work shirts in the spring, with the sleeves half-rolled revealing, after snows and cruel biting winds, the beautiful bare flesh of her forearms.

Lily with her hard, lean body and bright cornflower-blue eyes. She rode horses like a man but made love like a woman. In the privacy of their bedroom, she was soft, her voice gooey enough to get him to do anything gladly. He was the only one to see this side of her—not even their son, Christopher, had an inkling. He was acutely, almost painfully aware of the nature of her gift to him, but then his love for her ran so deep and strong that the first moment he had seen her take the stage for an audition at college he had been struck by a bolt of physical pain that had nearly felled him.

He was in the theater arts program then, learning the ins and outs of makeup design. Within a week, he would be painting her face for the stage, making her look older so that she could better fit the role she had won at the audition. She was a fine actress, even then, raw and untrained, for she had been born with the mind and the heart to recite lines as if they were her own thoughts and feelings.

He loved his work. The characters he created were for him more real than the actors themselves, whom he found vain and boring. When he was required to simulate blood or wounds he found novel ways of execution, for he dreamed of the violence that had caused these traumas, lived it, imagined it in such vivid detail that he never failed to win accolades from the faculty directors who over the four years came and went like clockwork.

Applying makeup to Lily was akin to making love to her. He felt strongly that he was transforming her not only outside but inside as well. She was, through him, becoming another person, an unknown quantity.

At those times he felt a peculiar form of intimacy that was transcendent. He felt as if he was killing her, only to have her splendidly resurrected when she made her appearance on stage.

At first, she hadn't seemed interested in him, or at least she had contrived to remain aloof. That was her reputation, he had learned. More than one of his friends and acquaintances had counseled him to steer clear of her. Perversely, their warnings had only served to make him want her more. Desire was like a flood-tide inside him, threatening to sweep him away.

"You want me, you may think you want me," she had said to him in those early days, "but I know what you want."

She had startled him, but like everything she said or did, hidden inside the shock of her words was the truth: she had been interested enough in him to do the re-search. She did not strike him as the kind of person to waste her time on things that didn't matter to her. He was right. Six months after graduation they were engaged.

By that time, he had switched from makeup to set design, wanting to re-create reality in the largest sense possible. He had become bored by the tiny tasks in-volved in remaking faces. He required a bigger canvas for his imagination. In his widely hailed designs could be detected not only symbols from the playwrights' work, but for every major character. It was as if he had imagined each character, carefully hiding the most potent part of him somewhere in plain sight.

A year after that, they had a June wedding. It was beautiful—or, rather, Lily was beautiful in her shimmer-ing satin gown with ephemeral tulle sleeves. There was, however, a flaw that marred the perfection. During the reception, he had gone to relieve himself and, upon returning, had seen Lily in close conversation with his cousin, Will. What enraged him beyond all reason was Will's hand rested on Lily's bare forearm. The white tulle of her sleeve had been drawn back like the intimate curtain in a boudoir, revealing that which should not be caressed by any outsider. It was unthinkable.

It took the best man and three of the ushers to wrench him off his cousin, whose face was by then a bloody pulp. Will couldn't even stand on his own, a fact that created a fierce elation in him as he was bound backward across the dance floor.

The band had been playing "We Are Family," and now they resumed, the first several bars as shaky as Will.

He stands spread-legged in front of the laboring air conditioner, which he is quite certain has had no Freon in it for years. At least the air, hot as it is, is moving. Lurid neon colors seep through the blades of the jalousie despite his best efforts to smother the outside world. There is a pool in the concrete courtyard below, or at any rate he thinks there is, remembering a blue-black oval he passed upon his arrival several days—or is it weeks?—ago. He could, he thinks, go down to the courtyard and fling his sweating body into the water. But perhaps that, too, is lukewarm like the water out of the faucet and he would sweat all the more with his exertions. In any case, he knows he will not take the chance. He is in his bunker now, the final resting place from which he has challenged his enemies to take him feetfirst.

Christopher was born six months after the wedding, but he wasn't a preemie. No, his birth was dead on time. He was a handsome child, with none of the gnomelike qualities many newborns exhibit. He had hair as blond as his mother's and her pink apple-blossom cheeks, but he had his father's musculature and sturdy build and, over the years, would grow into a larger, handsomer version of the man who had made him.

That is how he has always thought of himself in relation to his son, as if Lily was a mere receptacle for his seed, as if her genes had played no role in Christopher's physical or emotional makeup. Jesus, he hopes that is so.

And yet... He thinks of the day when Christopher found one of his early stage sets—a marvelous one-eighth size of colored cardboard, bits of wood and metal he'd done for the last act of *Death of a Salesman*. Christopher was—let's see—ten or eleven. The boy had plucked his old dog-eared copy off the shelf in his den-studio and had called his parents in to witness his performance. He'd played the part of Biff and he wasn't half-bad. Lily had encouraged him, of course, and for a while he'd taken acting lessons just as she had. But even then Christopher thought for himself. The chaos of acting, the publicness of performance proved too stressful. It was computers that fascinated him; he loved their precision and logic. For his first real project, he created software to change stage sets so that his father could fashion ever more intricate and complicated interiors and exteriors, cleverly mimicking reality in ways never before possible.

It was little wonder that this project—an artistic triumph, though with limited commercial value—led to a closeness with his son he could never have imagined. It was also the reason, he was convinced, that Christopher confided in him, rather than in the male companions his own age.

"They don't understand me, they don't have a clue as to who I am," Christopher told him one day.

And on others, during long walks, he confessed to his father his various love affairs. "They're all doomed, from the start," he said, "because even when I'm with them I can see how it's going to end, and this throws me into an agony of despair."

"Then, why don't you stop?" he had said.

"Because I can't," Christopher replied. "The first blush is transporting, there's no other feeling like it in the world."

He had been startled to discover that Christopher kept tokens of all his affairs—locks of hair, a few beads, an anklet, even the crushed butt of a cigarette on which was imprinted in pink the lips of his former beloved. He accepted this fetishism because he understood it, deeply and completely, but of course he never told Lily.

And then there was the time when he'd found Christopher standing at the open window of his room. It was in the dead of night, when the world was quiet and far away.

"What are you doing?" he asked his son.

"I'm imagining what it would be like to jump."

"Jump?" he had said, not quite understanding yet.

"Killing myself, Dad."

He had come to stand by his son's side. "Why would you want to do that?"

"Why do you think?"

Once again, he wasn't alarmed; once again, he understood. He also felt out of sync with the world, estranged and a stranger, sometimes even to himself.

He'd put his hand on Christopher's shoulder and felt as if it were his own shoulder. "Don't concern yourself, son. Everything changes."

"But it won't get better."

"That, no one can say."

Christopher had nodded and, closing the window, had said, "Thanks, Dad. Thanks for not lying to me."

For all its impotence, the air conditioner roars like the jet engines of the plane that brought him here. With the hot stream lifting the hairs on his forearms and chest, he looks down at his bare feet and thinks of death. There is nothing else left to think about, and now he wonders whether there ever was.

When had it become apparent that there was something wrong with Lily? Even though he has racked his brains for months, he hasn't been able to quite pinpoint the moment. Perhaps there was no one moment, perhaps, as in all other things in life his wife's demise was a death by ten thousand cuts. Because, until the very end, she had been the consummate actress. He was uniquely qualified to see her ruse—he who was closest to her, who should not have been able to be objective because she was his wife and his beloved. But she was to him a great, intricate clock, whose every tick, every tock he knew inside and out.

What eventually caught his attention were the tiniest details, so minute that not even Christopher had been aware of them. Only he, who was obsessed by her, who fetishized her—only he knew. But, really, he didn't know—not at first, anyway. But slowly the tendrils of suspicion took hold of him and would not let him go. So he began to pay special attention.

He recalls the time he went into her closet. He always went into her closet to search on his hands and knees for bits of her—a stray nail clipping or a strand of pubic hair. Eyelashes he loved best, not only for their exquisite scimitar shape but because they were something so intimate he could almost feel her heart beating when he held one on the tip of his finger. She existed in that one tiny follicle, as if she were a genie who had been put back into her lamp, to be with him for all time.

He'd made a light box of mahogany with beveled edges and mitred corners into which he put an 8x10 photo he'd taken of her on their honeymoon. Her eyes looked dewy and, behind the halo of her hair spread the fronds of Balinese palms, slightly out of focus, looking like Tjak, the Balinese bird with a human face. Behind this photo, he placed the ephemera he periodically collected from her closet, and some of them tended to cast unidentifiable shadows across her face.

That day, however, he found something else, a tiny scrap of paper with a mark on it. He thought it must be a bit of writing, though it wasn't English or for that matter any language that used Roman letters. The mark looked like a rune to him, something ancient and therefore unknowable. Thus his suspicions, having been previously awakened, were aroused.

In some ways, she was too perfect, and in light of his suspicions, her absolute perfection proved the deepest fissure in her simulation. In all ways, she was the perfect wife and mother. She cooked gourmet dinners, provided him with astonishingly imaginative sex, was always there for Christopher when he was ill or low, was so kind to his girlfriends that many of them kept in touch with her long after their liaisons with him had ended. She never complained when her husband went away on business trips and was grateful for the same treatment when she went away on her business trips.

The facade was complete, and life went on precisely as it should have. But nothing in life is perfect and, as Christopher was quick to understand, happiness is as ephemeral as a cherry blossom. In fact, it is his own opinion that happiness is illusory.

Take, for instance, the sex. While it had been true that in college he'd left a string of girlfriends behind him, his serial affairs were not at all motivated by sex, to which he had been indifferent. No, he'd been looking for something. At first, he hadn't known what it was, he only knew that each girl in her own way had disappointed him. Later on, it occurred to him that he was looking for a shadow, a kind of twin to himself, who possessed the qualities he himself longed for but did not have.

Lily had performed on him the most elaborate erotic rituals. It was not surprising that he came to enjoy them, then to actually crave them, but his burgeoning desire bound him to her, and this bitter revelation plunged him into despair.

As soon as he was able to see through the mirage of happiness everything changed. Lily, as it transpired, worked for the Agency, not Fieldstone Real Estate or, latterly, March & Masson Public Relations. Or, rather, she did work at the offices of Fieldstone and, latterly, March & Masson, but both entities were owned and operated by the Agency, stage sets as artfully aping reality as any of the ones he had designed.

There is a scratching at the hotel-room door, and he turns, facing his fate as if it were the lens of a camera. Let them come, his enemies, he is ready for them now, for if they break in they will find Harold Moss or Max Brandt. It will be of no moment to him and a bitter disappointment to them. He himself is gone, dissolved like candle wax beneath a flame.

* * *

Where was he? Oh, yes, Lily. Of course, Lily. His beginning and his end.

"I know what you want from me," she had said at the outset of their relationship, and she was right, she could see through to the hollow core of him. In fact, he is convinced this is why she married him. Since his core was hollow, she could fashion him into her ideal lover. She could turn him inside out and it wouldn't matter, because there'd been nothing there to begin with.

Years later, he had said to her, "What is it you want from me?"

It was night and they were in bed, naked and sweaty from their acrobatic exertions. She was still on top, reluctant to dismount. The night was still, as it always was when they made love, as if it had ceased to exist.

"I should have thought that was obvious. I love you."

A lie, but not, perhaps, the first one she'd told him, which might have been, "Don't look at me like that, it gives me the creeps," or then again, while he was making her up, while he was killing her, "You're nothing to me. I don't care whether you live or die." And then, reborn on stage, she had glanced into the wings at the precise spot where she knew he stood for each performance and had smiled at his shadow.

Actors were, of course, adept at creating their own reality, but lying, well, that was another matter entirely. It seems to him now, standing on the furthest shore of his life, in the stifling heat of summertime when it should be winter, that Lily became addicted to lying as others become addicted to heroin or cocaine. He suspected she had got high from lying—no, not suspected, *knew*, because in molding him she had given herself away, and he had known her as deeply and pro-foundly as she had known him.

Perhaps, in the end, this is how she had come un-done—not her lying to him, but the nature of her lies. And when the lies had altered, subtly but definitely, he had known. He'd followed her on one of her busi-ness trips and had seen her put something in a painted birdhouse affixed to a crooked wooden post out in the Maryland countryside. She'd left, but he'd stayed to watch. Twenty minutes later, a car had pulled up and a man got out. The man went straight to the birdhouse and when he'd pulled out whatever it was Lily had left for him, he depressed the trigger of his digital camera at 10X zoom.

The resulting photos he showed to the people at the Agency, who became immediately agitated.

Then he showed them the scrap of paper he'd found in Lily's closet.

"That's not a rune," they said, their agitation in-creasing exponentially. "It's Arabic."

He awakens into darkness and a rude snuffling, as if a large and hostile dog is just outside the door. He's off the bed in a shot. When had he drifted off to sleep? He cannot remember and, in any event, it does not matter. Time has crept on, but it is still the dead of night.

Reaching under the pillow, he brushes a water bug off the blued barrel of his semiautomatic pistol. Over the years, it has served him well, this weapon. On its grips is a series of notches, one for each of the people he has shot to death with it. In this way, the dead are always with him, like lovers who have disappointed him. In this way, he can confirm where he has been, how he has reached the place he is now. To anyone else, this train of thought might seem perverse, even illogical, but then he's never been foolish enough to put his faith in logic.

He rechecks the pistol, although there's really no need, his spycraft is precise, something in which he prides himself. It is fully loaded. He takes out a second clip, puts it in his left pocket, then another for good measure, which he puts in his right pocket.

At that moment, the room is flooded with noise and the door shudders on its hinges. He lunges for the jalousie, pulls it open. The night, fired by a million Buenos Aires lights, comes flooding in, nearly blinding him. He forgets his commitment to remain in the room and flings open the window. Beyond the crumbling concrete ledge is a black metal fire escape, onto which he swings. The noise from inside the room is deafening, and without a backward glance he hurls himself up the metal rungs, climbing breathlessly without pausing for even an instant to take in the high sky, the rearing black mountains. But when he gains the rooftop, the first thing he sees is the spangled ocean running up to spend itself on the wide swath of sand, whose color and curve matches exactly the shape of Lily's eyelash.

He looks around. The landscape he has ascended onto is flat as a bare stage, smelling of creosote and decayed fish. Here and there rise the squat shapes of ventilator housings, but in fact the rooftop is dominated by the skeleton that holds fast the enormous neon sign advertising the hotel: EL PORTAL, *the doorway,* as if it were a pleasure palace instead of a water-bug-infested hellhole. This he understands completely. It is nothing more than a stage set, a huge construct of brightly colored fantasy trying to mimic reality. But up close, its ugly black ironwork looms like a depressing image of urban sprawl.

Sounds come from below him, chaotic and harsh, and he backs away. Gun at the ready, he finds the nearest of the blocky ventilator housings and crouches down behind it. Anyone who follows him up will come into his sights. At his back the neon sign perks and sizzles, throwing off colored light like a dying star. He sees pigeons wheeling across the lurid sky. Far below him a dog barks, a forlorn sound he somehow comprehends.

All at once, there is movement above the parapet—a shape, a silhouette darker by far than the glittering night, and he squeezes off a shot. The shape, more visible now, resolves itself into a figure. The figure comes at him even as he squeezes off shot after shot. He throws away the empty clip, retreats to another ventilation housing as he slams home the second clip. Immediately, he begins firing again until that clip, too, is empty. Retreating to the crisscross metalwork of the sign stanchion, he reloads with his last clip. Clambering into the nebula of colored lights as if it were the last remnant of his past, he fires, this time knowing the figure will still come on, unwounded, unfazed and undeterred....

He awakens into darkness and a cold sweat, half his mind still paralyzed. In a way, the nightmare seems more real than his present reality. It is certainly more real than anything in his past. The pounding on the door comes as if on cue, as if his nightmare was presentiment. But he puts as little faith in the paranormal as he does in the rational.

No dogs snuffling, instead a human voice from beyond the barrier. He flicks off the safety of his gun and makes his winding way through the blizzard of torn, cut and folded magazine pages (he dare not trample them down!) to a spot just beside the door. He's onto them! He is too clever to stand in front of it, his enemies are all too likely to send a spray of machine-gun bullets through it, having lured him to it with the coaxing voice.

He takes a breath, lets it out slowly and evenly in precisely the same way he will soon squeeze the trigger of his weapon. Then he whips around the upper part of his torso so that he can put his eye to the peephole. He looks out, blinks, looks again, then whips his body back to safety. He hears the voice again—the familiar voice of his son.

"Christopher?" His voice is eerily thin, cracked from disuse.

"Dad, it's me. Please open the door."

He takes another breath, lets it out, striving to calm his mind. But it's no use, his son is here. Why?

"Dad?"

"Stand away from the door, son."

Risking another look through the peephole, he sees that Christopher has done as he asked. In the peephole's fish-eye lens he can see all of him now. Christopher is dressed in a lightweight linen suit over a white polo shirt. Polished loafers with tassels are on his feet. He looks as if he's just stepped off the plane.

"Dad, please let me in."

He wipes sweat off his face. Hand on the chain across the door frame, he pauses. What if his enemies have captured Christopher and are using him against his will? He'll never know, standing on this side of the door. He slides the chain off, unlocks the door and says, "All right, son. Come on in." Then he steps back, waiting.

Christopher comes through the door and, without being asked, shuts it behind him.

"Lock it, son," he says.

Christopher complies.

"What are you doing here?"

"I've come to get you, Dad."

His eyes narrow and his hand grips the gun with more force. "What d'you mean?"

"You killed Mom," Christopher says.

"I had to—"

"You had no orders."

"There was no time. She was a double working for—"

"Dad, you're mistaken."

"Certainly not. I saw her put the intelligence—"

"In the birdhouse," Christopher says. "That was you, Dad. You put the intelligence there."

He takes one terrible staggering step backward. "What?" His head has begun to hurt. "No, I—"

"I saw you do it myself. I took pictures—"

"That's a lie!"

Christopher smiles sadly. "We never lie to one another, Dad. Remember?"

His head hurt all the more, a pounding in the veins that cradle his brain. "Yes, I—"

"Dad, you've been ill. You still are." One hand held out in entreaty. "You thought Mom was onto you and you—"

"No, no, I found that scrap of paper with the rune on it!"

"The Arabic letter, Dad. That was yours. You're fluent in Arabic."

"Am I?" He presses his fingertips into his temple. If only his head would stop pounding he might be able to think clearly. But now he is unsure of the last time he's thought clearly. Could Christopher be right?

But then something odd and chilling occurs to him. "Why are you talking like this? You know nothing of your mother and me—of our secret life. You're a designer of computer software."

Christopher's eyes are soft, his smile all the sadder. "*You're* the software designer. That's why you were recruited to the Agency, that's how you were doubled—on one of your trips to Shanghai or Bangalore, they don't really know where, and right now it's not important. What is important is that you give me the gun so that we can walk out of here together."

A spasm of irrational rage causes him to lift his weapon. "I'm not going anywhere, with you or anyone else."

"Dad, please be reasonable."

"There is no reason in the world!" he shouts. "Reason is an illusion, just like love!"

And as he levels the gun at Christopher, his son whips a snub-nosed Walther PPK from behind his back and shoots him neatly and precisely through the forehead.

Christopher looked down at his father's corpse. At this moment, he was interested in what emotions he would feel. There were none. It was as if his heart had been muffled under so many layers of identity no event, no matter how traumatic, could reach it.

Agency protocol dictated that all evidence of terminations be immediately destroyed. This would be done, of course, his spycraft was precise, something in which he prided himself.

Looking around, he saw all his father's children, re-created in intricate and loving miniaturized detail from the pages of magazines he'd bought and scrounged from the hotel lobby.

Here was the set for *The Merchant of Venice,* here the one for *A Streetcar Named Desire,* there the set for the revival of *Carousel,* acclaimed for his father's innovative design. All the many shows were represented in miniature, so cleverly fashioned that for a moment Christopher was astonished all over again by his father's genius.

It was in the shower that he came across the set for *Death of a Salesman.* He stared at it for a moment, lines from Arthur Miller's pen running like an electronic news ribbon through his mind. After an unknown time he reached down. Retreating, he threw it on his father's body. Producing a bottle of lighter fluid bought for just this purpose, he poured it over the mass, soaking the corpse. Then, his back to the door, he threw open the lock and lit a match, watching it arc toward the end of all things.

Everything changes. But it won't get better.

He went out the side door of the hotel into the stinking dawn, the stench of lighter fluid and burning hair masking the reek of human excrement and decay. As he craned his neck, looking for the first gray tendrils of smoke, he decided to create a new legend for himself. When he passed through customs on his way home he would be Biff Loman.

The idea brought a smile to his face, and for that moment he looked just like his dad.

CHRISTOPHER RICE

Christopher Rice's first novel, the Gothic thriller *A Density of Souls*, was published when he was just twenty-two years old. Being the son of vampire novelist Anne Rice, his novel was met with a great deal of media attention and more than a fair amount of skepticism. But it was *The Snow Garden*, Rice's second *New York Times* bestseller, that cemented his reputation as a writer capable of bringing stories with fully realized gay characters to a wider commercial audience.

While his latest novel, *Light Before Day*, explores the seamy underbelly of Los Angeles's gay ghetto, Rice's consistent focus over the course of three books has been on the complex relationships that develop between straight and gay characters drawn together by a shared trauma. *The Snow Garden* focused on the murderous deceits that threaten a close friendship between a straight woman and a gay man. *Light Before Day* centered on the parental relationship that developed between a bestselling mystery novelist and his gay assistant. This same theme can be found here in *Man Catch*, where a young woman's sudden discovery of a loved one's closeted homosexuality brings a rain of violence down onto a tightly knit family unit.

Man Catch was a challenge for Rice. Unaccustomed to writing short fiction and often praised by his readers for detailed setting and atmosphere, he studied the efforts of Richard Matheson and David Morrell in an effort to tell the most fully realized story in the fewest words. At first, letting go of some of the texture and color Rice loves to include in his work was a frightening challenge. But ultimately, he says, it proved a deeply gratifying exercise.

MAN CATCH

From her table by the window inside the bustling Starbucks, Kate could see clear across the crowded parking lot and the traffic-snarled interstate to where the setting sun turned the San Bernardino Mountains into looming ghosts on the near horizon. After giving her his laptop computer, Rick had disappeared into the shopping mall next door; she assumed he was ensconced in the racks at Border's, perusing books on fishing or hunting, or one of the other strangely adult hobbies he had picked up from his father following high-school graduation.

This was going to be their first trip alone together, three days at a cabin near Lake Arrowhead, three days without parents checking to make sure they were sleeping in separate beds. In less than a month they would be at different colleges; every hour they spent together was too precious to be wasted in traffic.

Even though her boyfriend had insisted otherwise, Kate was confident they could find an alternate route to the cabin. As soon as she typed in the first two letters of Mapquest, the browser on Rick's computer automatically completed the address with the closest match from its list of recently visited sites.

www.ManCatch.com.

Convinced it was a Web site that taught lazy jocks like Rick how to manage their finances, Kate clicked on the entry. The screen filled with an image of a muscular half-naked Latino man reclining on a white bedspread, one hand draped over the bulge in his white briefs. According to the flashing pink banner above the man's head, ManCatch was the #1 site for man-on-man action in the country. She almost laughed out loud. Surely, Rick had visited the site by mistake.

Then she saw that the computer had been set to remember user names and passwords, not a surprise considering Rick had made it through four years of high school without memorizing a single locker combination. The user name in the entry blank was *Soaks-Guy*. S Oaks had to mean Sherman Oaks, the San Fernando Valley suburb where they had both grown up. The browser's history list told her that Rick had visited ManCatch the night before, at 1:30 a.m., when she had believed him to be asleep beside her.

At her house. In her bed.

Her breaths short and ragged, Kate clicked the LogIn button before she could convince herself not to. Suddenly, she was scrolling through profiles for Man-Catch members in which each man spelled out his sexual tastes in a coded language that combined hip-hop affectations with the shorthand her girlfriends used to pass notes in class. (*Lookin for hung dudes! U Can Play? Step 2 da front! HIV—here, U B2.*) Most profiles were accompanied by a photo. The first few were harmless enough, mostly shots of bare muscular chests, the heads cropped out, making the subject look like a Greek statue in lousy lighting. Then came several preposterously large erections.

A chair scraped the floor behind her. A silently furious mother was dragging her toddler-age son toward the exit. When the woman looked back and saw that it was a seemingly normal teenage girl who had just exposed her child to such filth, she looked both wounded and baffled, as if her tiny son had just flipped her the bird.

Humiliated, Kate scrolled up until the most offensive photographs were out of frame. She tried to make some kind of sense of what she was seeing. According to the history list, Rick had only made one visit to this site in the past three weeks. But the username and password suggested he planned on becoming a regular. Why then had he let her borrow his computer without a second's pause? Maybe he was a regular and had deleted all evidence of his other visits—except for one.

Nothing fires the imagination like betrayal, she realized. In digital clarity, she saw Rick, in only his paisley boxers, backing silently out of the half-open door to her room, holding his laptop in both hands as if it were the Holy Grail.

Her eyes locked on something she had missed. On the left-hand side of the screen, there was a long menu bar. It was clear Rick might be a regular; now she could find out if he had made any friends. When she clicked on the Buddy List button, only one name came up: *FunForRtNow*. Next to the name was a photograph of a short muscular brown-haired guy lying facedown on his bed. She thought he was naked at first, then she saw the red waistband of a jockstrap tucked beneath the exposed cheeks of his ass.

HOT JOCK LOOKIN 2 PLAY! YOU GAME?
5'11", 156, 27, 9" cut, in Studio City here. Into
young and old, u just gotta be fit, got it? (Fit =
work out 4 X a week or more!)A u gotta be hot!
No fats, flems or flakes. No time-wasters. No
hard partiers. Into porn, role play, lots a oral. Be
Clean! Be Cool.

The photo didn't shock her. But the nakedness of
the man's requests turned her stomach. Then it occurred to her that she was reading the wrong profile.

She was about to type *SoaksGuy* into the search
blank when something slammed into the window just
above her head. Rick was plastered to the glass as if
he had just been hurled against it by a nightclub
bouncer. When he stumbled back a few steps, he was
too busy laughing at himself to notice the expression
on Kate's face.

"So I was talking to my aunt on the phone," he
boomed as he approached her table. "She says there's
this awesome pond, like, a half mile from the cabin.
Totally easy hike, too." He slammed down into the
chair opposite hers and flattened his mess of black
curls with his palm. "She says it's so cool at sunrise
'cause the sun comes up, like, right over— Jesus. Are
you all right?"

Kate turned the laptop so Rick could see it. He
jerked back from the screen as if he had been stung.
Then his sleepy eyes turned to slits and his upper lip
tensed. He sucked in a deep, pained breath.

"Last night," she said. "One-thirty. I was asleep. I
thought you were, too."

"I *was!*"

"Your computer says you were *right here*," she said,

tapping the top of the monitor for emphasis. "Is it lying, Rick?"

He kept shaking his head and studying the screen in front of him as if his best defense could be found in FunForRtNow's profile. For the two years they had been together, she had consistently studied the way he acted around other girls, searched for smiles that might look like invitations, friendly pats on intimate body parts. She had been doing the wrong homework all along.

His wide eyes met hers. "It wasn't me, Kate," he whispered.

"Then who was it?"

His mouth opened slightly but nothing came out. He chewed his lower lip and brought one hand to the bridge of his nose. If he wasn't about to choke on his guilt, she certainly was. She pulled the laptop's power cord from the socket and scooped both items up off the table.

She was several paces from her 4Runner when he caught up with her. The second his hand met her shoulder, she whirled, lifting the computer like a base-ball bat, swinging it around her in a wide arc. For a split second, she wasn't sure how hard she had hit him. Then he hit the pavement ass-first, blood from his nostrils painted all over his lips. Before she pulled out of the parking lot, she checked to see if she had run over him. When she saw him struggling to his feet, she felt a dull sense of relief.

The interior rearview mirror offered a view of Rick's bulging duffel bag lying across the back seat. After the fourth call from him, she killed the ringer on her cell phone. She called her father. Her father would fix it. Her father would beat Rick within an inch of his life and find a way to blame his injuries on a strong wind. That morning, as she was packing, he had told her he would be entertaining clients late. It had seemed like an irrelevant detail at the time. Her dad liked to have his female assistant leave his greeting message, so Kate couldn't even take comfort in her father's soothing baritone voice. At the sound of the tone, her eyes misted and her throat clogged.

She hung up.

Her mother had flown to a convention in San Francisco two days before, where she was no doubt lecturing her fellow real estate agents on how to get ahead in life by sucking the air out of every room you entered. Her mother couldn't find out about this. She would just find a way to make it Kate's fault. Surely, Kate had missed something, some vital sign that her boyfriend was screwing other guys he met online. Surely, Kate could have planned for this contingency. Her mother loved plans. Right now, Kate's plan was to get home and crawl under the covers until her father arrived.

In downtown L.A., she hit a procession of brake lights and spent the next two hours in the slow crawl of chromium heading into the Valley on the 101 Freeway. It was a little past midnight when she reached her house, a Cape Cod-style cottage that sat on a meandering street at the base of the foothills. There was a good chance Rick might get a ride back from one of his friends and come looking for her, so Kate parked a block away and around the corner.

When Kate opened the front door, the alarm system let out a short burst of beeps. She was at the panel, ready to punch in the code, when the beeps stopped— not a warning that the siren was about to go off, just the perimeter alert that sounded every time a door or window in the house was opened. The house was dark. Her father had left without remembering to set the thing. That wasn't normal.

Her heart was racing. Even though she had been sitting in traffic for most of it, the drive home had left her feeling as if she had run a marathon. The door to her father's office was half-open. The mess of papers on his desk didn't look right; his computer was missing. That morning her father had said something about her mother taking the PC into the shop before she left town so that she could get the hard drive whipped; she wanted to buy him a new one and give the thing to her own mother as a Christmas gift.

Now that her eyes had adjusted to the darkness, she could make out a weak flickering light on the walls around her. It came from the second floor. At the end of the second-floor hallway, the door to her parents' bedroom was half-open. She could see a spread of tea candles on top of the credenza. There were many more that she couldn't see; they filled the entire bedroom with a ghostly luminescence. Whoever was in the bedroom had heard her come in and not blown out a single candle. This thought loosened the knot of fear in her chest. Maybe her father was in the tub.

Gently, she pushed open the door to her parents' bedroom. She was about to call out to her father when she saw a different man lying facedown across the bed, a dark stain curling out from under his head across the tan comforter. He was stocky and muscular and she could just make out his short cap of brown hair. Again, she thought he was naked until she noticed the red band of his jockstrap tucked under the cheeks of his ass. Hours earlier, she had seen a picture of the man on her boyfriend's computer screen and she almost whispered the words *Fun For Right Now.*

Before Kate could scream, a patch of darkness stepped forward from the bathroom door and lifted one arm in her direction. The silhouette seemed vaguely familiar at first, then Kate saw that her mother had tucked her long hair inside the back of her black sweater; it made a misshapen lump on the back of her head.

The guilt hit first. Kate saw the wide-eyed shock on Rick's face when she had confronted him. She had misread his pained breaths and wide-eyed fear as signs of guilt, when all the while Rick had known the truth and been afraid to tell her. Then she saw the two of them asleep in her bed just down the hall as her father padded silently out of her room with Rick's laptop in his hands. Because his own computer was in the shop. Kate tried to see through the halo of candlelight around the man's body, tried to detect some small motion that indicated life.

"Is he dead?" she asked.

"Would you like to hear what they did together? One time, I was away. You were asleep. In the yard, Kate. They did it in the yard while you were sleeping."

A car slowed outside, then turned up the driveway, tires crunching gravel. Her father was home, and Kate had walked right into a trap her mother had set for him. "Once I explain, you'll understand, Kate. I spent days talking to this young man, days finding out what he and your father did together. Once you hear, Kate, once you *know,* it will be very hard for you to be Daddy's little girl anymore."

Kate bolted from the room. Halfway down the steps she lost her balance. The hardwood floor at the foot of the stairs rose up to meet her face. The impact knocked the wind out of her. She lifted herself up onto all fours. A shadow dimmed the strips of leaded glass on either side of the front door. Keys rattled against the lock outside. "Kate," her mother said quietly and firmly. Kate could hear the challenge in her mother's voice. Maybe if she just let her explain. Maybe she could understand. Maybe then she wouldn't have to risk her own life for a father who was guilty of the indiscretions she had just accused her boyfriend of.

As soon as a crack of light appeared around the edge of the front door, Kate rose to her knees and hurled the front door shut, heard her father let out a surprised grunt. Steeling herself for the gunshot she was sure would come next, Kate dropped to the hard-wood floor.

"Well," her mother said quietly. "It looks like you've made your choice."

Kate heard the door to the master bedroom close. Then there was a quick sharp sound that Kate couldn't place. A movie sound. Her mind groped to give it a word. *Silencer.*

By then, Kate's father was standing over her, his jacket slung over one arm and his tie loose, his head cocked to one side like a puppy as he tried to make sense of the scene before him and the strange sound that had just come from his bedroom.

Kate didn't explain any of it for him. She let him go upstairs and discover the scene for himself, just as her mother had intended.

ALEX KAVA

When Alex Kava wrote her first novel, *A Perfect Evil*, she had no intention of making it the beginning of a new series. In fact, the character, FBI profiler Special Agent Maggie O'Dell doesn't enter the story until the seventh chapter. Instead of a series, Kava had simply based her story on two separate crimes that had occurred in Nebraska during the 1980s. One of the crimes, a serial killer who preyed on little boys, happened in the community where Kava was then working as a copy editor and paste-up artist for a small-town newspaper.

Years later, when Kava decided to write a novel, it was the same summer John Joubert—who thirteen years earlier had confessed to and was convicted for killing three little boys—was executed. The other crime, another little boy who was murdered in nearby Omaha several years after Joubert's capture, remains unsolved to this day. These two real-life crimes inspired Kava. However, because of *A Perfect Evil* and Maggie O'Dell's international success, Kava was compelled to develop a series. The results are four more novels featuring Special Agent Maggie O'Dell: *Split Second*, *The Soul Catcher*, *At the Stroke of Madness* and *A Necessary Evil*. Her one stand-alone thriller, *One False Move*, is also loosely based on a real crime.

Kava believes that truth is, indeed, stranger than fiction, which seems to be reiterated every time she begins research for a novel. One aspect of the Maggie O'Dell series that readers often comment on is the relationship between Maggie and her mother. It can best be described as challenging and confrontational, and definitely a far cry from what we perceive as a typical mother-daughter relationship. And yet, just like in real life there remains a bond, though sometimes unexplainable and often irrational. Here, in *Goodnight, Sweet Mother*, Kava takes Maggie and her mother on a road trip to illustrate that relationships, as well as perceptions, aren't always what they appear to be.

GOODNIGHT, SWEET MOTHER

Maggie O'Dell knew this road trip with her mother was a mistake long before she heard the sickening scrape of metal grinding against metal, before she smelled the burning rubber of skidding tires.

Hours earlier she had declared it a mistake even as she slid into a cracked red vinyl booth in a place called Freddie's Dine—actually Diner if you counted the faded area where an "r" had once been. The diner wasn't a part of the mistake. It didn't bother her eating in places that couldn't afford to replace an "r." After all, she had gobbled cheeseburgers in autopsy suites and had enjoyed deli sandwiches in an abandoned rock quarry while surrounded by barrels stuffed with dead bodies. No, the little diner could actually be called quaint.

Maggie had stared at a piece of apple pie à la mode the waitress had plopped down in front of her before splashing more coffee into her and her mom's cups. The pie had looked perfectly fine and even smelled freshly baked, served warm so that the ice cream had begun to melt and trickle off the edges. The pie hadn't been the mistake either, although without much effort Maggie had too easily envisioned blood instead of ice cream dripping down onto the white bone china plate. She had to take a sip of water, close her eyes and steady herself before opening her eyes again to ice cream instead of blood.

No, the real mistake had been that Maggie didn't order the pie. Her mother had. Forcing Maggie, once again, to wonder if Kathleen O'Dell was simply insensitive or if she honestly did not remember the incident that could trigger her daughter's sudden uncontrollable nausea. How could she not remember one of the few times Maggie had shared something from her life as an FBI profiler? Of course, that incident had been several years ago and back then her mother had been drinking Jack Daniel's in tumblers instead of shot glasses, goading Maggie into arresting her if she didn't like it. Maggie remembered all too vividly what she had told her mother. She told her she didn't waste time arresting suicidal alcoholics. She should have stopped there, but didn't. Instead, she ended up pulling out and tossing onto her mother's glass-top coffee table Polaroids from the crime scene she had just left.

"This is what I do for a living," she had told her mother, as if the woman needed a shocking reminder. And Maggie remembered purposely dropping the last, most brilliant one on top of the pile, the photo a close-up of a container left on the victim's kitchen counter. Maggie would never forget that plastic take-out container, nor its contents—a perfect piece of apple pie with the victim's bloody spleen neatly arranged on top.

That her mother had chosen to forget or block it out shouldn't surprise Maggie. The one survival tactic the woman possessed was her strong sense of denial, her ability to pretend certain incidents had simply not happened. How else could she explain letting her twelve-year-old daughter fend for herself while she stumbled home drunk each night, bringing along the stranger who had supplied her for that particular night? It wasn't until one of Kathleen O'Dell's gentleman friends suggested a threesome with mother, daughter and himself that it occurred to her mother to get a hotel room. Maggie had had to learn at an early age to take care of herself. She had grown up alone, and only now, years after her divorce, did she realize she associated being alone with being safe.

But her mother had come a long way since then, or so Maggie had believed. That was before this road trip, before she had ordered the piece of apple pie. Perhaps Maggie should see it for what it was—the perfect microcosm of their relationship, a relationship that should never include road trips or the mere opportunity for sharing a piece of pie at a quaint little diner.

She had watched as her mother sipped coffee in between swiping up bites of her own pie. As an FBI criminal profiler, Maggie O'Dell tracked killers for a living, and yet a simple outing with her mother could conjure up images of a serial killer's leftover surprises tucked away in take-out containers. Just another day at the office. She supposed she wasn't as good as her mother at denial, but that wasn't necessarily a bad thing.

Suddenly Kathleen O'Dell had pointed her fork at something over Maggie's shoulder, unable to speak because, of course, it was impolite to talk with a full mouth—never mind that during her brief and rare lapses into motherhood she constantly preached it was also impolite to point. Maggie didn't budge, ignoring her, which was also silly if she thought it would in any way punish her mother for her earlier insensitivity. Besides it had only resulted in a more significant poke at the air from her mother's fork.

"That guy's a total ass," she was finally able to whisper.

Maggie hadn't been able to resist. She stole a glance, needing to see the total ass she was about to defend.

He had seemed too ordinary to need Maggie's defense. Ever the profiler, she had found herself immediately assessing him. She saw a tall middle-aged man with a receding hairline, weak chin and wire-rimmed glasses. He wore a white oxford shirt, a size too large and sagging, even though he had tried to tuck it neatly into the waistband of wrinkled trousers—trousers that were belted below the beginning paunch of a man who spent too much time behind a desk.

He had slid into one of the corner booths and grabbed one of the laminated menus from behind the table's condiments holder. Immediately, he unfolded the menu and hunched over it, searching for his selection while he pulled silverware from the bundled napkin. Again, all very ordinary—an ordinary guy taking a break from work to get a bite to eat. But then Maggie had seen the old woman, shuffling to the table, holding on to the backs of the other booths along the way, her cane not enough to steady her. That's when Maggie realized her mother's pronouncement had little to do with the man's appearance and everything to do with the fact that he had left this poor woman to shuffle and fumble her way to their table. He hadn't even looked up at her as she struggled to lower herself between the table and the bench, dropping her small, fragile frame onto the seat and then scooting inch by inch across the vinyl while her cane *thump-thumped* its way in behind her.

Maggie had turned away, not wanting to watch any longer. She hated to agree with her mother. She hated even more the *"tsk, tsk"* sound her mother had made, loud enough for others at the diner to hear, perhaps even the total ass. Funny how things worked.

Maggie would give anything to hear that *"tsk, tsk"* from her mother now rather than the high-pitched scream she belted out from the passenger's seat. But, had she not been distracted by her mother's scream she may have noticed the blur of black steel sliding along-side her car much sooner. Certainly she would have noticed before the monster pickup rammed into her Toyota Corolla a second time, shoving her off the side of the road, all the while ripping and tearing metal.

Was that her front bumper dragging from the pickup's grille, looking as though the hulking truck had taken a bite out of her poor car? What the hell was this guy doing?

"I can't believe you didn't see him!" her mother scolded, the previous screams leaving her usual raspy voice high-pitched and almost comical. "Where the hell did he come from?" she added, already contradict-ing her first comment. She strained against her seat belt, reaching and grabbing for the Skittles candies she had been eating, now scattered across the seat and plopping to the floor mat like precious rainbow beads from a broken necklace.

"I didn't see him," Maggie confessed, gaining con-trol of her car and bringing it to a stop on the dirt shoulder of the two-lane highway. God! Her hands were shaking. She gripped the steering wheel harder to make them stop. When that didn't work she dropped them into her lap. She felt sweat trickle down her back. How could she not have seen him?

The pickup had pulled off the road more than three car lengths ahead, the taillights winking at them through a cloud of dust. Between the two vehicles lay the Toyota's mangled front bumper, twisted and discarded like roadside debris.

"Don't go telling him that," her mother whispered.

"Excuse me?"

"Don't go admitting to him that you didn't see him. You don't want your car insurance skyrocketing."

"Are you suggesting I lie?"

"I'm suggesting you keep your mouth shut."

"I'm a federal law officer."

"No, you said you left your badge and gun at home. Today you're a plain ol' citizen, minding your own business." Kathleen O'Dell popped several of the Skittles into her mouth, and Maggie couldn't help thinking how much the bright-colored candy reminded her of the nerve pills her mother used to take, oftentimes washing them down with vodka or scotch. How could she eat at a time like this, especially when it had only been less than an hour since they had left the diner? But Maggie knew she should be grateful for the recent exchange of addictions.

"I haven't been in a car accident since college," Maggie said, riffling through her wallet for proof of insurance and driver's license.

"Whatever you do don't ask for the cops to be called," she whispered again, leaning toward Maggie as though they were coconspirators.

She and her mother had never been on the same side of any issue. Suddenly a black pickup rams into the side of their car and they're instant friends. Okay, maybe not friends. Coconspirators did seem more appropriate.

"He sideswiped me." Maggie defended herself anyway, despite her mother being on her side.

"Doesn't matter. Calling the cops only makes it worse."

Maggie glanced at her mother, who was still popping the candies like they were antacids. People often remarked on their resemblance to each other—the auburn hair, fair complexion and dark brown eyes. And yet, much of the time they spent together Maggie felt like a stranger to this woman who couldn't even remember that her daughter hated apple pie.

"I *am* the cops," Maggie said, frustrated that she needed to remind her mother.

"No, you're not, sweetie. FBI's not the same thing. Oh, Jesus. It's him. That ass from the diner."

He had gotten out of the pickup but was surveying the damage on his own vehicle.

"Just go," her mother said, grabbing Maggie's arm and giving it a shove to start the car.

"Leave the scene of an accident?"

"It was his fault anyway. He's not going to report you."

"Too late," Maggie said, catching in her rearview mirror the flashing lights of a state trooper pulling off the road and coming up behind her. Her mother noticed the glance and twisted around in her seat.

"Oh fuck!"

"Mom!" For all her faults, Kathleen O'Dell rarely swore.

"This has not been a good trip."

Maggie stared at her, dumbfounded that her mother thought the trip had been as miserable an outing for her as it had been for Maggie.

"Promise me you won't play hero." Kathleen O'Dell grabbed Maggie's arm again. "Don't go telling them you're a federal officer."

"It'll actually be easier," Maggie told her. "There's a bond between law enforcement officers."

To this her mother let out a hysterical laugh. "Oh, sweetie, if you really think a state trooper will appreciate advice or help from the feds, and a woman at that…"

God, she hated to agree with her mother for a second time in the same day. But she was right. Maggie had experienced it almost every time she went into a rural community: small-town cops defensive and intimidated by her. Sometimes state troopers fit into that category, too.

She opened her car door and felt her mother still tugging at her arm.

"Promise me," Kathleen O'Dell said in a tone that reminded Maggie of when she was a little girl and her mother would insist Maggie promise not to divulge one of a variety of her indiscretions.

"You don't have to worry," Maggie said, pulling her arm away.

"My, my, what a mess," the state trooper called out, his hands on his belt buckle as he approached Maggie's car, then continued to the front bumper where he came to a stop. He looked from one vehicle to another, then back, shaking his head, his mirrored sunglasses giving Maggie a view of the wreckage he saw.

He was young. Even without seeing his eyes she could tell. A bit short, though she didn't think the Virginia State Police had a height requirement any longer, but he was in good shape and he knew it. Maggie realized his hands on his belt buckle wasn't in case he needed to get at his weapon quickly but rather to emphasize his flat stomach, probably perfect six-pack abs under the gray, neatly tucked shirt.

"Let me guess," he said, addressing Maggie even as he watched the owner of the pickup stomping around his vehicle. "You lost control. Maybe touching up your makeup?"

"Excuse me?" Maggie was sure she must have heard him wrong.

"Cell phone, maybe?" He grinned at her. "It's okay. I know you ladies love to talk and drive at the same time."

"This wasn't my fault." She wanted to get her badge from the glove compartment. She glanced back just in time to see her mother shoot her a cautionary look and she knew exactly what she was saying with her eyes, *"See, it's always worse when the cops get involved."*

"Sure, it wasn't your fault," he said, not even attempting to disguise his sarcasm.

"He was the one driving erratically." Maggie knew it sounded lame as soon as it left her mouth. The boy trooper had already accomplished what he had set out to do—he had succeeded in making her defensive.

"Hey, sir," he called out to the pickup owner who finally came over and joined them, standing over Maggie's mangled bumper, looking at it as if he had no idea how it had gotten there. "Sir, were you driving erratically?"

"Oh, for God's sake," Maggie said, then held her breath before she said anything more. She wanted to hit this cocky son of a bitch, and it had been a long time since she had wanted to hit somebody she didn't know.

"I was trying to pass, and she shoved right into me."

"That's a lie," Maggie's mother yelled over the top of the car. Both men stared at her, as though only now realizing she was there.

"Oh, good," the boy trooper said. "We have a witness."

"My mom's in the pickup," the guy said, pointing a thumb back behind him. They all turned to see a skinny, white leg sticking out from the passenger door. But that was as far as the old woman had gotten. Her cane hung on the inside door handle. Her foot, encased in what looked like a thin bedroom slipper, dangled about eight inches from the running board of the pickup.

"Well, I guess I'll have to just take a look and see what happened. See whose story's most *accurate*," he said with yet another grin.

Maggie couldn't help wondering where he had trained. No academy she knew of taught that smug, arrogant grin. Someone must have told him the look gave him an edge, disarmed his potential opponents; after all, it was tough to argue with someone who'd already made up his mind and was willing to humiliate you if you didn't agree. It was a tactic of a much older, mature lawman, one who could afford to be cocky because he knew more than he ever cared to know about human nature, one who could back up that attitude if challenged or threatened. This boy trooper, in Maggie's opinion, wasn't deserving of such a tactic.

As soon as she was close enough to see his badge and read his name tag, Maggie decided she knew a few tactics of her own. Three stripes to his patch meant he hadn't even made first sergeant.

"The skid marks should tell an accurate enough story, Sergeant Blake," Maggie said, getting his attention with a sharp look and no grin this time. It was one thing to know his name, quite another to address him by his rank. Most people didn't have a clue whether state troopers were officers or deputies, patrolmen or sergeants.

"Sure, sure. That's possible." He nodded. "I need to see both your driver's licenses before I check out skid marks." And he put his hand out.

Maggie resisted the urge to smile at what seemed a transparent attempt to gain control, to keep his edge. No problem. She already had her license ready and handed it to him. The pickup driver started digging in his shirt pocket then twisted and patted his back pants pockets, when suddenly there came a screech—something between a wail and a holler—from inside his vehicle. "Harold? Harrrold?"

They stopped and turned, but nothing more had emerged from the pickup, nothing besides the white leg still dangling. Then Maggie, her mother and Sergeant Blake all stared at Harold, watching as a crimson tide washed up his neck, coloring his entire face, his ears such a brilliant red Maggie wondered if they actually burned. But just as he had paid her no attention in the diner, Harold made no attempt to acknowledge the old woman now. Instead, he pulled out a thick, bulging wad of leather that was his wallet and began to rummage through it.

Maggie wasn't sure when her mother had wandered away. She hadn't been paying much attention to her. While Sergeant Blake took their driver's licenses and headed back to his patrol car, Harold had stomped up to the highway to see what evidence had been marked in rubber. After surveying the damage to his pickup once more, Harold shook his head, making that annoying *"tsk, tsk"* sound Maggie's mother had used earlier.

Maggie stayed in her own territory, wanting to tell Harold that he should be grateful. His damage was minimal compared to her ripped-off bumper and smashed driver's side. The gaping wound in her car's front end now had protruding pieces of metal shards like daggers. What a mess! There was no way she was taking the blame for any of this. So it had been several minutes before Maggie noticed her mother now standing in front of the opened passenger door of the pickup, her hands on her hips, tilting her head and nodding as if concentrating on what the old woman inside the vehicle had to say. Just then her mother looked back, caught Maggie's eyes and waved her over.

Maggie's first thought was that the poor woman was injured. Harold hadn't even bothered to check on her. Why hadn't she thought of it sooner? She rushed to the pickup, glancing over her shoulder, but both men were focused elsewhere.

The two women were whispering to each other. From what Maggie could see of the old woman, she didn't look as if she was in pain. However, there were several old bruises on her arms—old because they were already turning a greenish yellow. Her arthritic fingers tapped the seat with an uncontrollable tremor. She seemed even smaller and more fragile inside the cab of the pickup, curled into a hunched-over position.

"He does scare me sometimes," the woman said to Kathleen O'Dell, although her eyes were looking over at Maggie.

"It's not right," Maggie's mother told her, and then, as if only realizing Maggie was by her side, she said, "Rita says he hits her sometimes." She pointed to the woman's bruises, and Rita folded her thin arms over her chest as if to hide the evidence.

"The accident was his fault, Kathleen," Rita said. "He slammed right into your car. But you know I can't say that." She rubbed her shoulders as if they, too, were sore and bruised underneath her cotton blouse.

Maggie watched the two women, surprised that they spoke to each other as if they were old friends. Why was it that Kathleen O'Dell could so easily befriend a stranger but not have a clue about her own daughter?

"Rita says that sometimes he comes after her with a hammer at night," Maggie's mother whispered while she glanced around. Feeling safe, she continued, "He tells her she might not wake up in the morning."

"He's a wicked boy, my Harold," the old woman said, shaking her head, her fingers drumming out of control now.

"What's going on?" Harold yelled, hurrying back from surveying the skid marks.

"We're just chatting with your mom," Maggie told him. "That's not a problem, is it?"

"Not unless she's telling you lies," he said, a bit breathless. "She lies all the time."

Maggie thought it seemed a strange thing to say about one's mother, but Harold said it as casually as if it were part of an introduction, just another one of his mother's personality traits. He didn't, however, look as casual when he noticed Sergeant Blake approaching.

"Funny, she was just saying the same about you," Kathleen O'Dell said. "That you're the liar."

Maggie wanted to catch her mother's attention long enough to shoot her a warning look. No such luck.

"What's going on?" This time it was Sergeant Blake's question.

"She says you beat her." Kathleen didn't back down from confronting Harold, probably feeling safe with Maggie standing between the two of them.

"Kathleen, you promised," Rita wailed at her, another panicked screech.

Maggie met her mother's eyes, again hoping to stop

her, but she continued. "She said you've come after her with a hammer."

There was no grin on Sergeant Blake's face now, and Harold's had resumed a softer crimson color. This time Maggie knew it was anger, not embarrassment, and saw his hands at his sides, his fingers flexing and closing into fists.

"For God's sake," he muttered with an attempted laugh. "She says that about everybody. The old lady's crazy."

"Really?" Sergeant Blake asked and Maggie noticed that the young trooper's hands were on his belt again, but now only inches from his weapon.

"Two days ago she said the same thing about her mailman." Harold wiped at the sweat on his forehead. "For God's sake, she lies about everything."

Maggie looked back at Rita, who had pulled herself deeper inside the pickup. Now she had her cane in her shaking hands as if worried she might need a weapon of her own.

Maggie wasn't sure what happened next. It all seemed like a blur even to a trained law officer like herself. She had seen it happen before. Words were exchanged. Tempers flared and suddenly there was no taking back any of it.

She remembered Sergeant Blake telling Harold he'd need to go with him to the station to answer some questions. To which Harold said he had had enough of "this nonsense." Harold started to walk away, going around to the driver's side of the pickup as if to simply leave. Maybe a more experienced state trooper would have been more commanding with his voice or his presence, but Sergeant Blake felt it necessary to emphasize his request with a shove. Of course, Harold shoved back. Before Maggie could interfere, Harold lay on the ground, the back of his head cracked against the ripped metal of his own pickup. His wide eyes and that blank stare told Maggie O'Dell he was dead even before she bent over him to take his pulse.

Three hours later Maggie and her mother took Rita home, following the woman's directions, despite those changing several times en route. Maggie recognized her behavior as shock, and patiently waited for the old woman to issue a new set of directions. Otherwise, the woman hadn't said much. Back at the state police station, Kathleen O'Dell had asked her if there was someone they should call. Even after it was decided that Maggie would drive Rita home, Kathleen still kept asking if there was anyone who could come stay with her. But Rita only shook her head.

Finally they pulled up to the curb of a quaint yellow bungalow at the end of a street lined with huge oaks and large green lawns.

"I don't know what I'll do without that boy," Rita said suddenly. "He was all I had."

There was silence. Maggie and her mother looked at each other. Was it simply the shock?

"But you said he beat you?" Kathleen O'Dell reminded her.

"Oh, no, no. Harold would never lay a hand on me."

"You said he came after you at night with a hammer."

This time both Maggie and her mother turned to look over the seat at the woman who sat up in the back, grabbing for the door handle.

"My Harold would never hurt me," she said quite confidently, and she swung open the car door. "It's that wicked Mr. Sumpter, who brings the mail. I know he has a hammer in that mailbag. He's threatened to hit me in the head with it," she said without hesitation as she slammed the car door behind her.

Maggie and her mother stared at each other, both paralyzed and speechless. It wasn't until Harold's mother was climbing up the yellow house's front porch that Maggie noticed the woman no longer struggled. She was walking just fine, despite leaving her cane in Maggie's back seat.

GRANT BLACKWOOD

In his debut novel, *The End of Enemies*, Grant Blackwood introduced his hero Briggs Tanner, who, after witnessing the murder of a stranger, finds himself embroiled in a plot that takes him from Japan, to a remote island in the Pacific, and finally to the bullet-ridden back alleys of Beirut. In *The Wall of Night*, as the world marches toward a catastrophic war, Tanner returns to China to solve a mystery that has haunted him for twelve years. In *An Echo of War*, Tanner's search for a missing family member turns into a race to secure a biological weapon born in a secret bunker during the dying days of the First World War.

Here, in *Sacrificial Lion*, Blackwood introduces Henry Caulder, a British spymaster who slips into cold war East Berlin on an impossible mission. In the balance hangs the fate of Europe, and perhaps the world. But *Sacrificial Lion* is not just a tale of espionage, it's also a legacy of sorts, for Henry Caulder is the grandfather of Blackwood's newest hero, Sam Caulder, who, fifty-five years after Henry's fateful mission, will find himself entangled in a manhunt that pits him against rogue spies, mafia kingpins, Washington's power elite and a billionaire intent on controlling America's future. Blackwood plans several Sam Caulder adventures.

For both Caulders, past and present, the fate of the world hangs in the balance.

But each man is up to the task.

SACRIFICIAL LION

Moscow, January 1953

Henry Caulder knew by the sound of their footsteps they were coming to kill him.

Whether the spectacle was designed to instill fear or to uphold the image of Stalin's inescapable grasp, he didn't know, but every inmate in Lubyanka Prison recognized the ponderous march of the guard's boots in the corridor. It was a terrifying sound and an impressive sight, but Henry had been preparing for this day, and now all he felt was a sense of completion.

At least three men—perhaps many more—had gone before him, each receiving a single bullet in the head from a Makarov pistol. As most prisoners do, each man would have screamed his innocence to the end, until that last moment when he felt the cold steel circle of the muzzle come to rest on his skin.

The boots stopped outside his door. Henry took a

last look around. His cell was a bleak cliché: no windows, a straw mattress and a brimming waste bucket in the corner. The walls were painted a mottled gray and pus yellow. His only illumination came from what little light seeped around the edges of the door. He hadn't seen sunlight in forty days. To his surprise, that's what he missed the most. More than the torture, more than the starvation, more than the cold, he missed being outdoors.

His body was failing him. Since they'd started on him, he'd lost so much weight his ribs and collarbone poked from his skin. His nose and right hand were broken and his testicles…well, he hadn't been able to bring himself to look at them. The soles of his feet were bruised and swollen, his toes turning black. *Going to lose the nails on all of them,* he thought, chuckling. *Never be able to wear sandals again.*

He'd also developed a deep, racking cough. Pneumonia, perhaps. Perhaps something else.

The latch was thrown back. He let his shoulders slump and his face go slack. The door swung open. Standing there in full-dress uniforms were the two guards he'd dubbed Boris One and Boris Two. "You will come now," Boris One said.

Henry hobbled forward and fell in between them. He'd long suspected he was the only occupant of this block and now he saw he was right. Each door stood yawning, dark inside. Bare bulbs hung from the ceiling and trailed down the corridor to a gate. When they reached it, Boris One called out in Russian, "Open. Prisoner one-zero-nine-two."

The gate rattled back. They walked through and turned left. Henry felt his hands begin to shake. He clenched them. *You're okay…you've done some good.*

They reached a stairwell and started down. With each step, the light from above faded until, at the bottom, he found himself in darkness. Ahead was a lighted doorway. He stopped, his feet frozen. Behind him, Boris Two placed an almost gentle, coaxing hand on the small of his back. It was the first kind touch he'd felt in forty days. He felt tears well in his eyes. *Come on, Henry*.

He shuffled forward. At the door Boris One stepped aside, heels clicking together as he snapped to attention. Henry gulped a lungful of air and stepped up to the threshold. *Two months,* he thought. *God, was that all?* He'd come a long way since this had begun....

Knowing the Brahmins at MI6 wouldn't sign off on his plan, Henry took the first available plane out of London for Washington, D.C., where he took a taxi to the E Street offices of the recently christened CIA. He still thought of it as the OSS and probably always would. He had friends there, many of whom he'd jumped with behind enemy lines during the war as part of the Jedburgh commandos.

At the security shack he asked for Lucille Russo. The guard made the call, gave him a badge and directed him to Lucille's Quonset hut. She was waiting for him. "Henry, as I live and breathe! I thought you hated planes."

"I do—still do." Planes, parachutes and gunfire were affiliated memories. "I've got something in the works, Lucille. I need your help. Perhaps I could have a private word with you and Joe?"

Joe Pults was another Jedburgh friend, now in the CIA's Office of Special Operations. They found him reclined in his chair, feet propped on the desk. Seeing

Henry, he bolted up and strode over. "Henry? Henry Caulder? God, it's good to see you!"

"And you, Joe."

Lucille said, "Henry's got an op he wants to talk about, Joe."

Pults shut his door and gestured for them to sit. "Shoot."

It took but five minutes for Henry to make his pitch. "It's dicey, but if we pulled it off—"

"Jesus, Henry, I don't know what to say. What's your time line?"

"It should happen within the next couple of months—plenty of time if we move quickly."

"And your people?"

"I'm on a leave of absence."

Pults thought for a moment, then nodded. "Dulles is traveling. Let's talk to Beetle."

Walter Bedell "Beetle" Smith, former chief of staff to Eisenhower at SHAEF, had been appointed CIA director by Truman. Smith was a soldier at heart and Henry hoped that attitude would work in his favor. Smith listened to his plan, then said, "God, man, do you have a death wish?"

Standing against the wall, Lucille and Joe shuffled nervously. Henry simply smiled.

"Apologies," Smith said. "Okay, how many contacts?"

"Three." Henry gave him the names. "I doubt I'll have time to reach any more than that."

"You'd have to lay the groundwork just right."

"Yes."

"I know you speak German. How about Russian?"

"*Ya ischu devushku, kotoraya khochet lyubit i bit lyubimoy.*" *I am looking for a girl who wants to love and be loved.*

"Aren't we all," Smith replied. "You'd go naked?"

"Naked" meant without diplomatic cover. If captured, he'd be executed. "It's the only way," Henry said.

"Timeline?"

"Two weeks of prep here and three days on the ground."

"Tight schedule."

"I doubt they'll leave me alone any longer than that."

"Probably right." Smith gazed out the window for a moment. "You're sure about this?"

"General, we know they're coming sooner or later," Henry replied. "This is a golden opportunity."

"You have family?"

"My wife and I divorced in forty-two. My son, Owen, is twelve. His stepfather's a decent sort." *And I wasn't*, Henry thought. *Not much of a husband and not much of a father*. Since '39 he'd been gone more than home.

"Still," Smith said, "they—"

"They won't miss me, General. Let me do this. Please. It could make a difference."

"I'll have to run it by Ike." Eisenhower, who had been elected a week earlier, was in transition, preparing for his January inauguration. "In the meantime, Joe, you and Lucille get to work. Anything Henry needs, give it to him."

Ten days later Henry's cover, backstop documents, communication protocols and route were in place. The cornerstone of the plan, an executive secretary at the GSFG, or Group of Soviet Forces Germany, headquartered in Zossen-Wünsdorf, was being prepped by her CIA handler.

Two weeks after arriving in Washington, Henry landed at Tempelhof Airport and took a taxi to the CIA station on Baerwald Strasse, where he spent an hour with the chief of station. By dusk he was pulling up to the East German checkpoint at Chausseestrasse in the French-controlled sector.

He coasted to a stop before the barrier. On either side concertina razor wire stretched into the twilight, winking in the arc lights. A guard appeared beside the window and asked for his papers while two more circled his car.

"You are French?" the guard said in stilted English, the default language used at checkpoints.

"*Oui*—yes."

"Your purpose here?"

"It's in the letter. I'm a consultant with COMECON," Henry replied, referring to the Council for Mutual Economic Assistance. This alone would pique the immediate attention of the *Stasi*—the East German secret police—and the MgB—the current version of the Soviet's Ministry of State Security—but it couldn't be helped.

The guard handed his papers back. "Proceed."

The barrier swung upward and Henry drove into the Soviet Occupation Zone.

Having worked in Berlin since the end of the war, he knew its nooks and crannies. Even in the dark, the bleakness of the Soviet sector was palpable: buildings gray, streets gray, streetlights muted in the cold drizzle. It was as if the occupation had leached all the color from the landscape. In every vacant lot stood mountains of rubble from the bombing raids seven years earlier, and most structures still showed signs of war: bullet holes, gaping wounds from artillery, facades crumbling onto sidewalks. Here and there people walked in threadbare coats, heads down as they hurried home or nowhere. *How many?* he wondered. At last estimate, the *Stasi* had 50,000 agents and 125,000 informants throughout East Germany. One in six people on the street were *Stasi.*

The question was, could he do the job before they moved on him?

Henry had no trouble finding the safe house, an apartment off Wilhelm Pieck Strasse. He parked down the block and circled on foot to ensure he hadn't picked up any watchers, then climbed the alley stairs to the door and knocked. A female voice said, "*Ja?*" The language was German, the accent Russian. "Herr Thomas?"

Any name other than "Thomas" would have been the wave-off: *run and don't come back.*

Henry gave the correct response and the door swung open.

The agent known as ADEX was tall, blond and full figured. Henry had no idea what had motivated her to turn—likely one of the MICE: money, ideology, compromise or coercion—and he didn't care. Lucille and Joe had vouched for the handler, and the handler had vouched for ADEX. For the last four years she'd served in Logistics and Travel at GSFG.

"Welcome," she said. "My name is—"

"I don't want to know your name."

"Oh. Yes, of course. Come in."

Henry was in a hurry, but she wanted to chat. Most of them did. Isolation and fear were common among agents, especially here. After twenty minutes, she gave him the dossier. He asked her to make some tea, then scanned the file and put the details to memory. He walked to the woodstove and tossed the file inside.

"How did you come across this information?" he asked.

"Gossip, expense reports, that sort of thing. They come for meetings several times a week. What can I say? They like to talk." She smiled coyly and sipped her tea.

And more, perhaps, Henry thought. *Sexpionage at its best.* "And the other thing?"

Using her index and middle fingers, she mimed scissors. "Snip, snip. Done. Took it from his belt."

They chatted for a few more minutes, then Henry slid a folded newspaper across the table. Inside was an envelope. "Papers. You're leaving tonight. You'll be met on—"

"What? Tonight? Why?"

"If you stay, you'll be arrested. From here you'll walk to the eastern end of Prenzlauer Allee and stop. You'll hold the newspaper in your left hand. You'll be met." In fact, ADEX would be watched from the moment she stepped outside. If she deviated, she'd be snatched off the street. "Repeat that," he said.

"Prenzlauer Allee, eastern end, newspaper in my left hand."

"Good. Better get going."

She left. Henry finished his tea, then stretched out on the trundle bed and slept.

He awoke at two, left the apartment and started driving south. On the outskirts of the city he made his first mistake, speeding through a stop sign within sight of a Volkspolizei car. He pulled to the curb and waited as the VoPo officer checked his papers, asked his destination and gave him a lecture before sending him on his way.

He spent the remainder of the night touring the

German countryside, heading south and east, killing time. Two hours before dawn he reached Magdeburg and spent an hour servicing the dead drops. There was nothing to pick up, only drop off. Next he followed his map to Kleingarten, a park along the banks of Lake Neustadter. He parked, then ducked into a bus hut overlooking the path and waited.

His contact was on schedule. Colonel General Vasily Sergeyevich Belikov, hero of the Great Patriotic War and Commander of the Third Shock Combined Arms Red Banner Army, was a man of habit. Every morning without fail he walked his borzoi around Lake Neustadter.

Henry waited until Belikov was three hundred yards away then flipped up his collar and stepped onto the path. Hoarfrost coated the grass, and his footsteps kicked up billows of ice crystals that glittered in the sun.

Belikov was accompanied by four guards, paratroopers from the Ninth Corp, two preceding him and two trailing. Henry let his shoulders droop and adopted a shuffling gait—another tired and overworked German. As he drew even with the leading guards, they frisked him, checked his papers, then sent him along. He could feel their eyes on him, guns at the ready should he take a step toward their charge.

As he passed Belikov he let the blue button slip from his fingers. He bent to pick it up and called out, *"Entschuldigung Sie, bitte."* Excuse me, please.

The general turned around. *"Prastite?"* in Russian, then in German: *"Was?"* What?

"You dropped this," Henry said, button extended.

Behind him Belikov's guards were trotting forward, machine guns coming up. Belikov raised a hand, halting them, then said to Henry, "Pardon?"

"There, from your coat belt. It must have fallen off."

Belikov glanced down at the coat. "Oh…yes." He took the button from Henry's hand. "Thank you." He turned and walked on.

He was back in Berlin by late morning. As he crossed the Warshauer Bridge over the Spree, he caught the first whiff of *Stasi* watchers: two cars, one leading him and a second trailing a hundred yards back. In his rearview mirror he saw the passenger raise a microphone to his mouth.

No question now. They were onto him and probably had been since Magdeburg. As he was still an unknown to them, the leash was loose, but that wouldn't last long.

He spent two hours driving around the city, playing the delicate game of surveillance/countersurveillance. If he knew how big the net was, he might gauge how long he had. Conversely, if they suspected he was dry-cleaning, they might scoop him up. For now, his role had to be that of the oblivious quarry.

He spent the afternoon at the Pieck safe house. At six o' clock he left the city and drove north forty miles to Furstenberg, where he parked on a side street. Night had fallen and the lights along Leibninstrasse shone like yellow beacons. Only an hour from Berlin, Furstenberg had a lighter feel and the people on the streets were animated. He found the pub, the Schwarz Katze, halfway down the block.

The bar was crowded with Russian soldiers, mostly tankers and Spetsnaz, the elite of the Soviet Special Forces. The air was heavy with cigarette smoke, and in one corner a radio blared Russian folk music. Henry picked his way through the crowd to the bar and ordered a beer. Two minutes later a pair of civilians in black leather coats walked in and took a table near the back.

More obvious now, Henry thought. *Tightening the leash.*

It took but thirty seconds for him to spot the man he was looking for. General Yuri Pavlovich Kondrash, commander of the Second Tank Guards Army and the Twentieth Guards Spetsnaz Diversionary Brigade, sat alone, hunched over a bottle of vodka. Henry walked over, offered him a cigarette and struck up a conversation: Where was the closest butcher shop? What month was the Marigold Festival held? How often did the train run to Blindow?

Kondrash's answers were curt, but Henry had what he needed.

He was back in Berlin by 10:00 p.m. On the road he'd picked up more watchers, six men in three cars, bringing the total to ten he could see, and probably another dozen he couldn't. They were growing aggressive now, the lead vehicle only ten feet off his rear bumper.

Not long now, he thought, checking his watch. *God, let me finish.*

Remarkably, the Schiffbauerdamm theater, overlooking the Spree River and within sight of the Brandenburg Gate, had survived the war largely unscathed. Since '48 it had become the de facto center for East Berlin culture, from opera to ballet to theater. Friday night was opera, and according to the playbill given to him by ADEX, tonight's production was Wagner's *Tannhäuser*. Henry preferred a good western to the opera, but not so the man he'd come to see.

General Georgy Ivanovich Preminin, marshal of the Soviet Red Army and commander of the Group of Soviet Forces Germany, was Stalin's iron fist in East Germany. He was also the last piece of the puzzle Henry was hurrying to assemble.

He parked under a copse of linden trees behind a half-demolished church on Oranienburger Strasse and climbed out. The earlier drizzle had turned to freezing rain and the pellets ticked against the brim of his hat. He walked to the rear of the car and shined his penlight under the bumper. The transmitter was there, probably planted while he was in the Schwarz Katze. He ripped it off, crushed it under his heel and tossed the remains away. The move wouldn't save him, he knew, but it might buy him time as the *Stasi* quartered the area looking for his car.

He pulled the brim of his hat lower and started walking.

With the sleet, a thick fog had risen off the Spree. The Schiffbauerdamm seemed to float above the ground, mist swirling around its Gothic cornices. Lit from within, the stained-glass windows were rainbow-hued rectangles in the darkness.

From the alley Henry studied the parking lot until he spotted Preminin's car, a black ZIS-110 limousine with a hammer-and-sickle flag on each fender. Preminin's chauffeur/bodyguard stood under an umbrella beside the driver's door, smoking.

Henry heard the squealing of tires. Down the block a black Mercedes pulled around the corner, rolled to a stop and doused its lights. Two figures, cast in silhouette from the streetlight, sat in the front seat. Henry saw the tip of a cigarette glow red, then fade.

He pulled a pint of whiskey from the pocket of his trench coat, dumped half of it onto the ground, then took a gulp and swished it around his mouth. He tossed his hat away, dipped his hand in a puddle and mussed his hair, then stepped out onto the sidewalk.

Playing a drunk was a tricky performance but Henry had used the ruse before. Humming tunelessly, he stumbled off the curb and weaved his way toward Preminin's ZIS. Spotting him, the chauffeur flicked his cigarette away and slipped his hand inside his coat.

"Hey, nice car," Henry called in German. "What is it, eh? A Mercedes?"

"*Nyet, nyet,*" the chauffeur growled. "Go away."

Henry ignored him and shuffled around to the passenger side. The chauffeur followed, hand still inside his jacket. "*Nyet, nyet....*"

"Big bastard, whatever it is."

The ZIS's rear window was rolled down an inch.

Henry took a swig from the bottle. From the corner of his eye he saw the chauffeur moving toward him. Henry lurched forward and grabbed the upper edge of the window, pressing his face to the glass. "Big interior! Is that leather?"

"Get away from there!"

He grabbed a handful of Henry's coat. Henry let the slim aluminum tube slip from his hand. It bounced off the back seat and rolled onto the floorboard. The chauffeur jerked him backward. Henry let himself fall to the sidewalk. "Hey, what's the idea!"

"Go away, I said!"

"Okay, okay…"

Henry rose to his feet, brushed himself off and stumbled back across the street.

Behind him he heard an engine rev. Headlights

washed over him. He glanced over his shoulder. The Mercedes was accelerating toward him. He dropped the bottle and ran.

Having sprung the trap, the *Stasi* was everywhere. For the next hour Henry sprinted through parks and hopped fences; down alleys and up fire escapes and over rooftops. Sirens warbled, sometimes in the distance, sometimes close. At every turn, blue strobes flashed off wet cobblestones and shop windows. Henry kept going, picking his way north and west until he reached the alley across from the apartment.

Crouched behind a hedge, he watched for five minutes, waiting for the skidding of tires and the blare of sirens. None came. He trotted across the street. As he mounted the steps, a pair of headlights pinned him, then a second pair, and a third. Car doors opened, slammed shut. Booted feet hammered the pavement.

"*Schnell, schnell!*"

"*Halt!*"

Henry charged up the stairs, fumbled with the key, then pushed through the door and locked it behind him. Boots pounded up the stairs. The door shuddered once, then again. The wooden jamb splintered. Henry rushed across the room, dropped to his knees, pried back the baseboard. Glass shattered. He glanced over his shoulder. An arm was reaching through the window, groping for the doorknob. Henry pulled the packet from its hole, then carried it to the woodstove. Inside, a single ember glowed orange. He blew on it. A flame sprung to life. He shoved the packet inside. Too big. He folded it, tried again.

The door crashed open.

"*Halt!*"

He turned around and caught a fleeting glimpse of a rifle butt arcing toward his face.

Everything went black.

Blindfolded and shackled, he was taken to what he assumed was either *Stasi* headquarters on Normannenstrasse or to Hohenschoenhausen prison. No one spoke to him and no questions were asked. Around the edges of the blindfold he could see shoes coming and going in his cell, then he felt the prick of a needle and suddenly he was floating. Sounds and smells and sensations merged. He heard Russian voices, smelled the tang of cigarette smoke, felt himself being stripped naked.

His days became a blur as he teetered at the edge of consciousness. His world narrowed: the prick of the needle...the drug coursing hot in his veins...the rhythmic thump of steel wheels on tracks...the hoot of a train's whistle...the stench of burning coal. In that small, still-lucid part of his brain, Henry knew who had him and where he was going.

On the morning of the third or fourth or fifth day, the train groaned to a stop.

He was lifted to his feet and dragged down steps. He felt the crunch of snow under his feet and through the blindfold he could see sunlight. He was trundled into a car. After a short ride he was jerked out and marched down more steps, then a long corridor. He was shoved from behind. He stumbled forward and bumped into a wall. A door slammed shut behind him.

Henry put his back to the wall and slid down to the floor. *Lubyanka*.

* * *

He sat in darkness for three days. On the fourth day, two guards came for him. He was blindfolded and marched down a corridor, then several flights of stairs, then another corridor, ever deeper into the bowels of the prison.

He was guided into a room, where he was shackled to a chair bolted to the floor. His blindfold was removed. The room was small and square, windowless, with a single bulb hanging from the ceiling. A man in an MgB uniform stood before him. The man's epaulets told Henry he was a colonel. *Second Chief Directorate*, he thought. *Bad, bad news*.

"Good morning, Mr. Caulder," the colonel said in accented English.

Henry wasn't surprised they knew his name. He'd run dozens of operations in Berlin, either from the ground or at a distance, causing both the *Stasi* and the MgB a lot of heartache.

The colonel said, "I've been wanting to meet you for a long time."

"And now that you have, I assume you'll let me go?"

The colonel chuckled. "No, I'm afraid not. Let's have a talk, shall we?"

Over the next two days the colonel interrogated him twenty hours a day, at dawn, during the day, in the middle of the night, sometimes for twelve hours, sometimes only an hour. All the questions were variations on a theme: Why had he come to East Berlin?

Henry remained silent.

On the third day, the beatings began. He was hung by his wrists from the ceiling while a bald, heavyset man worked on him with a truncheon, pausing only to catch his breath or to let the colonel ask questions.

Still Henry remained silent.

At the start of the second week, he was brought again to the interrogation room. This time, however, he was stripped naked and shackled to the chair. The colonel stood in the corner, smoking, watching him. The bald man entered, carrying what looked like a birdhouse.

No, not a birdhouse, Henry thought. *Get a hold of yourself. You know what it is.*

A hand-cranked field phone.

The bald man attached wires first to the phone, then with alligator clips to Henry's testicles. He then nodded at the colonel, who walked over and stared down at Henry. "One last chance."

Henry simply shook his head.

The bald man started cranking.

He managed to hold on for another week. Once he started talking, it came in a flood, from his arrival at Tempelhof, to his meetings with Belikov, Kondrash and Preminin, to his capture at the Pieck apartment. Friendly now, the colonel walked Henry through the story again, and again, and again, looking for inconsistencies and contradictions. Finally, on the fifth day the colonel ended the questioning and dismissed the stenographer.

"Don't feel bad, my friend. You did your best."

For the first time in forty days, Henry Caulder smiled.

Now, standing at the threshold of the execution room, Henry felt that same smile forming on his lips. He quashed it and stepped forward. The space was

identical to the interrogation room, save two features:
The walls were draped in thick, heavily stained canvas, and off to one side lay a body bag.

"Good morning," the colonel said.

"That's a matter of perspective, isn't it?"

"Indeed. A poor choice of words. I wish it hadn't come to this, but I have my orders."

"Don't we all."

"We are enemies, you and I, but professionals nevertheless. You were doing your job and I was doing mine. Of course, they don't see it that way."

"They never do."

"It will be quick, I promise."

"What's going to happen to my people?" Henry asked. "Belikov, Kondrash and Preminin?" He already knew the answer, but he wanted to hear the words.

"It's already happened. They were convicted of treason and executed yesterday."

"And my network?"

"We're investigating each of their commands. We'll have confessions soon."

"I have no doubt," Henry said.

"On your knees, please."

Henry turned to face the wall and knelt down. He was waiting for the fear to come, ready for it to fill his chest like acid, but nothing happened. He felt peace. Suddenly a cough welled up in his chest. He heaved, bent double with the pain until the spasm passed. He wiped his mouth. His palm came back bloody.

"Pneumonia," the colonel said.

No, I don't think so, Henry thought.

Ironic that only now he was feeling the symptoms. The doctor had given him four months, no more, before the cancer would metastasize and spread from his lungs to his brain, then to the rest of his organs. Past that, he had a week, perhaps two.

For years both the American and the British intelligence communities suspected Stalin would eventually send the Red Army rolling across Europe, and the allies would be hard-pressed to stop them without going nuclear. The question was how to stop it before it started. For Henry, the answer was simple: Gut the Red Army of its best and brightest. Stalin's own paranoia had cocked the gun; all that remained was the gentlest of nudges on the trigger.

He'd purged the Red Army a dozen times since the twenties, killing hundreds of thousands of dedicated soldiers based on nothing more than suspicion and innocent association. Despite this, three of the most gifted had survived and had come to command key positions: Colonel General Vasily Belikov, General Yuri Kondrash and Marshal Georgy Preminin. When war came, these three men and their armies had the power to conquer Western Europe.

Of course, all three had sworn their innocence, but the MgB, ever ready to ferret out traitors to the motherland, and Stalin, ever wary of plotters from within, had all the evidence they needed.

Planning the operation, Henry had rehearsed the scenario from the MgB's perspective:

A British spymaster who has plagued them for years suddenly appears in East Berlin on a hurried mission.

A message intercept from a code the CIA believes still secure mentions an Operation Marigold and the activation of three agents: PASKAL, HERRING and ARIES.

In the weeks preceding the agent's arrival in East Berlin, CIA-backed Radio Free Europe strays from its normal programming and begins broadcasting what the MgB believes is plain-talk code, which includes multiple uses of the word *Marigold*.

Finally, coinciding with the agent's arrival in East Berlin, an executive secretary at GSFG headquarters vanishes.

Henry had little trouble envisioning the MgB's report to Stalin:

Once inside the Soviet sector, British agent Caulder was followed to Magdeburg, where he serviced three dead drops near the headquarters of the Third Shock Combined Arms Red Banner Army, after which he was photographed passing a message to Colonel General Vasily Sergeyevich Belikov. Upon Belikov's arrest, a false coat button was found on his person. Inside the button was a microdot containing a two-word message: PROCEED MARIGOLD.

In Furstenberg, Agent Caulder was seen talking with General Yuri Pavlovich Kondrash, commander of the Second Tank Guards Army and the Twentieth Guards Spetsnaz Diversionary Brigade. Witnesses state the word marigold *was passed between them.*

In East Berlin, Agent Caulder was photographed near the limousine of General Georgy Ivanovich Preminin, commander of the Group of Soviet Forces Germany. Upon Preminin's arrest, his limousine was searched, and found was a small tube containing a message: PROCEED MARIGOLD.

During questioning, Agent Caulder offered a signed confession disclosing the details of Operation Marigold and the complicity of Belikov, Kondrash and Preminin in a plot to foment an uprising in the Red Army and topple the Soviet government.

For his part, Henry had selectively and carefully broken every tradecraft rule in the book: He walked undisguised into a CIA station where he was photographed by *Stasi* watchers; he entered East Berlin from the French sector with a poorly backstopped cover letter; he was stopped by the VoPo, who noted his license plate and destination, which allowed the *Stasi* to intercept him in Magdeburg; he destroyed a tracking transmitter, a sure sign he was about to run; finally, he was arrested with espionage paraphernalia, including a cipher book and a partially encoded message containing the word *marigold*, false travel documents and a burst transmitter found hidden behind a wall.

From the start, Henry had been the right man for the job, but he knew if it were to succeed, the plan required a sacrifice—a man willing to punch a one-way ticket.

The cancer had made his decision easy.

He heard the scrape of the colonel's pistol sliding from its leather holster, followed by the clicking of heels on concrete. He imagined the pistol drawing level with his skull, the cold muzzle hovering over his skin. *No regrets, Henry. You made a difference. You went down like a lion.*

"Colonel," Henry said without turning. "A favor? One professional to another?"

A pause. Then, "What is it?"

"I'd like to see the sun one more time."

Silence.

Henry squeezed his eyes shut and held his breath.

"Very well, Henry," the colonel said. "Stand up, I'll take you."

* * *

In the months following Henry Caulder's arrest, hundreds of officers from units across the GSFG were tried and either executed or imprisoned for treason to the motherland. The purge spread quickly, first to associated commands, then to the civilian political ranks, and finally to GRU military intelligence. By the end of February thousands had disappeared into Lubyanka's basement.

On March 5, 1953, Joseph Stalin died in his sleep.

F. PAUL WILSON

F. Paul Wilson's urban mercenary Repairman Jack first appeared in his *New York Times* bestselling novel *The Tomb*. Here are some Jack facts:

The "Repairman" moniker was *not* his idea.

Jack is a denizen of Manhattan who dwells in the interstices of modern society. He has no official identity, no social security number, pays no taxes. When you lose faith in the system, or the system lets you down, you go to a guy who's outside the system. That's Jack. But he's not a do-gooder. He's a career criminal and works strictly fee-for-service.

Jack considers himself a small businessman and tries not to get emotionally involved, though he almost always gets emotionally involved. He has a violent streak that worries him at times. A firm believer in Murphy's Law, he thoroughly preplans his fix-its. But things rarely go as planned, and that makes him irritable.

He's low-tech—not a Luddite, but he believes

technology is especially vulnerable to Murphy's Law. He believes that men *are* from Mars, women *are* from Venus, and government *is* from Uranus.

Wilson left Jack dying at the end of *The Tomb*, but resurrected him fourteen years later in *Legacies*. Since then he has written seven more Repairman Jack novels. Born and raised in New Jersey, Paul misspent his youth playing with matches and reading DC comics. He's the author of thirty-two novels and one hundred short stories ranging from horror to science fiction to contemporary thrillers, and virtually everything in between. He lives at the Jersey Shore, and when not haunting eBay for strange clocks and Daddy Warbucks memorabilia, he dreams up another Repairman Jack tale, like *Interlude at Duane's*.

INTERLUDE AT DUANE'S

"Lemme tell you, Jack," Loretta said as they chugged along West Fifty-eighth, "these changes gots me in a baaaad mood. Real bad. My feets killin me, too. Nobody better hassle me afore I'm home and on the outside of a big ol glass of Jimmy."

Jack nodded, paying just enough attention to be polite. He was more interested in the passersby and was thinking how a day without your carry was like a day without clothes.

He felt naked. He'd had to leave his trusty Glock and backup home today because of his annual trip to the Empire State Building. He'd designated April 19th King Kong Day. Every year he made a pilgrimage to the observation deck to leave a little wreath in memory of the Big Guy. The major drawback to the outing was the metal detector everyone had to pass through before heading upstairs. That meant no heat.

Jack didn't think he was being paranoid. Okay,

maybe a little, but he'd pissed off his share of people in this city and didn't care to run into them naked.

After the wreath-laying ceremony, he decided to walk back to his place on the West Side and ran into Loretta along the way.

They went back a dozen or so years to when both waited tables at a long-extinct trattoria on West Fourth. She'd been fresh up from Mississippi then, and he only a few years out of Jersey. Agewise, Loretta had a good decade on Jack, maybe more—might even be knocking on the door to fifty. Had a good hundred pounds on him as well. She'd dyed her Chia Pet hair orange and sheathed herself in some shapeless, green-and-yellow thing that made her look like a brown manatee in a muumuu.

She stopped and stared at a black cocktail dress in a boutique window.

"Ain't that pretty. 'Course I'll have to wait till I'm cremated afore I fits into it."

They continued to Sixth Avenue. As they stopped on the corner and waited for the walking green, two Asian women came up to her.

The taller one said, "You know where Saks Fifth Avenue is?"

Loretta scowled. "On Fifth Avenue, fool." Then she took a breath and jerked a thumb over her shoulder. "That way."

Jack looked at her. "You weren't kidding about the bad mood."

"You ever know me to kid, Jack?" She glanced around. "Sweet Jesus, I need me some comfort food. Like some chocolate-peanut-butter-swirl ice cream." She pointed to the Duane Reade on the opposite corner. "There."

"That's a drugstore."

"Honey, you know better'n that. Duane's got every-thing. Shoot, if mine had a butcher section I wouldn't have to shop nowheres else. Come on."

Before he could opt out, she grabbed his arm and started hauling him across the street.

"I specially like their makeup. Some places just carry Cover Girl, y'know, which is fine if you a Won-der bread blonde. Don't know if you noticed, but white ain't zackly a big color in these parts. Everybody's darker. Cept you, a course. I know you don't like at-tention, Jack, but if you had a smidge of coffee in your cream you'd be *really* invisible."

Jack expended a lot of effort on being invisible. He'd inherited a good start with his average height, av-erage build, average brown hair and nondescript face. Today he'd accessorized with a Mets cap, flannel shirt, worn Levi's and battered work boots. Just another guy, maybe a construction worker, ambling along the streets of Zoo York.

Jack slowed as they approached the door.

"I think I'll take a rain check, Lo."

She tightened her grip on his arm. "Hell you will. I need some company. I'll even buy you a Dew. Caf-feine still your drug of choice?"

"Yeah. Until it's time for a beer." He eased his arm free. "Okay, I'll spring for five minutes, but after that, I'm gone. Got things to do."

"Five minutes ain't nuthin, but okay."

"You go ahead. I'll be right with you."

He slowed in her wake so he could check out the entrance. He spotted a camera just inside the door, trained on the comers and goers.

He tugged down the brim of his hat and lowered his

head. He was catching up to Loretta when he heard a loud, heavily accented voice.

"*Mira! Mira! Mira!* Look at the fine ass on you!"

Jack hoped that wasn't meant for him. He raised his head far enough to see a grinning, mustachioed Latino leaning on the building wall outside the doorway. A maroon gym bag sat at his feet. He had glossy, slicked-back hair and prison tats on the backs of his hands.

Loretta stopped and stared at him. "You better not be talkin a me!"

His grin widened. "But *señorita,* in my country it is a privilege for a woman to be praised by someone like me."

"And just where is this country of yours?"

"Ecuador."

"Well, you in New York now, honey, and I'm a bitch from the Bronx. Talk to me like that again and I'm gonna Bruce Lee yo ass."

"But I know you would like to sit on my face."

"Why? Yo nose bigger'n yo dick?"

This cracked up a couple of teenage girls leaving the store. Mr. Ecuador's face darkened. He didn't seem to appreciate the joke.

Head down, Jack crowded close behind Loretta as she entered the store.

She said, "Told you I was in a bad mood."

"That you did, that you did. Five minutes, Loretta, okay?"

"I hear you."

He glanced over his shoulder and saw Mr. Ecuador pick up his gym bag and follow them inside.

Jack paused as Loretta veered off toward one of the cosmetic aisles. He watched to see if Ecuador was going to hassle her, but he kept on going, heading toward the rear.

Duane Reade drugstores are a staple of New York life. The city has hundreds of them. Only the hoity-toitiest Upper East Siders hadn't been in one dozens if not hundreds of times. Their most consistent feature was their lack of consistency. No two were the same size or laid out alike. Okay, they all kept the cosmetics near the front, but after that it became anyone's guess where something might be hiding. Jack could see the method to that madness: The more time people had to spend looking for what they'd come for, the greater their chances of picking up things they hadn't.

This one seemed fairly empty and Jack assigned himself the task of finding the ice cream to speed their departure. He set off through the aisles and quickly became disoriented. The overall space was L-shaped, but instead of running in parallel paths to the rear, the aisles zigged and zagged. Whoever laid out this place was either a devotee of chaos theory or a crop-circle designer.

He was wandering among the six-foot-high shelves and passing the hemorrhoid treatments when he heard a harsh voice behind him.

"Keep movin, yo. Alla way to the back."

Jack looked and saw a big, steroidal black guy in a red tank top. The overhead fluorescents gleamed off his shaven scalp. He had a fat scar running through his left eyebrow, glassy eyes and held a snub-nose .38-caliber revolver—the classic Saturday night special.

Jack kept his cool and held his ground. "What's up?"

The guy raised the gun, holding it sideways like in the movies, the way no one who knew squat about pistols would hold it.

"Ay yo, get yo ass in gear fore I bust one in yo face."

Jack waited a couple more seconds to see if the guy

would move closer and put the pistol within reach. But he didn't. Too experienced maybe.

Not good. The big question was whether this was personal or not. When he saw the gaggle of frightened-looking people—the white-coated ones obviously pharmacists—kneeling before the pharmacy counter with their hands behind their necks, he figured it wasn't.

A relief…sort of.

He spotted Mr. Ecuador standing over them with a gleaming nickel-plated .357 revolver.

Robbery.

Okay, just keep your head down to stay off the cameras and off these bozos' radar, and you'll walk away with the rest of them.

The black guy pushed him from behind.

"Assume the position, asshole."

Jack spotted two cameras trained on the pharmacy area. He knelt at the left end of the line, intertwined his fingers behind his neck and kept his eyes on the floor.

He glanced up when he heard a commotion to his left. A scrawny little Sammy Davis-size Rasta man with his hair packed into a red-yellow-and-green-striped knit cap showed up packing a sawed-off pump-action twelve and driving another half a dozen people before him. A frightened-looking Loretta was among them.

And then a fourth—Christ, how many were there? This one had dirty, sloppy, light brown dreads, piercings up the wazoo, and was humping the whole hip-hop catalog: wide baggy jeans, huge New York Giants jersey, peak-askew cap.

He pointed another special as he propelled a dark-skinned, middle-aged—Indian? Pakistani?—by the neck.

Both the newcomers had glazed eyes, too. All stoned. Maybe it would make them mellow.

What a crew. Probably met in Rikers. Or maybe the Tombs.

"Got Mr. Manager," the white guy singsonged.

Ecuador looked at him. "You lock the front door?"

Whitey jangled a crowded key chain and tossed it on the counter.

"Yep. All locked in safe and sound."

"*Bueno.* Get back up there and watch in case we miss somebody. Don't wan nobody getting out."

"Yeah, in a minute. Somethin I gotta do first."

He shoved the manager forward, then slipped behind the counter and disappeared into the pharmacy shelves.

"Wilkins! I tol you, get up front!"

Wilkins reappeared, carrying three large plastic stock bottles. He plopped them down on the counter. Jack spotted Percocet and Oxy-Contin on the labels.

"These babies are mine. Don't nobody touch em."

Ecuador spoke through his teeth. "*Up front!*"

"I'm gone," Wilkins said, and headed away.

Scarbrow grabbed the manager by the jacket and shook him.

"The combination, mofo—give it up."

Jack noticed the guy's name tag: J. Patel. His dark skin went a couple of shades lighter. The poor guy looked ready to faint.

"I do not know it!"

Rasta man raised his shotgun and pressed the muzzle against Patel's quaking throat.

"You tell de mon what he want to know. You tell him *now!*"

Jack saw a wet stain spreading from Patel's crotch.

"The manager's ou-out. I d-don't know the combi-nation."

Ecuador stepped forward. "Then you not much use to us, eh?"

Patel sagged to his knees and held up his hands. "Please! I have a wife, children!"

"You wan see them again, you tell me. I know you got armored-car pickup every Tuesday. I been watchin. Today is Tuesday, so give."

"But I do not—!"

Ecuador slammed his pistol barrel against the side of Patel's head, knocking him down.

"You wan die to save you boss's money? You wan see what happen when you get shot inna head? Here. I show you." He turned and looked at his prisoners. "Where that big bitch with the big mouth?" He smiled as he spotted Loretta. "There you are."

Shit.

Ecuador grabbed her by the front of her dress and pulled, making her knee-walk out from the rest. When she'd moved half a dozen feet he released her.

"Turn roun, bitch."

Without getting off her knees, she swiveled to face her fellow captives. Her lower lip quivered with ter-ror. She made eye contact with Jack, silently pleading for him to do something, anything, *please!*

Couldn't let this happen.

His mind raced through scenarios, moves he might make to save her, but none of them worked.

As Ecuador raised the .357 and pointed it at the back of Loretta's head, Jack remembered the security cameras.

He raised his voice. "You really want to do that on TV?"

Ecuador swung the pistol toward Jack.

"What the fuck?"

Without looking around, Jack pointed toward the pharmacy security cameras. "You're on 'Candid Camera.'"

"The fuck you care?"

Jack put on a sheepish grin. "Nothing. Just thought I'd share. Done some boosting in my day and caught a jolt in Riker's for not noticing one of them things. Now I notice—believe me, I *notice.*"

Ecuador looked up at the cameras and said, "Fuck."

He turned to Rasta man and pointed. Rasta smiled, revealing a row of gold-framed teeth, and raised his shotgun.

Jack started moving with the first booming report, when all eyes were on the exploding camera. With the second boom he reached cover and streaked down an aisle.

Behind him he heard Ecuador shout, "Ay! Where the fuck he go? Wilkins! Somebody comin you way!"

The white guy's voice called back, "I'm ready, dog!"

Jack had hoped to surprise Wilkins and grab his pistol, but that wasn't going to happen now. Christ! On any other day he'd have a couple dozen 9mm hollow-points loaded and ready.

He'd have to improvise.

As he zigged and zagged along the aisles, he sent out a silent thank-you to the maniac who'd laid out these shelves. If they'd run straight, front to back, he wouldn't last a minute. He felt like a mouse hunting for cheese, but this weird, mazelike configuration gave him a chance.

He hurried along, looking for something, anything, to use against them. Didn't even have his knife, dammit.

Batteries…notebooks…markers…pens…gum…greeting cards…

No help.

He saw a comb with a pointed handle and grabbed it. Without stopping, he ripped it open and stuck it in his back pocket.

He heard Ecuador yelling about how he was going this way and Jamal should go that way, and Demont should stay with the people.

Band-Aids…ice cream…curling iron—could he use that? Nah.

Hair color…humidifiers…Cheetos…beef jerky—

Come *on!*

He turned a corner and came to a summer-cook-out section. Chairs—no help. Umbrella—no help. Heavy-duty spatula—grabbed it and hefted it. Nice weight, stainless-steel blade, serrated on one edge. Might be able to do a little damage with this. Spotted a grouping of butane matches. Grabbed one. Never hurt to have fire.

Fire…he looked up and saw the sprinkler system. Every store in New York had to have one. A fire would set off the sprinklers, sending an alert to the NYFD.

Do it.

He grabbed a can of lighter fluid and began spraying the shelves. When he'd emptied half of it and the fluid was puddling on the floor, he reached for the butane match—

A shot. A *whizzz!* past his head. A quick glance down the aisle to where Scarbrow—who had to be the "Jamal" Ecuador had called to—stood ten yards away, leveling his .38 for another go.

"Ay yo, I found him! Over here!"

Jack ducked and ran around a corner as the second

bullet sailed past, way wide. Typical of this sort of oxygen waster, he couldn't shoot. Junk guns like his were good for close-up damage and little else.

With footsteps behind him, Jack paused at the shelf's endcap and took a quick peek at the neighboring aisle. No one in sight. He dashed across to the next aisle and found himself facing a wall. Ten feet down to his right—a door.

EMPLOYEES ONLY

He pulled it open and stuck his head inside. Empty except for a table and some sandwich wrappers. And no goddamn exit.

Feet pounded his way from behind to the left. He slammed the door hard and ran right. He stopped at the first endcap and dared a peek.

Jamal rounded the bend and slid to a halt before the door, a big grin on his face.

"Gotcha now, asshole."

In a crouch, gun ready, he yanked open the door. After a few heartbeats he stepped into the room.

Here was Jack's chance. He squeezed his wrist through the leather thong in the barbecue spatula's handle, then raised it to vertical in a two-handed samurai grip, serrated edge forward.

Then he moved, gliding in behind Jamal and swinging at his head. Maybe the guy heard something, maybe he saw a shadow, maybe he had a sixth sense. Whatever the reason, he ducked to the side and the chop landed wide. Jamal howled as the edge bit into his meaty shoulder. Jack raised the spatula for a backhand strike, but the big guy proved more agile than he looked. He rolled and raised his pistol.

Jack swung the spatula at it, made contact, but the blade bounced off without knocking the gun free.

Time to go.

He was in motion before Jamal could aim. The first shot splintered the door frame a couple of inches to the left of his head as he dived for the opening. He hit the floor and rolled as the second went high.

Four shots. That left two—unless Jamal had brought extras. Somehow he couldn't imagine a guy like Jamal thinking that far ahead.

On his way toward the rear, switching aisles at every opportunity, he heard Ecuador shouting from the far side of the store.

"Jamal! You get him? You get him?"

"No. Fucker almost got me! I catch him I'm gonna skin him alive."

"Ain't got time for that! The truck be here soon! We gotta get inna the safe! Wilkins! Get back here and start lookin!"

"Who's gonna watch the front?"

"Fuck the front! We're locked in, ain't we?"

"Yeah, but—"

"Find him!"

"A'ight. Guess I'll have to show you guys how it's done."

Jack now had a pretty good idea where Ecuador and Jamal were—too near the barbecue section to risk going back. So he moved ahead. Toward Wilkins. He sensed that if this chain had a weak link, Wilkins was it.

Along the way he scanned the shelves. He still had the spatula, the comb and the butane match but needed something flammable.

Antibiotic ointments…laxatives…marshmallows…

Shit.

He zigged and zagged until he found the hair-care aisle. Possibilities here. Needed a spray can.

What the—?

Every goddamn bottle was pump action. He needed fluorocarbons. Where were the fluorocarbons when you needed them?

He ran down to the deodorant section. Everything here was either a roll-on or a smear-on. Whatever happened to Right Guard?

He spotted a green can on a bottom shelf, half hidden behind a Mitchum's floor display. Brut. He grabbed it and scanned the label.

DANGER: *Contents under pressure…flammable…*

Yes!

Then he heard Wilkins ambling along the neighboring aisle, calling in a high, singsong tone.

"Hello, Mr. Silly Man. Where aaaare youuu? Jimmy's got a present for you." He giggled. "No, wait. Jimmy's got six—count em—six presents for you. Come and get em."

High as the space station.

Jack decided to take him up on his offer.

He removed the Brut cap as he edged to the end of the aisle and flattened against the shelf section separating him from Wilkins. He raised the can and held the tip of the match next to it. As soon as Wilkins's face came into view, Jack reached forward, pressing the nozzle and triggering the match. A ten-inch jet of flame engulfed Wilkins's eyes and nose.

He howled and dropped the gun, lurched away, kicking and screaming. His dreads had caught fire.

Jack followed him. He used the spatula to knock off the can's nozzle. Deodorant sprayed a couple of feet into the air. He shoved the can down the back of

Wilkins's oversize jeans and struck the match. His seat exploded in flame. Jack grabbed the pistol and trotted into an aisle. Screams followed him toward the back.

One down, three to go.

He checked the pistol as he moved. An old .38 revolver with most of its bluing rubbed off. He opened the cylinder. Six hardball rounds. A piece of crap, but at least it was his piece of crap.

The odds had just become a little better.

A couple of pairs of feet started pounding toward the front. As he'd hoped, the screams were drawing a crowd.

He heard cries of "Oh, shit" and "Oh, fuck!" and "What he *do* to you, bro?"

Wilkins wailed in a glass-breaking pitch. "Pepe! Help me, man! I'm dyin'!"

Pepe…now Ecuador had a name.

"*Sí,*" Pepe said. "You are."

Wilkins screamed, "No!"

A booming gunshot—had to come from the .357.

"Fuck!" Jamal cried. "I don't believe you *did* that!"

A voice called from the back. "What goin on dere, mon? What hoppening?"

"S'okay, Demont!" Pepe called back. "Jus stay where you are!" Then, in a lower voice to Jamal: "Wilkins jus slow us down. Now find that fuck fore he find a phone!"

Jack looked back and saw a plume of white smoke rising toward the ceiling. He waited for the alarm, the sprinklers.

Nothing.

What did he have to do—set a bonfire?

He slowed as he came upon the employee lounge again. Nah. That wasn't going to work twice. He kept going. He was passing the ice-cream freezer when something boomed to his right and a glass door shattered to his left. Ice-cream sandwiches and cones flew, gallons rolled.

Jack spotted Demont three aisles away, saw him pumping another shell into the chamber. He ducked back as the top of the nearest shelf exploded in a cloud of shredded tampons.

"Back here! I have him!"

Jack hung at the opposite endcap until he heard Demont's feet crunch on broken glass in the aisle he'd just left. He eased down the neighboring lane, listening, stopping at the feminine-hygiene area as he waited for Demont to come even.

As he raised his pistol and held it two inches from the flimsy metal of the shelving unit's rear wall, he noticed a "personal" douche-bag box sitting at eye level. Was there a community model?

When he heard Demont arrive opposite him, he fired two shots. He wanted to fire four but the crappy pistol jammed. On the far side Demont grunted. His shotgun went off, punching a hole in the dropped ceiling.

Jack tossed the pistol. Demont would be down but not out. He needed something else. Douche bags had hoses, didn't they? He opened the box. Yep—red and ribbed. He pulled it out.

Footsteps pounded his way from the far side of the store as he peeked around and spotted Demont clutching his right shoulder. He'd dropped the shotgun but was making for it again.

Jack ran up and kicked it away, then looped the douche hose twice around Demont's scrawny neck and dragged him back to the ruined ice-cream door. He strung the hose over the top of the metal frame and pulled Demont off his feet. As the little man kicked and gagged, Jack slammed the door, trapping the hose.

He tied two quick knots to make sure it didn't slip, then dived through the empty frame for the shotgun. He pumped out the spent shell, chambered a new one and pulled the trigger just as Jamal and Pepe rounded the corner.

Pepe caught a few pellets, but Jamal, leading the charge, took the brunt of the blast. His shirtfront dissolved as the double-ought did a pulled-pork thing on his overdeveloped pecs. Pepe was gone by the time Jack chambered another shell. Looked back: Demont's face had gone pruney, his kicks feeble. Ahead: Jamal lay spread-eagle, staring at the ceiling with unblinking eyes.

Now what? Go after Pepe or start that fire?

Fire. Start a big one. Get those red trucks rolling.

But which way to the barbecue section? He was disoriented. He remembered it being somewhere near the middle.

Three aisles later he found it—and Pepe, too, who was looking back over his shoulder as he passed it. Jack raised the shotgun and fired, but Pepe went down just before the double-ought arrived. Not on purpose. He'd slipped in the spilled lighter fluid. The shot went over his head and hit the barbecue supplies. Bags of briquettes and tins of lighter fluid exploded. Punctured cans of Raid whirly-gigged in all directions, fogging the air with bug killer.

Pepe slipped and slid as he tried to regain his feet—would have been funny if he hadn't been holding a .357. Jack pumped again, aimed, and pulled the trigger.

Clink.

The hammer fell on an empty chamber.

Pepe was on his knees. He smiled as he raised his pistol. Jack ducked back and dived for the floor as one bullet after another slammed through the shelving of the cough and cold products, smashing bottles, drenching him with Robitussin and NyQuil and who knew what else.

He counted six shots. He didn't know if Pepe had a speed loader and didn't want to find out. He yanked the butane match from his back pocket and lit her up. He jammed a Sucrets pack into the trigger guard, locking the flame on, then tossed it over the shelf. He heard no *whoomp!* like gasoline going up, but he did hear Pepe cry out in alarm. The cry turned to screams of pain and terror as the spewing Raid cans caught.

Jack crept back and peeked around the corner.

Pepe was aflame. He had his arms over his eyes, covering them against the flying, flaming pinwheels of Raid as he rolled in the burning puddle, making matters worse. Black smoke roiled toward the ceiling.

And then it happened. Clanging bells and a deluge of cold water.

Yes.

Jack saw the .357 on the floor. He sprinted by, kicking it ahead of him as he raced through the downpour to the pharmacy section. After dancing through an obstacle course of ice pops and gallons of ice cream, he found Loretta and the others cowering behind the counter. He picked up the key ring and tossed it to Patel.

"Out! Get everybody out!"

As the stampede began, he heard Loretta yelling.

"Hey, y'all! This man just saved our lives. You wanna pay him back, you say you never seen him. He don't exist. You say these gangstas got inna fight and killed each other. Y'hear me? Y'hear?"

She blew Jack a kiss and joined the exodus. Jack was about to follow when a shot smashed a bottle of mouthwash near his head. He ducked back as a second shot narrowly missed. He dived behind the pharmacy counter and peeked over the top.

A scorched, steaming, sodden Pepe shuffled Jack's way through the rain with a small semiauto clutched in his outstretched hand. Jack hadn't counted on him having a backup. Hell, he hadn't counted on him doing anything but burning. The sprinkler system had saved him.

Pepe said nothing as he approached. Didn't have to. He had murder in his eyes. And he had Jack cornered.

He fired again. The bullet hit the counter six inches to Jack's right, showering him with splinters as he ducked.

Trapped. Had to find a way to run out Pepe's magazine. How? A lot of those baby semis held ten shots.

He peeked up again. Pepe's slow progress had brought him within six feet. Jack was about to duck again when he saw a blur of bright green and yellow flash into view.

Loretta, moving faster than Jack ever would have thought possible, charged with a gallon container of ice cream held high over her head in a two-handed grip. Pepe might have heard her without the hiss and splatter of the sprinklers. But he remained oblivious until she streaked up behind him and smashed the container against the back of his head.

Jack saw his eyes bulge with shock and pain as he pitched toward the floor. Probably felt like he'd been hit with a cinder block. As he landed face-first, Loretta stayed on him—really on him. She jumped, landing knees first on the middle of his back. The air rushed out of him with an agonized groan as his ribs shattered like glass.

But Loretta wasn't finished. Shouting, she started

slamming the rock-hard container against his head and neck, matching the rhythm of her words to the blows.

"NOW you ain't NEVER gonna point no GUN to my HEAD ever aGAIN!"

Jack moved up beside her and touched her arm.

"I think he's got the message."

Loretta looked up at him, then back down at Pepe. His face was flattened against the floor, his head canted at an unnatural angle. He wasn't breathing.

She nodded. "I do believe you right."

Jack pulled her to her feet and pushed her toward the front.

"Go!"

But Loretta wasn't finished. She turned and kicked Pepe in the ribs.

"Told you I was a bitch!"

"Loretta—come on!"

As they hustled toward the front, she said, "We even, Jack?"

"Even Steven."

"Did I happen to mention my bad mood?"

"Yes, you did, Loretta. But sometimes a bad mood can be a good thing."

TED BELL

Ted Bell wrote his first novel for children. In the pre-Harry Potter 1990s, Bell lived in London. The generally inclement weather kept his nine-year-old daughter indoors much of the time. Fine reading weather but, in the neighborhood bookstores, the children's fare was dominated by horror and "message" books. Where was *Treasure Island, Captain Blood* or their modern equivalents?

So Bell wrote a young-adult novel that recaptured the adventure and romance of his own childhood favorites. In *Nick of Time*, a boy of eleven and his seven-year-old sister conspire to thwart the Nazi invasion of their small Channel Island just prior to the Second World War. With the aid of a time machine, Nick and Kate also save Nelson's fleet from the wicked pirate Billy Blood. The book was optioned by Paramount Pictures and ultimately translated into seven languages.

After retiring from advertising, Bell began the Alex Hawke series of adult thrillers. Like his first novel, the new books recapture a lost sense of adventure and glamour. The hero of *Hawke* is Lord Alexander Hawke. As the series begins, three renegade generals abduct Fidel Castro, and turn Cuba into an immediate and frightening threat to the U.S. In the second of the Hawke series, *Assassin,* Alex Hawke battles an ancient cult of killers who are eliminating U.S. ambassadors and their families, prior to launching a horrific attack on America. The third Alex Hawke book, *Pirate,* debuted on the *New York Times* bestseller list. This time, Alex Hawke must stop a French-Chinese oil conspiracy and avert a nuclear showdown with America's latest global rival, China.

The Powder Monkey is a bit different. Here, we travel back in time to 1880. It's the tale of a lovelorn newspaperman's journey to the Channel Islands to learn the true story of the pirate captain Billy Blood's demise. In doing so, our hero learns how a small boy held captive aboard Blood's frigate, *Mystere,* is saved from certain death.

The boy's name is Alex Hawke.

And his dramatic rescue sets the stage for the further adventures of his later namesake.

THE POWDER MONKEY

London and the Channel Islands, 1880

I'm no hero.

But, I am the proud possessor of a large and rather good nose for news (I scribble for a wretched daily in London) that sometimes leads me to the very edges of peril. I had now the whiff of a cracking good story in my flared nostrils and was doggedly pursuing a most promising lead. Nearing my intended destination, in a freezing downpour, I had the ever-stronger sensation of an appointment with destiny.

At minimum, I believed, this latest venture might have a most happy result, namely, an influx of shillings to feed my woefully depleted coffers.

No, it was not some fleeting sniff of fame or any such nonsense that propelled me forward across that forbidding island's slippery scree. Rather, it was the fervent hope that I might soon possess sufficient funds to escape a grim warren of offices above Blackfriar's Tavern in Fleet Street. This was the joyless home to a tawdry little tabloid called the *Daily Guardian*.

It was there, under the mean and watchful eye of my editor, an ink addict named Mr. Symington Fife, that I pecked out my meager existence at tuppence a word. My accounts reflected my life's station, I suppose, for I currently had the princely balance of seven guineas, sixpence in the strongbox 'neath my bed. But, salvation appeared to be at hand.

As it happened, the *Guardian*'s chief competitor, a yellow broadsheet called the *Globe*, had last month announced a new subscription contest in honor of the upcoming seventy-fifth anniversary of Admiral Lord Nelson's great naval victory at Trafalgar. And, by Jove, I meant to win it!

The contest rules were straightforward enough. Any person who submitted a heretofore-unreported tale pertaining to the victory was eligible. The three most surprising and entertaining stories (they had to be historically accurate, of course) would be printed. The best would win a grand prize of seventy-five quid. A king's ransom in my humble view.

All I needed was a smashing tale of the battle and some proof as to its veracity. Of course, for the price of a pint, such rousing stories were easily come by in any pub or tavern. Proving them was another matter entirely. And so it was, with a heartful of hope and my nose twitching madly, that I had set out from London to Trafalgar in search of my liberation.

As you may have suspected, I am a city dweller. I am not, by any stretch, what one might call an "outdoorsman." No, I am hardly one of those stouthearted, broad-shouldered chaps one reads about in the penny novels, off felling trees in the Wild Yukon, scaling Alps or shouting "Sail, ho!" from a pitching mast-head. Rather, I'm one who likes his creature comforts and his books.

I reminded myself of this simple fact tripping over a smallish boulder I hadn't even noticed in my path. I suddenly pitched forward at a dangerous angle. Luckily, I managed to break the fall with my out-stretched hands, and came away with only minor abrasions and another lashing of wounded pride.

Every passing minute on this blasted island, it seemed, was meant to test my resolve. The footing was treacherous. Needles of horizontal icy rain stung my face; nonetheless, I pressed on. I stumbled and fell again. I got up. I walked on.

You see? By my lights, a cozy armchair by the fire-side is a far, far more suitable environment for adventuring than traipsing across the hostile plains of a frozen wasteland. Yet my trusty proboscis would not be denied, and so I pressed onward. The rain did ease a bit on toward evening, I must say. But, soon, the visibility dropped considerably when tendrils of fog nearly obscured the low-hanging sun. It was now merely a hazy yellow wafer sliding toward the sea.

Such dangerous terrain and weather as I encountered only served to fuel my misery and sap my confidence on that trek. Slipping and sliding across the island's rocky headland, I grew ever more tired and bone cold. Late in the day, more serious doubts about this adventure inevitably crept round the edges of my mind: one truly nasty fall and my frozen carcass wouldn't be found till next morning.

Still and all, I was determined to reach the old Grey-beard Inn before nightfall, for I had arranged a meeting with the proprietor there, a Mr. Martyn Hornby, at the hour of eight o'clock.

At quarter past the hour of seven, I was still on my feet, my face a mask of ice. Uncertain of my next turning, I dug my stiff fingers inside a pocket for my map, but it was soggy and ruined and came away in pieces. My course being westerly, with only the setting sun as my guide, I still believed I might arrive before darkness fell. Time would certainly tell.

The godforsaken place to which I had recently journeyed by sail is a tiny link in an archipelago located off the coast of France. This particular island, by far the smallest of the lot, took its name from the thick, pea-soupy fogs that persistently haunted the place.

It was aptly named Greybeard Island.

The place reminded me a bit of the Skelligs, if you know those two forbidding spires. I once chased down the rare Skellig tern there, the bird flitting about those two rock cathedrals set in the royal-blue Atlantic off the southwest shores of Ireland. The Skelligs are remote places, potent in their discomfort. One visit is enough for most, and more than enough for your faithful armchair correspondent.

But I kept putting one boot in front of another that frigid and gloomy evening for one reason. I fervently believed Mr. Hornby could alter the pitiful circumstances of my life.

Martyn Hornby, I had recently learned from his lovely daughter, Cecily, was one of a very small number of Royal Navy veterans of the Napoleonic Wars still alive. He was, as far as I could determine, the sole living survivor of the crew of the HMS *Merlin*.

This small forty-eight-gun English man-o'-war had fought a courageous and—I'd come to believe—pivotal naval battle against a massive French seventy-four-gun frigate back in '05. When I say pivotal, I do not speak lightly. I mean I believed that the *Merlin's* victory had changed the course of history.

And no one, to my knowledge, had ever heard tell of it!

Miss Cecily Hornby, a most charming woman in my eyes, had waxed eloquent in her discourse regarding this sea battle. Here, briefly, is what I know of the matter.

Seventy-five years ago now, back in the summer of 1805, a huge French frigate, *Mystere*, was lurking off this very coast. The reasons for the enemy's presence here at Greybeard Island were unknown. I did know she sailed under the command of the infamous Captain William Blood, an Englishman and a traitor of the first order.

Old Bill was an infamous rogue who had betrayed Admiral Lord Nelson, not for political reasons, mind you, but for a very large sum of capital offered by the French. Captain Blood's formidable services were now at the disposal of Napoleon and his Imperial French Navy.

William Blood was Admiral Lord Nelson's nemesis in those years. And it was only the purest of luck that put that villain at last in British gun sights.

England's very fate was in HMS *Merlin's* hands that day. Sometime in early July, the heavily armed *Mystere* engaged in a vicious set-to with the much smaller British ship. As I understood the thing, had not an obscure English captain named McIver and a mysterious passenger aboard *Merlin* known only as Lord Hawke eked out a victory that fine summer's day, we might all be speaking French.

Surely, I thought, this dramatic encounter, long lost in the swirling mists of history, was the prizewinning tale. For now, I could only dream it were true and hope to prove it.

Subsequent to Cecily's revelations, I commenced a feverish research at the Royal Navy College down at Greenwich. And, finding no record of the engagement, I had determined that, should Martyn Hornby's tale prove credible, I, Pendleton Tolliver, lowly chronicler of church bazaars, tea parties and missing felines, might soon be a wealthy fellow. And, one rewriting the history books in the bargain.

My mind was understandably excited.

Distracted by such thoughts, I slipped then, and nearly lost my footing on a sharply angled escarpment, at the bottom lip of which I spied a cliff, one that dropped some four hundred feet to the sea. Well, I clung to a vertical outcropping of glistening rock and paused, trembling on the edge of the precipice. Once my heart slowed to a reasonable hammering, I pressed on.

Darkness was fully upon me now, and I despaired of not bringing some kind of torch to light my way.

Historians, I was rapidly learning, need an adventurous streak. Tracking down and conversing with far-flung witnesses to history is neither for the faint of heart nor weak of limb. The would-be chronicler of forgotten events must be possessed of a degree of zealotry seldom found outside the pulpit or the sacristy. These, then, were my musings as a sudden thunderclap boomed behind me and lightning strokes danced on the far horizon.

Sodden, hungry, but still determined, I reached a fork in the road. In the gloom, I could make out no stone marker to guide me. To the left, a middling road of crushed stone led off through rain-swept fields to where the halo of a lighthouse shone in the far distance. To my right was a narrow, hard-surfaced pathway that angled sharply down. Below me, I heard the rush of unseen waves bursting themselves repeatedly upon jagged rocks.

The kindly ferryman at the village docks had told how the inn stood on a lower western bluff by the sea. So I chose the harder road descending narrowly along the towering cliff. There was little width to be had on this path, and in some spots it was little more than a shaley rock-cut ledge about ten inches or a foot wide.

The sheer face of rock to my right seemed to bulge, animated, as if it wished to push my body out into space. A trick of mind? Frightened well enough by heights, I inched along, trying to ignore the rising bile of panic and the agitated sea far below my feet. Not once, but now twice, I considered turning back, but quickly realized I had passed the point of no return.

Soon, but not soon enough I'll warrant, I came to a spot where could be seen a jutting arm of rock protruding into the black ocean. At the far end, a warm glow of yellow lights in the rainy gloom. The beckoning two-story house was aglow with promised warmth and food, and my steps quickened.

Realizing what a pitiful sight I would present, I paused outside beneath the pitched eave of the inn and tried to compose myself. I'd worn my one good woolen suit, threadbare but serviceable—at least when dry. My poor shoes, heretofore worn only on Sundays, were now ruined. Ah, well, I thought, pulling myself erect and wringing out my hat, I would just put the best face possible on things and hope for a miracle.

I pushed inside the inn's heavy wooden door and found the old Jack-Tar himself, clay-piped and pigtailed, sitting in silence by the fire. I pulled up a chair and introduced myself. Had I the good fortune of speaking to Mr. Martyn Hornby? I inquired with a smile.

"Aye, I'm Hornby," he said, removing his pipe. After a long silence in which clouds of geniality seemed to float above the man's head, he spoke.

"Weather slowed you up, I reckon," he asked, looking me up and down.

I admitted as much, apologizing for my tardiness, and, when the barman looked in, I ordered a pint of ale for him and a half of bitter for myself. I shed my oilskins and put my two numb feet up on the hearth. The fire felt welcome and the proprietor seemed a fellow who might warm to a story if well supplied with grog or ale.

He was a sturdy, handsome figure who looked to be in his late eighties. He wore faded breeches and a ragged woolen fisherman's sweater, much mended. He had a full head of snow-white hair, and his fine, leathered features were worn by years of wind and water. But, in the firelight, his crinkly blue eyes still held a sparkling clarity of youth, and I was glad of my perseverance on that final narrow ledge.

"Ye've come a long way, Mr. Tolliver."

"Indeed, sir, I have."

"My daughter's letter mentioned something about the old *Merlin*. And some newspaper contest you hope to win, I believe?"

I nodded. "I've a keen interest in your encounter with the French off this island, Mr. Hornby. I'd appreciate your recollections on that subject, if you'd be so kind. It might help my chances greatly, sir."

"Cecily said you saved her cat."

"I penned a short, albeit sympathetic, piece on the plight of foundling cats for my newspaper. Your devoted Cecily, a cat lover of the first magnitude, features prominently in my feline article and the story occasioned much favorable comment. We've since met a few times, she and I, and found each other's company most congenial. Just last month we learned of the contest and she shared the story of the *Merlin*. Fascinating stuff, sir. I decided I'd best hear the tale for myself."

"Aye," Hornby said, and then he fell silent. "I'm the last one…so I suppose I should tell it, if it's to be told at all. If my memory's up to it, of course." He gave a hearty shout for his barman in the next room.

The drinks soon arrived, along with a steaming meat pie for me, and we both sipped, staring into the merry blaze, each alone with his thoughts. Mine, at the moment, were solely of my poor tingling feet, more painful in the thawing than the freezing.

Suddenly, without warning, the man began to speak, eyeing me in a curious manner.

"How much do ye know, then, Mr. Tolliver?"

"Scarcely enough to suit me, sir."

"Well. You've come to the right place then. I seen it all, Mr. Tolliver. I was one of Captain McIver's powder monkeys, y'see, back in those glorious days, and—"

"Powder monkeys?" I said, unfamiliar with the term.

"Boys who would ferry black powder from the hold up to the gun crews when things got spicy. Listen. I'll tell you how it all started, Mr. Tolliver, if you want to start there at the beginning…"

I nodded, smiling encouragement, discreetly pulling my pen and a well-worn leather notebook from my pocket.

"We had a fair wind home to Portsmouth en route from our station in the West Indies where we'd recently captured a Portugee," Martyn Hornby began. "A spy."

"A spy."

"Aye, one much encouraged to speak his mind to

avoid the tar pot and cat-o'-nine-tails during the crossing. We eventually learned from his lips of a wicked plot, hatched in the evil brain of Billy Blood, the turncoat captain of the French frigate."

"That would be Captain William Blood?"

"Few alive today have heard the name, sir. But Old Bill was a holy terror in his day. Gave Lord Nelson fits at every turning, he did. His plot was this—our natural enemy, the king of Spain, and the scurrilous French meant to join their naval forces and surprise Nelson en route to Trafalgar, and send the outnumbered British fleet to the bottom. It would have worked, too, had it not been for the heroism of our captain. And a few ship's passengers."

"Passengers?"

"Hawke was his name. A peer of the realm, but an adventurous sort, being descended directly from the pirate Blackhawke. Him and a boy named Nick."

"Lord Hawke, you say?" I was scribbling furiously now.

"Long dead now."

"How did this Lord Hawke come to be aboard the *Merlin*, sir?"

"His young son, Alexander, had been kidnapped and held for ransom by the French. It was Bill's way to kidnap children of the aristocracy and extort great sums for their release. Hawke had learned Blood had his child aboard the frigate *Mystere* and Hawke was of a mind to rescue him. There was some mystery surrounding his lordship's presence on board, but Cap'n McIver gave him permission to come aboard at Bermuda, as I recall it."

"So, you were actually seeking out this frigate, *Mystere*, for more than military reasons?"

Hornby nodded in the affirmative. "See, we'd extracted from that blasted Portugee where Blood's ship might lie. And more. We knew he had geographical details of his scheme etched on a golden spyglass, and—"

"I'm sorry—etched on a spyglass?"

"Aye. And not just any glass, mind you, but one Bill stole from Admiral Lord Nelson himself the night of the mutiny! According to that damnable Portugee, the location of the intended naval ambush was so secret, Bill had scratched the longitudinal and latitudinal coordinates right into the metal barrel of his glass. Now, since Bonaparte himself had a hand in the planning of the thing, it was likely a cunning trap. We had to get our hands on that glass before Nelson and the whole British fleet sailed from Portsmouth…and, by God, we did!"

"But how?"

"Therein lies the tale, don't it, Mr. Tolliver?"

I took a quick sip of my drink and said, "This Lord Hawke, it was he, wasn't it, who saved the day? I mean to say, I know he figured prominently in Cecily's account of the action."

"Begging your pardon, sir, but it was the boy who accompanied him who carried the day. A scrappy one, he was, only one year older than myself," the old fellow said, tilting his chair suddenly backward at a precipitous angle against the wall. He was now much excited by the telling, and I feared a tumble and broken limbs.

"Another powder monkey, was he?" I asked, scribbling. "Aboard the British man-o-war?"

Another long silence as he gathered his thoughts and sipped his ale.

"No, not young Nicholas. Lord Hawke's fair-haired

ward, he was, came aboard at Bermuda with his lordship. Nick and me became fast friends soon enough, our ages being so similar. I was nine or ten, he was eleven, I believe. When we laid alongside that frigate after a vicious exchange of rippling broadsides, young Nick and myself secretly boarded the *Mystere* and found ourselves right into the thick of things, grapeshot and all. Never saw the like of such bloody struggle in all my years before the mast."

The old fellow was warming to his tale, waving a sloshing tankard of ale in one hand and a long thin bone of a pipe in the other. Somewhere, a ship's bell struck. The wee hours drew nigh. A fresh blow had rushed up to haunt the eaves, and the fire had died down somewhat, lending a discernible chill to the room.

"Please continue, Mr. Hornby," I said, getting to my feet and throwing another log or two onto the embers.

"Well, Nick had promised his guardian that he would remain belowdecks with me on the *Merlin* for the duration of the battle. I'd suffered a nasty head wound and was ordered by the ship's surgeon to stay out of things. However, a fire was raging below, one as was threatening the powder magazine, and it had made any notion of staying below problematical. So we sprinted up three decks and arrived topside only to find ourselves face-to-face with Snakeye himself."

"Snakeye?" I said, scribbling furiously. "First I've heard of him."

"A French pirate, had tattoos of snakes round his eyes and up his nose. Fearsome creature who was Old Bill's bloody right hand. He'd boarded us during the melee and he chased Nick and myself up into the rigging. We scrambled up our mizzenmast and out onto a yardarm. When the pirate followed, dagger in hand, we jumped. The two boats weren't more'n six feet apart and we both dived through a window opened on the French boat's stern quarter."

"This is quite good stuff," I allowed. "Then what?"

"Well, it was strangely quiet when Nick and me emerged from the aft companionway. We looked around *Mystere*'s aftermost deck and saw that it was near deserted, save the dead and wounded. The cannons on both vessels had ceased their thunder and for'ard we could see a press of sailors from both vessels gathered on her quarterdeck, with an occasional cheer in French or English, rising from their midst. We heard, too, the vicious sound of two cutlasses clanging against each other. A brutal swordfight from the sound of it.

"Anyway, I looked aloft and saw the Union Jack still fluttering from our maintruck. And, the battle-torn French flag was still flapping at the top of the enemy mizzen, so I knew Old Bill had not surrendered. This, despite the volume of lead we'd poured into him. Nick and I each took a cutlass off a dead sailor and we crept for'ard and climbed atop of the pilothouse so as to look down on the quarterdeck unobserved. We inched ourselves along on our elbows until we could just peek down and see the action not ten feet below. The crews of both vessels were pressing aft, trying to get a glimpse of the fight taking place at the helm and—"

"The main fighting had stopped?"

"Aye. A great sea battle had come down to a two-man war. Captain William Blood and Lord Hawke were locked in a death struggle. What a sight! Old Bill was a spectacle, wearing what must have been magnificent finery, white silk breeches and a great flaring white satin captain's coat, but now all this flummery was torn and soiled with blood and black powder. He had Nelson's spyglass, all right, jammed inside his wide belt. Hawke had a terrible gash down his right cheek and his shirtfront was soaked with his own blood. Still, he had his left hand rigidly behind his back, fighting Blood in classic dueling fashion, but with more fury in his eyes than I ever thought possible… Another drink, sir?"

"Yes, of course! Keep going though…"

Hornby called out for another round and continued.

"Hawke parried Blood's wicked blows each and all and thrust his cutlass again and again at the darting pirate. But, despite Hawke's genius-like finesse with the sword, it was immediately clear to us boys that this was the fight of his life, as Blood brutally laid on three massive resounding blows in quick succession.

"'It's finished, Hawke—surrender!' Billy cried, advancing, 'There's not a swordsman alive who can best Billy Blood! I'll cut yer bleedin' heart out and eat it for me supper!'

"'I think you shall go hungry then, sir!' Hawke replied, slashing forward. 'No, it's the brave kidnapper of small children who's finished, Blood.' Then, in the nick of time, Hawke deflected with his sword a tremendous cut that would have surely split him to the chine.

"'Look!' Hawke cried, 'Even your own crew has little stomach left for you, Billy Blood. See how these Frenchies stand idle, waiting to see their turncoated English captain's blood run in the scuppers?'

"Hawke, in a dancing parry and lunge, laid on a powerful blow and a great clang of iron rang out over the decks. It was true. Blood's men had all fallen silent, weapons at their feet, watching the battle with rapt attention. Our own Captain McIver, having dispatched the last pockets of resistance on deck, had now ordered a number of our marines to keep their muskets leveled at the few remaining French who hadn't yet thrown down their arms, in case they had any rash notions of coming to Billy's aid.

"'Lying dog!' Billy screamed, his face flushed furious red. He charged Hawke then like a wounded rhinoceros, bellowing at the top of his lungs. Hawke raised his cutlass to defend the ferocious blow, but Billy stopped short at the last instant and spun on his heel, whirling his body completely around and striking with huge force at Hawke's upraised blade. The sword was brutally ripped from his lordship's hand and went clattering across the deck."

"No!" I cried, finding myself right in the thick of the battle. I took a swig and leaned forward, eager for more.

"Aye," Hornby continued. "A cold hand gripped our young hearts as we watched Hawke retreating, completely defenseless against that murderous scalawag, and stumbling backward, tripping over wounded men lying about the decks awash with blood until he fell down.

"At that point, a young Royal Marine leveled his musket at Bill's heart, but Captain McIver pushed his barrel aside, shaking his head. It was Lord Hawke's fight, win or lose. Honor dictated that he finish it.

"'Captain Bonnard!' Billy cried, pausing to shout at his own Imperial French Captain of Marines, 'Why have your men ceased fighting? To watch this pitiful coward die? I order you to attack with vigor! Kill these English dogs.'"

Hornby paused, then stood and turned his back to the fire, warming himself.

"And there the battle turned, Mr. Tolliver. 'I'll take

no more orders from you, Monsieur Blood,' the
Frenchman Bonnard said, stepping forward and drawing his own blade. A cheer went up from his tattered
crew. 'We've hardly a soul with a will left to fight, a fire
rages amidships, and we are grievously holed below
our waterline. Any fit French captain would have seen
this mighty ship to victory this day, sir, but you have
precious little fitness in that regard. We had no chance
under your hand. We have suffered you long and long
enough, sir! Enough! You are unfit to command this
vessel, and I intend to negotiate her surrender on behalf of this crew. Throw down your sword, Captain
Blood, you are under the arrest of the Imperial French
Navy! Bo'sun, strike our colors, we are surrendering
Mystere to—'"

"Begging your pardon, Mr. Hornby," I said, "but
there were children held captive below, were they not?
What was to become of—?"

Hornby eyed me then and I lowered my head, most
sorry for my interruption.

"'Mutiny, is it then?' Billy said, and he threw back
his head and laughed. 'I'll slit your mutinous French
throats 'afore I'm done, but I'll begin with this English
swine!' He swung his gaze round on Hawke, then
lunged forward, his blade tip aimed at Hawke's heart.
Rapt, I was, and barely aware of young Nick climbing
to his feet beside me.

"'Lord Hawke! Up here!' Nick shouted, and everyone turned to see him standing atop the pilothouse.
He pulled the cutlass he'd borrowed from his belt
and threw it down to the empty-handed Hawke.
Nick's toss was short and the sword fell to the deck
at Hawke's feet. I saw my new hero bend to retrieve
it, but Bill was using the moment's distraction to

circle in toward Hawke, his sword poised for a murderous blow.

"Hawke and his blade were coming up as Blood's blade was coming down. The flat of Billy's sword caught Hawke hard across the shoulder blades, driving him back down to the deck. His head thudded hard and I could see he was stunned. His sword had landed a good fifteen feet away. Nick looked at me, and I could see in his eyes what he had in mind.

"It was only about ten feet from our perch down to the quarterdeck, and Nick timed that jump perfectly. He came down squarely on the shoulders of Captain Blood, straddling his head and clamping both hands over the enraged pirate's eyes. Blinded and snorting, Bill whirled about, staggering over the bodies of the dead. He shook that tenacious boy clinging to him, tormenting him, but Nick held on.

"Nick saw me then, peering down from the rooftop, and cried out, 'Down to the brig with you, Martyn Hornby! See if you can find Lord Hawke's boy and the children! His lordship and I have this well in hand.' Nick had somehow snatched the prized spyglass from Bill's waist…and then I saw Nick flying through the air as Billy had finally ripped him from his shoulders and flung him like a rag doll hard upon the deck.

"*Well in hand*, I thought, disbelieving. But I did as Nick said, and slid backward down off the roof, much as it pained me to leave that grave drama and then—"

"Wait!" I said, leaping to my feet and banging my shin on the hearthstone. "For all love, Mr. Hornby, you didn't leave your ringside seat at that very moment?"

"Mr. Tolliver, I was gone only a short while, and what I missed was filled in enough so's I feel I've seen what happened with my very own eyes, sir," Hornby said, seeming startled by my outburst.

"Well, then, please don't stop the tale there, sir," I said, returning to my seat. My pen hovered above the page, quivering to inscribe the conclusion of the adventure.

"'I'll have that glass back!' Blood roared, planting one of his gleaming Hessian boots squarely in the middle of Nick's chest. Bill poked the tip of his razor-sharp blade at him, prodding Nick's jacket. Then he slashed the boy's thin blue coat right through and the gleaming spyglass spilled out onto the deck, rolling away as Nick tried desperately to grab for it. In a flash, Blood's hand shot out like some inhuman claw and clutched it, raising it aloft where it shone in the sun.

"'No!' Nick shouted. 'That's Nelson's glass!' He was clawing at Blood's leg, trying to rise from the deck, but Billy still had him pinned with his boot pressed painfully in the boy's stomach and Nick could only twist frantically like a spider impaled. Then Nick reached inside his jacket for a bone-handled dagger Lord Hawke had given him for protection. He plunged that blade deep into the fleshy part of Old Bill's calf. Roaring in pain, Blood didn't see Hawke approach from behind.

"'The boy said the glass belongs to Nelson,' Hawke said, the point of his cutlass in Billy's back. 'I'll thank you to return it to him. Now.'

"'Your tongue has wagged its last,' Bill said, whirling to face Lord Hawke. They eyed each other. Bill lunged first, his blade going for Hawke's exposed gut, but this time it was Hawke who spun on his heel in lightning fashion, whirling his body with his flashing cutlass outstretched. And then an awful sound, the sound of steel slicing through flesh and bone. The sound of steel *through* flesh and bone!

"There was an enormous howl of pain, and Billy held up a bloody stump of his right arm.

"On the deck lay Blood's still-twitching hand, bloody fingers clenched round the shining golden spyglass."

I stood again and looked down at old Hornby, who was staring into the fire with gleaming eyes.

"Ho! Hawke had Nelson's glass?"

"Aye, we had it, for all love. The longitudinal and latitudinal coordinates of the ambush, scratched into the gold in code. But the Portugee spy, he'd given up that code long ago. Hawke read off the numbers plain as could be and a marine wrote 'em down."

"And that's the end of it?"

"Not quite, sir. A bit remains to be told."

"What, then?" I asked, almost pleading, for surely I could already see his story appearing under my byline in the *Globe*. "Please continue, Mr. Hornby, I beg you."

"Ah, well, I suppose I should finish it, shouldn't I? Because, you see, I myself reappear in the story." He chuckled, threw back a swig, and got on with it.

"On the quarterdeck, the French captain Bonnard went down on one knee and presented the sword of surrender to Lord Hawke. Hawke took it and spoke, but there was no trace of pride about him.

"'Captain Bonnard, on behalf of the *Merlin* and His Majesty's Royal Navy, I accept your surrender. I will present your colors and sword to my captain forthwith. You are a gentleman and it has been my honor to do battle with you, sir.'

"The French struck their colors and every English heart lifted as the Union Jack rose against the blue sky at *Mystere*'s topmast. Hawke stepped to the binnacle and raised the surrendered flag of France into the air.

"'My brave shipmates and comrades,' Hawke

began, 'I hardly know how to express my gratitude for your gallant—'

"'Father! Father!' came a tiny voice that pierced the silence in a way that made Hawke's heart leap up into this throat so quickly he could scarce get another word out.

"And then Hawke saw the sailors part and a small ragged boy racing across the deck toward him, followed by a grinning powder monkey who was living his finest hour. I was a bit bloodied by my most recent encounters with Snakeye and his men standing guard below at the brig. But I had done my duty and I was smiling, sir, believe me, as all the wee children came pouring up onto the decks, laughing and gulping the sweet air.

"'Oh, Father, it's really you!' the small boy cried, and Hawke leaped down from the binnacle, falling to his knees and embracing his boy, Alex, as if he'd never let him go."

A silence fell then, only a patter of rain on the roof could be heard.

"A marvelous tale," I finally said, looking over at Hornby. He seemed a bit overcome.

"My tongue hasn't wagged so in years," he said, looking a might done in. "My apologies."

"You do yourself credit, sir. Is there more?"

"Soon enough, the barky was under way again, and she had a fine heel to her, and, looking aloft, I saw clouds of billowing white canvas towering above, pulling hard for England. A corps of drummers dressed with magnificent battle drums launched into a stately military tattoo that rolled across our decks. *Merlin* was a fine, weatherly ship and I recall thinking that, if this breeze held, we'd have no trouble completing our do-or-die mission. We'd reach Portsmouth in time to personally warn Nelson of the intended ambush."

"And you did, did you not?"

The old fellow leaned forward as if he had a further confidence to impart, and I saw his eyes welling.

"We did, sir, and I was honored to be present at St. James's Palace on the occasion. Afterward, Lord Hawke himself came over to me, Alex in his arms. He bent down and looked me straight in the eye.

"'Magnificently done, young Mr. Hornby,' he said, and handed me a canvas packet, but my eyes were too blurry to know then what it was. Years later, I hung it there, on the wall there beside the hearth. D'you see it?"

I rose from my chair and went to inspect the item, glinting in the shadowy firelight.

"Yes, I see it, Mr. Hornby," I said. I reached up and fingered the old leather strap, careful lest it crumble under my touch.

Lord Hawke's gift that day to the young powder monkey, Martyn Hornby, once a shining treasure, was now a tarnished memory of glory hung by the hearthside. It was Lord Nelson's spyglass.

"Go on, Mr. Tolliver, put it to your eye. That's history there in your hands, sir!"

I lifted the glass from the nail where it hung, and that's when it happened. The strap parted and the glass slipped from my fingers and smashed against the hearthstone. The lens popped into the air, spinning like a tossed shilling, and I reached out and snatched it.

"Sir!" I cried as I bent to retrieve the dented tube. "I'm dreadfully sorry!"

"No worry, Mr. Tolliver," he replied kindly. "It's seen far worse. Look closely, you can see Bill's inscription there by the eyepiece."

But something far more intriguing had fallen from the tube. A thin, yellow roll of parchment, tied with a black ribbon.

"Mr. Hornby," I said, trying to control my emotions, "there appears to have been a message of some kind inside. Were you aware of it?"

"A message, sir?" he said, getting slowly to his feet. "Let's have a look."

I untied the ribbon with utmost care and spread the letter upon a table. We both looked down in utter disbelief. The letter was signed and dated by Napoleon himself! Here is what it said:

Captain Blood,
Make for Cadiz at once under a full press of sail. Once our fleets are united with Spain's, England is ours! Surprise Nelson en route to Trafalgar and all will be over. Six centuries of shame and insult will be avenged. Lay on with a will! His Majesty counts as nothing the loss of his ships, provided they are lost with Glory...
N.

I said in a daze, "Astounding, sir. And proof of the tale!"

"Yes. Proof enough, I should think."

We were both silent, staring down at the remarkable document.

"How much is the Globe's prize then?" Hornby asked, puffing his pipe in a contemplative fashion.

"Seventy-five pounds, sir."

"A goodly sum."

I took a deep breath and said, "Mr. Hornby. There is one last piece of business I must discuss with you.

Cecily and I—well, Cecily and I are to be married. Sorry. What I mean to say, sir, is that I've come here because I should very much like your permission to ask for your daughter Cecily's hand in marriage!"

He stared into the embers and made no reply. I was sure he found me, shabby as I was, a poor match for his beautiful daughter. It seemed he couldn't even summon the energy to deny me my hopes. I got to my feet and stretched my weary bones. I closed the notebook and slipped it inside my breast pocket, patting my jacket, finding some measure of hope and reassurance for my future there.

I was about to head upstairs in search of an empty bed, for I was sorely tired, when Hornby got to his feet.

"You're a good man, Penn Tolliver. An honest soul. Cecily said as much in her letter. I told her I should like to find that out for myself. It was I who suggested you make this long journey in fact."

"Well, sir, I don't—"

"Take the Napoleon letter, lad, as your proof. You'll win the prize, all right. It's yours. I've always wondered these many years whether or not it was worth anything. Now I see that it is worth a great deal, indeed."

"You knew of the letter?"

"Of course. It's how Captain McIver and Hawke proved the existence of the plot to Lord Nelson himself!"

"But, Mr. Hornby, this letter is worth thousands of pounds! Ten thousand at least! Perhaps more! I cannot possibly accept it."

He put the battered glass into my hands and closed my fingers around it.

"Take it, lad."

"And, about Cecily, sir? I don't mean to push, but— I do love her very much, sir, and I can only pray that in time you could come to accept me as someone who only has her best—"

"I'd be honored to have you in the family, Mr. Tolliver."

The old man put his head back against the cushion and was fast asleep before I was halfway up the stairs, flying up them, a happy man, determined to get a bright and early start next morning.

After all, I was a young man with a future.

M. DIANE VOGT

Legal thrillers have always provided high drama and intense conflict. As a child, M. Diane Vogt was a devoted fan of Perry Mason. Every week, Vogt and her dad would watch Erle Stanley Gardner's Mason outsmart the bad guys on television, matching wits with Mason in the process. Those evenings were at least in part responsible for Vogt becoming a lawyer and, many years later, writing legal thrillers. She is the author of the highly acclaimed and popular *Judge Wilhelmina Carson* series.

Vogt believes that fictionalization of the legal world is necessary to good stories. But, like Gardner, she takes little dramatic license with the lawyers she portrays and the world they inhabit. From an insider's perspective, she shows what actually happens in lawsuits, courtrooms and lawyers' offices, not just in criminal matters, but in civil cases—where most people collide head-on with the law.

Karen Ann Brown is a young lawyer disillusioned with the law's compromises enough to leave her job as a prosecutor and strike out on her own. She now works as a "recovery specialist," with a cover identity as a travel writer. Karen is forced to make tough choices when her clients' needs are thwarted by gaping holes in the law, particularly concerning children abducted by their parents. *Surviving Toronto* was inspired by the plight of Vogt's good friend, who was embroiled in a futile ten-year custody battle. It's a tale of irrational anger and rage, something all too familiar to many divorces.

But, luckily, Karen Brown is watching.

SURVIVING TORONTO

Dressed in black, Karen Brown was indistinguishable from her surroundings. Ambient light was nonexistent in the expensive, quiet neighborhood, where *crime* should've been nonexistent. The microwave clock glowed 3:00:15 a.m.

She switched the Sig-Sauer's grip to her left hand, raised her right to rub her sore neck and stretched her shoulders. Man, she hated custody battles. But this one was different, not because of the challenge, but the parties.

Karen leaned back, ankles crossed, heels propped on the kitchen table, and settled in to wait through the remainder of the third night.

Jeffrey London, as malevolent a bastard as ever drew breath, was far from stupid. He would try again to steal his daughter. If not tonight, then tomorrow or another night soon. She felt it. And she knew Jeffrey. Instinct and preparation had saved her life before. She wouldn't ignore them now.

Combating boredom, her thoughts wandered to Jeffrey when she'd been in love with him. He was her first college romance and she'd felt as treasured as a rare art object, although the warning signs were there. A chill ran through her. How narrowly she'd escaped his bondage when he dumped her for sexier, younger, more fun-loving and naive Beverly.

Ten years later, Karen felt not only grateful to have escaped, but guilty. *Survivor guilt* was what psychologists called it. Irrational perhaps, but real enough. Jeffrey had to marry someone. Karen had tried to warn her, but Beverly's inexperience prevailed and the two began the destructive tango that led them all here.

Karen knew exactly why she'd accepted this job. A second chance to save Beverly and her child before Jeffrey destroyed them. Maybe Beverly had forgotten her worth, but Karen would not.

At 3:34:17, as if her thoughts had conjured him, she heard Jeffrey's heavy tread on the squeaky plank decking. Karen pressed the remote button to activate the security camera outside the back door. The night vision would record everything in an eerie green glow.

Karen blended with the darkness and waited, holding the Sig in her right hand, ready to use it. But not too soon. Only when he left the premises with Deidre would he be guilty of kidnapping.

Should she be forced to confront him before then, he'd claim he wasn't taking Deidre anywhere. Beverly was the custodial parent, but Jeffrey had bought and still owned this house. Technically, he wasn't trespassing and he could visit whenever he chose. His twisted lies had persuaded Beverly to excuse his behavior before.

Karen timed him. Jeffrey spent exactly twelve seconds forcing the lock and opening the back door. She smiled to herself. He should have tried the old key. She'd made sure it would work.

The alarm began its incessant bleat. Karen breathed silently, disturbing the air as little as possible. Jeffrey had the instincts of a predator. He would sense her presence if she made the slightest sound.

He crossed the tile to the alarm panel next to the refrigerator. He rapid-punched the six numbers of his wedding date, the code he and Beverly had chosen when he still lived here. Before their bitter divorce. The alarm stopped. He turned, never glancing in her direction.

Arrogance was Jeffrey's Achilles' heel. It simply didn't occur to him that anyone would be watching. She grinned to herself inside the black ski mask she wore over her head and face.

She watched Jeffrey climb the stairs and cover the short distance to the first door on the right. He paused. The night-light illuminated him enough that the camera would record perfectly. He showed his face to avoid frightening his daughter, to keep her quiet and not awaken her mother. Beverly's sheer terror tomorrow morning when she found Deidre missing was much of what the sadistic asshole wanted to accomplish. He wanted Beverly off balance and afraid. He would always control her and Deidre as surely as if they were confined to prison.

He glanced around, maybe assuring himself that he'd made it this far, that Beverly slept soundly down the hall. Then he faced the door to Deidre's room, opened it and crept inside.

He emerged shortly with the sleeping girl in his arms. She was dressed in white pajamas. Strawberry curls framed her cherubic face and cascaded down the back of his arm. She didn't stir.

He eased the door almost closed, leaving it as Beverly had when she saw Deidre last, and descended the stairs in silence. Karen waited. Her right hand held the Sig firmly pointed in Jeffrey's direction. She'd shoot him if he forced her to.

If Jeffrey saw her, he would do something stupid. Something that might hurt Deidre. The child's safety was paramount.

He snuck out the back door and closed it without a sound. Karen activated the tiny camera she wore in a pendant around her neck, waited until she heard the creaking boards under his feet and hurried out behind him. She followed him to the street where he'd parked a dark SUV.

Jeffrey was bent over, placing Deidre in the back seat when Karen came up behind him.

"Move away from the car. Much as I'd like to shoot you…" She allowed her deep, husky voice to trail away.

He stepped back, cavalierly raised both hands palms out.

"Turn around," she said quietly, hoping not to awaken Deidre. He complied. He saw the gun, pointed now at his chest. "Smile," she said, picking up the pendant and pointing the micro camera directly toward him. "A picture's worth a year of testimony, isn't it?" She photographed Deidre sleeping in the vehicle, too.

She'd argued with Beverly and Beverly's sister, Brenda, for hours about this part of their plan. Beverly had cried, said she didn't want her child's father incarcerated. She wasn't desperate enough yet. But Karen knew she would be. Released and alone, Jeffrey would take his daughter again, not because he loved her, but because he owned her. Deidre would never be safe from him. He should have gone to prison for battering his wife. Or when he stole Deidre the last two times. But Beverly had refused to testify. Now she had proof, when she needed it.

Jeffrey stared at Karen, wary but unafraid. Her lanky frame was indistinguishable from a man's in these clothes. And she held an equalizer pointed at his heart. Did he recognize her voice? Probably, although they hadn't talked in years. She could almost see him calculating his next move.

"If you ever set foot in Florida again, the video of tonight's escapade will be delivered to the U.S. Attorney's Office. You'll die in prison."

He smirked. He wasn't afraid of her. Karen's hand itched to smash the gun into his face, but she kept calm.

"Move to the front of the car." He sidled to the center in front of the grille. Her gaze never leaving him, the gun steady, Karen bent down and lifted the little girl. She stirred, but didn't waken.

When she was sure Deidre was secure in her grasp, Karen distanced herself from the SUV. "Get in and drive away."

Hands in his pockets, Jeffrey sauntered around to the driver's side and opened the front door. Instantly, the car alarm sounded, repeated long blasts of the horn. The cacophony awakened Deidre. When she saw the black-clad apparition holding her, she began to cry and kick, yelling, "Let me go! Let me go!" Karen grabbed her tightly to keep her from taking them both down to the ground, but the gun didn't waver.

"Hush, Deidre. It's me, Aunt Karen. It's okay. Be quiet now."

"Aunt Karen?" the astonished child cried, tears and screams coming to a shaky, tentative halt.

Jeffrey now had one leg in the SUV, his weight shifted toward the driver's seat. He pressed the key fob to silence the blasting horn, and then flashed a sardonic grin. "How nice to see you again, Karen."

She stiffened and extended the gun, her intention clear. "Don't forget what I told you, Jeffrey. No contact. Go."

"You think I take orders from you?" He slid into the SUV, started the engine, rolled down the window and threw a stare of pure hatred at Karen. She shivered imperceptibly. She'd made an open enemy. Somehow, he would prove he controlled her, too, along with everything in his world, no matter what the cost.

All pretext of the gentleness he'd shown his daughter gone, he said, "You'll be sorry you screwed me, Karen."

"I've been sorry about that for years."

Just back from Europe, the news flashed across her computer as she worked on revisions to *Karen Brown's Guide to Switzerland*, courtesy of Tampa P.D.'s Internet subscription active calls for service. A domestic-violence call in a Carrollwood neighborhood. The first officer at the scene found a woman shot and a five-year-old girl missing. An Amber Alert went out at 3:30 a.m. Karen glanced down at the clock on the screen. Twenty-five minutes ago. Wasting no time on useless recriminations, she left immediately.

Thirty minutes later, she reached Grouper Circle, a few houses scattered around the cul-de-sac bordering Lake Grouper. Tampa P.D. cruisers blocked the Dolphin Avenue entrance. Karen parked her red 4Runner and slipped her Sig under the front seat. She had a license to carry but no need to make this tense situation worse.

She grabbed her laptop and approached the first officer she saw. "Hey, Randy," she said, to avoid startling him in the darkness.

"Counselor." He nodded. "What's your interest?"

"Beverly London is a client. Came to offer support."

"She don't need it," Officer Wilson told her bluntly.

Karen closed her eyes. A short moment of mourning was all she permitted herself for now. "Suspects?"

"Nasty divorce. Custody problems with the daughter. That your angle?"

Karen nodded.

"Bet on the ex," Randy said. "Real piece of shit. Restraining orders, my ass."

Nobody needed to tell her how inadequate the law was at protecting women from men like Jeffrey. "Can I go up?"

He nodded.

"Who's primary?"

"Jerry Scanlon."

Karen made her way down the short street to the brick colonial at the end. She saw two unmarked cars, an ambulance and people milling around. Officers, crime-scene technicians, photographers. A couple of detectives interviewing one of the neighbors, probably the one who'd called in the gunshots. She walked up the sidewalk to the threshold and stared into the open front door.

Beverly London's body lay on the tiled foyer floor, clad in a neon-yellow nightgown, eyes open, frozen in surprise. Two entrance wounds were visible in her chest and abdomen. Lots of blood had pooled. Bullets probably severed the femoral artery. No way Beverly would have survived, even if she'd been found immediately. But she'd been there a while, long enough for all the blood to have congealed.

Karen caught Detective Scanlon's attention. "I hear you gave up law, writing travel books now," he said, a question in his tone that she'd answered too many times before. *Why?* That's what he wanted to know.

"I like writing travel books," she said. She was still a member of the bar. That's all he needed to know.

"Not enough money in the writing to keep you in cabernet?"

"Something like that."

He sized her up as if he'd never seen her before, although the two had worked together frequently during her short stint in the prosecutor's office. He waved toward the body. "Not a pretty scene."

"There are security cameras throughout the house and grounds." She pointed to the camera hidden in the wall sconce on the side of the front door. When his eyebrows rose in question, she nodded. "Mine."

"We're not through processing yet." He let her pass.

Karen moved carefully through the kitchen, Deidre's room, Beverly's room, and the door that led outside to the attached garage. She located the surveillance cameras and removed the memory sticks. The cameras recorded in a loop, replacing images every three days until the sticks were changed.

She opened her laptop, booted up and slipped the memory stick from the kitchen camera into the slot first. The images downloaded quickly. She and Detective Scanlon watched video of the dark kitchen, but nothing more.

"It was a long shot," he said by way of forgiveness. Methodically, Karen downloaded data from the other four and continued searching. "Look there." She pointed to the screen. The intruder had come in through the garage door. Jeffrey London. No doubt about it. *He's a bold bastard,* she reminded herself.

They studied the digital images on the tiny laptop screen. She felt a sick déjà vu as she watched Jeffrey invade the house, disarm the security system, climb the stairs, enter Deidre's room and return carrying the sleeping girl, just as he had the night Karen saw him from the kitchen chair.

"Dammit!" she muttered. She blamed herself. She should have forced Beverly to turn Jeffrey in last year. If she had, Beverly would be alive now.

"Look…" Scanlon pointed to the image.

She shook off her recriminations and watched Jeffrey reach the bottom of the stairs, his body twisted to the right, toward the garage door. Light flooded the foyer.

Camera three captured the entire scene. Beverly stood very near the same location where she was lying now. "Jeffrey!" her voice screeched from the laptop's inadequate speakers. Karen winced.

Deidre awakened, looked around, sleepy-eyed, disoriented. "Daddy?" she said, as if she was surprised to be held in his arms. Which surely she was. He hadn't seen her in fourteen months, and the last time was under harrowing circumstances.

"Put her down, Jeffrey," Beverly's panicked voice instructed.

He chuckled, changed direction and strode toward the front door.

Beverly grabbed his arm, jerking it from under Deidre's legs. Jeffrey grasped the child tighter, held her close to his chest. Then he yanked his right arm from Beverly's grasp, reached around his back, slipped a .38 from his belt and shot her twice.

Beverly fell to the floor. Deidre screamed, "Mommy! Mommy!" and thrashed wildly.

Jeffrey held on to the frightened girl. He strode through the front door and out of camera range. The screen reflected the empty foyer. After an excruciating few seconds, Beverly's faint groans stopped.

Moments of stunned silence followed before Scanlon laid a hand on Karen's shoulder. "We'll get a warrant and an APB. Any idea where he's taken her?"

Numb, she said, "He's a Canadian citizen. Lives in Toronto. Wealthy. Probably flew here in his private plane."

Scanlon sighed, resignation showing in the slump of his shoulders. "If he gets her to Canada before we catch him, that's a big problem."

"Why?"

"Canada won't extradite him for a crime that carries the death penalty. And we won't waive the death penalty unless he pleads guilty and accepts a life sentence."

Karen's despair overwhelmed her. "I can see that happening all right."

Scanlon nodded. "Sarcasm won't help. There are some alternatives. None is perfect, and they all take time."

"You'll understand if I don't think spending the next two years cutting through bureaucratic red tape to get Deidre back through channels is a great solution."

She cued up the last of the video again and checked the time stamp on the image. "He's been gone more than six hours. By private plane, he could easily be in Toronto already." Karen knew Jeffrey wouldn't have risked planning to return on a commercial flight.

"We'll check the airlines to be sure," he paused. "Otherwise, I'm afraid we're hosed here."

Karen felt a slow burn rising from her toes to the top of her hair. Every nerve ending alert. Beverly dead. Deidre missing. Jeffrey London gone.

Case closed?

Not a chance.

After the fifth lap, cold rain pelting her body, punishing her for screwing up, Karen began to feel a bit better. Although her racing days were long over, swimming still cleared her head. The water slid past her wet skin. She completed a dive and turn underwater, gliding through the silky depths back to the surface, flawlessly resuming the forward crawl. She used the steady rhythm that allowed her mind to strategize. The problem wasn't finding Jeffrey but extracting Deidre from Canada. And then keeping the girl away from Jeffrey. She finished fifteen laps while the plan worked itself out.

When she left the practice of law, disillusioned and angry with its compromises and failures, she'd turned to writing travel books, seeking a totally different life. She quickly discovered she loved the work. It satisfied her in a way she'd never expected. And it allowed her to work privately as a recovery specialist, unencumbered by the rules lawyers were required to follow.

The lifestyle suited her. She traveled to research her books, but she carefully selected worthy clients and fashioned solutions for them that achieved desired results. Clients like Beverly London and her sister, Brenda.

Karen frowned and shook water from her eyes. Jeffrey would never leave *his* child alone unless he was in prison or dead. There was no middle ground. She must resolve that problem, too. She needed a final solution.

Karen swam, one arm over the other, legs kicking, diving and turning, ignoring the wind that chilled her whenever she rose above the water. Her plan resolved, she finished with ten laps of relaxing side strokes. Finally, she floated on her back, allowing the icy rain to drench her face. The cool air now felt refreshing because she knew what she was going to do.

Karen waited several months, long enough for Jeffrey to relax into complacency before she flew from Tampa to Buffalo. At the airport she rented an anonymous-looking gray sedan. She'd avoided a nonstop flight to Toronto. Although faster and easier, she'd be dependent on flight schedules for the return. Since 9/11, airport security had become irritatingly problematic. She'd be required to prove Deidre's identity, which would make them easier to stop and trace. No, driving into and out of Canada was best.

Reluctantly, she rejected buying an untraceable gun on the streets of Buffalo. Taking a gun into Canada was a serious crime. Canadian citizens weren't allowed to carry concealed weapons. Even owning them was severely restricted. If she was caught she'd be arrested and probably imprisoned. Deidre would certainly be returned to her father. No, the risk was too great. She'd take Deidre away from Jeffrey permanently using guile alone. She refused to fail again.

Karen drove to Lewiston, New York, and checked into a mom-and-pop motel. She rented the room for two nights. Tomorrow, she'd test her plan. The following day, she'd execute it.

She slept lightly for four hours, then dressed casually in khaki slacks, pink shirt, blue blazer and running shoes. She grabbed her shoulder-length blond hair into a ponytail and studied herself in the mirror, pleased by the guileless soccer-mom effect she'd created.

It was dark at 5:00 a.m. as she drove toward the Lewiston-Queenston Bridge. Jeffrey would expect her to take the shortest route to and from Toronto. She intended to oblige. Drive time was seventy-five minutes, barring construction or heavy traffic.

The border crossing went well. Off season, during the week, the area was almost deserted both ways. Very few travelers meant only one of the two customs booths were open. As in most of the small tourist towns, the Canadian customs officer simply asked her name, nationality, where she was going and when she planned to return. She'd offered the typical tourist's response for a visit to Niagara Falls and paid the toll. He'd waved her through without asking for ID. *May the return be so easy*, she thought.

She reached the private school where her research revealed Deidre was enrolled. After circling the block twice to be sure Jeffrey wasn't lurking and didn't have Deidre under surveillance, she parked in front. She had a clear view of the playground while waiting for 10:15 a.m. It nagged her that Jeffrey seemed to have allowed Deidre out of his control. Was he that sure of himself? Had he arrogantly assumed she had given up? What was she missing?

At 10:15 a.m., a young woman led twenty energetic children out the door to the playground. She spotted Deidre. When she saw the little girl with the strawberry curls for the first time, Karen's eyes teared. She wiped her eyes with her fingers, willing the tears away. No time for sorrow now. The job demanded her full attention.

Deidre seemed quiet and unfocused, but functional. Eyes dull and heavy-lidded, she stood apart from the other children clutching a rag doll under her left arm and sucking her right thumb.

A low flame of suppressed anger began in Karen's stomach. Deidre's parents had been locked into their own rage, unable to put Deidre's life first. The child would never be normal again. Deidre was a victim of a tragic struggle. All Karen could do now was try to mitigate the damage. And get the bastard responsible.

Like every good lawyer, she'd analyzed the risks, then constructed plan A and plan B. With plan A, she and Deidre returned home without Jeffrey's interference, luring him back into the U.S. where authorities would arrest him. Plan B provided an alternative if Jeffrey attempted to thwart her. He would be dealt with at the border crossing. At least, in theory.

Yet again, she regretted the decision she'd had to make about the gun and prayed her alternative would work, even if it cost her her own life.

As always before executing the final stages of retrieval, Karen slept fitfully. Finally, at 4:00 a.m., she gave up the effort.

She arrived at the school two hours early and parked down the street, waiting for Deidre's arrival. Just before nine, a station wagon stopped. A young woman helped Deidre out of the back seat, and held her hand as they walked to the school's front entrance. The woman was gentle with Deidre, but Deidre demonstrated no affection when they parted. Deidre walked into the school, slowly and alone, dragging the rag doll with her. The woman returned to the station wagon and left.

When the children entered the playground for recess, Karen left her car and strolled over. She called to Deidre twice. The child looked up. A broad grin slowly lit her face. Deidre loped toward her.

"Aunt Karen!" she said, crying as Karen picked her up and hugged her, too tightly. The child felt thinner inside her clothes. Karen's sadness, followed by hot anger, returned.

Within a few moments, Karen had explained to Deidre's teacher that Deidre had a dentist's appointment and produced a forged note from Jeffrey allowing her to take the child. The teacher looked at Karen carefully, but released Deidre, probably in part because Deidre continued to hold on to Karen as if she never wanted to let go. Less than fifteen minutes after Karen first saw Deidre on the playground, they were driving toward Lewiston. So far, plan A seemed to be working.

Constantly checking the rearview mirror, she retraced the route she'd taken the day before. Deidre, securely belted in the back seat, had returned to her subdued behavior. She talked quietly to the rag doll she'd brought along with her. About an hour into the drive, her eyelids closed, her chin gently touched her chest and she fell into the rhythm of sleep. A bit of drool slid from the corner of her mouth onto the doll's head. She was so young, so sweet. So undeserving of this mess. Karen clenched the steering wheel so tight her hands cramped.

Was Jeffrey controlling her with medication of some kind? Another thing to despise him for. She glanced at her watch. Just like yesterday, she was right on time.

When they approached the border crossing, Karen located the passports, prepared to show them if she had to. She'd seen no sign of Jeffrey or anyone following her for the entire return trip, which worried her.

Jeffrey was crazy, violent, controlling. She'd expected him to know where Deidre was every second, and to come after her. Or at least, Jeffrey should have learned Deidre was abducted and reasoned that Karen would take the shortest route back to the U.S.

So far, she hadn't seen Jeffrey. But her senses were on alert. She'd learned never to underestimate him. There was something she'd missed. Somehow, she believed, when they reached the border, he'd be there. Plan B. Could she pull it off?

Supremely focused now, she drove over the bridge without noticing the spectacular views of Niagara Gorge. At the U.S. checkpoint, the line of vehicles moved swiftly through the single open kiosk. She looked into the cinder-block customs building, which also housed the duty-free store. She saw one officer behind the counter, and one clerk in the store waiting on a customer.

While she watched, the customer carried a bottle of liquor in a plain brown bag to the rusty battered panel van in front of her and got in. The panel van belched smoke when it backfired, and its muffler had long ago surrendered to the rust belt.

Midweek, off season, at lunchtime, the entire area was relaxed, thinly patrolled and almost deserted. She hoped this would make Jeffrey more obvious, if he appeared and tried anything.

Karen mentally rehearsed the lie she'd tell if the customs officer asked her more than routine questions. Yesterday, the process was casual, easy, intended to encourage tourism, not to thwart a kidnapper.

Two cars ahead passed through the checkpoint. When the panel van jerked toward the kiosk window, Karen pulled up and waited at the yellow line. The van blocked her view of the officer. She glanced again toward the duty-free store. She saw a lone figure, vaguely familiar, standing outside.

Jeffrey. He'd shaved his head and wore sunglasses. She didn't know how he'd found her, but he had. A tracking device on Deidre somewhere? Regular calls to the school just to check on his daughter? However he'd managed it, he was here now. She had to move. Adrenaline made her heart pound and sweat bead on her brow. Plan B. *Stay calm.*

Checking the rearview, she realized she'd have to move forward. An eighteen-wheeler six feet behind blocked any alternative.

The officer in the kiosk seemed to be chatting too long with the occupants of the van. But she couldn't see him, and he couldn't see her. She tapped the steering wheel impatiently.

Mimicking the guy who'd joined the van, Jeffrey strolled toward her car. Quiet panic fluttered in her chest as she watched him. Did anyone else see him? He reached the door, looked directly into her eyes as if to mesmerize her, grasped the handle and lifted it.

The locked door didn't open. Then he glanced into the back seat where Deidre slept, covered by the blanket Karen had brought, still holding the doll. A smirk creased his face. It was the doll. That's where he'd hidden the tracking device. *Bastard. You think you're so clever. We'll see.*

Karen lowered the back window and Jeffrey stuck his left hand on top of the glass. "Go away, Jeffrey, while you still can. If you try anything here, they'll kill you. Your choice."

He laughed. "You're kidnapping my child, Karen. Do you really think they'll take your side over mine?"

While he held on to the glass and the door handle Karen punched the accelerator. The car leaped forward. Jeffrey lost his balance. She slammed the brake.

The car's quick jerk threw him to the ground. Her actions, and Jeffrey's, were blocked from the customs officer's view by the panel van, which moved forward now, slowly, through the gate. Maybe surveillance cameras saw him. Surely, the border guards would protect her and the child. She hoped.

The officer waved her ahead. She released a breath and eased to a stop next to the booth, left hand on the wheel.

"What's your citizenship, ma'am?" the kindly old officer asked.

"U.S." She glanced in the right-side mirror. Jeffrey had risen from the ground. His stare carried a malevolence she could feel. *Bastard. Go away. While you still can.*

The customs officer glanced into the back seat now, too, where Deidre slept. At the same time, he noticed Jeffrey, hands in the oversize pocket of his sweatshirt, not moving, saying nothing.

The officer became more alert. "How about the child, ma'am?" Another officer came out of the building, hand on his gun, waiting. They had seen him try to enter her car. It was working. Plan B was working. *Thank God.*

"U.S., too." Small rivulets of sweat tickled her armpits. *Let us go, Jeffrey, and live to try again.*

"Picture ID?"

Karen reached into her handbag, retrieved the passports and handed them to the officer. He examined the blue-jacketed folders. "Your name is Karen Ann Brown? And hers is Deidre London?"

"Divorce," she said. Jeffrey simply stood there. What was he thinking? Was he willing to die to thwart her?

The officer glanced at Jeffrey again. "Do you have her birth certificate?"

She furrowed her brow with consternation. "I didn't think you'd need it."

He closed the passports and gestured toward the building. "I'm sorry, ma'am. Park over there and go inside where they'll verify your identification." Then he nodded at Jeffrey, who stood stock-still, feet braced shoulder width apart, hands still inside his big front pocket. "Do you know him?"

Now. Now was the time. "He's got a gun."

Before the officer could react, Jeffrey slowly extracted his hand from the sweatshirt and pointed the gun at her head.

"Get down! Get down!" the officer shouted, squatting beside the car's engine block, the only place safe from gunfire.

Jeffrey chose death. The deafening noise of shots rang out. Bullets entered the rear glass. One grazed her arm as she fell sideways. Another exited inches from where her head had been an instant before. The pain seared through her as blood soaked her blazer and ran down her arm. Deidre began to scream.

Border guards acted immediately. They shouted for Jeffrey to drop his gun. He didn't. A guard shot and hit Jeffrey in the leg. He went down, and kept shooting. Bullets tattooed the back of the sedan. *Idiot! You'll hit Deidre!*

After an excruciatingly long few seconds, the customs officer in the booth drew his weapon, and two additional officers ran out from the building. "Drop your gun! Drop your gun!"

Karen looked into Jeffrey's eyes. Either of them could have changed things at that moment. But they didn't. She jammed the accelerator to the floorboard. The sedan lurched forward, broke through the wooden gate and raced onto American soil.

Jeffrey shot at Karen's car again. As she'd known they would, the guards returned fire.

Karen mashed the brake, jerking the sedan to a stop behind the solid walls of the U.S. Customs station. Applying pressure to her throbbing, bleeding arm, she managed to open the back door and unsnap Deidre's seat belt. She slid the hysterical child onto the pavement. Determined, Karen held Deidre close until the deafening gunfire stopped.

In the brief silence, Deidre's screams became sobs. Karen struggled to rise while holding the girl, despite the searing pain in her arm, and stumbled back to the kiosk. Jeffrey lay on the ground, blood running from his mouth, lifeless eyes staring straight at her. Her first thought was, *Thank God*.

Karen's anger flared, leaving no room for remorse. He'd chosen to die rather than let Karen take Deidre. He'd intended to get all three of them killed.

A few weeks later, Karen joined Brenda, who sat watching Deidre on the Land of the Dragons playground. The family resemblance was unmistakable. Both were clearly from Beverly London's gene pool. In Deidre, Karen saw some hint of Jeffrey, too. How could a wonderful child have emerged from two such damaged parents?

"She looks happy, doesn't she?" Brenda asked with a wistful tone. Deidre was in counseling and taking medication that the psychologist hoped would help her to work through the traumas she'd endured at her parents' hands.

To reassure her, Karen said, "Don't worry so much. She's young. With luck and love, she won't remember most of it."

A tear rolled down Brenda's cheek. Her lips quivered. "She won't have much to remember about her mother."

Karen closed her eyes against tears of her own. She had risked her life so that Deidre might thrive. Now, all she could do was hope. "It's up to you to keep Beverly alive for her."

Together, they watched Deidre climb the rope ladders and slide down the dragon's tail, laughing when she landed on her butt in the sand.

"Beverly was so smitten. And he loved her, too." Brenda stopped, bewildered. "What went wrong?"

Karen rubbed her sore arm to stop its pulsing. Like Jeffrey's effect on his child, Karen's wound would hurt for a long time and leave a permanent scar. She rejected sweetening the truth. To defeat Jeffrey forever, Brenda must do her part. "She knew he was dangerous before she married him. She ignored her instincts and deceived herself. The best thing you can do for Beverly now is to make sure Deidre doesn't repeat that pattern."

And I'll be watching.

CHRISTOPHER REICH

Numbered Account was Christopher Reich's first book. And not just his first work to be published, but the first Reich ever tried to write. He never took an English class in college. The drawers of his work desk did not contain drafts of earlier novels, short stories or aborted screenplays. *Numbered Account* was it for him. One chance to make it as a writer or return to the salt mines of the financial world—more mergers and acquisitions—more back to work. "The struggling writer, the starving artist…that's the other guy," Reich liked to say.

Numbered Account came from Reich's own wanderings of the snowy, cobblestone alleyways of Geneva, on his way to and from work at the Union Bank of Switzerland. There, he learned the sophisticated art of handling money for the richest people in the world. For Reich, the seeds of *Numbered Account* were planted on his first day of work. But it was six years later before he realized that some people are cut out for fourteen-hour days and he wasn't one of them. So Reich decided to write a novel and always knew that it was going to be a thriller. To his credit, *Numbered Account* went on to become a *New York Times* bestseller.

Assassins, the story for this collection, finds the hero of *Numbered Account*, Nick Neumann, back on Swiss soil with a new mission. This is the first time Reich has written about Nick since 1997. All thriller writers know that it's never wise to fall in love with any particular character. Who knows when they might turn a corner and walk right into a knife, or a gun, or a poison-tipped umbrella?

So Nick Neumann should tread carefully.

ASSASSINS

Nick Neumann sat stiffly in the corner booth, back pressed against the leather banquette, shoulders pinned in the finest Swiss tradition. He was tired and hungry, and he wished the dinner would come so he could get on with the job. He placed his hands on the tablecloth, willing himself not to adjust the cutlery or examine the stemware. The heavy sterling knives and forks and spoons were, he noted, perfectly placed. The glasses were made of Austrian crystal, and absent the slightest smudge. Whenever he wondered how he had survived so long, the answer always came back the same.

Details.

Turning his head, he let his eyes wander the restaurant. At a few minutes past seven, the Kronenhalle was nearly full. It was a Friday, and the weather had been unseasonably cool for early October. He had always thought of the Kronenhalle as a cold-weather restaurant. The tightly placed booths, the bold lighting, the crisp tablecloths, the bustle of waiters across the hardwood floor, the chef guiding his gleaming wagon down the narrow aisles, and of course, the hearty cuisine. All of it conspired to create a cozy formality, a warm and convivial antidote to rain and snow and biting wind.

Expertly, he scanned the dining room for a familiar face. The men were ruddy, well fed and prosperous. The women were elegantly dressed, and, if not as beautiful as their Parisian or Roman counterparts, as immaculately coiffed. He recognized no one and admitted to relief. Anonymity was a cornerstone of his profession.

Neumann checked his watch. He had ordered eleven minutes ago and his appetizer had not yet been served. Not long by any measure, but he was more nervous than the assignment demanded, and anxious to see it to its completion.

Zurich.

Years ago, he had lived in this city. He had worked at a prominent bank. He had fallen in love. He had killed a man and put another in prison. His stay had been short—a few months, no more—but his memories of it had proven long-lived. It was those memories that made him restless and antsy. Not for the first time, he wondered if he should have turned the job down.

Just then, the table rocked slightly as the chef arrived with his wagon. A wineglass teetered and Neumann rushed to stop it from overturning. *Point against.*

"*Gerstensuppe?*" The name on the smock read "Stutz." Wrong man.

"*Bitte,*" said Neumann, not caring to meet his gaze.

With ceremony, the chef dipped his ladle and poured a generous cup of soup. The aroma of beef stock and barley tickled Neumann's nose. The brass stockpot was polished as well as a symphony instrument. *Point in favor*.

Neumann picked up his soupspoon and began to eat. He noted the broth's consistency, the pleasant aftertaste of sherry and mark. The temperature was ideal. The flavor full bodied but clean. Invariably, he dined alone. It was one of the challenging aspects of the job. Still, if he must dine by himself, at least he dined well. He never arrived in a city without having laid out his culinary itinerary in advance.

Details.

Tonight, the *gerstensuppe* would be followed by a warm *nussli* salad with chopped bacon and crumbled Stilton cheese, and as an entrée, the specialty of the house, *zurigeschnetzltes mit rosti*. For dessert, there would be chocolate mousse and coffee. Besides an aperitif of champagne, he did not drink. A man in his profession was wise not to dull his senses.

It was then that he saw him.

There, across the room, removing his trench coat and hanging it on the rack, was Milos the Greek. He was grayer, his posture bent more than in the past, but it was him, all the same. There was no doubting the sharp nose, the tortoiseshell glasses, the hair combed and parted with military precision. Neumann had taught himself never to stare, but for a moment he couldn't help himself.

The Greek was in Zurich.

Calmly, he continued with his soup. He tore off a roll and buttered his bread. He sipped his flute of champagne. But all the while he kept a discreet eye on the Greek who, like him, was seated alone at a table in the main *salle*, back to the wall with a view on the entry and exit. Another man with a past. A fugitive unsure where and when an enemy might appear with retribution foremost on his mind. A professional who did not welcome surprises.

When Neumann looked up from his soup, the Greek was smiling his sly smile, his hard gray eyes locked on his own. He had been spotted, too. A shiver passed through him. Recognition was a constant risk. Some wore disguises: wigs, mustaches, spectacles. Some even tinted their hair and dressed against type. But not the Greek. He'd never made his identity an issue. Neumann had decided he wouldn't either. For better or worse, his face was a liability to be factored into his assignments.

Neumann raised his eyebrows and gestured toward the empty seat across from him. For a moment, the Greek hesitated. There was no etiquette governing what two men in their profession were to do should they meet. They had never been formally introduced, yet by reputation they were well acquainted. These days it was a small world, and in their rarefied circles, smaller yet.

The Greek was renowned for his hawk's eye. It was said that he was able to spot the smallest slipup, the split-second lapse that led to a target's demise. When he found the killspot, he was merciless.

Neumann knew his own reputation, as well. They said he had an uncanny ability to pinpoint the larger flaws, the structural weaknesses that would compromise the target. Bravado was his strong suit. Even the long-entrenched *Capos*, protected by their armies of minions and bully boys, were not safe from his reach. Some questioned his abilities, claiming an American didn't possess the finesse for the work. Not in Europe. They said he was best left to the gunslingers in

Las Vegas and Miami Beach. The loudmouthed impresarios in Manhattan. And the braggarts in Beverly Hills. Six years in the trade said they were wrong.

The Greek shrugged, rose from his table and ventured across the room. "Finally, we meet," he said, offering an arthritic hand.

Neumann stood. "A pleasure. Won't you join me?"

The Greek sat down and spent a long moment placing the napkin in his lap, adjusting his necktie, pulling the cuffs from his sleeves. Finally, he looked up. "I trust you ordered the specialty of the house."

"Each year I think of choosing something else, but can't quite force myself to do it."

"In summer, I prefer the Dover sole. I ask them to grill it, then add lemon juice. Never any butter."

"I'll make a note of it." But Neumann was sure to keep his hands away from his jacket for fear of upsetting the uneasy truce.

The Greek leaned forward, beckoning with his trigger finger. "I've heard rumors."

Neumann shifted uncomfortably. "Oh?"

"They say that you enjoy your work as much as I do."

Neumann considered this. "It's a living."

The Greek laughed richly. "A paltry one for the services we provide. We cull the weak from the strong. I think of it as 'natural selection.' Tell me one thing. Are you satisfied?"

"More or less. You?"

"After so many years, there can only be one answer. However, I find that it's hard on the soul. I only think of the bad ones. I feel as if my hands were covered in blood. So many dreams destroyed. I sleep poorly."

The waiter arrived. The Greek made sure to hear the specials, then said, "The same as my friend."

"And the champagne…Veuve Clicquot is acceptable?"

"Eminently." The Greek measured Neumann with a respectful eye. "You're here on assignment."

"Unfortunately. And you?"

"I can't afford to quit. A tip…Rome…Sabatini…the trout isn't bad."

"Beirut…Alfredo's…minced lamb and couscous. Passable."

"You travel to Beirut?"

"The region's a bit unstable, but if you know your way around, it can be lucrative."

The Greek motioned toward his jacket. "May I?"

Neumann studied the cut of the coat, then said, "Yes."

"My memory isn't what it used to be." The hand dug out a small notepad and jotted down a few words. "Did you hear about Yuri? He let one off the hook."

Neumann didn't bother hiding his shock. Yuri's reputation was second to none. He was ruthless, daring, and always relentless. A master. "Was he terminated?"

"There are no second chances in this game. At least, he can be thankful it was quick."

"What happened?"

"They lured him back to the head office in Paris. The Boss likes to do it in person." To make his point, the Greek made a grotesque pantomime of slashing his own throat. Despite himself, Neumann winced. The Greek removed his glasses and spent a long moment polishing them with his napkin. "And now you and I together in Zurich?" he said absently. "After the same target. Hardly a coincidence, I imagine."

"Probably not."

"Contract or freelance?"

"Contract. You?"

"Same as ever."

"And so?"

"We do what we must do. It is our calling. May I wish you luck."

"Likewise." Neumann smiled to himself, viewing the assignment with added relish. He'd always enjoyed competition, the zest of going face-to-face with another as well trained.

The meal arrived. Heaping portions of sliced, infinitely tender veal bathed in a delicate cream sauce were portioned onto generous wedges of lightly fried potatoes. He picked up his knife and fork, hesitating at the last instant. "A Bordeaux? After all, for one of us, it is to be his last meal."

"The LaTour '79 would be suitable."

"Eminently," said Neumann.

Afterward, the two men strolled across the Limmat Bridge. The rain had frozen to sleet. A stiff wind blew off the lake. Winter was near.

"And so?" asked the Greek.

"One star," declared Neumann. "Very good in its category."

"Two," said the Greek. "Worth a detour to visit."

"Never!" Neumann looked at Milos, bent, satisfied, content, and in that instant, knew that his own skills were superior, that he would triumph, and that the Greek would make the lonely trip to Paris and give up his badge as an inspector for the Michelin *Guide Rouge*.

"It's true, then, what they say," Milos whispered, his tired voice hardly audible above the wind.

"What's that?" asked Neumann.

"You're an assassin."

BRAD THOR

Brad Thor spends a lot of time in Greece and has always wanted to set a novel there. When he was approached to write for this anthology, he knew right away that he wanted to write about an idea that came to him in the Greek Islands several years ago.

For decades a terrorist organization known as 17 November wreaked havoc throughout Greece. In fact, the United States still spends more money defending its embassy in Athens than any other embassy in Europe. It started in 1975 when the organization assassinated the CIA's Athens station chief with what would become its trademark .45-caliber pistol. Since then, the group has claimed responsibility for twenty-one murders, four of which were U.S. diplomats. Though 17 November's initial attacks were directed at senior U.S. officials and Greek public figures, they eventually expanded their targets to include ordinary citizens, foreign businesses and European Union facilities.

Thor was always perplexed by the government's inability to make any progress in bringing 17 November to justice. For years, no member of the organization had ever been arrested, and no clues as to who was orchestrating their attacks had ever been found.

A breakthrough occurred in 2002 when a bomb being carried by a forty-year-old icon painter prematurely detonated in the Athenian port of Piraeus. The bomber was also carrying a set of keys and a prepaid telephone card, which led police to an apartment in downtown Athens packed with antitank rockets, missiles and other weapons. Within two weeks, police uncovered a string of 17 November safe houses, two of which contained additional caches of weapons, disguises and the group's signature .45-caliber Colt 1911 semiautomatic pistol used in some of their most high-profile assassinations.

Since those successes things have been relatively quiet in Greece, but intelligence officials are concerned that several members of the organization may have slipped through their net and have gone deeper underground. These same officials worry that if and when these last remaining members do surface again, it will be with a terrible vengeance.

Which brings us to *The Athens Solution*.

THE ATHENS SOLUTION

June 12
Athens, Greece

U.S. ambassador to Greece Michael Avery picked his way through the late-afternoon throng of tourists clogging Athens's famous Plaka district. Behind him, a team of CIA operatives mixed within the crowd, while two streets over, in a nondescript van, a contingent of heavily armed Diplomatic Security Service agents and NSA communications experts followed as closely as they dared. Avery had been told to come alone, but both the Departments of State and Defense would hear nothing of it. Too much was at stake.

With his crisp white sport shirt and blue blazer, Avery looked like any other upscale Westerner visiting Greece during the height of the tourist season. He even had a small backpack casually slung over one shoulder. But unlike the other backpacks around him, his contained an encrypted laptop, complete with a wireless modem and sophisticated remote-viewing application.

He was passing a small outdoor café with a nice view of the Acropolis and the majestic Parthenon atop it when his cell phone rang.

"Stop here and take a table," said a voice with a heavy Greek accent. "You know what to do next."

Yes, the ambassador did know what to do next. A CD ROM and final set of instructions had been delivered to the embassy that morning. The instructions indicated that the CD could only be used once and that any attempts to copy or crack it before the appointed time would result in all of its data being destroyed.

Avery sat down at a table and, after ordering coffee, removed the encrypted laptop from his backpack and powered it up. The CD whirred in its tray. Within moments an instant-message screen appeared and the words, "Good afternoon, Mr. Ambassador. Thank you for coming," flashed.

Back in the van, the NSA communications experts could see in real time exactly what the ambassador was seeing, thanks to the laptop's remote-viewing application, and began trying to locate the source of the transmission.

Are you prepared to transfer the funds? appeared next.

How do we know the merchandise is authentic? typed Avery.

One word was returned, Watch.

The ambassador's screen split into two separate windows. Next to the dialogue box, an image came up entitled JFK/ATC. He discreetly tilted his head and spoke toward the microphone sewn into the lapel of his blazer, "Are you getting this?"

"Loud and clear. So is Washington," replied one of the techs in the van. A satellite uplink was beaming everything back to the States for verification.

Avery pressed the mini-earpiece farther into his ear as he anxiously awaited word. Seconds later, it came.

"Verification complete. Mr. Ambassador, you are looking at a live picture of JFK's Air Traffic Control system."

Knowing what would happen next sent chills down Michael Avery's spine. His hands shook as he typed the following message, We are ready to proceed.

One by one, aircraft started disappearing from the screen.

Ninety seconds later, the NSA man's voice came back over the ambassador's earpiece. "JFK is reporting a major ATC system malfunction. They're losing track of aircraft left and right. The merchandise is authentic. You are authorized to complete the transaction."

Initializing funds transfer, typed the ambassador as he began the predetermined sequence. The green status bar seemed to take forever. When the *Transfer Successful* message finally materialized on the screen, aircraft flying in the New York area began reappearing on ATC radar.

Simultaneously, a third window appeared on the ambassador's laptop. In it, he could see a live picture of the device the United States had just paid so handsomely for. As the image widened, he could see the Parthenon in the foreground.

"We're on it," said one of the NSA men over Avery's earpiece as the van took off to claim the merchandise.

The ambassador continued to watch the feed as a pair of hands came into view, picked up the device and secreted it inside the nearest trash can, as agreed, for pickup.

"Sir," said one of the CIA operatives as he approached the table. "There's a car waiting. We'd like to get you back to the embassy."

Avery nodded his head and was just about to shut down his laptop when he noticed the live image from the Acropolis was moving. There were jerky flashes of legs and feet as someone moved the camera and repositioned it overlooking the road below. Seconds later, the white embassy van with the Diplomatic Security Service agents and the NSA team entered the frame.

"Jesus Christ," said Avery. "It's a trap. Get them out!"

The CIA operative who had been sitting in the café looking over the ambassador's shoulder grabbed both him and the laptop while shouting into his radio, "Beachcomber, this is Point Guard. You've been compromised. Abort now. Repeat. You have been compromised. Abort!"

Before the men in the white van could respond, they heard what sounded like a giant knife tearing through the fabric of the afternoon sky. The ambassador grabbed the laptop back just in time to see a shoulder-fired missile slam through the windshield of the van and explode.

The CIA operative, code named Point Guard, didn't waste any more time. He steered the ambassador out of the café and down the closest side street as he radioed the driver of their car to come get them. The other operatives headed for the Acropolis as people ran out of the shops and restaurants around the Plaka in response to the explosion.

As Point Guard and the ambassador turned the next corner, the pair could see the embassy's dark, armor-plated BMW and began running even faster. They were *almost* there.

Suddenly, a motorcycle screamed out of a nearby alleyway. Point Guard reached for his gun, but he was too late.

One week later
Dodecanese Islands
Southeastern Aegean, Greece

Lying in the tall grass one hundred meters from a sprawling, whitewashed villa, Scot Harvath used the Leupold Mark 4 scope and Universal Night Sight of his SR25 Knights Armament battle rifle to search for any sign of Theologos Papandreou, the man U.S. Intelligence had fingered as the mastermind behind the murder of Ambassador Avery and his multiagency security detail.

As a Navy SEAL, and now as a covert counterterrorism operative for the U.S. government, Harvath had spent the better part of his professional life pulling a trigger. One of the sadder truths he had learned was that there were a lot of people in the world who needed to be killed. He tried to remind himself that more often than not, the people on the receiving end of his lead-tipped missives were beyond reasoning with. They posed serious threats to the stability and safety of the civilized world and had to be taken out.

Tonight, though, Harvath had his doubts. Something didn't feel right.

Before leaving D.C., Harvath had been fully briefed on the murder of Ambassador Avery. Two years prior, a Greek company headed by a man named Constantine Nomikos had approached the United States to partner up on a technology venture. They were developing a revolutionary new system to better track their fleet of next-generation tanker and cargo ships worldwide. Nomikos needed heavy access to satellite and radar systems to further his research. While reviewing the project, the U.S. had noted several excellent military applications and immediately jumped into bed with them. It wasn't until later in the development process that the Defense Department discovered the device's full potential.

Anything with an electronic guidance system—aircraft, missiles, ships—could be rendered completely invisible to radar. But that was only the half of it. The device could also override guidance systems and remotely control an object's course, speed, trajectory—you name it. With the right satellite uplinks, a missile could be diverted off course or a plane could be hijacked without terrorists ever having to set foot on board.

The Defense Department deemed it one of the most exciting and dangerous pieces of technology ever developed. They also gave it its code name, the *Achilles Project*.

Two weeks prior to Ambassador Avery's assassination, the device had been stolen from Nomikos's research and development facility near the Athenian port of Piraeus. Shortly thereafter, an unidentified organization contacted the U.S. embassy in Athens and offered to sell it back to the United States. Avery and his team had been participating in an operation to recover the device when they were killed.

Despite the fact that a firebomb had been tossed into the car after the shooting and the bodies were burned beyond recognition, ballistics reports indicated that the weapon used to kill Ambassador Avery, as well as the CIA operative accompanying him, was a .45-caliber automatic—the same .45 caliber used in a string of high-profile assassinations attributed to the Greek terrorist organization 21 August.

The name 21 August corresponded to the organization's first attack. On August 21, 1975, they shot and killed the CIA's Athens chief and deputy chief of station.. In a long and rambling letter to a left-wing Athenian newspaper, they claimed credit for the murders, spelled out their Marxist-Leninist beliefs and outlined their plans for ridding Greece once and for all of any Western—specifically American—influences.

Be that as it may, the current president of the United States had different plans for 21 August. He was furious that in a country of only eleven million, the Greeks couldn't seem to lay their hands on what every Western intelligence agency agreed was a cell of no more than ten or fifteen people. The "Athens Problem," as it had become known in Western intelligence circles, had been a problem for too long, and he wanted it stopped. He wanted 21 August neutralized before they could mount any more attacks against American interests or, God forbid, sold the Achilles device to one of America's enemies.

The CIA had tentatively identified Papandreou, an associate of Constantine Nomikos, as a key personality behind 21 August. Evidence also suggested he had a hand in the attacks upon Ambassador Avery and his team. The dots didn't connect for Harvath as cleanly as he would have liked—and certainly not cleanly enough to base a decision to take a man's life, but nevertheless, he had his orders. He had been sent to Greece to take Papandreou out as quickly as possible and recover the Achilles device by any means necessary. Adding to the mission's urgency, the CIA had just learned that 21 August had a buyer for the device—an unidentified Jordanian national, and the transaction was going to take place any day.

Still dubious about the intelligence the U.S. had gathered from its Greek sources, Harvath glanced at his Kobold tactical wristwatch and wondered where the hell his target was. Papandreou should have been here by now.

Suddenly, the sound of the ocean crashing on the rocky beach below was replaced by the sound of tires crunching down the villa's long gravel drive. Harvath readied his rifle and pressed himself flatter against the damp earth. He prayed to God his superiors back in Washington weren't making a mistake.

A blue Land Rover rolled to a stop before the large double doors of the house. When the driver's door opened Harvath peered through his scope, but it was no good. He couldn't see the man's face. He'd have to wait for him to exit the vehicle.

"Norseman, can you properly ID the target?" said a voice over his headset, thousands of miles away in the White House Situation Room.

"Negative," replied Harvath. "Stand by."

Pressing his eye tighter against his scope, Harvath strained to get a positive identification on Papandreou so he could do his job and pull the trigger.

"Norseman, satellite is giving us only one, I repeat *one* individual in that vehicle. Can you confirm the subject's identity? Do we have our man?"

Command-and-control elements in the rear always wanted to know everything that was going on in the field. Harvath, though, couldn't give them a play-by-play *and* pay full attention to his assignment, so he gave them the field operative's polite equivalent of *shut the hell up*, "Clear the net."

The chatter on his headset fell silent and Harvath watched as the driver began to exit the vehicle. From where he was positioned, he'd have to wait until the man came around the Land Rover and made it to the double doors of the villa before he had not only a clear view of his face but also a clean shot to take him out.

"Ten seconds until subject ID," said Harvath, more for his own benefit than the men and women gathered in the Situation Room.

Three more steps, Harvath thought to himself as the man rounded the grille of the Land Rover.

It was hot and Harvath could feel beads of perspiration collecting on his forehead. *What if this wasn't the right guy?*

As the man's head came into view, Harvath took a deep breath, held it, but delayed applying pressure to the trigger of his SR25. *A few more steps*, he thought to himself. *A few more steps.*

Suddenly a shot rang out and Harvath's target fell face-first in a spray of blood onto the gravel drive.

"What the—" Harvath whispered into his microphone.

"Norseman," came the voice from the Situation Room. "What just happened?"

Harvath scanned the area as best he could with his scope. "We have another shooter on-site and the subject has been downed. Who else is on this job?"

"You're the only operator on this assignment," replied the voice from Washington. "Can you ID the target?"

Harvath stared through his scope at the man lying in the driveway. "Negative. A positive ID is impossible from my position."

Moments later the voice responded. "Norseman,

you're going to need to change your position ASAP and get that ID."

"The subject's facedown in the gravel."

"Then get down there and lift him up."

Harvath tried to keep his anger in check. "We've got an active shooter. I need you to pinpoint him for me first."

"Negative, Norseman," said the voice from the Situation Room. "No can do. All the infrared satellite is showing is you and the subject adjacent to the vehicle."

"No heat signature from a recently discharged weapon?" asked Harvath, though he knew if they could see it, they'd tell him.

"That's a negative. No heat signature."

Whoever that shooter was, he was very good and being very careful.

Harvath was truly up against it. There was no way he could move to the driveway, not when the other sniper could be out there waiting for someone to approach the body.

Though he was trained to expect the unexpected, an additional shooter was something Harvath hadn't banked on. Nevertheless, the idea that somebody else might be after the Achilles device was perfectly reasonable, but none of that mattered now. Harvath needed to identify the guy in the driveway and make his way into the villa where the device was supposedly being kept, and to do that, he was going to need a distraction.

Waiting for him two hundred meters offshore was the *Amalia,* a weather-beaten Greek trawler manned by the only two people in Greece Harvath could trust, Ben and Yannis Metaxas. Harvath had met Ben while his SEAL team was training in the Aegean with the Greek navy. The two had become fast friends, and to this day Harvath still spent a good amount of his vacation time every year kicking back at Ben's beach bar on the island of Antiparos.

Changing his radio frequency, Harvath raised Ben out on the *Amalia* and told him what had happened and what he needed him to do. When Ben's flare broke over the water four and a half minutes later, Harvath was already up and running.

He never bothered ID'ing the body—it would have been suicide. Instead, Harvath grabbed the man by the collar, kicked open the villa's double doors and dragged him inside the courtyard. It was only then that Harvath rolled the body over. There was no mistaking the man whose photo he had seen during his briefing in Washington, Constantine Nomikos. *What the hell was he doing here?* Harvath examined him. Head wounds always bled profusely and he looked like he had lost a lot of blood. Harvath doubted he would make it.

"Goddammit," he mumbled under his breath. Nomikos had picked a hell of a time to come visit his old pal. Changing freqs, Harvath clued the Situation Room in on the development.

With no other vehicles inbound, Harvath was told to shift to locating the Achilles device. *Easy for them to say,* he thought. Somewhere, very nearby, was a killer who was most probably sent to Papandreou's villa with the same orders as he was.

With the Metaxas brothers offshore on the *Amalia*, Harvath had no direct backup. He could only rely on himself. He was in the process of rigging a booby trap when the landscaping lights illuminating the neat rows of olive trees throughout the courtyard dimmed and went dark. Harvath had been in this game long enough to know there was no such thing as coincidence. The other sniper had just cut the power. That could only mean one thing—he was about to breach the villa. Harvath needed to move.

Finding the front door unlocked, Harvath quickly made his way inside and searched for the study. Five minutes later, he had uncovered Papandreou's safe. While he knew more than most about safecracking, tonight it made no difference. Secreted behind a false panel was an American-made Safari-brand safe. Safaris were the best and Harvath knew he had no choice but to blow it. The only question was whether or not he'd brought along enough C4.

Considering Safari's impregnable reputation, Harvath prepared to use everything he had. If he overestimated and it resulted in him damaging the Achilles device inside, then so be it. He knew Washington would be glad just to know the device was out of commission.

Taking cover behind Papandreou's desk, Harvath blew the door off its hinges in an enormous explosion. Once the smoke had cleared, he rushed forward only to discover that it was totally empty.

The CIA was positive the device was being kept at the villa—most likely in Papandreou's safe, but apparently that location had seemed too obvious.

Knowing that blowing the safe had drawn the attention of the other sniper, Harvath quickly exited the room and began making his way down the hallway, his SR25 up and at the ready.

He passed several rooms, and was about to pass the kitchen when something caught his eye and caused him to back up. In the middle of the kitchen floor was a trapdoor standing wide open. After double-checking the SureFire flashlight mounted to his rifle, Harvath swept into the kitchen and made his way down the stone steps beneath the trapdoor.

The steps led him into a low-ceilinged, rough-hewn corridor illuminated by a string of bare bulbs. From what he could tell, a generator somewhere at the end of the corridor was powering the lights.

Harvath hated tunnels. They provided little cover and had a rather undesirable propensity for funneling enemy fire right at you.

Hugging the wall, he made his way toward a fissure of some sort at the end of the corridor. He was now well beyond the grounds of the villa above and could smell saltwater from somewhere off in the distance.

He entered the fissure and had to crouch to make it through, but when he emerged thirty-five meters later he found himself in a brightly illuminated grotto with a narrow strip of sandy beach. Upon it were parked two heavily armed, high-end Farallon DPVs, or Diver Propulsion Vehicles. The lingering doubts Harvath had harbored about Papandreou's innocence were beginning to melt away.

From the far end of the beach, a flash of sparks and a high-pitched, grinding whine caught Harvath's attention. A figure dressed in black was using what appeared to be a circular saw to carve into a metal canister propped between two large rocks. Harvath's instinct was to call in what he was seeing to Washington, but he had lost all radio contact the minute he had entered the first subterranean passage.

A million questions raced through his mind, the answers to which appeared to be on the beach.

Harvath found a narrow footpath and carefully picked his way down, never once taking his eyes off the figure so intent upon opening the metal canister wedged between the rocks. When his feet hit the sand, Harvath moved forward as silently as a shadow.

With sparks flying and the grinding of metal upon metal, the black-clad figure never noticed Harvath's approach. When the suppressor of Harvath's SR25 was pressed up against the back of the man's wet suit, he let the saw fall to the ground.

Harvath told the man to turn around slowly, and when he did, Harvath was rendered nearly speechless. "Ambassador Avery," he stated. "I don't understand. I thought you were dead."

An aura of shock was replaced by one of dignity and power as the silver-haired ambassador replied, "Obviously I'm not. Who the hell are you?"

"My name's Harvath. I was tasked by the Pentagon to find your killers."

"The Pentagon? They couldn't find their ass with both hands. I suppose you've also been tasked with retrieving the device."

There was something about looking into the eyes of a dead man that caused Harvath to mentally pull back and play it dumb until he could get a handle on what was going on. "The *device*, sir?"

"Don't bullshit me," commanded Avery. "That's what this is all about. Put your weapon down and give me a hand. We haven't got much time."

"Where's Papandreou?"

Avery was silent and so Harvath repeated, "Where is Papandreou, sir?"

"Somebody took him for a swim," said the ambassador, motioning over his shoulder toward the water. "I don't think he's coming back any time soon."

Harvath looked to where the beach dropped off into the deep water of the grotto. Several feet below the surface he could make out the shape of a man wrapped multiple times in what looked like heavy anchor chain. Pieces of the puzzle were starting to fall into place.

"And Nomikos?" asked Harvath. "Let me guess. Someone was just trying to help him clear the wax out of one of his ears."

"Who cares? They were both 21 August. All that matters now is that we get the device out of here ASAP."

The hair on the back of Harvath's neck was standing up. He didn't like this. Steadying his SR25 on the center of the ambassador's chest, he ordered, "Get your hands up where I can see them."

"What the hell are you doing?"

"Taking you into custody."

"No, you're not. I've got an assignment to complete. If you get in my way and fuck this up, I'll make sure you burn for it."

"Just the way you did in Athens?"

The ambassador fell silent and the only sound that could be heard throughout the grotto was the steady hum of the generator.

"I ought to put a bullet in you right here," continued Harvath, his mind rapidly cobbling together a picture of what must have happened. "Good men on your detail died. And for what? Money?"

"Lots of money," came a voice from behind. "Twenty-five million and counting."

Harvath turned to see the head of the ambassador's security detail, the agent known as Point Guard. In his hands he carried a fully automatic French FA-MAS with a heat shield over the barrel. The man was enormous—almost twice Harvath's size and was wearing an Infrared reduction suit.

Though he didn't mean to, Harvath laughed.

"What's so funny?" demanded Point Guard.

"I was just thinking of that old joke about the difference between a BMW and a porcupine, except in the case of you and the ambassador, this time the pricks actually *were* on the outside."

Point Guard stepped up to Harvath and wiped the smile off his face with a butt stroke from the MAS across his jaw.

Harvath saw stars and fell to one knee.

"We've all gotta do what we've all gotta do," said the ambassador as he stripped Harvath of his weapons and equipment and tossed them into the water.

"And in your case," added Point Guard as he kept him covered, "you've gotta join Mr. Papandreou for a little swim."

Harvath spat a gob of blood from his mouth and said, "Probably not a good idea. I just ate before I got here."

"Very funny, wiseass."

"Why don't you tell me how long you've been working for 21 August."

The ambassador smiled. "We don't work for them. They work for us. Our associate, Mr. Papandreou, screwed up very bad a while back and we offered not to turn him in if he would be our eyes and ears inside the organization."

"Did the State Department or CIA know about this?"

"Of course not, Papandreou was too valuable an asset to be shared."

"And he used his friendship with Nomikos to steal the device?"

"Yes, but Nomikos was no angel. He was the chairman of 21 August."

Harvath was stunned.

"Papandreou had suspected for quite some time that his cover within the organization was blown," continued Avery. "He knew that they were going to come for him eventually. In fact, I suspect that was why Nomikos showed up here tonight. Looking back on it, we probably should have done away with Papandreou much sooner and gotten out of the country, but we had other loose ends to tie up and hindsight is always twenty-twenty."

"So you and Papandreou put this plan together yourselves? The hit on your detail, your car?"

"We threw a couple of bodies in the car," replied Point Guard, "swapped out our dental records and then firebombed them so only the bullets would survive to tell the tale."

Harvath had to hand it to them. "And the entire trail led right back to 21 August. You skated with the money *and* the device, ready to start a new life anywhere you choose."

"Precisely," replied Point Guard.

"And the Jordanian buyer?"

"Will be meeting us in a hotel on Sicily in three days," said Avery, "so I'm sure you can appreciate that we need to get on with our business."

As Point Guard grabbed a length of anchor chain from a nearby pallet and began to approach, Harvath tried to stall for more time. "So that's it? Papandreou double-crosses Nomikos and 21 August, after which you double-cross him, and your country, then fake your deaths and make off to sell the device to some character who is very likely to be an enemy of the United States?"

"Well said," replied the ambassador as he accepted Point Guard's assault rifle so the man could bind Harvath with the heavy chain.

Harvath made a move to take Point Guard's legs out from under him and get control of his sidearm, but he wasn't fast enough. Point Guard dodged left and brought an elbow crashing down into Harvath's temple, causing him once again to see stars. As he fell to the ground, he felt clumps of sand between his fingers made moist not from seawater but from the blood running from his mouth.

Point Guard worked quickly, wrapping the anchor chain around Harvath's wrists and ankles and then began half dragging, half carrying him into the grotto's saltwater pool. All Harvath could think about was staying alive, but no matter how hard he struggled he couldn't get free.

As Harvath felt the bottom dropping away beneath the bigger man's feet, he knew that any moment now he was going to be let go.

Drowning seemed like one of the most ignoble deaths a SEAL could face and yet that was exactly what was rushing headlong to meet him.

Harvath summoned all of his strength and tried for one more major contortion of his body. If nothing else, maybe he could get a hold of the sick son of a bitch who was about to drown him and take him down, too.

He counted to three and then as fast and as hard as he could rolled his shoulders forward, his hands grasping for any item of his killer's clothing. As he did, there was a *snap*, followed by a searing pain in his upper arm. Somewhere in the back of his mind, something told him he had just torn something very serious, but he didn't care. All that mattered was staying alive.

Harvath tried again, struggling with all of his might to break free, and then heard another *snap*. A second later, blood began to drip into his eyes. As he looked up, he saw something bracing his killer's throat and blood pouring out all over. It was only a quick snapshot and before Harvath knew what had happened, the powerful hands that had been dragging him deeper into the water let go.

In an instant, the heavy chain pulled him to the bottom. It happened so quickly he had barely enough time to fill his lungs with air. He tried desperately to locate the upward slope and inchworm his way back to the beach, but it was no use. The sand was too soft—each time he moved he only dug himself in deeper.

His chest felt like it was pinned beneath a thousand tons of concrete. Every fiber of his body was screaming for oxygen. His vision was dimming at the edges and he knew it was only going to be a few seconds before his mouth automatically opened in one final, desperate attempt at life and his lungs sucked in a hopeless quest for air.

Harvath prepared himself for the end and as he did, he felt something strange bump his back. It felt distinctly like the nose of a shark, which shouldn't have come as any surprise since the grotto most likely opened up onto the sea.

The bump came again, followed by another. Soon, he felt himself being pulled away. He strained to see the animal, but his vision was almost black and the water was filled with blood.

The great beast propelled him forward and he had the eerie sensation of breaking the surface. Immediately, he was jolted by a heavy impact followed by a searing pain in the same spot in his upper arm where he had felt a similar pain moments ago. A popping sound that reminded him of gunfire, but which he knew were actually teeth snapping bone came next and Harvath told himself it would all be over soon. Finally, there was quiet. Deep, cold, *the end is finally here* quiet.

It was at that moment that Harvath's eyes shot open and he began sucking in hot, greedy gasps of air. Thrashing in the shallow water, he looked to his left and swung to his right, trying to find the shark.

"Easy," said a voice from above as a pair of weathered hands began unwinding the chain from around his wrists and ankles.

Harvath looked up and saw the face of Ben Metaxas. "Ben, what the—"

"Careful, my friend, don't move," he said.

"Why? What's going on?"

"I'm not as good a shot as Yannis, I'm afraid."

Harvath didn't understand. "What are you talking about?"

"Your arm," said Ben.

Looking down at his arm, Harvath saw a long metal shaft and realized what had pierced the throat of his killer—a speargun. Harvath's own wound was almost as serious. The spear had gone straight through his left bicep and almost punctured his rib cage.

"It was very difficult pulling you out of the water."

"But how did you get here?"

Ben held up his mask and swim fins. "There was another boat offshore. We saw a man bringing out supplies from inside this cave. When we couldn't reach you on the radio, we decided to take a look."

Harvath remembered the ambassador. "The other man. What happened to the other man?"

"The man on the beach?"

"Yes."

"He's dead," said Yannis as he made he way back toward them. "I shot him with this." Yannis held up Point Guard's weapon.

"What about the canister?" asked Harvath, fighting back the shock beginning to take over his body.

"He dropped it in the tunnel. Don't worry."

But Harvath was worried. They had to secure the canister and get the hell out of there. "We need that canister. Go get it."

Harvath collapsed onto the beach and waited for Yannis to come back with the Achilles device. While he lay in the sand, Ben did his best to work the spear free of Harvath's arm and dress his wounds. It was an incredibly painful procedure.

The longer Yannis was gone, the more Harvath began to worry. When he did finally return, it wasn't with good news. "I can't find it."

"What do you mean?" said Harvath as Ben helped him to his feet.

"The canister is gone."

"That's impossible. We're the only ones here."

"I don't think so. There's a trail of blood leading down the corridor and up the stairs into the kitchen."

Upon hearing that piece of information, the bottom dropped out of Harvath's stomach. "We've got to get upstairs."

Harvath led the way as quickly as he could through the low tunnel, down the corridor and up the stone steps into the house. The trail of blood couldn't be missed. He used the beam of his SureFire to trace it back through the house, out into the courtyard, and right up to the spot where Constantine Nomikos's blue Land Rover had been sitting less than half an hour before. There was no sign of the Land Rover, the device or Nomikos.

Harvath reached for his radio only to realize that Ambassador Avery had pitched it into the water, along with the rest of his gear.

Defeated, Harvath leaned back against the outer wall of the courtyard. He tried to tell himself that it would be impossible for a man as high profile as Constantine Nomikos to hide forever, but Harvath had been around long enough to know that with enough money, anything in life was possible.

He had also been around long enough to know that the good guys didn't always win.

RAELYNN HILLHOUSE

Raelynn Hillhouse's spy fiction draws upon her extraordinary life experiences. As a former smuggler, Hillhouse has slipped through some of the world's tightest security. From the Uzbek-Afghan border region to Central Europe, she's been followed, held at gunpoint and interrogated. Six months before the Libyan Intelligence Service's East Berlin office orchestrated the bombing of Pan Am 103, one of their operatives attempted to recruit her as a spy. Another foreign government later tried, too, but failed.

Hillhouse loves cold war intrigue, but has recently been fascinated by how the war on terror has transformed modern espionage, adding new players, while decreasing the role of traditional ones. Her debut, *Rift Zone*, a cold war thriller, received widespread critical acclaim. Her next thriller, *Outsourced*, deals with a Pentagon operative who infiltrates a for-profit, private military corporation suspected of selling seized arms to terrorists. He becomes a target in the multibillion-dollar war on terror, and the only one he can trust is his ex-fiancée. Unfortunately, she's been hired to kill him.

While researching *Outsourced*, Hillhouse came across a little-known event that kept nagging at her. She knew her main character, Stella, had somehow been involved in an incident that marked the first time the United States was targeted by fundamental Islamic terrorists. Two weeks after American hostages were seized in Iran in 1979, the U.S. embassy in Pakistan was overrun by Islamic extremists, razed, and two Americans and two foreign nationals lost their lives. This all-but-forgotten incident was actually a key event in the origins of modern terrorism, and was pivotal for Stella, whose life would become entangled in the complex struggle.

DIPLOMATIC CONSTRAINTS

Islamabad, Islamic Republic of Pakistan
November 21, 1979

Khan heard the muezzin wail from the loudspeakers, calling the faithful to midday prayers, and he pedaled faster. Students streamed into the mosques. He counted a dozen men wearing the same dark green sweater vests, and smiled. The wardens had received their uniforms; after prayers, the weapons would be distributed. He wished he could personally give them their final instructions, but knew he was taking a risk being seen on the campus. But he couldn't deny himself prayers with his brothers. Not today. Not on the biggest day of his life. Khan jumped from the bicycle running and shoved his way into the packed courtyard. As he washed himself at the fountain, he overheard fragments of conversations, "Death to the American dogs, death to Carter, death to the Zionists."

He saw eyebrows knit, jaws clenched, eyes glaring. Their anger was contagious. Khan was overjoyed.

Inside the American embassy compound, a waiting room afforded Stella not only a panorama of cows grazing on dry scrub, but also a view of the main gate. Several dozen young men loitered in the tree-lined street, apparently oblivious to the news of the siege in Mecca and the rumors that the U.S. and Israel were behind the capture of Islam's holiest site. She hoped that the pastoral scene didn't change after midday prayers.

The windowpane appeared too thin to be bulletproof and would shatter with the first brick. Either embassy architects hadn't given much thought to security or their local contractor had cheaper ideas. The antishatter laminate had small bubbles under the film. She couldn't get the hostages in Tehran out of her mind as her fingernail scraped at one corner of the laminate; it easily separated from the glass.

A man strolled over to her. He was taller than she had first guessed, someone used to concealing his height. Clean-cut, athletic build and a burn scar on his left forearm—a soldier or spy. He, too, was waiting on the CIA's deputy chief of station, so she guessed spook.

"Strange-looking critters, aren't they?" He pointed to the red, humpbacked cows and water buffalo. "You don't see Sahiwals back home. I knew an old boy in the Panhandle who tried to beat the drought with them. They're lean. Made some of the toughest steaks you ever ate."

"I'm a vegetarian."

"I'm Congressman Tom Rack." He extended his hand and looked her over as if admiring a prize heifer.

"Stella." She turned back toward the street. The

number of people had grown to over one hundred and more were arriving every minute. Some carried signs, but kept them at their feet, turned away so she couldn't read them.

They're waiting for something.

Bernie Thompson walked into the waiting room and greeted Stella.

"Great to see you," Stella said, "but we'll have to make it another time. I want out of here before that crowd starts up. I don't want to get caught in a situation like Tehran."

"Welch and I just got back from driving around looking for demonstrations and everything was quiet."

"Take another look."

A half-dozen Punjab Transport Corporation buses pulled up. Passengers were smashed against the fogged windows. "I have to fire off a cable, but we need to talk," Thompson said. "Give me two minutes. Only two minutes."

The masses swelled around Khan, crunching every centimeter of space. Each breath was a struggle, but he kept shouting as loudly as he could, "Death to the American dogs." He shook his clenched fist in beat with the crowd, their anger pounding the embassy walls. "Death to the Americans." The words became a mantra, and thoughts of his mission, thoughts of his family, thoughts of everything, fell away. "Death to the Americans." Khan had only one thought. He and the mob were one.

Death to Americans.

"Death to America," he said, gasping. The multitude began to move, sweeping him along. He shuffled ahead, unable to see where he was going but sure he was moving toward the embassy, toward the Americans. As they passed through the gate, bodies squeezed tighter, pressing harder and harder, crushing against his chest. He struggled for breath but still he mouthed, "Death to America."

The furnishings in Thompson's office were American, although the workmanship was definitely local. Stella had long ago noticed that drywall wasn't a strength of Third World craftsmen who were accustomed to the single-wall construction of the tropics. Several blotches of spackle showed through the thin white paint, and in one corner the drywall didn't quite reach the ceiling. Thompson sat at his desk, but Stella stood and kept an eye on the uneasy streets below. She realized that she'd seen several men wearing hunter-green sweater vests. When she took a closer look, she saw one key a walkie-talkie. "Bernie, they've got a command-and-control structure. I'm out of here."

Thompson's phone rang. "Hold on a minute. Let me check the back gate for you," he answered, then paused. "That many. What about the service gate?" His face hardened, as if the muscles were assuming their own battle stations. "Send a man to the roof. I want to know what we're facing."

"Bernie—" Stella approached his desk, holding up a hand. "Some are carrying Enfields." The turn-of-the-century single-bolt action rifles had helped hold the British Empire together and they remained a powerful symbol among former subjects. In the right hands, they were highly accurate.

Thompson continued, "You copy that, Gunney? Enfields. You know the Rules of Engagement. Unless the DCM changes them, you can only fire to protect yourself. Good luck." He slammed the phone down. "Looks like we're going to rock and roll."

They studied the swelling masses. So far, everyone remained behind the metal-piping barricade surrounding the compound. The crowd was focused upon a commotion at the gate, but two women seemed to be looking straight at them. Suddenly, one stepped aside. Metal glistened in the sun, and Stella understood.

"Down!" Stella tackled the former high-school linebacker and they slid toward his desk. The window exploded. Shotgun pellets sprayed the drywall. A few shards of glass flew into the room, but the laminate held most of the fragments.

They stared at the cratered wall, then looked at each other. She caught a brief, unnerving glimpse of raw fear in his face. He briefly shut his eyes, shook his head, but didn't speak. The unyielding face of the hardened operative returned.

The office door burst open and Rack crawled into the room, hugging the floor. "Anyone hurt?"

Stella lowered the blinds, then turned off the lights. "I'm fine. Bernie?"

"I'm okay."

"Have you got a rifle?" Stella said. "I'll take out the shooter. I'm not bound by your Rules of Engagement."

"Neither am I," Rack said. "Give me whatever firepower you've got."

"Firing into the crowd would incite things further," Bernie said. Chants could now be heard through the broken window. "There are some shotguns in the marines' case. Self-defense only. Understand?" Bernie reached into a desk drawer, removed a set of keys and tossed them to Stella. "You're under my command. Gear up while I protect my agents." Lying with his belly on the floor, Bernie dialed the combination on the wall safe. He opened it, grabbed a box crammed with index cards and scooted over to his shredder. He stuffed the growling machine, nearly choking it.

A brick flew into the room. Stella jumped but continued inching toward the gun locker. She unlocked the case, passed Rack a 1200 Winchester pump-action shotgun and took one for herself. She held the stock in her right hand and pointed the barrel toward the ceiling. She pumped the wooden slide back and forth to assure herself that the gun would work when she needed it. Rack leered at her. "In your dreams, Congressman." She flashed him a smile and pumped the shotgun one last time. "In your dreams."

Khan lost himself in the crowd—in his crowd. He speculated that they numbered in the thousands, but could really only see those pressing against him. A towering shesham tree was about ten meters away and it would make a good perch from which to survey the event if he could make it up to the first fork.

The chants were so loud, but he thought he had heard a gunshot. He wound through the masses toward the tree, at first excusing himself, then pushing and shoving until he hit another wall of bodies—hot, sweaty, smelly bodies. The throng constricted around him like a python. He raised his fist in the air and gasped the words *Death to America.*

Stella listened as the mob chanted over and over, faster and faster, until the words blurred into a whirlwind of rage. "I counted three marines on my way in.

And did I understand that you don't have security cameras on the roof?"

"We have two cameras, one on each gate, and six marines total," Bernie said.

Rack snorted. "Hell, the Tulsa Wal-Mart has tighter security than that." He loaded shells and chambered a round.

"The host government provides police protection."

"Like in Tehran?" Rack said.

A half-dozen gunshots went off in rapid succession. Stella pushed herself flat against the floor, even though she knew it wouldn't make much difference. When the gunfire stopped, she peeked outside. Thousands of fists shook in rhythm with the chants. A separate group near the gate moved back and forth in unison. She glimpsed a battering ram as it smacked into a brick pillar. Chips of brick and mortar flew into the air.

"They've broken through! What's the emergency plan?" Stella tugged at Bernie's arm. He yanked papers from their files, threw the manila folders to the ground and stuffed the documents into the shredder.

"Go to the vault and wait for rescue. Only shoot in self-defense."

Stella nodded, although she was going to make damn sure she got there, even if it meant laying down fire to hold protesters at bay. No one was going to take her hostage.

"Death to America," the mob on the street chanted in harmony, but the protesters already within the embassy walls were out of sync. The crowd fanned out into the compound, and so many were pushing from behind, Khan had to keep moving. It parted momentarily at a mulberry, so he jumped into the tree's wake.

He doubled over for a moment and caught his breath and thoughts. He hadn't planned on participating in the riot, only instigating it. But he had lived through enough monsoon rains to know how hopeless it was to fight the rising floodwaters.

Death to America.

Stella was in top physical condition, but she was breathless as she entered the cramped vault. Over a hundred people were crammed into it, including not only American officials, but Pakistanis who worked for the facility. Some stood, others sat on the floor; everyone contributed to the stale air. Stella turned the shotgun's barrel toward the ceiling and followed Thompson to the CIA code room, weaving through the group, careful not to step on anyone.

Inside the smaller room Congressman Rack was smashing computers and other machines with a sledgehammer. The sound echoed off the steel walls. She knew the CIA operatives wouldn't destroy their cryptographic equipment unless they believed there was a real chance the vault was somehow going to be overrun. *Not good.*

They squeezed into the chamber and Rack stopped and looked up. "Good to see you, Bernie. I really didn't want to be the ranking officer in here."

"I did what I could for our friends, but I'm not sure I got all the payment records," Thompson said. "Any word from our host government?"

"Bill's been stonewalled by the Foreign Ministry. When pushed, Babar said they've sent a runner with a message to President Zia. Seems he's off bicycling somewhere."

"A runner. Hi-tech. What about General Ahktar?"

"You know Zia. Where the president goes, the generals are in tow—insurance against another coup attempt."

Stella stood uncomfortably close to Thompson. "So what's the evacuation plan? Is there a hatch to the roof?"

"My predecessor installed one, but don't count on the Marines," Thompson replied. "We're dependent upon our host—"

"The bicycling dictator?" Stella said. "Don't you guys follow politics? We yanked his military aid for knocking off Bhutto. He has to live with those fundamentalists out there. You don't think he's going to turn on them to help us? That would be political suicide—even for a military dictator. Right, Congressman?"

Rack nodded. "He's not about to break up the party. If I were in his shoes, I'd pedal faster and wait for it to burn itself out, and us along with it."

"What the hell do you want me to do?" Thompson raised his voice, then paused, and, with a calculated breath, returned to the measured drone of a bureaucrat. "Our emergency plans call for falling back to this position and waiting for rescue."

"Those plans went into effect before Tehran. We're sitting ducks in a big steel pot and the water's gonna boil. We need to go on the offensive before they're entrenched. Hold the building or at least—"

A marine wearing a duty uniform and carrying a shotgun interrupted. "Sir, I have a man pinned down at Post-2. They're prying the grilles off the cafeteria windows and squeezing through. They're crawling all over the compound. Sir, permission to use force?"

"Only Ambassador Hummel or DCM King can authorize force," Thompson said.

"That's bullshit," the congressman said.

Thompson pointed at Rack. "You shut the door." He continued, "Gary, has anybody found Hummel or King?"

"They went home for lunch right before the fun started. The diplomats in the other room have them on the phone. You know Hummel. He'll never authorize it—and it would take too long to try."

"Sir," the marine said. "It's Sergeant Molson trapped down there—the one whose wife just had twins."

"Bernie, you can't work for two agencies at once," Stella said. "You gonna let the diplomat's caution rub off and tarnish the operative in you?"

Thompson pursed his lips and squinted an evil eye. At that moment, she knew he hated her. He said, "I've got a Dragunov in the Agency's private collection. Take it and do whatever you need to do—quietly."

"Your best resource management would be to get me and the Dragun into a little fresh air on the roof," Stella said.

"Jesus, you can't snipe from the roof of a U.S. embassy."

"The rifle doesn't exist. I don't exist. I don't see the problem."

"Will you help Molson or not?"

"Whoa." Rack held up his hand. It was twice the size of Stella's. "Are you out of your mind sending this girl to do a man's job? Give me the rifle."

Stella's face grew warm. "You ever fire one of these, Congressman?"

"You don't need a trained sniper to take out rioters at thirty yards."

"You need someone who knows what she's doing to tame a Dragun indoors," Stella said.

Thompson opened a locker and removed a sleek, black case. Stella reached out for it. So did Rack.

"Sorry, Congressman." He handed it to Stella. "She's the man for the job. But no one will stop you from checking the hall to make sure it's clear before she goes out." He passed a smoke grenade and gas mask to her.

Stella turned toward the marine. "You have a flak jacket?"

"Not here, ma'am."

"Can you get me radio contact with the sergeant?"

"No, ma'am. He's on a land line."

"Tell him to use tear gas when I signal him, then run like hell to the vault."

"What's the signal?"

"He'll know." *As soon as I do.*

Stella snatched up a large rubber band from atop a file cabinet. Rack eyed her as she pulled her shoulder-length hair away from her face and into a ponytail. She missed some, allowing a few wisps to frame her face. Now the girl was ready for the man's job.

Khan scraped his arm as he climbed the mulberry tree. The crowd was magnificent, topping ten thousand, and he could see three more buses down the street. They had only imagined stirring up fervor for the Islamic revolution; no one had thought as far as occupying the embassy like their Shia brothers in Tehran. Today's protest was a single event, but if they could leverage it with hostages, they could steal the show from the misguided Ayatollah Khomeini and energize their brothers around the world with their message. The Iranians had seized the embassy with a mere five hundred. They were many times this size and growing. It was regrettable that his students were so disorganized, but Khan was certain he could change that.

* * *

Rack stepped from the vault first, a shotgun pressed against his shoulder and said, "Clear!"

Stella slipped past him and set the rifle case and a shotgun on the linoleum floor. "Thanks, Congressman. You can go back inside now."

Rack didn't budge. She guessed he was waiting for a glimpse at the gorgeous weapon. She flipped open the latches. "Okay, Congressman. She's a beauty, but it's time for you to move on."

"I'm not going anywhere until that boy's safe."

She slammed the case shut. "Follow my lead and stay the hell out of my way." She opened the nearest office door and stashed the sniper rifle behind a coatrack, covering it with a sweater.

"What the fuck are you doing?"

Stella held the gas mask with two hands and smoothed out the face piece with both thumbs, opening it to its fullest extent. She seated her chin into the chin pocket, pushed it against her face, pulled the harness over her head and felt for the center patch. Satisfied, she pulled it off and placed the straps over the front of the lens.

Rack adjusted his own mask.

He knows what he's doing.

She dumped the contents from her purse and stuffed the grenade and half-mask inside. She picked up the shotgun.

"What was all of that Dragun-taming BS back in there?" Rack asked.

"Only a fool would choose a Dragunov over a shotgun for close-quarter combat." She sprinted toward the stairwell, a long lock of hair dancing against her cheek. "A Dragun is meant to have a good wind at its back and sunlight streaming toward her. She's like a wild bird. You don't cage her."

Stella reached the bottom of the stairway, glanced up at the security camera and then peeked through the fire door's small rectangular window. Five men were in the hall, two carried Enfields, a rotten choice to clear rooms. An older man was going door to door, looking for unlocked rooms. He turned a doorknob and signaled the riflemen into position. One of the Arabs kicked the door open with a kung fu thrust. The group rushed into the office. One remained behind, aiming the rifle down the empty hall.

Rack whispered to Stella, "We can take them all out."

"It's not right. They're students."

"They've got guns and fingers on the triggers." Rack raised his shotgun.

Stella put her hand on the barrel of Rack's gun and pushed it down. "They don't have a clue what they're doing."

Just as she turned toward the security camera, movement caught her eye. She jerked her head back to the window. Two women marched from an office, followed by three armed men. One wore traditional Islamic dress; the other sported Farrah Fawcett hair and a short skirt.

The first American hostage.

"Damn!" Stella whispered. The throbbing of her heart seemed to shake her entire body. She recalled her father's training. *Paint the picture you want them to see.* Stella took out the smoke grenade, pulled the pin and dropped it on the stairwell floor. "Your mask. Now."

"You crazy?" Rack pulled the respirator over his face.

After a few seconds' delay, the grenade spewed

white smoke. Stella looked again at the security camera, extended both arms parallel to the floor and pumped her fists toward her ear three times, as if flexing her biceps. She prayed Sergeant Molson was monitoring and caught the military's visual signal for gas.

Smoke filled the stairwell. "Fire!" Stella shouted in Urdu, then thrust her chin into the mask, seated it and exhaled. Careful to stay clear of the burning phosphorous, she opened the door and held it long enough for a cloud to billow out. Like a skilled cricket player, she grasped the gun by its barrel and knocked the white-hot grenade into the hall with the butt. She glided across the corridor and yanked down hard on the fire alarm. An ear-piercing ring filled the hall. She winced.

Down the hall a tear-gas canister rolled across the floor. Within seconds the gas mixed with smoke. Lost in the thickening haze, rioters bumped against one another, scrambling to find their way out of the building. The marine dashed to the stairwell as ordered.

"Help!" the American woman shrieked.

Stella ran toward the cries. The Pakistani still held her hostage by the wrist. Stella dug her thumb into the pressure point between the Pakistani woman's thumb and index finger until she found bone. The woman released her grasp.

Just then, Rack appeared. He picked up the hostage and carried her to the stairwell.

Stella twisted the Pakistani woman's hand around and pressed down, bending it backward. Stella led her without further resistance to the stairs. The stairwell was smoky, but nothing like the thick cloud in the hall.

On the third floor, Rack pushed up his mask. "What the hell are you doing with her?"

"Get your own hostage—she's mine."

* * *

Stella escorted the Pakistani woman to the office where she had stashed the Dragunov. As soon as she let go of her, the woman collapsed to the floor in a coughing fit. Barely able to hold her head up, she vomited from the tear gas. Stella calculated that she had a couple of minutes to work without interference. She crouched below the window and inspected her surroundings as she crawled over to lock the door.

Before she reached it, she sensed someone in the hall. She stopped and aimed the shotgun.

"Friend!" Rack's deep voice boomed above the din of the fire alarm.

Stella lowered the shotgun, now certain he had military experience.

"Get your pretty ass back into the vault," Rack said. "I don't know what the hell you're thinking, but taking this woman as a hostage isn't going to mean shit to them."

"Cover the hallway while you're standing there." Stella inventoried the office. Its standard furnishings provided no unusual options.

"That mob will rip you apart," Rack said.

"You know as well as I do they're going to loot this place, then torch it. Maybe I'm wrong, but I'm not sticking around." She rifled through a desk drawer. A private collection of Snickers bars, Cadbury chocolates and a bag of Fritos was stuffed behind a cash box. She ripped the wrapper from a candy bar and bit down. She tossed Rack a Snickers, then shoved the rest of hers into her mouth.

"You're nuts." Rack looked out the window, then lowered the blinds.

"Eat it. If you're with me, I'm not going to risk your

blood sugar tanking." She glanced at the woman who was still throwing up from the tear gas.

"Who the hell are you?" Rack asked her.

"A girl who needs the wind at her back and sunlight streaming toward her." She flashed him a smile, then opened a metal supply cabinet. "I *am* going to get out of here." She found duct tape. "Guess this is the best I'm going to do."

"I don't like leaving everyone behind in that vault."

"You'll figure out a way to spin it before election time rolls around. If I could save them, I would. Bernie's the ranking officer—he has to stay. But the others are diplomats. They'd rather be taken hostage than fight their way out."

A chunk of brick smacked against the bent blinds. Stella didn't jump but only glanced up. She crawled over to the heaving woman and gently patted her back to reassure her while she removed her light gray headscarf. She continued talking to Rack. "If you're with me, you need to find your own costume. I'm sure there are several donors still groping around down there." Stella coughed. Smoke and tear gas were beginning to blow upstairs. "Lock the door when you go. And try to pick up one of the Enfields to add to the illusion."

Stella tied up the woman and pulled on her *jilbab* to begin her transformation to a modest Muslim woman. Her arms stuck four inches out of the sleeves and the hem hit between her ankles and knees, a racy length she would have to compensate for with her posture. She tied the scarf around her head, shoving every strand of hair under it.

As she was about to leave, Rack returned, depositing an armful of white clothes and an old rifle onto the desk. "Here's hoping that one of these pairs of Paki pj's fits."

"No friends with you?"

"I don't do hostages—slow you down too much." Rack thrust his arm into the sleeve. The seams ripped. He tried the other one on, but he could barely shove his large hand through the narrow opening. "I might have just screwed myself when I gave the diplomats our guns and told them to lock the vault."

Even the most hard-core rioters avoided burning buildings, but Stella took only enough time in Thompson's office to use his CIA-issue disguise kit to darken their fair complexions and to rinse color through Rack's blond hair and long sideburns. He wore a wool skull cap and a pair of white *kurta* pajamas that Thompson had stashed in his office, no doubt for a clandestine rendezvous. Aside from the gas mask, he made a pretty good local, albeit a large one.

Stella ran as quickly as the long, tight *jilbab* permitted. She put on the gas mask, pulled up the coat and bounded down to the first floor. The hallway was empty of intruders but filled with tear gas and smoke. They didn't want to risk going out a door and allowing more rioters inside. They had to find where they had broken in.

She crept into an office. The windows were partially broken, but the grates were intact. She crossed the corridor and entered another office, catty-corner from the one she had checked. She searched the ground floor in a modified star pattern, careful not to move along the same line, always staying a shade to the oblique.

Rack found her, motioning that he'd discovered the

rat hole. She signaled him that she needed a moment. He disappeared into the cafeteria.

It was time to add the finishing touch to her costume: a typewriter. In a land where most people paid scribes to type their papers, she would be the envy of the other looters.

She stepped inside an office, then froze. Two men lay motionless on the floor. One wore only his underwear. One of their heads was turned a little too far to the left. Necks were not easy to break. *The congressman's trained—if he's a congressman.*

She grabbed an IBM Selectric typewriter. Hiking up the *jilbab*, she stepped over the bodies. She shuddered.

The hallway was still empty and the door that Rack had entered was shut. She put her hand on the knob, then stopped herself. Rather than enter as Rack would expect, she slipped inside the kitchen and slinked over to where she could see Rack. He crouched behind a serving counter, studying the crowd outside. She crept into the room, staying below the tables, out of sight of the protesters. Rack spotted her and waved.

The cafeteria wasn't as cloudy as the hallway, but enough gas and smoke lingered to make breathing miserable. Stella put her hand on the gas mask with the dread of someone about to jump into an icy pond. She counted to three, then pulled it off. Her reluctant body inhaled. She coughed. Her eyes wanted to clamp shut but she held them wide open. When they emerged from the window, they had to appear as if they had braved the smoke of a burning building.

She stood on tiptoe and spoke into Rack's ear. "If anyone looks at us too closely, here's what to do…"

* * *

"Ladies first," Rack whispered when they got to the window.

Stella handed him the typewriter. She wanted to hike up the *jilbab* so her legs could maneuver, but she didn't dare break character. A mob circled the building at a cautious distance. Thousands of eyes were watching their egress.

The windowpane was shattered and pieces of glass jutted out from the frame. She knocked away debris. Perching on the sill, she swung her legs out in tandem, then dropped to the ground.

Rack lowered the heavy typewriter to her, then jumped down. He swaggered with the rifle over his shoulder and his pants riding up on him. Stella slouched, but the *jilbab* was several inches too short. They were the only show to watch as they crossed the fifteen meters between the building and the crowd.

They were too exposed.

They weren't going to make it.

She tugged at Rack's pajama sleeve.

Suddenly, Rack threw his head back and shouted at the top of his lungs, *"Allahu Akbar."* He pointed the Enfield into the air and fired. *"Allahu Akbar!"* His voice boomed.

Stella held her breath.

Rack emptied the rifle into the air, then waved it above his head.

"Allahu Akbar! Allah is great!" The crowd erupted with cheers and joy shots. As they delved into the anonymous safety of the mob, Stella shouted as loudly as she could, *"Allahu Akbar!"*

This time, she meant it.

ROBERT LIPARULO

In the first draft of Robert Liparulo's thriller *Comes a Horseman*, the coprotagonists—FBI agents Brady Moore and Alicia Wagner—were helped out of a particularly hairy situation by police sniper Byron Stone. Byron was a moody fellow, renowned as much for his reticence as for his skill with a rifle. Ultimately, pacing considerations trumped Liparulo's (and early readers') affection for Byron, and his scenes wound up being edited out.

Byron, of course, wasn't happy. He nagged at the edges of Liparulo's mind, always asking the same questions: What makes me so gloomy? How did I become so proficient with a gun? What's my story? After a while, Liparulo started jotting down answers, eventually explaining Byron's life in the notes, outlines and fragments of three yet-unwritten thrillers—*Recoil, Recon* and *Return*.

While Byron Stone draws blood from Liparulo's own heart, he's also a compilation of Liparulo's acquaintances, including a SWAT sniper and an

FBI sniper (imagine *their* disagreements). These two shared the qualities of quiet, nearly impenetrable machismo and subtly troubled spirits. The taking of lives made them each respect life that much more. They would kill only when it would save more lives, or a more innocent life. But this creed allowed them only to pull the trigger. Bad guy or not, a life is a life, and to hell with how tough snipers act, their souls ache for each of the ones they ended.

A sniper's knowledge that his job is necessary, crashing headlong into his humanity—this was the conflict Liparulo wanted to explore with Byron. *Kill Zone* does not answer all of Byron's questions, but it opens a window on the police sniper's moral struggle.

KILL ZONE

The sweaty, beard-stubbled face wavered behind the sniper's crosshairs. The suspect's eyes flicked around—to the kids, weeping in a corner; to the apartment door, propped closed with a chair because he had broken the latch when he kicked it in; to the window, where he seemed to expect the peering faces of would-be rescuers. Forget that it was five stories up, with no fire escape.

Keep looking, buddy, the sniper thought. *All the better to keep you in my sights.*

It was bad enough that the gun-brandishing creep had provoked the wrath of the city's SWAT team; now he had Byron Stone's rifle pointed at him. Most folks would have told the offender to jump out the window and get done with it.

Byron was as comfortable with a rifle as an accountant is with a mechanical pencil. From his eighth birthday, when he was bequeathed his granddaddy's .22 for plunking at cans and groundhogs (and stray cats when no one was looking), through boot camp,

Ranger training, sniper school and the police academy, he figured he hadn't gone longer than a week without shooting a gun. Breathing required more thought.

Now he was poised across the street and a floor up from the commandeered apartment. He could see the perp, scruffy and likely drunk, holding a woman in front of him with a thick arm around her neck. In his other hand was a pistol, which he alternately held to the woman's temple and pointed at the kids. The sniper panned to the next window. The children were still there. The boy was little, no older than three. The girl was about eleven, his own son's age. They were terrified.

He panned back to the man who was threatening them. He tensed. The woman was no longer struggling. She was hanging like a doll in the man's grip. There was no blood and he'd heard no shot. Could he have strangled her? Broken her neck? She lifted her hand to touch her captor's arm, and Byron relaxed slightly. She had simply realized the futility of fighting, or was too exhausted to continue. Now she was only partially blocking the man's face from Byron's view, instead of randomly flailing her head around, which wasn't the brightest idea in situations involving snipers.

He watched the perp jerk her this way, then that, waving the gun like a conductor's baton. It appeared to be a .38 snub-nose revolver, what they used to call a Saturday night special—cheap, but lethal.

Eyeing the scene through the scope's optics was like watching a television program with the volume turned off. The networks would have dropped this show a long time ago. The acting was melodramatic, the plot was nonexistent. In fact, Byron did not know the story at all. Was this a lovers' spat gone off the deep end? A fouled drug deal? Maybe the guy had chosen a door at random: some people meet their soul mates in chance encounters; the woman and her children had met the devil. Whatever ill wind blew the man to that apartment also stirred people like Byron, people who made it their life's work to stop bad guys from preying on innocence.

Byron noticed the woman was wearing a waitress's uniform, light blue with white trim. A name tag clung to her left breast, but her constant flailing prevented him from reading its inscription. He felt a pang of sympathy for her. Two kids. A dead-end job. Living in a one-room dive, in which the "kitchen" amounted to a few appliances and a countertop running along one wall of the living room; he could see its pink tiles, a plastic grocery bag of something lying like a disemboweled stomach on the counter, an open bag of bread. And now this.

He drew a bead on the man's head. He was going for a clean kill, one that would short-circuit even the death spasm that could cause the hostage-taker's finger to twitch on the trigger and grant him one last victim. That meant severing the nervous system pathway, an inch wide, at the back of the skull—on a wildly moving target. Between the rifle's muzzle and the target were a hundred and twenty yards of gusty winds and a pane of glass. If the bullet managed to zing past the hostage's head to find its mark, a final barricade of tooth and bone would try to deflect it away from the brain stem, so crucial to the hostages' safety.

"Piece of cake," Byron whispered as he aligned the crosshairs on the man's philtrum, the dimple between nose and upper lip.

His heart seemed to thump especially hard, causing Byron's aim to jerk away from the man's head. He knew the spasm, imperceptible to anyone but him, was no involuntary physical tic—the kind that ended the careers of surgeons and snipers. This one came from deep within, from a bit of conscience that told him the object in his sights was flesh and bone.

Perspiration tickled his scalp. The sweatband along the inside edge of his cap would keep it from blinding him. He allowed his eyes to close. For only a second, then two. Vision, again…and the man's head in the scope. Byron's stomach cramped.

A creak of wood reminded him he was not alone. His spotter—the second half of every police sniper team—stood on a chair behind him, watching the scene through powerful binoculars. Usually, the spotter gave periodic updates on wind velocity and direction, SWAT team movements, the position of hostages. In this case, he would have confirmed the children's whereabouts so the sniper's attention could have stayed on the target. But this spotter was different. He had been silent for the nearly three hours the two had been in position.

Three hours. Sometimes an operation lasted only minutes.

More often, it was a waiting game.

Upon receiving a brief sketch of the situation, Byron had selected this building, and after rejecting three other locations, settled on this abandoned room. The fading ghost of something rotting lingered in the air, but his nose had acclimated to it. Carefully, he had cut the pane from the window, because raised windows tended to draw suspicion, and shooting through glass decreased accuracy. He'd hung cheesecloth over it like sheer curtains to hide behind, without affecting his tightly focused view through the sniper-scope.

Then he'd made a platform to lie on from a door and two chairs. His vantage point and stability were perfect.

Through it all, the spotter had quietly observed. And that was okay; Byron preferred checking things out for himself.

For the first two hours, he'd waited for the word: *red* to stand down, *green* to shoot. Some fifty minutes ago, he'd received the go-ahead. Apparently, the creep had a long history of violence. Earlier in the day, before taking the woman and two kids hostage, he'd stabbed his former employer with a screwdriver. Somewhere, a tactical-unit leader had gathered intelligence from sniper teams, police investigators, a psychologist, a hostage negotiator. He had determined there was sufficient cause to effectively sign the guy's death warrant.

Byron wasn't so sure. Against sniping wisdom, he never forgot that his targets were human, men (usually) who'd been boys full of hope and wonder, who probably loved someone and was loved back, who had somehow lost their way. Given the choice, he'd rather see a peaceful resolution. But the choice wasn't his. It was in the hands of the guy on the other end of the scope. If he continued to threaten others, if it looked as though he would cause them serious harm, it was Byron's duty to eliminate him.

So for three hours, Byron had held his position, ready, vigilant.

"Shoot 'im, man," his spotter whispered. He had grown impatient. "You got the green light."

Byron ignored him.

In the scope, the man half turned from the window and seemed to yell at the door. Byron adjusted his aim to a spot just above his ear, where the side neural motor strip lay, another instant-incapacitation spot. He nestled the rifle stock more firmly in the pocket of his shoulder. He had already adjusted the scope's Bullet Drop Compensator for distance and the difference in their elevations. The wind was a concern. It was rising and dropping like gusts through a valley. He had spotted a rag caught on a telephone wire. Its flapping gave him a sense of the wind speeds, and he could see it without lifting his head from the scope by opening his other eye. He would move the crosshairs slightly to the left to adjust for the wind at the time of the shot—a method of compensation called Kentucky Windage.

The perp abruptly spun and fired two shots through the apartment door. The negotiations weren't going well. Byron maintained his composure. He pressed the tip of his finger against the trigger. He knew precisely how many ounces of pressure he was applying to the trigger's four-pound pull, and when it would slam the firing pin into the bullet. His lips moved in silent prayer.

Riding a surge of adrenaline, the man threw the woman to the floor below the window. Her mouth open in a scream Byron could not hear, he raised the pistol toward her.

The rag was almost horizontal in a strong wind. Byron adjusted. He took in three-quarters of a breath, held it—and pulled back on the trigger. The rifle *cracked!* and kicked against his shoulder, which was well muscled for just such times. He didn't even feel it. He was frozen in what marksmen call the follow-through: no movement for a full second after firing to prevent starting the after-shot procedure a hair before the bullet left the barrel, causing it to miss its mark. He saw the bullet impact and the target go down. He chambered another round, watching for movement through the scope.

"Direct hit to the head," he called to his spotter, who responded, "Suspect down."

The spotter yelled into his mic, then yanked the earbud plug from his radio handset, and a buzz of voices filled the room.

The door of the apartment across the street burst open. Men and women streamed in. They gathered around the body, some of them kneeling, pointing at the hole perfectly placed below the suspect's nose. A policewoman with short-cropped hair inspected the bullet hole in the window. She looked up toward Byron's position, his "hide." She smiled and waved. Behind her, a burly-looking cop with a mustache hoisted up the body, holding it for Byron to see. Someone else gave him the thumbs-up.

A chill skittered along his spine, and he shook it off.

After three hours of mentally filling in the gaps to make the target as real as possible, it was a difficult task to start thinking of it again for what it was—an animatronic target mannequin, used for high-level training and top-flight competitions.

Puppeteers, situated safely away from the target, controlled its movements. He peered once more through the scope at the face of the pretend hostage-taker. The latex skin looked genuine enough. Even the eyes had rolled back, the mouth had dropped open. It didn't look so different from the real corpses he had seen.

The woman cop was dragging the woman mannequin from the room. He panned to the other window. The kids were huddled in place, now just looking like sad dolls. The illusion of reality, so strong in Byron's mind, was wearing off. When he looked again, a photographer was trying to snap pictures of the suspect-mannequin's wound while someone else danced with it.

He released his grip on the rifle. It rocked on its bipod and settled on the sandbag below its stock. Joints popped and muscles protested as he rolled onto his side to look back at his "spotter"—actually, a fine marksman himself who'd volunteered to help judge this contest.

"Jack, I'm getting too old for this," he said.

Jack came around the side of the platform and extended his hand. "My man, that was incredible." His voice, deep and smooth, made the words sound true. They squeezed each other's hands. For a second Byron thought Jack might try to butt heads, or some such crap. Blowing the heads off things had that effect on men. Instead, Jack pivoted and planted his butt on the platform beside Byron. He fished a pack of cigarettes out of a breast pocket and tapped one out. He offered the pack to Byron.

Byron stared without seeing. His mind had returned to the shoot, the perp, the hostages. He rolled back to his scope.

Beside him, Jack said, "You got this thing bagged up, dude." A cloud of white smoke drifted into Byron's periphery. "That idiot Hanson took off the perp's ear. Schumann, that prima donna acting like his farts don't stink because he won National, and everyone said he'd take this one. Sorry cuss plugged a hostage."

He kept rambling, a talker released from a three-hour vow of silence, but his words became background static in Byron's ears.

The kid-dolls reminded him of a time when it wasn't make-believe, when he hadn't been so perfect with his aim, when the perp had retained enough life force to empty his Glock.

One of the kids jerked his head to look directly at him. His heart wedged into his throat.

The kid jumped out of view. Byron panned to see a cop dragging it by one leg toward the apartment door.

He closed his eyes and moaned internally. Could he ever do this without investing so much of himself? He doubted it.

"Dude." Jack elbowed his hip. He turned. "We gotta— What's with you?"

Byron pressed his fingers to his cheek. Wet.

"Bug or something flew in my eye…this *smoke*." He waved his hand, clearing away a thin tendril.

Jack glared, suspicious. He stood. "Let's get outta here, man. Grub's on, beer's flowing."

Byron nodded, and pushed up onto his knees. He looked out through the cheesecloth. The windows into the kill zone were dark.

STEVE BERRY

History, action, long-lost secrets, intricate conspiracies and international settings—these are the main ingredients in a Steve Berry thriller. His debut, *The Amber Room*, dealt with a legendary Russian treasure, a room paneled entirely in amber, stolen by the Nazis in 1941. *The Romanov Prophecy* answered the question—What happened to the two children of Nicholas II, the last tsar of Russia, whose remains have never been found? *The Third Secret* revolved around the Catholic Church, Marian visions and shocking divine messages.

In his fourth thriller, *The Templar Legacy*, Berry introduced Cotton Malone, a lawyer/agent who worked with the Justice Department for many years in a special unit known as the Magellan Billet. Deciding the risks were too great, Malone retires out early, moves to Copenhagen and opens an old-books shop. Unfortunately, trouble seems to follow Malone, and *The Templar Legacy* is just the first of several adventures Berry plans for Malone and the cast of supporting characters. *The Devils' Due* is a tale from before Malone retired, when he was still active with the Magellan Billet.

Another unique situation with far-reaching consequences.

Typical for Cotton Malone.

THE DEVILS' DUE

Cotton Malone stood on the balcony and calmly watched the books burn.

He was standing next to Yossef Sharma, president of a tiny central Asian nation nestled firmly between Afghanistan, China and a host of other American enemies. Which was why Washington had, for years, conveniently ignored Sharma's excesses, including his audacious plan to burn nearly every book in his country.

"We've been collecting for the past month. The people have brought them from every town and village." Sharma spoke a mixture of Russian and Arabic unique to the region. "Tonight, there are fires in every quarter of the nation. All to rid us of Western influence."

"I almost think you believe that crap," Malone said, not taking his eyes off the spectacle.

"After tomorrow, possession of a single book, excepting the Koran, will be punishable by imprisonment. And if my people are anything, they're obedient."

Malone continued to watch as people, bundled in

coats and jackets, picked their way over slippery cobbles to heap more books onto the blaze. Clatter from flutes and tambourines added to the surreal spectacle.

"That crazy obedience," Malone said, "more than anything else, explains your current predicament. The world believes this place is another Afghanistan, and you know what that led to."

"Lucky for me, and this country, *you* know that to be false."

He smiled. "More lucky for you."

Malone was a navy commander turned lawyer turned Justice Department operative, assigned to a covert division within Justice known as the Magellan Billet. Twelve specially trained agents, all lawyers, working under a no-nonsense lady named Stephanie Nelle. On the outside, Nelle reminded most observers of their grandmothers, but inside she possessed the resolve of a Roman centurion. When he was first assigned Malone had thought the tour would be both limited and boring. But that was ten years ago, and the past decade had been anything but dull. Tonight was a good example. Here he was, standing on the balcony of a presidential palace beside a uniformed despot, while an immense bonfire fueled by books roared below, each breath from the cool, arid air laced with the scent of smoke and sorrow.

"You tell your government," Sharma said, "that I'm doing what I have to in order to survive. This nation is Muslim and these people demand a strong leader." The president motioned below. "You think they're burning those books because I ordered it? Never. It's because they want to."

Malone was no stranger. Twice he'd worked here, both times directly with Sharma. Malone had actually become interested in the country—a mountainous region of over a hundred thousand square miles, home to four million people, 8.5 percent of whom were Sunni Muslims. He'd studied its history and knew about its expansive tradition of writers, poets and composers, most dating back to the Middle Ages. But yesterday he'd painfully watched while the entire national archive had been cleared. The loss of so much knowledge was incalculable, but a United Nations protest had been swiftly rebuked by Sharma. Now Malone's stomach turned. It was like friends were burning below. He was a confirmed bibliophile. Books meant something to him. His home back in Atlanta overflowed with them. He loved everything about them, and many times lingered a day or two after an assignment to peruse rare-book shops.

In disgust, he allowed his gaze to drift away from the fire to the picturesque remains of mosques and other architecture lining the plaza. He knew that many of the buildings had stood since the nineteenth century, surviving the Soviet takeover in 1922, a Muslim rebellion in 1935, the fall of communism in 1991 and an Islamic revolution a year later. Finally, he faced Sharma and said, "Why am I here?"

"To see this happening."

He doubted that. And that, as far as he was concerned, was the trouble with central Asia. Truth was an underrated commodity.

"And to give you this."

Sharma reached over to a small table and lifted up a book. The binding was tooled with brass fittings in excellent condition. Malone accepted it and studied the cover. In English was written, *Canterbury Tales*.

"I thought you might like that."

Sharma knew him well. One of his favorites. "After tomorrow, I'll go to prison if I have this."

Sharma smiled. "For you, an exception. I know how much you love them. It's a seventeenth-century edition. For some reason we had it shelved in our archive."

He carefully balanced the book in his palm and was about to open it when Sharma stopped him. "Not here. Later."

He thought the comment strange.

"There's another gift. Inside. Especially for you. So later, back at your hotel."

He knew better than to question. So he nodded in understanding, slipped the tiny volume into his jacket pocket and turned his attention back to the bonfire.

Malone returned to his hotel room. The fire was still burning strong after two hours, when he and Sharma vacated the balcony. He locked the door and removed his jacket. Its brown leather smelled of ash.

He sat on the bed and studied the copy of *Canterbury Tales*. A second Speght edition, dated 1602. A text read and owned by the likes of Milton, Pepys, Dryden and Pope. Worth in the neighborhood of ten thousand American dollars, provided a copy could even be found.

Yet he was now holding one.

Given to him by Yossef Sharma.

He opened the book and, toward the center of the dingy yellowed pages, found a scrap of paper. He freed it and read the feminine English script.

In the mountains, to the north, visit the ruins of Rampur. Arrive at noon tomorrow. Someone wishes to speak with you, alone.

Sharma had gone to a lot of trouble to pass him this message. He apparently wanted Malone to go—which was the real reason why he'd been invited to the country—but did not want any fingerprints of his on the effort.

Typical Sharma. The man was a friend of the United States, but no one, other than a few with the highest security clearance, knew that. To the world Yossef Sharma was an oppressive ruler of an unimportant nation, but for years he'd quietly provided the West with some of the best intelligence out of central Asia. He possessed a superb spy network and the price for his services was the privilege to run his country as he saw fit. Of course, his efforts at generating utter chaos among his much larger neighbors was protected by one lucky truth—none of them had time to bother with him.

But now this.

What was Sharma up to?

Malone awoke early and prepared himself for the journey north. He secured a car from the American embassy along with a road map and noted that Rampur lay about two hours away, across some of the highest ranges in the country. The drive from the capital wound across Alpine terrain, through narrow passes where snow still lingered even now, in August. Cave entrances honeycombed many of the precipices.

He drove leisurely, taking care to ensure that he was not being followed. He motored through flat-bottomed valleys that housed compact villages, where he spotted more remnants of last night's carnage in piles of smoldering books.

He found Rampur.

Earlier, at the American embassy, he'd learned that

Bactrians in the first century, Arabs in the seventh, Turks in the tenth, then Mongols, Afghans, Russians and Soviets had all, at one time or another, claimed the site. Alexander the Great himself even laid siege to its walls. Currently, the surrounding forested hillsides, mountains and valleys were owned by the government, and a sign a few miles back had warned about loitering. Another sign, posted just off the pavement ahead, specifically forbade any entrance to the ruins. But Malone had been invited, so he stepped out into the brisk thin air and stuffed his Billet-issue Glock into a shoulder harness beneath his jacket. He knew that wild boar, brown bears and snow leopards all patrolled these mountains. But he was more concerned with two-legged predators, the kind that toted automatic weapons.

A gravelly path wound upward and required a steady foot and the practiced head of a mountaineer to negotiate. Thunder rumbled in the distance and he stopped to grab his breath, admiring distant snow-covered peaks that matted the horizon.

Another sign noted the beginning of the archeological site and again warned of no entrance. Beyond, an aimless accumulation of limestone slabs, most of which were once walls and towers, lay piled upon one another. Thorny bushes grew in clumps among the weathered stone, colored by summer irises and edelweiss. No evidence existed of any recent archeological exploration. In fact, the desolate spot, overhung by cliffs, appeared long abandoned.

He checked his watch.

11:57 a.m.

"Mr. Malone," a male voice called out.

He stopped walking and touched the Glock inside his jacket.

"I was told you speak this language," the voice said in Arabic.

"You were told right."

"I was also told you're a man to be trusted."

He knew that honor, however misguided, was important to the central Asian culture. "I try to be."

Twenty feet ahead, a man stepped into view. He was tall, maybe six and half feet, with an olive complexion. He wore a dingy white robe that draped his lanky frame. Wrinkles scored his forehead, as straight as if drawn with a ruler, and his dull, silver-gray hair and beard hung shaggy. A black turban wrapped his scalp and he hobbled forward with the aid of a long stick.

Malone aimed the Glock.

He knew the man's full name. Usamah bin Muhammad bin Awad bin Laden. But the West called him simply Osama bin Laden. What had Sharma said? *Someone wishes to speak with you. Someone, indeed.*

"I assure you, Mr. Malone. I'm no threat."

He was actually wondering about others.

"And I'm alone."

He kept the gun level. "Forgive me if I don't believe you."

Bin Laden shrugged. "Believe what you wish. I asked for this meeting and I came alone, as I asked you to do."

He decided that if the goal was to kill him he'd be dead already, so he lowered the Glock. "Why am I here?"

"I'd like to surrender myself to you."

Had he heard right? The entire United States military was looking for the fugitive standing before him. At last count, rewards of over twenty-five million dollars had been offered. And bin Laden simply wanted to surrender?

"Why would you do such a thing?"

"I'm tired of running."

"Since when?"

Bin Laden grinned. "I learned about you. We're about the same age. I'm forty-nine, you're five years younger. Haven't you ever wanted to stop what you're doing?"

Actually those thoughts were occurring to him more and more of late, but he wasn't going to discuss his doubts with a murderer. "What do you want?"

Bin Laden shuffled over to one of the boulders and sat. Malone came closer, but kept some distance, still wary.

"Your military. Your president. They want me dead. They want to show photographs of my corpse to the world. That wouldn't be so bad. I'd be at peace and my followers would have my death to avenge. I'd continue to lead them even from the grave. Not a bad fate. There are others though with different plans. These *others* want to prevent such a glorious ending for me."

Malone couldn't care less.

"They want me dead, but they want no one to know. In fact, they actually want to keep me alive, even after I'm dead. You see, my continued existence, even if only a perception, is far more valuable to them than my public death."

Malone had read briefing reports of how bin Laden was a master at oratory, so he told himself to listen with care—debating with the devil had never been productive for anyone.

"I want to cease my wanderings. I want to become your prisoner. I'll be tried in a court. That's your way. There, I'll have a forum from which to speak. More important, my followers will know I'm alive. And when you finally execute me, they'll know I'm dead. Either way, I win."

"We may not execute you."

"But those *others* certainly will."

He flushed the poison from his ears. "Sharma knows you're here?"

Bin Laden nodded. "These ruins have been a great refuge. No one has ever looked in this country for me. Sharma is *your* friend. You trust him, though you want no one to know that. So I chose this as my haven. Now, with my blessing, Sharma offers me to you. But he wants no credit. You found me. You captured me. That's the way it will be. I've sent many martyrs to die for our cause—"

"Am I supposed to be impressed?"

Bin Laden seemed unfazed by the interruption. "Look around you, Mr. Malone. Ancient battles occurred here. Mainly with bows, spears and stones. The custom was, after a battle, for warriors to bring the heads of the slain to their officers for a reward. Great honor came from having the most heads."

"You should know."

His enemy's stern face melted into a grin. "Many heads have been brought to me. Now it's my turn to do the bringing."

"But you want your death to be a spectacle."

"No leader wishes to die in obscurity."

"Why me?"

"Sharma says you're...a good man."

His mind swirled with possibilities as he tried to decide what to do next. Bin Laden seemed to read his thoughts.

"You have arrangements to make. I understand. Do

so. But know this. I'll surrender to you tomorrow, here, at noon. And only to you. Alone."

He raised the Glock. "Why not now?"

"Look around you, Mr. Malone."

His gaze strafed the ruins. On the cliffs above him he spotted eight turbaned men with automatic rifles.

"Thought you said you came alone?"

"I lied. But you're still breathing, which shows that I'm telling the truth about surrendering. Tomorrow, here, noon. Alone."

And the devil shuffled away.

Malone returned to the capital and, from the American embassy, immediately made contact with Stephanie Nelle at the Magellan Billet offices in Atlanta. He told her what happened, and six hours later he was informed that an army special forces unit would covertly enter the country from Afghanistan by 7:00 a.m. the following morning. He had no intention of taking possession of bin Laden alone, nor did the military want to be absent when that happened. So he'd made, as bin Laden had said, *arrangements*.

Malone met the unit at a prearranged point on the highway north of the capital. It consisted of six soldiers and two officers, all dressed in nondescript civilian clothing. Colonel Rick Cobb was in charge, a slender man with reddish-blond hair and deep-set green eyes. Malone explained what he wanted the unit to do, then left them on the side of the road as he drove off for Rampur.

At precisely noon Malone strolled back into the ruins. A pall of impenetrable mist shrouded the precipice and shielded the cliffs overhead. He stepped with caution, waiting to see what would happen.

Bin Laden appeared, just like yesterday. Today, Malone wasn't going to chitchat. "Ready to go?"

"As promised."

He withdrew his Glock.

"That's not necessary."

"Makes me feel better."

His prisoner shrugged. "Then, by all means."

"Your friends here today?"

"Until we're safely away. Then they'll be gone."

It took twenty minutes to hike down to Malone's car, the going slow because of bin Laden's cane-assisted gait. Before loading the Arab into the passenger's seat Malone frisked him. Bin Laden seemed to expect the violation and did not resist.

They left Rampur and started the drive back for the capital. About halfway, Malone spied the same battered cars on the side of the highway. He eased onto the shoulder and parked behind them.

The doors to both opened and the American unit poured out.

"Friends of yours?" bin Laden calmly asked.

"Your keepers."

"The deal was I surrendered only to you."

"I lied."

Malone left the following day. President Sharma attempted no contact, but he expected none. The announcement that Osama bin Laden had been captured would come through the White House, and the American military would receive full credit. Contrary to what bin Laden may have thought, Malone neither expected nor desired public acknowledgment.

Nor, he knew, did Sharma.

Both their jobs were done.

Two weeks passed with no announcement. Malone was dispatched to Germany, then to Bulgaria, Australia and Norway. After another two months and still nothing, he decided to see what was happening. Stephanie Nelle was likewise curious, so she made an official inquiry.

"Cotton, they don't know what we're talking about," she told him over the phone from Billet headquarters.

He was between planes in London. "Stephanie, I drove the SOB in my car. He was sitting beside me. I turned him over to an army colonel."

"I gave them the name of the officer. Rick Cobb. He's a colonel, assigned to special forces, but that day he was on leave in the United States. Nowhere near you. That's been verified."

"You get a description of him?"

She told him, and it in no way matched the man to whom he'd handed over bin Laden. "What the hell's happening here? They playing games with us?"

"Why? The president would give his left nut to have bin Laden in custody."

Malone heard what bin Laden said to him. *These others want to prevent such a glorious ending for me.*

"I need to talk to Sharma. I'll get back to you."

Malone found an Internet portal in a business alcove of the international terminal. There, he connected his laptop and sent an e-mail, which he knew was precisely how Sharma liked to communicate. The president hated telephones—*uncontrollable*—and preferred to retain a hard copy of all his messages. So Malone kept his message simple:

MY GIFT IS GONE.

His plane was not for another two hours, so he sat and waited. Interestingly, the response came in less than ten minutes.

REVISIT THE RUINS.

Malone knew that was all he was going to get. Obviously, Sharma had been expecting contact. Malone had been on his way back to Atlanta for three days of rest before his next assignment.

Not anymore.

Late autumn had a firm grip on the Pan Mountains as Malone parked at the base of the ridge that led up to the Rampur ruins. The air was a solid forty degrees cooler than it had been three months ago, and snow draped the surrounding peaks in long veils.

He reached beneath his parka and withdrew his Glock. He had no idea what was waiting for him, but he had to follow Sharma's lead.

He climbed in measured steps, careful on the frozen earth. He entered the site and allowed his senses to absorb the same barren desolation. He pressed on and explored, his mind alert.

Automatic gunfire startled him.

Bullets ricocheted off boulders.

"Far enough, Malone," a man said in English. "Let your gun hit the ground."

He released his grip and turned. "Colonel Rick Cobb" hopped down from a narrow cliff and descended the stacked boulders.

"I was told you returned to the country yesterday," Cobb said. "So I knew you'd be here today."

"I like to be punctual."

"Funny, too. What a guy."

"And you are?"

"Colonel Rick Cobb. Who else?"

"You know I don't buy that."

"That's all you're going to get."

"Okay, Colonel Rick Cobb, you plan to tell me what happened to bin Laden?"

"How about I show you?" Cobb motioned with the rifle. "That way."

Malone walked past more mounds of rubble and turned a corner. A cold breeze raked his limbs and dried his lips. He spotted a blackened splotch of earth near where an outer wall once stood. Weather was rapidly erasing the traces, but it was clear something had been burned there recently.

"All that's left," Cobb said. "Shot him myself, right about where you're standing, then we burned the murdering asshole till there was nothing left."

"And the purpose of that?"

"Damn, you have to ask? He killed Americans. He was an enemy of the state."

"You're no soldier."

"Soldiers have rules, and rules have a nasty way of interfering with what's right. I work outside the rules."

"Bin Laden said you were after him. He told me you wanted him dead, but for no one else to know. Care to tell me the point?"

"Come on, you're a bright guy. America is spending tens of billions of dollars on the war on terror. More money than anyone can even comprehend. It's like manna, my friend—straight from heaven."

Malone was glad his suspicions now seemed confirmed. "And there are a lot of corporations getting rich."

"Now you're thinking. Have you looked at the stock prices for some of the defense contractors? Through the roof. Lots of smaller companies are making a fortune, too. Can't let that end."

"And you work for them?"

"They all got together and decided to hire one team. The best in the business. Hell, we developed a better intel network than the government. Took us over a year, but we finally got close to bin Laden. We damn near got him twice. About eight months ago, though, he dropped from everybody's radar. Gone. We were beginning to worry, until you called in."

"We contacted the military that day, through official channels, not you."

Cobb nodded. "That you did. But we have friends real high on the food chain. After all, this is a gold mine for the military, too. *Nobody* wants this gravy train to end. So they called us and, luckily, we were nearby."

"So you brought him back here and killed him."

"Good a place as any. His people ran like scalded dogs after you two drove off. I sent a few additional men to keep an eye on this place. So instead of driving south to the Afghan border, we just doubled around and came here. Over and done with it in two hours. His body burned fast."

Something else he wanted to know. "Why use real military-personnel names? We checked, there's a Colonel Rick Cobb."

The man shrugged. "Makes it easier to move around. Damn computers allow everybody to be monitored. We choose the guys on leave. Our friends at the Pentagon kept us informed. Like I said, can't let the gravy train end."

"Why would it?"

"Get real. You know the answer. Americans have short memories. They get blown up on 9/11, they invade a few places, kick some butt, then capture Saddam. Next thing they want is it all to end. Public opinion is already fading. Politicians are feeling the heat. That means budget cuts, priorities shifting—all bad things for my employers. Last thing they need is for bin Laden to be corralled. No. Keep him out there. Make him a threat. Let 'em wonder. Stalin did the same thing with Hitler after World War II. He knew the bastard was dead, but fueled everyone's fear that the devil may still be alive and kicking. All to keep his enemies off guard."

"So you now control bin Laden's existence."

"Every damn bit of it. And we plan on making him quite the badass."

"What are you doing here?"

"Waiting for you. I have a message. My employers want you to stop snooping around. Leave it be."

"Why would I?"

"'Cause you got squat to show for anything. What are you going to do? Claim you captured bin Laden? You'd sound like a nut. No body, no photo. There's nothing left of him for any DNA match with one of those twenty or so kids he supposedly fathered. It's over. Let it be. Move on."

"And if I don't?"

"We're not in the habit of killing our own, but we're not opposed to it either."

"You're no better than he was." He started to leave, but Cobb quickly blocked the way. "I'd move if I were you."

The gun came level. "You a tough guy, Malone?"

"Tough enough I don't need a rifle to protect myself from you."

He stood rock still. He wasn't going to let Cobb know for a second he was scared. But who wouldn't be? The dark end of a rifle barrel was not a pleasant sight.

Cobb lowered the gun.

Malone had guessed right. They wanted him alive. Who better to start the ball rolling than some American agent who claimed bin Laden surrendered to him and that there was some sort of conspiracy designed to conceal bin Laden's death. The military would deny the assertions and, in the process, supercharge the world's fear of bin Laden. He'd have nothing for proof and they'd have the terror of the past.

Easy to see who'd win that battle.

"Go on, Malone. Get out of here. Go tell the world what you know."

Not a chance.

He slammed the heel of his boot into Cobb's right knee. The move clearly caught the man off guard. Maybe he'd thought him incapable? He heard bone break and he planted a fist into the jaw. Cobb cried out in agony as he crumpled to the ground, clutching his wounded leg. Malone lifted the rifle from the ground.

"I'll say it again. You're no better than he was. He killed for Allah. You do it for profit."

"The...devil...got his due."

Malone slung the rifle out into the open air, beyond the crumbled wall, and left.

Malone zipped his suitcase shut and checked out of his hotel. Downstairs, he stepped out into the frigid evening and searched the crowded street for a taxi to the airport. One appeared and he quickly climbed into the back seat. The driver eased his way through stop-and-start traffic. Darkness came quickly this time of year to central Asia and night had enveloped the city by the time they stopped at the terminal. He handed the driver forty rubles and was about to leave when the man said in Russian, "Mr. Malone, my president has something for you."

He stared at the driver from the rear seat as the man handed him a brown envelope.

"He also said to wish you well."

Malone thanked the man and added another twenty rubles for his trouble. Sharma's reach was extensive, he'd give the man that. Through the envelope he felt the distinctive outline of a CD. Inside the terminal he checked his bag, then, with his carry-on draped over his shoulder, headed for the gate. There, he opened the envelope and saw that it contained a disk, along with a note. He read the message, then inserted the CD into his laptop.

On the screen appeared a video. He watched while the phony colonel named Cobb shot Osama bin Laden. Then, with the help of the other paramilitary members, whose faces Malone recognized, Cobb burned the body. The screen went dark, then a new video began. This one featured him and Cobb hours earlier. Malone found his earphones and switched on the audio. The sound of their voices was excellent and their entire encounter, including Malone's assault, was recorded.

Then the screen went black.

He shook his head.

Yossef Sharma had been watching. Though he was the head of a nation that possessed no means of adequately protecting itself, the president was a clever man. He'd wanted the United States to have bin Laden because that's what bin Laden wanted. But that had not happened. So Sharma had delivered another gift. One that Malone would this time personally hold on to until the moment was right. A little legwork would be needed, but it shouldn't be hard to track down Cobb, his cohorts and their employers. After all, that was the Magellan Billet's specialty.

He read again the note that had been included with the disk.

MAKE SURE ALL THE DEVILS GET THEIR DUE.

Damn right.
He stood and headed for his plane.

KATHERINE NEVILLE

Katherine Neville's award-winning first novel, *The Eight*, is widely regarded as a cult classic, translated into thirty languages. That story begins at the dawn of the French Revolution when a fabulous, bejeweled chess set, once owned by Charlemagne but buried for a thousand years, is dug up by the nuns of a French abbey and scattered around the world to preserve its mysterious powers. The nonstop suspense moves from the 1790s of the French Revolution to the 1970s of the OPEC oil embargo. The plot itself is a giant chess game, and the characters are pieces and pawns.

When Neville began her long-anticipated sequel, she was glad that she could retrieve many fascinating historic figures, characters like Benjamin Franklin who, due to earlier schedule constraints, she'd had to limit to walk-on parts. But even despite the recent flurry of additional histories, biographies and films heralding Franklin's three hundredth birthday, Neville's research offered her a big surprise that, inexplicably, none of the experts appeared to have noticed. When it came to her character's well-documented, almost obsessive, penchant for creating or joining private clubs, here was an enigmatic gap in his life.

The Tuesday Club fills that void.

THE TUESDAY CLUB

Franklin would not have been Franklin without
a club, and his club in France was the Lodge of
the Nine Sisters.
—Carl Van Doren, *Benjamin Franklin*

August 31, 1784, 7:00 a.m.
Auteuil, France

Today, the day of the crisis, was a Tuesday.

As always, thought Mme Helvetius with irony,
things went more to the mark in French—*non?* For example, in French, the name Tuesday was *mardi*, Mars
Day, the day of the god of war. And given the impending crisis, and the message she'd just received, any
thought of Mars spelled more than it seemed—indeed, it could spell *la calamité!*

Although Mme Helvetius had been awaiting such
a message for months, it was so cleverly coded that

even the messenger who'd brought it from Scotland could not understand it. Still, given his urgency, she knew it could only mean that what she had expected was about to happen, quite soon, something that could ruin all her well-crafted plans, that might place their entire enterprise—their very lives—in danger.

But to deliver the message right away would require a deception.

In stealth, she let herself out the side French windows of her private salon to where her gardener's large white mule stood patiently, saddled and waiting. The mâître d'hôtel of her estates—a very bossy man, indeed (servants today carried themselves with more pretensions than the nobility ever dreamt of)—had insisted she must take care, if traveling in secrecy and alone.

She understood that the extensive entourage within her household would be inflamed with curiosity if they saw her depart so early. She hoped they all believed in a clandestine tryst she'd never taken pains to deny. At home or abroad, these days, every room and road in France was riddled with spies, acting on behalf of one fractious faction or another: to be cautious was to be wise.

Nonetheless, Mme Helvetius felt a complete fool in this ridiculous disguise, dressed as she was in the faded blue costume borrowed from her milkmaid (which smelled rather rich) and a dilapidated straw hat. Done up like a strumpet, astride a big white mule—she, Anne-Catherine de Ligniville-Autricourt, Mme Helvetius—one of the wealthiest women in France and, at one time, among the most beautiful. Well, that had been another day. And she was, assuredly, another woman.

With impatience, Mme Helvetius prodded the mule to go faster through the rolling hills and vineyards still drenched with dew, along the dusty, winding road from her *banlieue* of Auteuil, just outside Paris, to its neighboring suburb of Passy. When she noticed the mule eyeing a heavy bunch of grapes along the road, she tapped his rump firmly with her hand, muttered, *"Obstiné,"* under her breath, and jerked at the reins.

Although she might be anxious to reach her destination, Mme Helvetius couldn't help thinking about the strangeness of the message running unbidden through her mind like a long-forgotten melody. The oddity of it—so peculiar, like nothing she'd ever thought of. Whatever could it mean? There was only one person, she knew, who could decipher it. She must get to him—and quickly.

The mule was so slow, it seemed hours before Mme Helvetius at last spied the sun breaking over the eastern cliff. And there, high on its perch above the river Seine, lay her destination: Le Valentinois. Tucked like an ostentatious jewel into its lavish setting of gardens and follies, plashing fountains and octagonal pools, the famous château was a bastion of extravagance that would rival a pasha's palace.

Mme Helvetius felt the chill she felt whenever she came here, which was more often than she cared think of. Given the criticality of her mission, she was grateful she'd come in this attire, so she might eschew the carriage entrance and enter through the gardens where she wouldn't be recognized. For Le Valentinois, despite its opulence, was known as the nest of gunrunners, speculators, thieves and spies—a notorious circle formed and fed upon war and crisis, of the sort they'd just come through in Europe.

This circle was ruled by the most dangerous man of all: the château's wealthy, mysterious owner, Donatien le Ray de Chaumont. Given the importance of her message, she prayed she was not walking with open eyes into a trap. At whatever cost, she must deliver the message in private, before the household was stirring. She must get the message to Franklin at once—here in his private wing of the château.

Only Dr. Franklin would know what they must do— what action the club must take when it met tonight— that is, once he had deciphered the message in that song.

8:00 a.m.
Auteuil, France

One might be lonely in Paris, thought Abigail Adams with chagrin—but one could surely never be alone!

Wherever one tried to move, crowds of unwashed bodies closed in about one. The streets were a cesspool. No wonder the Parisians wore more lace around their necks than a Dutch tablecloth—within easy reach of their noses, to block the smell! Hadn't her dear Mr. Adams fallen deathly ill each time he'd crossed the waters here from America?

And the women! There were forty thousand of them licensed as whores (she blushed even to think the word) who'd been sanctioned to "ply their craft" within the very city gates.

And the boxes! A horror she'd gleaned from the churchwardens themselves: boxes set out on designated street corners for women to drop their unwanted children into. An improvement, they said, upon the "old days" of the philosopher Rousseau, when babies had been left on church steps to die of exposure— some frozen so hard, they had to scrape their little bodies off the stones. O, iniquity!

After just a few days in Paris, Abigail felt, before exposing them further to this rotten decadence, she should take herself off with her own two children, Nabby and Johnnie, for a steam cleaning at a thermal spa.

So thank heavens, Abigail sighed in relief, from now on they would not have to spend another moment in the sordid sink. Her dear Mr. Adams had secured them a place in the country, at Auteuil.

The house was quite impressive—fifty rooms! Replete with gardens and servants, far across the river from the city's turmoil. There was an extra plum in the pudding, too, for just next door to their new residence lived the woman whom Dr. Franklin had once described to Abigail as "a true Frenchwoman, free of all pretension…the best person in the world." Her name was Mme Helvetius.

It did seem to Abigail, despite the lady's heralded modesty, that Mme Helvetius had a few gifts and accomplishments of her own to boast of. Among these she was still considered, at nearly age sixty, to be among the most beautiful women in France. It was said that the poet Fontenelle, on his hundredth birthday, had sighed, "Mme Helvetius makes one long to be eighty again."

Abigail had learned, too, that the lady's late husband was a famous philosophe who'd planned to found a club of distinguished dignitaries and scientists. Upon his death, his widow, Mme Helvetius, had drawn upon her own fortune to fund the club's creation: "The Lodge of Nine Sisters" it was called, referring to muses of the arts and sciences. As its official founder, Mme Helvetius was the only woman admitted to the Lodge's private meetings. Though these were by invitation only, they were far from secret, for the club boasted among its early members Lafayette, Voltaire and Dr.

Franklin: the doctor had tapped its financial connections for monies needed to ensure the success of the American Revolution.

Her new neighbor here in Auteuil must be a great lady indeed, thought Abigail as she dressed to depart for her day at Le Valentinois—Abigail couldn't wait to meet her. But hadn't Dr. Franklin said that Mme Helvetius's club always met on a Tuesday?

So Abigail might make her acquaintance, even tonight.

9:00 a.m.
Bois de Boulogne

John Adams truly loathed Anne-Catherine de Ligniville-Autricourt, Mme Helvetius. Like his attitude toward most French aristocracy, he'd despised her nearly from the day they'd first met.

Cantering on his gray gelding through the Bois de Boulogne, as he did each morning, Adams thought of this woman who had wreaked so much damage, over all these years upon the American mission to France. Naturally, he couldn't share these feelings with Abigail—though he'd never kept secrets from his dear spouse before. But La Helvetius, like so many of these useless upper-class women, had captivated the great Dr. Franklin with her so-called "gaiety and charm." The doctor was besotted with all things French.

Adams knew he must exercise caution in his dealings here on the continent. He'd been recalled once by Congress, from a previous mission, due to complaints by the French minister, Vergennes, about his comportment in diplomatic circles. But Adams had always suspected it was Franklin himself who'd gotten him recalled. For the doctor, who'd lived much of his life abroad and had soaked up the sins of each land, could no longer abide Yankee honesty and directness.

Adams could only pray that, if not he, then at least Thomas Jefferson would be able to talk some sense into the good doctor, regarding the critical treaties that they three were to forge with England and France. And there was something more.

There was a fly in the molasses when it came to this blighted French mission. Adams suspected it had been there for quite some time: there was a spy—perhaps even a double agent—working all this while in Passy, right under the nose of Benjamin Franklin. As God himself knew, that residence, Le Valentinois, was fraught with dire possibilities. Not only Chaumont, its arms-dealer owner, was suspect. But also Franklin's own twenty-two-year-old grandson who lived there, Temple Franklin, a youth whose father William (Ben's bastard son) was himself a Royalist exiled from America.

In John Adams's view, however—of the elitist aristocrats, Royalist sympathizers and nouveau riche the doctor always sucked into his orb in that retreat at Passy—the most dangerous of all was Mme Helvetius. And for very good reason.

The Sieure Helvetius, her late husband, had made his fortune by royal sinecure, hadn't he? He was one of the "Farmers General," those who'd been given exclusive rights, monopolies, one might say, over all sale and purchase of goods produced or imported by France. The same people who still held sway, today, over American trade with France and her dominions.

As for La Helvetius, she'd even established a secret society to help her circle of vipers maintain control—a club whose members had the audacity to call themselves liberals, Freemasons!—when half its founders came from the nobility of France!

As Adams patted the flanks of his steaming horse and prepared to make toward Passy to attend his morning meeting, he smiled at a private thought: He imagined his wife, a preacher's daughter, meeting La Helvetius for the first time.

It might happen today, mightn't it? After all, today was a Tuesday.

10:00 a.m.
Passy, France

Benjamin Franklin plucked his knight from the chessboard and set it down beside his opponent's rook. He tapped his finger on the table for attention.

"If you take that knight with your castle, my friend, it's mate in three," he announced to Thomas Jefferson, who'd glanced across the board in surprise. "But if you don't take my knight," Franklin added with a wry grin, "then I'm afraid it will still be mate in five."

"My dear Jefferson," said John Adams, standing at the wall of windows overlooking the vast, manicured gardens of Le Valentinois, "that's the third game you've lost in a row. If your skills at negotiating treaties—for which Congress sent us to France, after all—are no better than your skills at chess, we may as well pack up our portmanteaus and go home."

"Nonsense," said Franklin, putting the chess pieces back in order on the board. "Jefferson hasn't had the practice I've had. When I play chess, I brook no distractions. Why, I've played a full evening, whilst Mme Brillon, my erstwhile *amour*, sat in a state of deshabille, soaking in her bath!"

Franklin laughed uproariously, then he saw Jefferson rubbing his unpowdered head of thick hair with both hands.

"Too much mental stimulation for one morning, I'm afraid, and not enough accomplishment," Jefferson said, adding apologetically, "I seem to feel one of my migraines coming on."

"Willow bark," said Franklin. "It contains a pain-killing ingredient specific to headaches. I never disturb the servants this early, but I'll ring for them to find Bancroft, the secretary of our embassy—high time you met—and he shall make you a willow tisane. The chap's a medicinal genius," Franklin assured Jefferson. "Worked on a plantation in Guiana. He's patented all sorts of textile dyes made from barks and tropical plants. I sponsored his election, years ago, to the Royal Society in London—he's been our covert British agent ever since."

"But how do you know you can trust the fellow?" asked Adams. "Some say Edward Bancroft's a war speculator, only out to profit himself. If he takes our money, he may do the same with the French or British. Should he be privy to communiqués from Congress? And take notes of our private councils?"

"My dear Adams—" Franklin was already pulling the bell cord, as if shrugging off such concerns "—everyone in France is a spy of some kind. You'll find that a few things have changed since your last foray to this continent. For one, there's no war going on, upon which one might speculate—either financially or philosophically. We keep eyes on the British only to make sure they won't begin one! For another, here at Le Valentinois, we live life so openly and blamelessly that there is really nothing to spy upon!"

No sooner had Franklin released the bell cord than

the door to the outer hall popped open. There stood Edward Bancroft, splendidly outfitted in lacy jabot, satin breeches and powdered wig—dressed, as always, for a fancy ball. Adams shot a wicked glance toward Franklin, who ignored it.

"Dash me," said Franklin with his same wry smile. "It seems the walls have ears. My dear Bancroft, we were just speaking of you!"

"I must possess better powers than Professor Mesmer," said Bancroft, returning the smile. "Only a moment ago, whilst in the small salon, I had the intuitive feeling I was wanted here in this room. Now I find you—uncustomarily dressed at this hour—and locked away with some colleagues. By all appearances, you three gents are already working up a storm of intrigue before your secretary's arrival."

"Nothing of the sort," Franklin assured him. "We were playing chess. May I present Mr. Jefferson— lately arrived from America?" Bancroft took Jefferson's proffered hand as Franklin added, "And, of course, Adams here is not unknown to you—though his wife and daughter, who've just set foot on these shores, will be joining us to dine."

"I've had the pleasure of their acquaintance moments ago," Bancroft told him.

"Yes," explained Adams. "My family wanted to arrive early. John Quincy had promised to take the doctor's little grandson, Benny, for a ride in Mr. Jefferson's trap."

"As we've so many young folk, my dear Bancroft," said Franklin, "you might ask the servants for an earlier meal than our usual two o'clock repast. Oh, and while you're at it, a willow bark tisane for Mr. Jefferson."

The instant John Adams was sure that Bancroft was out of earshot, he struck out again: "Do you not find it odd that your secretary was lurking at the door, just when his name came up in conversation?" he demanded of Franklin.

"*Our* secretary," Franklin corrected him. "He is paid by the mission. And I don't find it strange, when I was just ringing to find him myself—"

"Good Lord!" cried Jefferson, peering out the library's French windows. "There is a barnyard animal eating your costly roses, and the wench who's astride him clearly can't manage the beast!"

The two men went to the windows. There, at the center of the jewel-like garden, a middle-aged woman sat astride an obdurate white mule, yanking at the reins. When this got her nowhere, she swung her leg over the saddle in apparent exasperation, dismounted like a man, and still grasping the reins forcefully, she uprooted a bunch of flowers from a nearby garden bed and shoved them into the mule's muzzle. The beast, instantly diverted by the fresh buds, took a healthy mouthful.

Franklin smiled a strange, private smile.

"I believe that I am acquainted with that 'wench' out there—though not with her beast," he informed his companions. "I may add, in my experience, the lady has assuredly mounted animals superior to that one." He laughed as he saw the astonished faces of Adams and Jefferson.

"Do you not recognize her?" Franklin asked Adams. When the latter shook his head, Franklin clarified: "It is Notre dame d'Auteuil."

"Madame Helvetius?" cried Adams, aghast.

When Franklin nodded, Jefferson said, "Not the wife of the philosophe! But why is she dressed as a farmer's wife?"

"Ah, the upper classes are always a mystery, aren't

they?" said Franklin. "Our charming queen, Marie Antoinette, has a peasant farm on the grounds of the palace, where she plays at being a poor shepherdess. Rousseau has made these 'natural' ideas so popular."

But privately, Franklin couldn't imagine why Anne-Catherine Helvetius would arrive here in this fashion, astride a recalcitrant mule. The situation did not bode well.

Suddenly he saw that Mme Helvetius had lashed her mule to a tempting-looking lemon tree with lush green leaves. While it was occupied, she was headed on foot—with a swiftness that almost resembled stealth—straight for the garden entrance to the salon, where the others Bancroft had mentioned would be waiting.

What in blazes was the woman thinking, prancing about in the garden instead of using the customary entrance? And where was her driver? Where was her cabriolet? Action seemed called for on Franklin's part—and quickly.

"Enough for the morning, gentlemen, I can rest here no longer," he announced, rubbing his leg as if to plead his eternal gout. "Let's attend to the others, shall we?"

And, leaving the two men to collect themselves, he hobbled swiftly out the door.

He was too late—at least, too late to halt the explosion.

Echoing down the long gallery of mirrors and many-paned windows that led from the library came a piercing shriek that had emanated from within the salon. Franklin knew it could only be Anne-Catherine Helvetius:

"O, mon Dieu, ou est Franklin? Et qui sont ces dames-là?"

A bit more commotion from within—raised voices, the sound of a door opened and banged shut, then a moment of silence. Franklin stepped up his painful gait along the corridor. All at once, Anne-Catherine Helvetius came hurtling down the hall toward him, her idiotic straw hat askew. In her flush of excitement, she nearly collided with him.

Grasping her by the arms, Franklin said, "My beloved friend…" But then he caught a whiff of her. "What is that interesting aroma—a new *eau de parfum?*"

Helvetius glared up at him in fury.

"My milkmaid's dress! I am *en camouflage!*" she said, trying to keep her voice down. "That *cafard* of a mule. I have been on his back for hours. And now this—a roomful of women. You never entertain so early—and so many guests! I do not wish to intrude, but this is of great urgency, *mon ami…*"

"*Au contraire*, my beloved *madame*," Franklin assured her, "you're always a welcome guest. I pray you'll join us for an early dinner." Casting an eye again at her attire, he added with amusement, "I am sorry to inform you, however, *madame*, that no cows will be available for milking—we were not planning to hold our meal alfresco!"

"*Canaille!*" cried Mme Helvetius, stamping her foot.

"*Madame!* Your language!" Franklin cautioned with a saucy grin.

With her next words, he looked as though he'd been seized with an attack of kidney stones, on top of the gout.

"*Faites attention!*" she told Franklin, sotto voce, lest prying ears overhear: "*Le message est arrivé!*"

"The message!" he nearly cried aloud. "Then we should not be seen here…"

Just then came the distant sound of the library door closing, followed by clicking footsteps approaching.

"My colleagues arrive," whispered Franklin. "What is the message?"

"C'est encodé!" Mme Helvetius whispered back, her silvery eyes enormous.

"Of course it's encoded!" snapped Franklin, pulling in irritation at the long tail of his own hair that clung to his shoulder. "What is it?"

When Anne-Catherine stood on tiptoe and put her lips to Franklin's ear, he caught another whiff of her attire—earthy, like a barnyard, but not altogether rank.

"'Frère Jacques,'" Mme Helvetius whispered.

The silence was broken only by the footsteps approaching the corner, where they would soon be exposed, huddled together here in the open hall.

"A name?" Franklin whispered back. "No other clue? Just 'Brother Jacques'?"

"Non, non, mon ami," she breathed in impatience. *"C'est une chanson!"*

"A song is the message?" said Franklin in confusion. But when Mme Helvetius hummed the first notes under her breath, he said, "Ah, I see—very clever!" With a quick pat on her rump, he said, "Make haste. To the salon, by the far door. I shall join you."

In swift comprehension, she vanished into the east hall just a moment before Adams and Jefferson rounded the corner. With his colleagues close at heel, Franklin entered the salon just as Mme Helvetius appeared breathlessly through a door at the opposite side of the crowded room. All the guests and family members turned to greet Franklin. Though his own heart was beating like a Mohican drum, he shot Mme Helvetius a confident smile across the room. He knew exactly what he must do.

12:00 noon
Le Valentinois

Benjamin Franklin looked around the table at the assorted group who had collected, as customary, for the seven-course afternoon repast at the expense of his host. Today it was a few hours early—but then, time was of the essence, was it not?

Here at the table were those who would soon represent the past: the owner of this magnificent château, the pudgy millionaire Donatien le Ray de Chaumont, who had an ax to grind: he was still outraged with the American Congress, which had never paid his bills to supply arms for the Revolution. Beside Chaumont, his attractive wife—the mistress, some said (*de temps en temps*) of the naval hero John Paul Jones. Then the revolutionary playwright Beaumarchais, author of huge hits, *The Marriage of Figaro* and *The Barber of Seville,* a man who had run more munitions into the British colonies than any other, in aid of the revolution. Mme Helvetius was seated between Franklin himself and John Adams, with Abigail at Adams's far side—looking annoyed by Notre dame d'Auteuil's blithe bantering to her husband—part of her inane camouflage.

Thomas Jefferson sat at the side of the table that Franklin viewed as the future. Beside Jefferson was young John Quincy Adams, seventeen, who seemed to dote on the Virginian's each word. Quincy's sister, Abigail the younger—Nabby Adams—who at age nineteen seemed to have captivated Franklin's twenty-two-year-old grandson, Temple. And Benny Franklin Bache, Franklin's other grandson, the youngest at the table at age fifteen, who was bracketed at the other side by Edward Bancroft, the mission's secretary and sometime spy.

After the soup course had been served and the servants had departed, Franklin announced portentously, "Thirteen at dinner, an inauspicious number—for it reminds one always of that other supper where the host said, 'Tonight, one of you shall deny me and one of you shall betray me.'"

Mme Helvetius shot Franklin a steely sideways glance. Then, unilaterally changing the subject, she picked up her spoon with a charming smile, removed a bit of crayfish from her bowl and deposited it on her plate.

"This month does not have an *R*," she informed the group. "One should never eat *les crustaces* in months spelled without *R*—they may contain poison."

"But, Grandfather," said Benny Bache, as if she had not spoken, "do you really expect someone to deny or betray you tonight? And even if you did, it surely wouldn't be any of us, here at this table."

"I have reason, my child, to believe precisely that," Franklin assured his grandson. "In support of this view, I must mention that I have recently received an encrypted message..."

He paused, for Mme Helvetius was choking on her soup; Chaumont dashed around the table with some Madeira from the sideboard, and poured it into her glass. She swilled down several large gulps—more than the Adamses had ever seen a woman put away at one sitting. When things had calmed a bit, John Quincy Adams chimed in, "Dr. Franklin, we all realize that an encrypted message must be held in the greatest secrecy. Especially if it might pertain—as you seem to believe—to someone in this room. I confess I am fascinated with codes. And Mr. Jefferson here, like you, is an expert of sorts. He has promised to help train me in the basic ideas while my family and I are in France. I'd be glad if you could tell us only two things. How did you know that the message was encrypted? And have you been able to decipher what it means?"

Franklin was wolfing down his crayfish soup with gusto—with seeming disregard for whether the month was spelled with an *R* or not—also disregarding his painful gout and kidney stones, which he referred to as his "Grit and Gravel."

"Your first and second questions both have the same reply," Franklin said, setting his spoon aside from his empty bowl. "I knew it was encrypted, and I know what it means because I have the key!"

There was much commotion, which afforded Mme Helvetius the opportunity to give Franklin a healthy poke in the ribs. As he leaned to peck her cheek, he whispered, "Say nothing at all—the game has just begun." She lapsed into silence.

"Today is a Tuesday," Franklin said. "As many of you know, Mme Helvetius, who sits by my side, for decades held philosophical salons on that day with her husband in their Paris mansion. You may also know that Madame is the founding sponsor of an elite lodge of Freemasons, here in France, known as the Loge des Neuf Soeurs. This club, of which I am an initiate and twice a grandmaster, also meets on Tuesdays, and continues to perform many useful services for our United States. What significance can we assign to this day of the week?"

"It's the day of the Norse god, Tiw, which is Mars in French," said Quincy.

"Indeed," agreed Franklin. "But there is something more."

The servants had arrived to remove and replace the plates. When they had passed the platters of duckling, truffled foie gras, quail, rabbit and legumes, they topped off the wineglasses and departed. Only then did Franklin take the floor.

"I once attended the meeting of another such club, in another time and place," Franklin began. "It was nearly thirty years ago, in 1754, that I had reason to leave my home in Philadelphia and travel to points south. At that time, there was no inkling that one day— a day not far in our future—we colonists would revolt against the mother country and form a new republic. Indeed, at the moment we were having more trouble with the French, who were fortifying the Ohio River Valley. And with the Indians, whom they were also fortifying, with French weapons and Louisiana rum.

"In a few years, a young soldier named Washington would fire the first shot in the French and Indian War. As that war soon dragged all of Europe, even India, into a Seven Years War leading to our own revolution, it would truly become the first 'shot heard round the world.'

"In January of that year, I'd just attended a summit of some of these disgruntled Indian nations—only to learn, on my return to Philadelphia, that I'd been appointed deputy postmaster for the colonies, an important role. As there was another Indian conference looming in a few months, at Albany, I determined it would be a prudent time right now for me to make a quick tour of postal facilities throughout the southern colonies. Among the most important of these was Annapolis, on the Chesapeake Bay.

"My reputation as an inventor preceded me—as the discoverer, only a few years back, of harnessing lightning from the skies. The instant the *Maryland Gazette* announced the new deputy postmaster's arrival in the bustling waterfront community, I received a flood of invitations from political, social and scientific societies.

"The most mysterious of these was from a group of gentlemen claiming to be none of the above. Rather, they represented themselves as amateur musicians, many of Scottish descent, who met twice a month to compose and perform music. As these meetings always took place on Tuesdays, they had dubbed their little group 'The Tuesday Club.'" As Franklin began his tale, the only sound to be heard was that of cutlery scraping on plates…

The Tuesday evening that I joined the group was a dismal, rain-splashed night on the waterfront. The founder of the club, who greeted me at the door, was a native of Edinburgh, a recent transplant to our shores: one Alexander Hamilton—no relation to our congressman and war hero by that name. The Hamilton name is a powerful one in Scotland. I soon had cause to understand what that might mean, in the grander scheme.

The members, whose names I've long forgotten, played amusing songs all the night. We were dubbed with secret names—I was called Electrico Vitrifico, I recall, for my bringing of the power of lightning to earth. They had made a model of my glass 'armonica for playing watery tunes. There was a supper, much drinking of alcohol, and between, some Freemason ditties were sung. Since I'd been a chartering member of Philadelphia's lodge in the 1730s, I recognized myself to be among the brethren, and felt well at ease. There is nothing better than the camaraderie of a club.

It was late that same night, after most of the young gents had returned to their households, when I found myself alone with Hamilton's inner clique, as it were. It was then that I came to pose the most important question: "What song is it that you've asked me here to listen to?"

The members, by all appearances, were exceedingly pleased by my remark. They stood one by one to sing, a cappella, a familiar rondel or canon of ancient origin. First they sang in French, then in English, a song like this:

Frère Jacques, Frère Jacques,
Dormez-Vous? Dormez-Vous?
Sonnez les Matines, Sonnez les Matines,
Din-Dan-Don, Din-Dan-Don…

Are you sleeping? Are you sleeping?
Brother John, Brother John,
Morning bells are ringing, morning bells are ringing,
Ding-Ding-Dong, Ding-Ding-Dong…

As each singer finished his repeats of the song he took his seat, one by one, until only a sole singer was standing, singing the last chiming bell. When he, too, was seated, the men all looked at me in silence. Only the sound of rain could be heard, pattering on the roof. I was the first to speak:

"Simple ditties like this one, gentlemen," I said, "have long been used to communicate hidden meaning across time and place. In the case of 'Frère Jacques,' as I now perceive, it is a meaning that may, indeed, have been hidden for a hundred years or more. Not only a secret is hidden—perhaps even a conspiracy of sorts, from the Latin conspirare, 'to breathe together'—suggesting a mystery of the kind that oughtn't be more than whispered. But I believe I do comprehend your mission, and I shall assist you, my brethren, in any way I can."

They applauded this comment, and each man came up in turn to give me a "brotherly" handshake. When the others had departed, their leader, Hamilton, offered to see me home in his carriage. As we drove to my lodgings, only the sounds of the clopping horse hooves on cobbles broke the silence. Despite the wintry season, you could smell the fresh aroma of salt in the air.

"My dear doctor," Hamilton addressed me as we moved through the deep black velvet of the Annapolis night. "I wonder if you do understand completely what we meant tonight, in singing that old nursery song for you?"

"Why yes, I think I do," I told him. "You've sung me a charming French song, with a very poor English translation. For in French, I do not need to point out that the word 'Jacques' does not mean 'John' as it might in English—it means James. And 'matins' are not 'morning bells,' but a canonical hour of both the Catholic and Anglican Churches—the call to prayer, just after midnight, with the related offices of devotion.

"Brother James," I went on to suggest, "would be James the Greater, brother of Jesus in Holy Scripture, who founded the first Celtic Church in Spain (Santiago, as they call him there) as well as those ancient parish churches of the French Pyrenees.

"You are mostly Scotsmen here by origin, are you not?" I added. "It seems to me that the Scots, in recent memory, have been aligned with only one dynasty of great power and ancestry, and with whom the Scottish royal families have intermarried on numerous occasions—that is, with the French. There was Mary of Guise, who married the king of Scotland two hundred years ago—and then her daughter, Mary Queen of Scots, who married the French dauphin. And of course, young Mary's Scottish son, James Stuart, the successor to Queen Elizabeth who became

King James I of England." I turned to Hamilton in the darkness of the carriage, and added, "Given the canon of the song, this is the true 'James' that your chantey refers to—is it not?"

"It is," Hamilton replied quietly. "It is, indeed."

It took no Doctor of Philosophy to read the meaning in that message. But it did take a bit of initiation into other hidden significance. The Tuesday Club was asking my future aid, as a brother, in the time of their need...

Franklin paused in his story to look about the room of attentive listeners, then he added with effect, "This very same *chanson* was delivered to me, only this morning, from Scotland. I at once recognized its import—for nearly thirty years ago, I'd been warned by a club of Scotsmen, an ocean away from here—a warning that has now come home to roost.

"As we know, my friends, for more than one hundred years, the Scots have continually struggled to expel the Hanover usurpers from the throne of England and to restore the Scottish blood. From the English Civil War right down to the battles of Bonnie Prince Charlie, the son of the last King James who tried to seize England again only nine years before my trip to Annapolis!

"This song's deeper meaning was that my fellow Masons at Annapolis were initiates into an ancient, hidden rite of masonry known only to Scotland. Some call it the Rite of Strict Obedience, others the Rite of Kilmarnock, named for an earl who founded the rite and who was executed, nearly one hundred years ago today, for supporting the Stuart return to the throne. The Tuesday Club knew the meaning of Brother Jacques, and seemed prepared to implement its logical outcome—as they might, even today.

"But how many realize," Franklin asked his fellow diners, "that that same Bonnie Prince, Charles Edward Stuart, who claims the British throne, lives only kilometers from where we sit? At St. Germain en Laye, on the road from Paris to Versailles. There the Stuarts have remained under the protection of the Bourbon kings for one hundred years, ever since their ouster from Britain's throne."

"You don't mean to suggest," interjected John Adams indignantly, "that the exiled Stuarts are still a factor in European politics?"

"Europe—no," agreed Franklin. "It is America that is forefront in my mind. Our newly fledged country has, as yet, no true ruler—no chief of state. General Washington, everyone's choice, has—like Julius Caesar—thrice been proffered a kingship, and thrice declined. A great man, who is married to a long-barren wife with useless offspring of her own. Shall he produce the necessary dynasty to keep us safe?"

"Dynasty?" cried Adams, leaping to his feet. "Why have we fought a revolution? Are you gone mad, sir?"

"Look about you, my friend," said Franklin coolly. "Is there a country on any continent that exists with no line of succession? What would ours be? Kings deal with kings. Washington knows this—that is why he's sent a private delegation to ask whether the Stuarts are prepared. My message suggests that the Stuarts are prepared—their ship departs for the coast by the canonical hour of Matins—that is, by midnight, this very night! They are bound for America, and the children of the Kilmarnock Order will greet them when they arrive."

Adams was blathering, tugging at his wife's arm, as the younger folk around the table scrambled to their feet.

"This is monstrous!" Adams informed Franklin. "I shall see you tomorrow, sir, when you've had time to reflect!"

Franklin nodded gravely as the Adamses took their leave.

Taking Mme Helvetius by the arm, he retired to the salon as customary, to bid all his guests adieu before his afternoon nap. But as he passed the windows, Franklin noticed that the French contingency—his hosts, the Chaumonts, and the playwright, Beaumarchais—had stepped into the garden and were close at heads with the American mission's secretary. After a moment, Beaumarchais reentered the house as the others were still collecting their things to depart, and he took Franklin aside.

"Look here, my dear doctor," said the dashing playwright, "we're flustered at this turn of events. Though no one believes a Scottish king is in the stars for America, it will create a furor if true. You mentioned that your message suggested a spy among us. However did you deduce such a thing from a nursery song?"

"Ah, a mere ruse," Franklin assured him. "I know who the spy is, you see! Despite the revolution, I'm afraid there are those in our ranks who remain Anglomanes. I've had this particular gentleman recalled to America more than once, but our Congress keeps sending him back. I wasn't surprised that he left our company so abruptly today—off to send a message to his friends across the channel, no doubt!"

"You mean Adams?" whispered Beaumarchais in amazement.

"Please don't share it with a soul," Franklin said. Then he turned to Mme Helvetius, a short distance away. "A game of chess before my siesta, my dear?"

Midnight in the Gardens of Le Valentinois

The gardens were beautiful by night, thought Franklin. "Canonical hour!" He laughed to himself at his own cleverness. It was the best time to be abroad in the world. Beneath the star-filled August sky, a breeze ruffled the citrus trees. Moonlight drenched the pools and fountains a milky white. In the distance, the river Seine snaked across the land like a serpent of liquid silver.

At first sight, no one would imagine that this fairyland was only a short carriage ride from the steaming streets of Paris. Franklin knew he was fortunate, indeed, to have a host like Chaumont. When it came to intrigues and money, the man was a true rapscallion, but he wasn't the worst of his lot.

As he strolled along the promenade, Franklin took Mme Helvetius's arm.

"You did well this afternoon, my friend," Franklin told his companion. "I refer not only to your prowess at chess, but to your flair for intrigue." He paused to sniff at her clothes, and added, "I've become quite attached to that fragrance. Might we send your milkmaid by some afternoon to share tea with me in my boudoir?"

"*Vieux cochon,*" Mme Helvetius replied with a naughty smile. But as she glanced over the railing into the lower gardens, she tensed. "I thought everyone had long gone. Who are those men down there by the pool?"

Far below, at the edge of the cliff that rose from the Seine, was the large, octagonal pool designed by Donatien le Ray de Chaumont, with its famous, water-driven carillon of bells, which struck the hours. Close together at the pool's edge, two figures were sitting in shadow.

"It is Jefferson and John Quincy Adams," Franklin explained. "I asked them to stay on and meet me here to watch the show. They told the boy's parents he'd be staying in town at Jefferson's rooms. Come, let's descend to join them."

"But isn't it dangerous to involve others?" asked Mme Helvetius.

"Just as dangerous as a game of chess," Franklin replied. "And very like it. Young Quincy wants to learn the art of encryption and decryption. What better opportunity than tonight?"

When they reached the spot, Jefferson and young Adams rose to greet them.

"Dr. Franklin," said Quincy. "I believe we've broken most of your code, and Mr. Jefferson's headache has quite vanished in the process. But we've still a few questions."

"Broken my code?" scoffed Franklin. "Very well—out with it, if you please."

John Quincy glanced for approval to Jefferson, who nodded for him to proceed.

"First, the delivery of the message by Mme Helvetius," said Quincy proudly. "She tried to arrive privately. When all the world recognized her, you admitted you had a message. But to throw the spy off the trail, you focused on the French version of the song, thereby diverting attention from the words in English—'Are you sleeping, are you sleeping, Brother John, Brother John.' That would give a wholly different meaning."

"And precisely what would that be?" said Franklin, with a pleased smile.

"The mention of 'Brother,'" explained Quincy. "It's the word by which Freemasons greet one another, with no titles like Seigneur, for all men are thought equal, regardless of their circumstances of birth. Then

there was the repetition 'Brother John, Brother John.'
This would refer to the two patron saints of the Freemasons—St. John the Baptist and St. John the Evan-
gelist—whose saint days are celebrated at summer
and winter solstices, indicating a message meant for
Masonic, not just Scottish, ears. So 'Are you sleeping,'
and 'Morning bells are ringing' would mean 'Wake
up, Brothers!' I'm afraid in our decipherment, this is
as far as we've come."

"Excellent!" Franklin commended him. "You have
covered much ground."

"But, my dear doctor," said Jefferson, "we don't
know the real meaning of the message sent by the
Masons of Scotland. For surely if there was a spy in
our midst, as you say, your story by now has likely
raised many eyebrows among London's cohort at this
side of the channel—'Bonnie Prince Charlie sailing on
the morning tide to become first emperor of the
United States!' Do you think anyone swallowed that?"

"I hope so, for it's quite true!" said Franklin. "I
should know. I myself was initiated into the very Rite
of Kilmarnock I spoke of, not long after my evening
in Annapolis in 1759, when I went up to St. Andrews
University on the Scottish coast to receive my
honorary doctorate. The Bonnie Prince still has an
enormous following there, and in America—though
not, of course, with General Washington, myself or
our fellow Masons. The arrival of a prince of the blood
on our shores could be devastating at this moment—
so soon after our revolution, with as yet no fixed government and a gaggle of factions bickering like
brainless geese. Hence, the urgency of my warning
from the Scottish Masons. What better hope have we
than to stop the problem before it arrives? And what

better chance than to place a bug into the ear of King George III and his British Secret Service? The idea of a Scottish king on the throne of his former colonies should frizzle George's wig something proper!"

"So one coded message was hidden within another," Quincy observed. "'A coup is under way, and the Masonic brethren must awaken to the call!'"

"It has traditionally been our way," Franklin agreed, "to conceal layers within layers…often within other layers."

"But who shall bell the cat?" asked Jefferson. "Who is the spy that carried your message away into British hands this afternoon?"

"I'm afraid I had to suggest someone to divert attention," Franklin said. "So I chose your father, Quincy. Please forgive me. In fact, it's our secretary, Edward Bancroft. We have long followed his movements. Bancroft leaves Le Valentinois each Tuesday night and retires to the gardens of the Tuileries at the heart of Paris. There, at eleven-thirty, under cover of darkness, he deposits a packet of papers inside the hollow of an old oak tree—a packet containing all the intelligence he's gathered from us in the week. The British Secret Service pays him five hundred pounds per annum to spy upon us, and we pay him to spy on them. It's the only way we can be certain that the British are receiving the news we want them to know. When you, my dear Jefferson, replace me in this French mission, I pray you may find him useful!"

Jefferson laughed modestly. "As I often say, I can only succeed you—no one can replace you. It seems now you're a master of the French art of espionage, too. But if that message was calculated to trick the British into thwarting a Jacobite plot, something remains unexplained. Why did you invite us to meet you in the gardens here tonight?"

At that moment, the carillon of water bells from Chaumont's octagon pool began striking the hour of twelve. When the tones had died out, Franklin said, "Invite you? Why, to attend the salon of Notre dame d'Auteuil, of course!"

Mme Helvetius had stood all this time gazing down at the river. Now she said, "The Loge des Neuf Soeurs. They arrive with the water bells."

Slipping from shadow on the river below, they saw a long boat rowed by nine sturdy men that was pulling toward the moonwashed pier.

"Nine muses, and a carillon of bells in E-flat major," Franklin explained to Jefferson. "That is the missing code that you and young Johnnie here were seeking. In both versions of our ditty, one hears three chimes of the bell, three notes that are repeated: Din-Dan-Don…Ding-Ding-Dong. These three notes represent the Masonic code—the number three. Masonic songs are always written in E-flat major, containing a musical signature of three flats—with the E itself being the third note of the octave music scale. The repetition of the bell, three and three, represents three-squared, which is nine, reflective of the name of Madame's lodge down there, filled with musings and dedicated to muses." He laughed.

"But then, at last, as in any code," Franklin added, "there is always that final question which explains all the rest."

Jefferson had joined Mme Helvetius in gazing down at the nine men below, who had lashed down their boat and were disembarking on the pier. Despite the warm night, they were shrouded in black. For a time, no one beside the pool spoke. It was Jefferson who broke the silence.

"Tuesday," was all he said.

"Precisely!" agreed Franklin in astonishment. "What made you think of it?"

"And what does it mean?" asked Quincy breathlessly.

"The message was not about something that would happen on a Tuesday," Jefferson explained. "Nor was it about a Tuesday. No—just as the doctor's Annapolis frères had meant to communicate to him—the message is 'Tuesday'!"

"*Ah, oui!*" said Mme Helvetius in comprehension. "The Day of Fire!"

"Tuesday," Jefferson added for John Quincy, "was the day in the ancient calendar dedicated to fire. Delphi was the Greek temple of fire, conquered by Apollo, the sun god. The number three forms a triangle, a pyramid, a temple of fire, as its name suggests. And while there are many music scales that contain three flats or sharps, the E that Dr. Franklin mentioned is the only one of these carved above the door of the Delphi temple—a sign so ancient that no one has ever learned what it signified…"

"And do not forget," chimed in Mme Helvetius, "we French have a royal family descended from a Sun King, too! But, like others, this light does not burn so brightly any longer. Perhaps it is time to replace it with a new flame."

"Good Lord!" cried Jefferson. "You are both speaking of revolution! A revolution in France! In Europe! Tuesday really does refer to fire—and Mars, the god of war!"

"I'm afraid," said Franklin, "that I am a very old revolutionary. You know what they say of revolutionaries—'Once it is over, we must vanish, for the fire that destroys cannot build.' But you, my noble colleague, have wits so full of fire they've made your hair fiery red!" He patted Jefferson on the shoulder. "Do not forget, my friend—three knocks, three bells, three points that form a triangle. A square of triangles creates a pyramid of fire. The conflagration is coming. We've already lit the match! Now, come join our colleagues—and may the god Mars protect us all!"

Franklin headed with Mme Helvetius down the stone steps to the pier, but he added to Jefferson, "When you yourself are Sun King, which may be sooner than you think, you must not pause while crossing that fiery river Styx. Just remember, you can always call upon friends, as long as you can hum a tune!"

And Franklin and Mme Helvetius went off down the steps in front of the others, singing "Frère Jacques," all the way.

DOUGLAS PRESTON & LINCOLN CHILD

Gone Fishing features one of Douglas Preston and Lincoln Child's favorite characters, Lieutenant Vincent D'Agosta, of the New York City Police Department: a working-class cop from Queens with a heart as big as the ocean. D'Agosta made his debut in the team's first thriller, *The Relic*, alongside their famous Special Agent Pendergast of the FBI. In the Paramount film made from that novel, Pendergast was cut from the story entirely, leaving Vincent D'Agosta (played by Tom Sizemore) as the unrivaled star. It was the character's fifteen minutes of fame, so to speak—and events in D'Agosta's life seemed to go downhill from there.

After reappearing in *Reliquary*, the sequel to *The Relic*, D'Agosta disappeared for six years (and five novels). Disappointed at not making precinct captain, D'Agosta quit the force and moved with his family to a small town in British Columbia to live his dream: writing crime fiction. He published two highly regarded novels that didn't sell. Desperate, broke, and separated from his wife, he moved back to New York to reclaim his old job, only to discover the NYPD was under a hiring freeze. He ended up a lowly sergeant in the Southampton, Long Island, police department, chasing beer-swilling teenagers and loose dogs in a dune buggy. His break came when the sleazy art critic Jeremy Grove was found burned to death in his Southampton mansion. D'Agosta's work on the case, alongside his old friend Agent Pendergast, won him back his position in the ranks of the NYPD—a story recounted in Preston and Child's thriller, *Brimstone*.

Gone Fishing is the first short story Preston and Child have written together, and the first time D'Agosta appears without Pendergast. The story begins with the theft of a priceless Inca sacrificial knife from the Museum of Natural History and ends twenty-four hours later in a clearing in the woods of northern New Hampshire, amidst a scene of transcendental horror.

GONE FISHING

The Ford Taurus hissed along the slick road, topped the hill and emerged from the woods. A sudden panorama of farms and green fields spread out below, a cluster of white houses and a church steeple along a dark river.

"Speed limit's forty-five," said Woffler, voice tense.

"Don't get your undies in a bunch," Perotta replied. "I was born driving a car." He glanced over at the carpenter: the man's face was white, and the faggoty earring he wore in his left ear—a gold ring with a red stone on it—was practically trembling with agitation. Woffler and his whining was starting to get on his nerves.

"I'm not worried about your driving," Woffler said. "I'm worried about getting stopped. You know, as in *cops?*" And he nodded pointedly at the velvet bag on the seat between them.

"Yeah, yeah." Perotta slowed to fifty as the car descended the hill toward the town. "Need a potty break, guy?"

"I could use something to eat. It's dinnertime."

A diner lay at the near end of town in what looked like a converted gas station. Six pickup trucks sat in the dirt parking lot.

"Welcome to Buttcrack, New Hampshire," said Perotta.

They got out of the car and approached the diner. Perotta paused in the doorway, surveying the clientele.

"They grow 'em big up here, don't they?" he said. "Or do you think it's inbreeding?"

They took a booth next to the window, where they could keep an eye on the car. The waitress came waddling over. "What can I get you folks?" she said, smiling.

"How about menus?" Perotta said.

The smile disappeared. She nodded toward the wall. "It's all up there."

Perotta scanned the board. "Gimme a cheeseburger, fries and a side of grilled onions. Make it rare. Coffee."

"Same for me," said Woffler. "Except I'll take my burger well done. And no onions."

The waitress waddled off and Perotta followed her with his eyes. As she passed a far booth he saw a man with tats and a tank top staring at him. He was a big man, pumped up. Something about him made Perotta think of prison.

He considered staring the scumbag down, then decided against it. This wasn't the time. He turned back to his partner.

"We did it, Woffler," he said in a low voice. "We freaking did it."

"We haven't done anything yet," Woffler replied. "Don't talk about it in here. And don't call me by name."

"Who's listening? Anyway, we're hundreds of miles

from New York City—and nobody's even noticed it's missing yet."

"You don't know that."

They sat in silence. The man with the tats lit up a cigarette and no one told him to put it out. Within minutes the waitress came out with their burgers, slid them on the table.

Perotta checked, as he always did. "I said rare. R-A-R-E. This is well done."

Without a word the waitress picked up his plate, took it back into the kitchen. Perotta noticed the guy with the tats was staring at him again.

The plate came back out and Perotta checked. Still not rare enough. He began to signal the waitress when Woffler stopped him.

"Will you just eat your burger?"

"But it's not rare."

Woffler leaned forward. "Do you really want to make a big scene right now, so everyone'll remember us?"

Perotta thought about that for a moment and decided that Woffler might be right. He ate the burger in silence, drank the coffee. He was hungry. They'd been driving since before dawn, stopping only for gas and candy bars.

They paid, and Perotta stiffed the waitress. It was the least he could do, a matter of principle. What was so hard about making a hamburger rare?

As they got in the car, the tattooed man emerged from the diner and walked over. He leaned an arm into Perotta's open window.

"What the hell do you want?" Perotta asked.

The man smiled. Up close, Perotta could see the guy had an old tracheotomy scar right below his Adam's apple. His teeth were the color of urine.

"Just wishing you a nice trip. And offering a piece of advice." He spoke pleasantly, rolling a toothpick around in his mouth.

"And what advice might that be?"

"Don't come back to our town again. Ever."

"No chance of that. You can keep your Shitville, or whatever you call this dump."

He jammed his foot down on the accelerator, fishtailing out of the parking lot and pelting the man with dust and gravel. He glanced in the rearview mirror: the guy was slapping dust from his arms but didn't seem to be making a move to follow them.

"Why do you always have to make a spectacle of yourself?" Woffler asked. "You just left two people in that town who'll have no problem identifying us in a lineup, even months from now."

"How's anyone going to know we ever came through here?"

Woffler just shook his head.

The road entered another forest, the damp asphalt shining like blued steel in the dying light. With one hand on the wheel, Perotta reached over with the other and tipped up the velvet bag, letting the object slide out. Even in the dim light, the glow of the artifact seemed to fill the car. Perotta had read the label on the case at the museum a dozen times; he could practically quote it by heart. It was an Inca Tumi knife, used in human sacrifices to cut through the breastbone of the victim. The blade itself was made of copper and badly corroded; but the elaborate handle, cast in massive gold, was as fresh as the day it was hammered. It depicted the Sican Lord, the god of death, with staring ruby eyes and a grimace of turquoise teeth.

"Will you look at that?" he said, chuckling. "Two million bucks."

"If we can fence it."

"There's gotta be some Arab sheikh or Japanese businessman out there who collects this stuff. And even if we can't, we can always pry the stones out and melt the thing down. Those rubies are probably twenty carats each. I bet we could get fifty grand for them, plus a shitload for the gold."

"Fifty grand's a lot less than two million."

"Woffler, I'm getting a little tired of your negativity. No one made you do it."

Woffler looked out the window at the blur of dark woods. "I don't know. It seemed like a good idea at the time."

"And it *was* a good idea. A freaking brilliant idea! We saw our chance and took it. You liked building cases at the museum for twenty bucks an hour? As for me, I got tired of shaking doors and checking IDs."

"You aren't worried about Lipski?"

"Screw him. He's just a middleman. The real buyer's that guy in Peru."

"What about him? How's he going to react?"

"What's he gonna do? Fly up here and comb America for us? Nah, he's going to assume Lipski ripped him off and put a cap in his ass."

"He sounds like somebody important."

"If you want my opinion, the guy's a psychopath. Probably wants the knife back so he can rip out a few more hearts, just like his ancestors. I bet he doesn't even know we exist."

"Even if he doesn't, Lipski does. And he's going to be looking for us."

"You think he'll find us at Passumkeag Lake? I'd like

to see him, with his Armani suits and handmade shoes, stomping around the New Hampshire woods trying to find two guys bass fishing in the middle of nowhere." Perotta laughed. "I really would."

"Slow down, we're coming to another town."

They flashed past a sign that said Waldo Falls. Just to shut Woffler up, Perotta eased down to the speed limit.

They passed a row of white farmhouses, a church, a firehouse, a neat town square with a Civil War monument and a rusted cannon.

"Welcome to beautiful downtown Dildo Falls," Perotta said. "Can you believe people live in a place like this?"

"As a matter of fact, I can."

In a moment they had left the town behind them and were back in the endless north woods. Perotta started to accelerate, then abruptly slowed again. "Jesus, will you look at that," he said, pointing. "It's like a time warp."

A battered VW bus was pulled off the road in a muddy turnout. It was covered with peace signs, feminist symbols, painted pot leaves and psychedelic flowers. A man with long greasy hair sat smoking in the driver's seat. He watched them go by.

Perotta gave a couple of honks as he passed.

"What'd you do that for?"

"Didn't you see the bumper sticker? *Honk If You're Pro-Choice.* Hey, I'm pro-choice. Line the girls up and let me choose," he cackled.

"Why don't you just hang a sign out the window, saying, 'Obnoxious museum thief on his way to cabin hideout?'"

"Whaddya mean?"

"What I mean is, every town we go through, Perotta, you do something to attract attention."

"Look, will you lighten up? In case you hadn't noticed, it's over. We did it. Quit worrying and enjoy the vacation. When the heat's off, we can figure out how to fence it, or melt it down, or whatever. In the meantime, we've gone fishing."

Woffler sighed heavily. His face looked gray. "I'm no good at this."

"You'll do better next time."

"There won't be a next time."

The side road wound through the dark trees and then suddenly they were at the lake, walled in on all sides by hemlocks. Perotta eased off the gas. The rented cabin stood off to the right, with a sloping wooden porch. A needle-strewn path led to a crooked dock on the bouldered shore. The pond was deathly still in the falling twilight and the water was black.

Perotta shut off the car and turned off the headlights, and they sat there in silence a moment while the engine ticked and cooled. There was no other sound save for the steady drone of insects. After a moment they got out of the car and took their luggage and bags of groceries inside.

The cabin was cool and musty, all the furniture draped in sheets dotted with dead flies. Woffler cleaned up while Perotta cooked up a pot of pasta with tomato sauce and fresh basil. After dinner they started a fire and sipped from snifters full of Chivas. The Tumi knife lay on the coffee table, gleaming in the reflected firelight, the ruby eyes flashing and jumping.

"Feeling better?" Perotta asked.

"I'm getting there."

He nodded at the knife. "How many beating human hearts you think they cut out with it?"

"We should hide it."

"Nah, let's enjoy it for a moment."

They lapsed into silence. Perotta took another sip of scotch, enjoying the fiery sensation as it slid down his gullet. Here they were in the deep woods, four hundred miles from New York, and every mile had taken them farther into the boonies. The fire popped and crackled on the grate. He gave a sigh of satisfaction.

When the soft knock came at the door, almost below the threshold of audibility, it startled Perotta so much he slopped half his drink into his lap.

"Who the hell—?"

Woffler was already up, hand on the Tumi knife. He slipped it into the velvet bag and disappeared into the bathroom. Perotta went to the window, flattened himself sideways, opened the curtains, and peered out.

"Who is it?" Woffler asked as he came out of the bathroom.

"Nobody. There's nobody there. What'd you do with it?"

"In the toilet tank."

Perotta went to the door. Hand on the knob, he hesitated a moment. Then he opened it and stepped out on the porch.

The hemlocks were like a dark wall all around the cabin, and they sighed in the night breeze. The surface of the lake gleamed like ruffled velvet in the moonlight.

He stepped back inside, stared at Woffler. "It was a knock, right?"

"Sure sounded like one."

Perotta reached for a tissue, dabbed at his wet pants. "Maybe it was a branch or something."

They sat back down at the fire. Perotta took another slug of Chivas, but the spell was broken.

"How long you figure we have to stay up here?" Woffler asked.

"Don't know. Three, maybe four weeks."

"Think the heat will be off by then?"

"One way or another."

"What does that mean?"

"It means that Lipski—"

And then the soft knock came again. This time, Perotta sprang up and rushed the door, throwing it open.

Nobody.

"Go see if someone's around back of the cabin," said Woffler.

"I'll need a flashlight first."

They searched through the kitchen drawers and finally found one full of flashlights and packages of batteries. They went back into the living room and stood there, uneasy.

"You think it's some kids?" Perotta asked.

"We're ten miles from the nearest town. And they wouldn't be out messing around on a weeknight."

"Maybe the landlord's a practical joker."

"The landlord," Woffler said stiffly, "is eighty and lives down in Westchester County."

They stood there, uncertain what to do next. Finally Perotta went to the door, opened it and shined the light into the dark woods. The beam played feebly among the dark trunks.

"There!" Woffler said from behind him.

"I didn't see anything."

"It was right there. Something white, moving."

Woffler came forward now, playing his own flashlight beam into the woods.

"Hey!" Perotta yelled. "Who's out there?"

He could hear his voice echoing faintly back from the far side of the pond.

Woffler walked to the edge of the porch and shined the flashlight into the wall of trees. "There!" he said, stabbing with his beam.

Now Perotta thought he saw something, too. It looked like the figure of a man in white.

"Go see who it is," he said.

"Me?"

"You're the one that saw him," Perotta reasoned.

"I'm not going out there."

"The hell you aren't. Look, somebody has to stand guard here. Don't worry, I'll watch your back."

Reluctantly, Woffler walked down the steps and slowly made his way toward the edge of the woods, twenty-five feet away. He stopped, swung his beam around. Then he took a step into the trees.

"There's someone in here," he called back, uneasiness clear in his voice. "Someone was spying on us, and look—there are footprints in the wet needles."

"Follow him. Find out what the bastard wants."

"But—"

"*Do* it."

Woffler hung back a moment, hesitating. Then he stepped forward and disappeared into the woods. Perotta waited on the porch, watching the beam flicker and bob through the trees until it was gone, swallowed up by the woods.

Suddenly it seemed very quiet.

As he waited on the porch, he started to feel a little uneasy himself. He tried to push the feeling aside. Nobody, he reminded himself, could know they were there: nobody. Woffler had rented the cabin online, using a bank account he'd set up in the name and social security number of a dead man. They had planned it down to the last detail. Woffler was good at the details; Perotta had to admit he never could have pulled it off himself.

He wondered if the guy with the tattooed arms had followed them up here and was trying to pull some shit. But that run-in was almost thirty miles back, and he was sure they hadn't been followed.

He checked his watch. Ten minutes to ten.

Where the hell was Woffler?

Maybe it *was* Woffler. Maybe all his anxiety was just an act. Maybe he hadn't really seen anything in the woods. Maybe this was all an excuse for him to run off with the artifact himself. He might have rented another car, stashed it somewhere nearby.

Perotta skipped back into the house, ducked into the bathroom, pulled the cover off the toilet tank. The knife was there all right, wrapped in its sodden velvet pouch. He replaced the cover and walked thoughtfully back out to the porch.

Could it be Lipski, after all? It didn't seem likely. Sure, Lipski knew by now they'd pulled some shit on him—they were supposed to deliver the knife before 5:00 p.m.—but how would he know where they'd gone? And it sure as hell wasn't the rich Peruvian Lipski claimed to be dealing with, the one who wanted the artifact back for his ancestors or something like that. It was way too early for him to know he'd been screwed.

He supposed it *could* be Lipski. But how could he trace them? Through Woffler's car, maybe? That was the one weak link. But who'd seen the car? And how could anyone know they'd end up at the lake? The only way would be if they'd been followed.

He checked his watch. Five past ten.

"Woffler?" he called out. "Hey, Woffler?"

The dark wall of trees sighed back.

He cupped his hands. "Woffler!"

His voice echoed back, distant and lost.

He shined his flashlight into the woods, but there was nothing.

"Shit," he muttered.

He turned, went back inside, took a slug of Chivas, took the longest knife he could find from the kitchen and slid it into his belt. Woffler should have taken a weapon. Stupid.

He threw another log on the fire, paced about, picked up the snifter, then put it down without taking another sip. He'd better stay sober; he might need his wits.

He sat down, stood up again. Then he went back out and stood on the porch.

"Woffler! Yo!"

Ten-fifteen. He'd been gone almost half an hour.

This was bullshit.

Heart beating fast, he walked down the steps and headed toward the spot where Woffler had vanished into the trees, shining his light on the ground. It had rained recently, and the soft ground, covered with a thick carpet of tiny hemlock needles, retained the clear outline of Woffler's footprints, and those of someone else—someone with smaller feet.

"Hey, Woffler!"

In the ensuing silence, he could hear the faint lapping of the lake. He took a few tentative steps into the woods.

A very distant call came drifting back through the trees, so faint he couldn't distinguish it. It wasn't an echo.

"Woffler! Is that you?"

A sound came back—a distant answering cry. But it was high pitched: almost, Perotta thought, like a scream.

"Jesus," he muttered.

He shined his light ahead. The two sets of footprints went off into the trees. He swallowed a little painfully. Might as well hurry up and get this over with.

He began hiking fast, following the tracks. The trail wound between huge tree trunks, and the air smelled of pine pitch and damp earth. Once or twice he passed some boulders, as tall as he was, draped with lichen and moss.

"Woffler!"

Perotta quickened his pace. It was stupid to have sent Woffler out there in the first place. He was a city boy, didn't know the first thing about woods. He was probably lost and panicking.

The footprints began skirting a swamp. An owl hooted off in the darkness.

"Woffler, you coming back or what?"

No answer.

He shined the light around, slapped at a mosquito. The trees stood all around him like massive dark pillars. Where the ground became swampy there were thick mats of sphagnum moss. The footprints ran along the soft verge of the swamp, and then they veered in sharply, becoming holes where the feet had sunk through the moss into the mud.

"Jesus." He stopped. Why would Woffler go into the swamp like that?

He shined the light around again, and saw something white, like a mushroom, at the edge of the swamp. He took a step closer. It wasn't a mushroom, after all. It was a shell, a white oyster shell. He bent over and picked it up, then immediately dropped it again, horrified at the rubbery feel.

It fell on the moss, upside down. From this angle, he could see that blood was smeared along one side. It was fresh blood, shiny and intensely red in the glare of the flashlight. Heart pounding, Perotta picked up a stick and turned it over.

It was an ear. A human ear, severed at the stump, with a gold earring through the lobe, set with a red stone.

With an involuntary moan, Perotta took a single step back. It was like a bad dream, the kind of nightmare where something strange and terrible was happening but you were paralyzed, unable to move, unable to get away, no matter how hard you tried.

And then, suddenly, he found movement. With a sharp cry he ran wildly, blindly, through the trees, crashing through brush, clawing through ferns.

He ran and ran until he could run no more, and then he fell. He lay on the sodden ground, breathing so hard his sides burned and he moaned with each exhale, the loamy smell filling his nostrils, choking him. He clawed his way back up and turned around and around, playing the light over the tree trunks. He had no idea where he was; he'd lost the trail. And now he remembered the kitchen knife. He fumbled at his belt, drew it out.

"Woffler!" he screamed. "Where are you? Answer me!"

Nothing.

He played the light over the ground. The ground was heavy with pine needles here, and there were no footprints. Like a goddamn idiot, he'd gotten himself lost. Even if he'd wanted to, there was no way he could retrace his trail.

He tried to calm his pounding heart, get his hyper-ventilating under control. It probably was Lipski, after all. That was the only answer. Maybe the little shit had suspected them from the beginning, followed them all the way up. That would explain the small footprints.

Shakily, he began to walk downhill, in the direction he hoped would lead him back to the lake. If he could find the shore, he'd be able to see the lights of the cabin and find his way back to the car and get the hell out.

He saw a sudden movement, a flutter of white, through the trees.

"Woffler?"

But he knew it wasn't Woffler.

"I'll cut you!" he screamed, backing up, brandishing the knife. "Don't come near me!"

He turned and ran away from the fluttering movement, slashing through waist-high ferns. He ran and ran and then stopped again, heaving for air, shining the light around wildly, turning and turning.

Another flutter of white.

"Get away from me!" He backed up against a tree, the yellow beam of his flashlight jerking and flitting about the trunks.

"Lipski, look. You can have the knife, it's in the toilet tank inside the cabin. Go ahead. Just leave me alone."

Silence.

"Lipski, you hear me?"

The forest was so silent. Even the wind had ceased breathing in the hemlocks. The cloying smell of wet moss and rotting wood filled his nostrils.

"I was stupid. I admit it. *Please.*" He gave a choking sob.

He heard a faint sound and saw movement out of

the corner of his eye. Suddenly, a bloody hand shot around from behind the tree and seized his shirt.

"Get away from me!" he screamed, flailing his arm and slashing with his knife, wrenching himself free, his shirt buttons popping. He backed away from the tree, shakily holding the knife out ahead of him, his shirt open and hanging loose. "Don't do this to me, Lipski," he choked out. "Don't."

But now he wasn't sure it was Lipski.

The flashlight. He had to turn it off. He had to get away, move in darkness. He started walking, not fast, and turned the light off. But the deep blackness of the forest seemed to smother him, and a feeling of dread and terror overwhelmed him, and he snapped it back on.

Perotta caught sight of something low to one side. He swung the beam over in a panic, thinking it was the attacker, crouching and ready to spring. He stopped, frozen by horror at what the flashlight revealed.

The beam illuminated a very white foot, severed at the ankle. Perotta stumbled back with a retching sound. The beam jumped from that to another thing lying on the pine needles: an arm. And farther on, two-thirds of a head, cleaved at an angle, with one halfway forced-out eye, white showing all around.

The other piece of the head lay some feet away, with the second staring, surprised-looking eye.

"Oh, *Jesus!* No, no!"

A voice came from behind him, and he swung around with an inarticulate gargle. But there was nobody there; the voice seemed disembodied, coming from everywhere and nowhere at once, as if the demonic forest itself were speaking. In the extremity of his horror Perotta turned around and around, unable to get a fix on it.

"That's what they do to them, you know," the voice was saying, soft and hoarse. "Take a good look—that's what they do to them. And now, that's what *I'm* going to do to *you*."

Lieutenant Vincent D'Agosta, NYPD, watched the M.E. place the last piece of victim number two in a wet evidence container. It had taken them quite a while to sort through which piece belonged to who. The hot summer sun barely filtered through the branches of the tall hemlocks, creating a green, humid atmosphere that reeked of death. The flies had arrived in force and a steady drone filled the cathedral-like woods, like a low undertone to the hiss of radios and the murmur of the forensics team as they did the final walk-through before closing down the scene.

D'Agosta heard the soft press of footsteps and turned to see the local cops coming back up the hill.

"They were staying in the McCone cabin," one of them said. "We got their wallets, IDs, car, the works. Two employees of the Natural History Museum."

"Yeah?"

"Looks like we're almost done here. Thanks for coming up so quickly, Lieutenant."

"Appreciated the call," said D'Agosta.

"We heard on the radio about that heist at the museum," the other cop said. "When we found that artifact in the tank, we put two and two together and figured you'd be interested."

"Yeah." D'Agosta looked down. "Interested."

"Is that golden knife really worth millions?" the first officer asked, trying to keep the eagerness out of his voice.

D'Agosta nodded.

"Looks like they double-crossed the wrong person."

"Maybe," D'Agosta said. *But this took work*, he thought to himself. *A whole lot of work. You could send a message with a lot less effort. And why was the artifact still in the toilet tank? That was the first place anyone would look.*

The M.E. began carting the body bags and evidence lockers back out toward the road. It had been a long day.

"Let's get back to the station," the first officer said. "Finish up the paperwork. Once that's been processed and the evidence boys are done, we'll release the knife to you, Lieutenant."

D'Agosta stood for a moment, staring at the sticky, torn-up killing ground. It was as if the earth itself had been cut, violated. He fetched a sigh and turned to follow the others. His part was over. The Tumi knife was found. As for the double homicide, it wasn't his jurisdiction.

On the way out, D'Agosta paused by the first officer. Almost against his will, he said, "This is just the first. There'll be more."

The officer looked up sharply. "What do you mean?"

D'Agosta nodded back toward the woods. "What happened back there had nothing to do with the museum theft."

A hesitation, a firming of the mouth. "Thank you, Lieutenant, for your opinion."

D'Agosta could read the skepticism and annoyance in the officer's eyes. With a sudden feeling of weariness, he turned and walked toward the car and driver that would take him back to the local airfield, where his NYPD chopper was standing by. Suddenly, he couldn't wait to get back to New York City: to the heat-packing crackheads, ATM-camera flashers, Hummer-driving pimps, two-dollar murderers, turnstyle jumpers, grandmother decapitators, three-card-monte scammers, nightclub arsonists, hit-and-run stock-brokers, dog rapists and all the other freaks he knew so well and loved. Anything was better than these woods—and this killer.

The Fisherman sat behind the wheel of his VW bus, waiting in the muddy turnout at the side of the road. The police cars had come and gone, and now the road from Waldo Falls was silent. It was twilight and a layer of mist had formed, drifting through the trees, beading up on his windshield.

He adjusted his wig, pulling it down tighter, grasping the long locks of polyester hair and giving them a tug. Then he lit up a Marlboro and waited.

It was a while before a pair of yellow headlights appeared, heading out of town. He stubbed out his cigarette and watched the car materialize in his rearview mirror. It was a foreign car, a Toyota, which was good. They would buy Jap over American.

As the car passed it honked.

The man waited until the taillights had disappeared around the gentle curve. Then he put the VW into gear, started up the windshield wipers and eased it onto the road. He allowed himself a slow, crooked smile, and a prayer of thanks to the Lord for once more presenting the opportunity to serve Him.

The Fisherman had just hooked another killer of the unborn.

Author Biographies

Ted Bell is a native Floridian. He began his career in advertising as a copywriter at Doyle Dane Bernbach in New York. He has also worked in Chicago, where he was president of the Leo Burnett Company, and later served as vice chairman and worldwide creative director of Young & Rubicam in both London and New York. Ted is the *New York Times* bestselling author of three action-adventure thrillers: *Hawke*, *Assassin* and *Pirate*. The series features the dashing British intelligence agent Alex Hawke. Ted lives in Florida where he writes thrillers, reads and messes about in boats. Visit Ted at his Web site, www.tedbellbooks.com.

Steve Berry, a *New York Times* bestselling writer, lives on the Georgia coast. He's a lawyer who has traveled extensively throughout the Caribbean, Mexico, Europe and Russia. Steve's thrillers include *The Amber Room*, *The Romanov Prophecy*, *The Third Secret* and *The*

Templar Legacy. His novels have been feature selections for major book clubs, chosen as BookSense picks, and have been sold in thirty-two countries. Visit his Web site at www.steveberry.org.

Grant Blackwood caught the writing bug while reading Clive Cussler's *The Mediterranean Caper*. He's a U.S. Navy veteran, having spent three years on active duty aboard a guided-missile frigate as an operations specialist and pilot rescue swimmer. He's been writing for nineteen years and lives in Minnesota, where he's working on a new thriller series.

Previously a television director, trade union organizer, theater-lighting designer, stage manager and law student, **Lee Child** has been an author for nine years and has published ten Jack Reacher novels. He was born in England but now lives in New York City and the south of France. Currently his books are sold in forty-one countries and have all been international bestsellers.

David Dun, a native of Washington State transplanted to California, where he manages a law practice, acts as general counsel to a large, privately held corporation, and writes. He is the national bestselling author of five action-adventure novels, *Necessary Evil*, *At The Edge*, *Overfall*, *Unacceptable Risk* and *The Black Silent*, which are currently published in eight languages. When he's not parked at a desk, he enjoys cruising the waters of Washington State and British Columbia.

New York Times and *USA TODAY* bestselling author **Heather Graham** majored in theater arts at the University of South Florida. After a stint of several years in dinner theater, backup vocals and bartending, she stayed home after the birth of her third child and began to write, working on short horror stories and romances. Since then, she has written over one hundred novels and novellas. Her books are currently published in twenty languages. Graham loves to travel and enjoys anything that has to do with the water, including being a certified scuba diver.

After twelve years as a Miami trial lawyer, **James Grippando** is now the national bestselling author of ten suspenseful thrillers. *Got The Look* is his fifth book featuring Miami criminal defense lawyer Jack Swyteck, a series that critics have applauded as "John Grisham meets Robert Ludlum." He's also the author of a thriller for young readers, *Leapholes*, the first novel for children ever to be published by the American Bar Association. James was the 2005 recipient of the Distinguished Author Award from Scranton University, and his novels are enjoyed worldwide in over twenty languages. He lives and writes in south Florida.

Denise Hamilton is a Fulbright scholar and *Los Angeles Times* reporter who turned to crime and thriller writing after her two children were born. Her bestselling Eve Diamond series has been short-listed for the Edgar, Anthony, Willa Cather and Britain's prestigious Dagger awards. Her book *Last Lullaby* was a *Los Angeles Times* Best Book of 2004. Visit her at www.denisehamilton.com.

Raelynn Hillhouse has run Cuban rum between East and West Berlin, smuggled jewels from the Soviet Union and forged Eastern bloc visas. A native of the Missouri Ozarks, Raelynn has lived for over six years in Europe, has traveled in over forty countries and is fluent in several languages. She earned her Ph.D. in political science at the University of Michigan and is a former professor and Fulbright fellow. She has not only faced the barrels of Kalashnikovs, but has also been caught in the crossfire of border guards' snowball fights. Raelynn lives in Hawaii on the slopes of Mauna Loa volcano. Her debut thriller, *Rift Zone*, received widespread national acclaim.

Gregg Hurwitz is the bestselling author of *The Tower*, *Minutes to Burn*, *Do No Harm*, *The Kill Clause*, *The Program*, and most recently, *Troubleshooter*. His novels have been feature selections for all four major literary book clubs, chosen as BookSense picks and translated into seven languages. Gregg adapted *Rogue Warrior* for Jerry Bruckheimer Films and *The Kill Clause* for Paramount Pictures. He holds a B.A. from Harvard in English and psychology, and a master's degree in Shakespearean tragedy from Trinity College, Oxford. He's published numerous short stories, articles, reviews, and academic articles, and lectured at Harvard, UCLA and USC. Visit his Web site at www.gregghurwitz.net.

Alex Kava is the author of the international bestselling series featuring FBI profiler Maggie O'Dell and the critically acclaimed thriller, *One False Move*. Her novels have sold almost two million copies and have been published in twenty countries. They have appeared on the *New York Times* and *USA TODAY* bestseller lists, as well as making bestseller lists across the globe. Alex divides her time between Omaha, Nebraska, and Pensacola, Florida.

J. A. Konrath is the author of the Lieutenant Jacqueline "Jack" Daniels thrillers. His short stories have appeared in dozens of magazines and anthologies, and he currently teaches fiction writing and marketing at the College of Dupage in Glen Ellyn, Illinois. He lives in Chicago with his wife, a few kids and dogs. Visit him at www.JAKonrath.com.

John Lescroart is the *New York Times* bestselling author of sixteen novels, including thirteen in the Dismas Hardy/Abe Glitsky series of books set in San Francisco. He lives with his wife and their children in northern California.

Robert Liparulo is an award-winning author of over a thousand published articles and short stories for such publications as *New Man*, *Reader's Digest*, and even *Modern Bride*. He has written (and sold) screenplays, celebrity profiles and investigative exposés, but he always returns to his first love, fiction. As testament to his vivid and fast-paced style, his debut novel, *Comes a Horseman*, ignited a bidding war in Hollywood for the movie rights—months before its publication. Liparulo lives in Colorado with his wife, Jodi, and their four children. Find him online at www.robertliparulo.com.

David Liss is the author of two bestselling novels featuring Benjamin Weaver—*A Conspiracy of Paper* and *A Spectacle of Corruption*—in addition to two stand-alone thrillers, *The Coffee Trader* and *The Ethical Assassin*. His books have won numerous awards, including the Edgar Award for Best First Novel, and they have been translated into more than a dozen languages. *The Devil's Company* will be the third Benjamin Weaver novel. Liss lives in San Antonio, Texas.

Eric Van Lustbader is the internationally bestselling author of *The Ninja, Art Kills, The Bourne Legacy, The Bravo Testament* and twenty-six other novels, both thrillers and fantasy, plus a host of short stories. He graduated from Columbia College in 1968 and spent fifteen years in the pop music industry. He has also been a New York City schoolteacher. For more information, visit him at www.ericvanlustbader.com.

Dennis Lynds, aka Michael Collins, wrote the Dan Fortune series that began in 1967. There are now nineteen Dan Fortune books, the most recent being *Fortune's World*, a collection of short stories spanning from 1963 to 2000. His most recent thriller, *The Cadillac Cowboy*, featured a new protagonist whose name may or may not be Ford Morgan. As Mark Sadler, John Crowe, William Arden and Carl Dekker, he published another eighteen crime novels and thirteen juvenile crime novels. As Dennis Lynds, he published three novels and two collections of stories, the most recent being *Talking To the World*. A fourth Lynds novel, *Pictures On a Bedroom Wall*, is forthcoming. Lynds won the

Mystery Writers of America Edgar and has been nominated for two more. Born in St. Louis, he was raised in England. Later, his parents, both English actors, returned to the States and he grew up in Los Angeles, Denver and New York City. Sadly, Dennis died in August, 2005, leaving behind his wife, bestselling novelist Gayle Lynds.

New York Times bestseller **Gayle Lynds** is the author of eight international espionage thrillers, including *The Last Spymaster*, *The Coil* and *Masquerade*, which have been published in twenty countries. Lynds is generally considered the first woman to write successfully in the thriller field since Helen MacInnes. With Robert Ludlum she created the *Covert-One* thriller series. She is a member of the Association of Former Intelligence Operatives and is a cofounder of International Thriller Writers, Inc. You can visit her at www.GayleLynds.com.

Chris Mooney was twenty-eight when he published his first thriller, *Deviant Ways*. He is also the author of *The Missing*, *World Without End* and *Remembering Sarah*, which was nominated for a Barry Award and the Edgar Award for Best Novel. Visit him at www.chrismooneybooks.com.

David Morrell is the author of *First Blood*, the award-winning novel in which Rambo was created. He holds a Ph.D. in American literature from the Pennsylvania State University and was a professor in the English department at the University of Iowa, until he gave up his tenure to devote himself to a full-time writing career. David has published twenty-eight books, which have been translated into twenty-six languages. His numerous bestselling thrillers include *Creepers*, *The Brotherhood of the Rose* and *Extreme Denial*, which is set in Santa Fe, New Mexico, where he lives. His *Lessons from a Lifetime of Writing* is an analysis of what he has learned during his thirty-seven years as a writer. He is a cofounder of International Thriller Writers, Inc.

Katherine Neville was for many years an international consultant and computer expert, numbering among her clients and employers the Department of Energy, the Nuclear Regulatory Commission, OPEC, IBM, the Algerian government and the Bank of America. She has also been a professional model, portrait painter and commercial photographer. Katherine's first novel, *The Eight*, has been translated into nearly thirty languages and was recently voted one of the top ten books of all time, in a national poll in Spain. Her second book, *A Calculated Risk*, was a *New York Times* Notable Book, and *The Magic Circle* was a *USA TODAY* and an international bestseller. Katherine lives in Virginia, Washington D.C., and Santa Fe, New Mexico.

Michael Palmer is a graduate of Wesleyan University and Case Western Reserve University School of Medicine. He started writing as a hobby in 1979 and has since published eleven novels of medical suspense, all international bestsellers. His work has been translated into thirty languages, and *Extreme Measures* was made into a film starring Hugh Grant, Gene Hackman and Sarah Jessica Parker. He's an avid tennis player and scuba diver, and holds the rank of bronze life master in bridge. Palmer lives in Massachusetts with the youngest of his three sons, Luke. **Daniel James Palmer,** Michael's middle son, holds a master's degree in communications from Boston University, and is a musician, songwriter and software professional. He lives with his wife and son in Southern New Hampshire, where he mountain bikes and plays tennis.

In one of the more unusual—and successful—writing collaborations in recent memory, **Douglas Preston** and **Lincoln Child** have coauthored ten bestselling thrillers over the past fifteen years. They met when Child, then a young editor at St. Martin's Press, asked Preston, a writer for the American Museum of Natural History in New York City, to pen a nonfiction history of the museum. The two later teamed up to write *The Relic,* set in a fictitious natural history museum, which was made into a hit film by Paramount Pictures. Their protagonist, the eccentric and brilliant Special Agent Pendergast, has become a cult hero among thriller readers. They also work solo: Child has written two thrillers and produced numerous ghost story anthologies, while Preston has written four nonfiction books and three thrillers, as well as occasional articles for the *New Yorker* magazine. Child is an aficionado of motorcycles, rare books, fast cars and exotic parrots, while Preston is a horseman and a member of the elite Long Riders' Guild. Both writers like to point out that they graduated from college with a "useless" degree in English literature.

Christopher Reich was born in Tokyo. A graduate of Georgetown University and the University of Texas at Austin, he worked in Switzerland before returning to the United States to pursue a career as a novelist. He's the bestselling author of five acclaimed novels, *Numbered Account*, *The Runner*, *The First Billion*, *The Devil's Banker* and *The Patriot's Club*. He lives in California with his wife and children.

Christopher Rice is the *New York Times* bestselling author of *A Density of Souls*, *The Snow Garden* and *Light Before Day*. He is also a regular columnist for *The Advocate*. *The Snow Garden* won a Lambda Literary Award. Rice lives in West Hollywood.

James Rollins is the *New York Times* bestselling author of numerous thrillers, including *Map of Bones*. You'll often find him underground or underwater as an amateur caver and scuba diver. From these hobbies sprang his earlier thrillers *Subterranean*, *Amazonia*, *Ice Hunt* and *Sandstorm*.

M. J. Rose is the international bestselling author of eight thrillers, including *The Halo Effect*, *The Delilah Complex* and *The Venus Fix*. She has been a finalist for the Connecticut Book Award and the Anthony Award. She has also coauthored two nonfiction books and is on the board of International Thriller Writers, Inc. Her work has also appeared in Wired.com, *O, The Oprah Magazine*, and *Poets & Writers*. She is presently published in ten countries, including Japan, Israel and Russia. In addition, Rose runs the popular Buzz, Balls and

Hype and Backstory blogs and is the creator of Author-Buzz.com. Visit all of these at www.mjrose.com.

James Siegel is the *New York Times* bestselling author of *Derailed* and *Detour*. His first thriller, *Epitaph*, was nominated for a Shamus Award as best first novel. *Derailed*, with Clive Owen and Jennifer Aniston, was released in 2004 as a major motion picture, and *Detour* is in production.

Brad Thor, a native of Chicago and a graduate of the University of Southern California, is the *USA TODAY* bestselling author of *The Lions of Lucerne*, *Path of the Assassin*, *State of the Union* and *Blowback*. He and his family divide their time between Park City, Utah, and the Greek island of Antiparos. Visit his Web site at www.bradthor.com.

M. Diane Vogt is the author of the acclaimed Judge Wilhelmina Carson legal thrillers. The Chinese government purchased and translated Diane's fiction and non-fiction as an entertaining read, reflective of American life and the legal system. A lawyer in private practice for more than twenty-five years, Diane has represented the world's largest corporations as well as individuals and governments.

F. Paul Wilson is the award-winning, *New York Times* bestselling author of thirty books and over a hundred short stories spanning horror, adventure, medical thrillers, science fiction and virtually everything in between. More than seven million copies of his books are in print in the United States and his work has been translated into twenty-four languages. He also has written for the stage, screen and interactive media. Wilson is the creator of the popular Repairman Jack thrillers.